"Hey, Cam."

The voice I haven't heard in almost five years sounds like it's coming from down a long, dark tunnel, and I realize it's because my heart is pounding so hard it's thundering in my ears. It's the same raspy, deep voice I've heard in my head in the middle of the night, no matter how much I didn't want it there. It's the same soothing sound I spent over twenty years of my life wanting to listen to forever, coming from the same man I wished would be my forever. The sound is like music to my ears and I want to beg him to say something else, just so I can hear him again and know that he's really here, and really within touching distance.

I can't stop looking at Everett, standing here a few feet away from me. He's still wearing his dark brown hair shaved short on the sides and a little longer on top, the thick, messy strands falling all over the place on top of his head, making me want to reach up and run my fingers through them. His hair is the only similarity to the Everett I used to know.

That thought suddenly makes the tears in my eyes dry up and all the emotion I felt at seeing him again vanish in the blink of an eye. How dare he just show up here after all this time after not one word in almost five years. How dare he go from being one of the most important people in my life to someone who threw me away and never looked back. Who couldn't even be bothered to reach out to me when our best fucking friend died.

I resist the urge to close the distance between us and throw myself in his arms, dying to feel the heat from his body and the beat of his heart against my own, reassuring me that he's real.

"What the hell are you doing here?"

Praise for Tara Sivec's novels

WISH YOU WERE MINE

"Emotional and poignant, *Wish You Were Mine* will leave your heart soaring as you wipe away a final tear. My new favorite Tara Sivec book."

—**Mia Sheridan,**
***New York Times* bestselling author**

"Filled with angst, sizzling chemistry, and a plethora of emotion."
—**Harlequin Junkie**

THE STORY OF US

"The best book I have read all year. Heartbreaking and hopeful. Highly recommend."

—**A. L. Jackson,**
***New York Times* and *USA Today* bestselling author**

"Emotional and real! I couldn't read *The Story of Us* fast enough and know it will stay with me forever. Five heart pounding stars!"

—**Aleatha Romig,**
***New York Times* bestselling author**

"This is a story of an undying, unending love that was strong enough to heal even the deepest of scars. I highly recommend it to anyone looking for beautifully written, heart-wrenching and healing romance to fall in love with."

—**Aestas Book Blog**

"I fell hard for these characters, I felt their every emotion, their every up and down, and coupled with Tara Sivec's knack for storytelling, I would wholeheartedly recommend this book to anyone in a heartbeat."

—**Natasha is a Book Junkie**

wish
you were
mine

TARA SIVEC

FOREVER
New York   Boston

Copyright © 2017 by Tara Sivec
Excerpt from *The Story of Us* © 2017 by Tara Sivec
Cover design by Elizabeth Stokes. Cover copyright © 2017 by Hachette Book Group, Inc.

Forever
Hachette Book Group
1290 Avenue of the Americas, New York, NY 10104
forever-romance.com
twitter.com/foreverromance

First Trade Paperback (POD) Edition: November 2017
First Mass Market edition: July 2019

Forever is an imprint of Grand Central Publishing. The Forever name and logo are trademarks of Hachette Book Group, Inc. The publisher is not responsible for websites (or their content) that are not owned by the publisher.

The Hachette Speakers Bureau provides a wide range of authors for speaking events. To find out more, go to www.hachettespeakersbureau.com or call (866) 376-6591.

ISBNs: 978-1-5387-0000-6 (mass market), 978-1-4789-2016-8 (ebook)

Printed in the United States of America
OPM
10 9 8 7 6 5 4 3 2 1

*For my husband, who I've loved since I
was twelve years old.*

*Thank you for showing me every day that
falling in love with your best friend can
be a wish come true.*

Acknowledgments

Thank you to my agent, Kimberly Brower, for loving this story even when I hated it as soon as I finished writing it. Thank you for talking me down from the ledge through all the hundreds of rewrites and edits and different versions of *Wish You Were Mine* until everything clicked and it became something I'm so incredibly proud of.

Thank you to my absolutely wonderful editor, Michele Bidelspach, for helping make this story better and one I love so much more after you gave it your magical touch.

Thank you to Jessica Prince for all the plotting phone calls and texts, and for not wanting to kill me every time I changed my mind about how this story should go.

Thank you to the best beta readers in the world: Michelle Kannan and C. C. Wood. I could never write a story without you kicking my ass when something sucks, and giving me a huge ego boost when something is good.

Thank you to all of the members of Tara's Tramps for your unwavering support, and for all of your posts, which make me laugh when I'm sad, or run out to the store to stock up on eye bleach.

Thank you to the fabulous women of FTN. For your support, your love, your help, and everything in between.

As always, thank you to my family, who remind me to shower and feed me when I'm on a deadline.

Last, but certainly not least, thank you to my readers. Thank you for letting me do what I love. Thank you for continuing on this crazy ride with me whether I make you laugh, make you cry, or make you read with all the lights on. I love you all, and I'm so incredibly blessed that you allow me into your lives and into your hearts and let me tell you my stories.

wish
you were
mine

Prologue

Dear Everett:

If you're reading this, I'm dead.

Sorry, that's probably not the best way to start off a letter to my best friend, after my sudden and horribly tragic death. You'll surely never, ever be able to move on, because I was such an amazing person, but there it is. You know I've never been one to mince words. And while we're on that subject, you're an asshole.

It's been four years since we've seen you. FOUR. I get it, believe me, I do. The first time I met you, when we were ten years old, you told me you wanted to be a doctor. For sixteen years I listened to you talk about how you wanted to do something with your life you could be proud of. We're all proud of you, Everett. Proud that you accomplished what you set out to do, proud that you took charge of your life and made something of yourself. But you can't stay away forever.

I don't know what happened between you and Cameron the night you left, but I know she hasn't been the same since. Neither one of us has. The Three Musketeers has been missing one of its members for four years, and if you aren't here already, it's time for you to come home.

Yes, I'm guilting you into coming home because I'm dead.

Finished.

Gone.

Never coming back from the Great Beyond.

Do you feel guilty yet? You should. Because Cameron misses you, even though she won't admit it. I've tried my best to make her happy without you here. She puts up a good front about not giving a shit that you've been gone for so long, but I know she's lying. She needs you now, more than ever. She needs you to get that stick out of your ass, suck up the reasons you've stayed away from us, and come home.

I'm not going to be there to make her laugh, wipe away her tears, or cheer her on when she does something amazing. I am officially passing the baton over to you. It's your turn now. You've traveled around the world, you've saved lives, you've become a goddamn hero to strangers. Now it's time to be a hero back here at home, where you belong. It hasn't been the same without you. We haven't been the same without you, and now that I'm gone, you can make it up to me by GETTING YOUR ASS BACK WHERE YOU BELONG.

And just so you know, I read your box of wishes. You know the ones we swore we'd never, ever read until we were all old and gray. Dude, I'm dead, so you can't be pissed at me for that. But I am so pissed at you from beyond the grave for never telling me about that shit. I mean, I knew, of course I knew. I'm not blind or stupid. But all these years when I thought you were just being an idiot and refusing to admit how you felt, or figured you must have changed your mind and moved on, you were actually admitting everything to those fucking stars! I'm your best friend and you didn't even tell me. Is that why you stayed away for four years? If it is, you're an even bigger asshole than I thought. It's time to stop wishing on those fucking stars every year and make your dreams come true by actually doing something about it.

Brace yourself, because I'm going to say a few things now that will make me sound like a pussy. Just remember, I'm doing this for you and I'm still a manly man.

I know what it's like to look at a woman and, suddenly, everything makes sense.

I know how it feels to love someone so completely that you have no idea how you survived before her.

I've had that love returned tenfold, and even though I know I don't deserve it, I've done everything I could to make sure I don't fuck it up. You know, aside from the whole dying thing, but what can you do?

Don't fuck this up, man. Cameron has been hurt enough. She's going to be hurting even more after I'm gone and I need you to pick up the pieces and put them back together. I need you to give her everything I won't be able to anymore.

I'm sorry I won't be there to see Cameron kick your ass for staying away for so long. Be careful, she's developed a mean right hook over the years. But go easy on her, man. She's going to pretend to be okay, pretend like everything is fine and she's fine and her whole damn life *is fine…you know how she is. Always more concerned about everyone else than she is about herself. But she needs you now, more than ever.*

I'm sorry I didn't tell you I was sick the last time we talked on the phone, but what would have been the point? It's not like you could have done anything about it, aside from sitting here and watching me die. I don't want you to remember me like this. It's bad enough Cameron has to have this picture of me in her head for the rest of her life—I won't do that to you, too. I want you to remember me as the devastatingly handsome, perfect specimen of man that I was. I want you to remember the good times, the laughter, growing up together at the camp, and me being full of life instead of confined to this fucking bed with barely enough energy to write this damn letter. Don't you dare feel guilty about not being able to save me. I know you're an amazing doctor, but sometimes, cancer wins.

Come home, Everett. Come home and finally do something about those wishes.

You can't save me, but you can come home and save our girl.

Aiden

Chapter 1

EVERETT

How do you know when you've reached your breaking point?

Watching children die right in front of their parents' eyes?

Telling someone that they're sick, but you don't have the resources to help them?

Seeing countless people get infections from unclean water and live in horrible conditions, and the only thing you can do is hand them pills and wait for them to get sick again?

Trying your hardest to travel to every third world country you could possibly think of to avoid going home, only to find out your best friend since you were ten years old died of pancreatic cancer?

And because you didn't even know he was sick, you weren't there to help. Never got a chance to apologize for being such a shitty friend. Never got a chance to say good-bye.

How much is too much?

I take another swig of vodka and let my head thump back

against the wall, wondering how much more I can take. I've been trying to numb the pain with booze since I came back to the States. It works for a little while. The blur of vodka when it pumps through my veins makes me forget about everything for a few minutes.

A few minutes of peace.

A few minutes of not hearing the cries of babies or the pleas of mothers begging me to save their children.

A few minutes of not seeing Aiden's face in my head, smirking at me and calling me an asshole.

A few minutes of not thinking about her.

One-hundred-and-eighty seconds when I can close my eyes and feel nothing.

With my ass on the floor and my legs sprawled out in front of me, I close my eyes and let the quiet oblivion take over, but it's gone too soon. It never lasts long enough. Not anymore. Not after that letter he wrote.

That fucking letter.

I open my eyes and my body breaks out into a cold sweat when I see it crumbled up and tossed a few feet away from me. The letter I've been rereading for the last three months, ever since it showed up in my mailbox in Cambodia, exactly two weeks after Aiden died.

My eyes stay glued to the ball of paper, Aiden's shaky and uneven handwriting peeking out of the crushed page. I bring the vodka back up to my lips and try to drink away the pain and misery swirling around inside of me. It doesn't even burn anymore when it goes down, and I can almost fool myself into believing the water bottle I poured it in really contains just water. I don't know why I bother trying to hide it at this point. My brother, Jason, has seen all the empty vodka bottles I've hidden under my bed and out in the garage behind shelves and boxes. In the trunk of my car yesterday, he found an entire box of empty liter bottles, which I'd meant to take out to the garbage dump and get rid of, but never got around to it. Probably because I was too drunk to drive there.

I laugh when I think about the intervention he had with me yesterday morning. He went in my trunk to borrow my jack for a flat tire he needed to change before he left for work, and saw that damn box of bottles. He made me promise to stop drinking. He made me promise to get help. Of course I agreed. He's my baby brother. I live here with him in our grandparents' old house until I can get back on my feet. A house my grandmother left to me when she moved away, the place Jason was forced to stay in and take care of while I was always gone. And he's still here, taking care of the house and taking care of me instead of moving out and getting his own life. He puts up with my sorry ass day in and day out, and he deserves so much more than having a drunk for a brother who can't get his shit together.

And I kept my promise. For almost twenty-four hours, I didn't touch the one last bottle of Tito's I had stashed on the top shelf of my closet. I gritted my teeth through the pain of withdrawal, and I threw up every ounce of water I tried to get in my system, but I did it. I pushed through it for Jason. I sucked it up for my little brother, who'd survived the same shitty childhood I had, but never got to escape like I did. I dealt with the shakes and the headaches and the puking and the fever so I wouldn't have to see that same tired, disappointed look in his eyes when he got home from another day of work while I just sat my useless ass on his couch.

"You weren't supposed to die!" I scream at the letter, still lying a few feet away, taunting me to crawl over to it and read the words inside again. "Why in the hell didn't you tell me sooner?!"

The water bottle of vodka crinkles in my hand when I squeeze my fingers around it and angrily bring it up to my mouth, chugging it until it's almost gone.

Aiden's voice is buzzing in my ear like an annoying housefly you can't swat away. It just keeps coming back and coming back, pushing me over the edge until I want to cover my ears and make it stop. The alcohol isn't working. His voice just won't go away.

You're an asshole.
I hope you feel guilty.
Come home.
Come home.
Come home.

I *am* an asshole. I *do* feel guilty. And I'm home. I got on the next flight out of Cambodia as soon as that damn letter arrived, not even bothering to call home, just wanting to get back here before it was too late. I acted without thinking and of course I was too late. Two weeks too late to say good-bye, too late for the funeral, too late to make amends, too late to do anything but pick up a bottle and try to forget all the mistakes I'd made. It's been exactly three months and two weeks to the day my best friend died in his sleep when his body just couldn't fight anymore. Three months and two weeks to the day that he stopping existing.

I've spent every waking moment since I got home trying to forget about the pain Aiden's death caused, and then a few hours ago a box of photos fell from the top shelf of my closet when I was looking for something. It came crashing to the floor, spilling memories of Aiden all around my feet. Aiden laughing at me during a game of basketball when we were ten, Aiden smiling at the camera with his arm wrapped around one of his many dates when we were in high school, Aiden smirking as he holds up his college diploma. Every memory of him seeped into my brain and squeezed the life out of my heart until that fucking letter I'd shoved into the back of my dresser drawer started taunting me to read it again. I could almost feel Aiden standing next to me, telling me I deserve to be miserable for the shit I've pulled. I was trying to do better and he just shows up in my brain, provoking me and pushing me to fuck it all up, make me forget about the promise I made to my brother until nothing else mattered but taking a drink so I could make it all go away. I came home, just like Aiden wanted, and all I want to do is leave.

"Do you really want me to take care of our girl now, Aiden?!" I shout toward the ceiling. "I bet she'd be really happy to see me show up at the camp like this."

I laugh at my words, wondering if it's the booze or my fucked-up head that's made me start talking to myself like a crazy person.

"You weren't supposed to die. You were always supposed to be here," I mutter, my throat clogging with tears when I look over at his letter again.

I took everything for granted, and I have no one to blame but myself. I walked away from my two best friends and never looked back because I was a coward. I always thought in the back of my mind that one day I'd be able to get over my shit, get over how I felt about Cameron, come back home and they'd both be waiting for me, ready to forgive me for being an idiot. But now that's never going to happen.

Aiden is never going to be there with a smirk on his face and a sarcastic comment at the ready. Cameron is never going to forgive me. For not being there while Aiden was sick, for not doing everything I could to try to save him, and for not going to her right when I got home.

I should have gone to her. We should have been able to

mourn Aiden together, but I couldn't deal with my own pain, let alone hers. I *still* can't deal with my own pain.

No one understands what it's like to come back home after you've been on the other side of the world, experiencing horrors no one back here sees or even realizes is happening. People here live in their happy little worlds, going about their happy little lives, and they forget there are men, women, and children without basic necessities, like clean water, so they, too, can have those happy lives.

Jason doesn't understand, even though he tries to.

No one understands what it's like to be back here. What it's like to have nothing to do with your free time but think and feel guilty about the people you couldn't save in another country, or the person you should have saved right here at home. To feel like you're constantly living in a nightmare where every thought and every memory is a film reel of all the ways you fucked up.

I'm so tired of feeling this pain. I just want relief. I just want to feel nothing at all. My eyelids grow heavy and my vision starts to blur as darkness and the sweet bliss of numbness covers my body like a warm blanket.

"Goddammit, Everett! Son of a bitch..."

I hear my brother's voice, and even though it sounds muffled and far away in my drunken brain, I can still hear the anger in it. I don't even realize I've slumped over onto my side until I feel Jason's arms come under me and slide me back upright against the wall.

"Open your eyes. Open your fucking eyes!" Jason shouts close to my face.

The darkness surrounding me disappears when I blink my eyes open as his palm smacks against my cheek.

Sadness, worry, anguish, and fear.

That's what I see written all over my brother's face as he

looks at me and shakes his head. I want to apologize to him that he found me like this, but what's the point? He's found me in similar situations many times since I got home, and my apologies aren't worth shit at this point.

I want to tell him that I don't want this crutch of alcohol. I don't want to need it, feeling like it's the only way I can survive the pain. The pain in my gut, the pain in my head, and the pain in my heart. Without drinking, it all comes back until I want to claw at my skin and scream until my throat is hoarse. I open my mouth, but the words won't come.

He sits down next to me and kicks his legs out in front of him, mirroring my own.

"What was it this time? Flashback? Bad dream?" Jason asks quietly, listing off all the excuses I've given him over the last few months when he's smelled the alcohol on my breath or found me passed out on the couch.

I lean forward to grab the letter from Aiden, but the room spins and I have to quickly lean back against the wall before I puke. Instead, I lift my arm and point to it.

He looks away from me to the crumpled-up ball of paper, letting out a big sigh before reaching over to grab it. I watch silently as he uncrinkles it and smooths it out against his thigh. I stare at his face, blinking a few times to keep it in focus, as he reads through the letter.

"Jesus Christ," he finally whispers. "Where did this come from?"

I clear my throat and look away from him to stare at the opposite wall in our grandparents' living room before answering him.

"It came when I was in Cambodia. Two weeks after he died."

Jason doesn't say anything for a few minutes, and I take the time to look around the room. I always loved this house growing up. An old farmhouse on the outskirts of Charleston, it was filled with happy memories and good times, the complete opposite of the home we shared with our mother in New Jersey. I looked forward to spending every summer here with our grandmother. She baked us cookies, she fed us home-cooked meals, and she paid attention to us. She loved us and she cared for us and she did everything she could to make us happy.

This house that was once full of dreams now feels like hell. I can't stand these four walls that surround me, caging me in, not letting me get away from the memories and the pain.

"I'm sorry, Everett. This letter is…shit. I don't even know what to say about this thing. Why didn't you tell me? Is this why you've been drinking yourself into a coma since you got home?" Jason asks.

"It is what it is," I shrug, ignoring the drinking comment. "He's right. I'm an asshole, but there's nothing I can do about that now."

My brother scoffs, pushing himself up from the floor to stand over me. It hurts my head to look up at him. The overhead light is shining in my eyes and stabbing into my skull, and I curse when I have to shield my eyes to see his face.

"I know I'll never understand everything going on in that head of yours. I know I'll never be able to sympathize with all the shit you saw over there. And I know the sadness I feel about Aiden being gone is nothing compared to what you feel," Jason tells me. "But enough is enough. You were doing something you loved over there and you didn't know he was sick. Even if you had, you couldn't have done anything about it. He had the best medical team money could buy, flown in from all over the world. What he had, even your fancy medical skills couldn't have fixed. You're still alive and you need to start fucking acting like it. I'm sorry that letter hurt you, but I'm not sorry Aiden wrote it. He's right. You need to get your head out of your ass."

I can feel anger start to replace my buzz, and I clench my hands into fists in my lap. I don't want to hear this bullshit coming out of his mouth. I know I deserve it, but I don't want to hear it.

"What the fuck happened to the promise you made me yesterday?" he asks, snatching the water bottle out of my hand and hurling it across the room.

It smacks against our grandmother's oak curio cabinet filled with her good china and drops to the floor, the last few sips of vodka leaking out onto the hardwood floor.

"It hurts," I whisper, looking down at my balled fists, unable to look him in the eyes anymore.

"Of course it hurts, you dumbass! It's called alcohol withdrawal for a reason. It's not supposed to feel good, but I guess you don't even want to try," he fires back.

Jason squats down next to me and grabs my chin, forcing me to look at him.

"I'm sorry Aiden's gone. I'm sorry you're hurting and you feel guilty for not being able to save him. But *screw you* for not even trying. I was too young to remember losing Dad, but watching Mom fade away and drink herself to death was bad enough. You can go fuck yourself if you think you're going to leave me behind, too. If you won't do it for me, do it for Cameron. She lost Aiden, too, you know. What do you think will happen if she loses you as well?"

With that, he gets up and walks away. The angry stomp of his construction boots banging against the hardwood floor makes me drop my head into my hands to stop the damn thing from feeling like it's going to explode.

I want to go back to the people that need me, but my employer won't let me.

I want to stop hearing Aiden's voice in my head, but he won't let me.

I want to drown myself in booze, but my brother won't let me.

No one will just fucking let me be.

My brother has no idea what he's talking about. Cameron will be fine without me, just like she's been for the last four years. She doesn't need me. She's never needed me.

Everyone needs to just fucking Let. Me. Be.

Chapter 2

EVERETT

Wishing in the past…
Ten years old

"My name's Aiden Curtis, I'm ten, and my daddy's rich," the kid who just walked up to me says.

He's as tall as me, and we have the same dark brown hair and blue eyes, but his clean black dress pants and fancy white dress shirt prove his daddy really is rich. I feel like a bum standing in front of him in a pair of dirty and tattered jeans that are two sizes too small for me and a T-shirt stained with grease and mud.

I want to punch him right in the mouth, but Grandma always says I should never be the one to throw the first punch and start a fight, but I should always throw the last one and defend myself.

"Is your daddy rich, too?" Aiden asks, grabbing the basketball out of my hands and tucking it under one of his arms.

I really wish this kid would hit me already. I don't care if his family just moved in down the road and his parents are friends with Cameron's parents, which means he'll be here at the camp all the time. I still want to punch him.

"Aiden! Don't be mean. Everett doesn't have a daddy anymore."

The scowl I was shooting at Aiden quickly turns into a smile when Cameron walks up between us. I don't really like girls. They're loud and annoying and always giggling, but Cameron is okay, even if she is just a baby and only seven. She's always covered in dirt, always has hay stuck in her hair from the horse barns, always getting in trouble for climbing trees too high, and she can whoop my butt in every activity here at camp, including archery. It should be embarrassing that a little girl can shoot arrows and play basketball and swim better than me, but for some reason it isn't.

"You've got hay in your hair again, Cam," I tell her, pointing and laughing at the pieces sticking out from her messy ponytail.

She just shrugs, puts her hands on her hips, and turns to face Aiden.

"You should apologize to Everett," she informs him.

It doesn't even feel weird that I'm letting a girl stick up for me. I've known Cameron since she was an actual baby. She wasn't even a year old the first time my grandma brought me to the camp her parents own. I've spent every summer with her for the last seven years. For some reason, out of all the hundreds of kids at the camp, Cameron has always stuck to me like glue. And since she's good at sports and stuff, it's not annoying at all. It's like having a girl for a little brother.

Aiden immediately wipes the smile off of his dumb face as Cameron keeps glaring at him, and he gives me a sad look.

"I'm sorry about your dad. If you want, my dad can buy you whatever you want if we're friends. He's got a lot of money."

I think about the PlayStation all my friends at school have that my grandma says we can't afford, the one my mom doesn't even know I want, and I immediately agree to Aiden's friendship request. It doesn't take much for a ten-year-old to lose interest in a fight.

"What do you want to be when you grow up?" I ask.

"Rich!" he replies with a laugh. "What do you want to be?"

I look down and kick a rock away with the toe of my shoe.

"A doctor, like my dad was. But I can't. My mom doesn't like it when I talk about being like my dad," I tell him quietly.

Cameron moves closer to me and rests her head against the side of my arm.

My dad was a doctor for the Army. Ever since my dad was killed in the war when I was three, my mom hasn't been the same, which is why I spend so much time with my grandma, why she started bringing me to Cameron's parents' camp. My mom gets really upset when I talk about being a doctor like him, even when I tell her I don't want to be in the Army and that I'd never die like he did. I don't want to be a soldier, but I want to save people like him. She cries a lot and locks herself in her room for days, so I don't talk about it anymore. But it feels good to be able to say it out loud to someone else and not feel bad about it.

"You can do whatever you want when you get older. I can't wait until I get older and no one can tell me what to do. If you want to be a doctor, you should be a doctor. You can give people shots and cut them open and you'll be so cool and be so rich. Doctors make a lot of money." Aiden smiles.

"You think being a doctor will make me cool?"

Aiden nods. "Definitely."

I smile at him. "Okay, we can be friends."

"Yay!" Cameron cheers, clapping her hands together and jumping up and down. "Aiden and I have been playing when you're not here, and I'm so happy you like each other, too. Now we can all play together! I'm gonna make a wish on a star tonight that we're going to be the bestest of friends forever and ever and I know it will come true!"

Aiden and I both laugh at how happy Cameron is. He hands me back the basketball and asks if we want to play a game, which just makes Cameron even more excited. Aiden's face lights up with a smile as he watches Cameron dance all around us, talking nonstop about all the best friend things we're going to do and how she's going to kick our butts in basketball.

I like doing stuff that I know will make Cameron happy, and it looks like Aiden will be good at helping me with that. When he wraps his arm around her shoulder, he calls her "kid" and tells her not to beat us too badly in basketball. And Cameron looks up at him and smiles brighter than I've ever seen.

I'm glad we have a new friend to hang out with and he thinks I'll be cool as a doctor, but something makes me feel weird about watching the two of them standing there together like buddies without me. I quickly walk over to the other side of Cameron and wrap my own arm around her shoulder until the three of us are standing side by side.

"Promise me we'll be best friends forever, no matter what," Cameron demands, looking up at Aiden, and then turning her head to look up at me.

Aiden and I share a look over her head and we both shrug.

"Sure, Cam. We'll be best friends forever, no matter what," I agree.

"Yep, no matter what. Even if you are a girl," Aiden adds.

Cameron frowns and pulls away from us, punching him in the stomach. I laugh out loud when Aiden bends over, clutching his stomach and howling in pain. Cameron finally gives me the same smile she gave Aiden a few minutes ago, and the weird feeling I had goes away when she holds out her hands and I toss the basketball to her.

"Rule number one, Aiden. Never tick Cameron off or she'll punch you," I tell him, patting him on the back and grabbing his arm to help him stand back up.

"Thanks for the warning," he groans, rubbing his hand across his gut as we get into position in front of the basketball hoop.

Cameron, Aiden, and I spend the rest of the day playing H-O-R-S-E, and just like always, Cameron wins every game. Aiden doesn't whine or complain, he just keeps challenging her to another game, and just like that, I don't mind agreeing to Cam's request that the three of us should be best friends forever.

Chapter 3

CAMERON

You ruined my life.

I read aloud and roll my eyes at the one-sentence, type-written note I just opened from the unmarked envelope, shoved between the stack of bills that just came. I'd like to rip the paper to shreds and toss it into the garbage, but instead, I shove it into a manila folder in the bottom drawer of my desk with all the others until I have time to make copies and give them to the local police.

"Well, at least this one is direct and to the point," my friend and coworker, Amelia, says from her seat in the chair across from my desk. "Why can't they be more specific? Tell us exactly *how* you ruined their life. Did you pull out in front of them at an intersection? Were they behind you in line at the grocery store when you took eleven items to the 'ten items or less' line?"

I can't help but laugh at the serious look on her face. It feels good to laugh. I haven't had much to laugh about lately, and I can always count on Amelia to cheer me up.

"I will have you know I only took more than ten items through that line once and it was an emergency."

"Was it a wine emergency?" she asks with a raise of one eyebrow.

"Maybe..." I trail off with another laugh.

"You have too much stress in your life right now. I think what you need is a visit from your *special friend.*"

She gives me a knowing wink, even using air quotes around the words *special friend.*

"Let's just call it what it is. Grady is a booty call. I need a visit from my booty call and I'm one step ahead of you. I was just getting ready to send him a text."

Amelia gives me a high five and I try not to feel guilty when I send the text. He knows the score. He agreed to it and I have nothing to feel guilty about.

After we share a few quiet minutes, Amelia gives me a soft smile.

"Don't let it bother you. You know some people just don't understand what you do here."

Amelia Sparks came to our camp with her five-year-old son three years ago, needing something to help them both cope when her husband came home from deployment, and we became fast friends. So when Amelia lost her job as a hostess at a restaurant in downtown Charleston last year, I immediately offered her the position of activities director, which had just become vacant. She's been a godsend in more ways than one, around here at the camp and in my life, especially lately. Just looking at her now, so different from when I first met her, I know the feeling is mutual.

When she first walked into this office, her long brown

hair was in a messy ponytail, there were bags under her eyes, which were bloodshot from crying, and she was so skinny I immediately took her into the house and made her sit down and eat something. She whispered when she spoke and she was too nervous to meet my eyes when I tried to engage her in conversation. It took me a month to finally get her to tell me that her husband wasn't handling being back home very well. He was always angry and always drinking, taking his pain and his fear out on her and their son, Dylan. With the help of our counselors, she and Dylan found strength and happiness, despite what was happening back home. Amelia learned how to take charge of her life and let go of the husband—who refused to get help—and put their family back together.

Her freshly highlighted brown hair falls in gentle curls around her shoulders, her makeup is beautiful and flawless, and the weight she put back on when she said good-bye to her depression gives her curves that I envy. She smiles easily and often, and she does whatever she can to pull me out of my own unhappiness, living her life to the fullest and making sure I'm doing the same.

I'm not, but it's not for lack of trying on Amelia's part.

"I'm fine," I reassure her with a smile, sliding the bottom desk drawer closed. "It's not the first angry note we've ever received, and it certainly won't be the last."

Now that my parents are semiretired and I've taken over running the camp for them, I continue handing the notes over to the police as a precaution, just like my parents have always done. Nothing bad has ever happened and I highly doubt anything ever will, but you can never be too safe when you run a camp filled with children. It still pisses me off that anyone would be angry about what we do here. Whether it be people who are against the camp in principle, someone who has a political agenda and hates anything involving war and soldiers, or someone who knew someone that went here, we've seen it all.

My parents turned the plantation my mother grew up on into the Rylan Edwards Camp for the Children of Veterans and Deployed Soldiers. When my father came back home from the war, he seemed like he had healed from the torture and abuse. But he was anything but fine. He spent months trapped in his own personal hell in his mind, seeing things that weren't there and pretending like everything was fine so he could win back my mother's love. His only focus was getting back to the woman he was forced to leave behind when he went off to war, and nothing else mattered to him, including his own health. With my mother's help, he learned how to let go of the past and the pain, walk back into the light, and learn to live without regret. As soon as my father became well again, they knew there was nothing they'd rather do with their lives than create a safe place for other veterans and their families, to help them heal and teach them how to live again, without the pain and the guilt.

The outpouring of love and support they received was enormous. But you can't make everyone happy, and along with love and support came a few bitter and angry individuals over the years. There will always be eccentric right-wing people and throw-back hippies who think what we do here is a political statement, and make it clear how displeased they are with us.

There will also always be family members who don't appreciate the things we provide for their loved ones at Camp Rylan, no matter how much it benefits everyone. Not only do we provide a safe and happy place for children of military personnel, whether they are deployed, wounded, or deceased, but we also provide counseling as well. Over the years, we've had a few people, after participating in the counseling we provided, decide to make changes, which sometimes meant parting ways with their spouse or loved one, just like Amelia did with her husband.

Sometimes those decisions aren't taken very well by all the parties involved. People get angry. People get upset. People want someone to blame. I try not to let the angry letters, e-mails, and phone calls we receive bother me, because I know how much those people are hurting. I know how hard it is for them to go off and fight a war and then come home and realize nothing will ever be the same again. I grew up in a very loving household, but my parents never sheltered me from the PTSD my father went through and continues to struggle with to this day. Even though he got better, he still has hard times every once in a while. There are still sleepless nights, or nights he wakes up screaming from a nightmare. I can relate to all of the campers on a personal level, which makes it so much harder to handle when someone doesn't take the advice we give, or doesn't believe in what we do.

But I know the good always outweighs the bad in the end, and the thankful and appreciative messages we receive are always far more numerous than the nasty ones.

Aiden used to always tell me this was a thankless, depressing job and he never understood how I handled it day in and day out. He would always joke that he made more than enough money and he would happily share it with me so I could be a woman of leisure and do something fun with my life instead of something he thought was depressing.

My eyes flit over to a framed picture of him on the corner of my desk, and it's a struggle to keep myself in check and not break down in tears. With my hands in my lap, I fiddle with the ring that Aiden gave me. I should have probably put it away in a jewelry box after he died. It was too flashy and not really my style, but I wore it for him, because he gave it to me. I refuse to take it off now because looking down at it and touching it make me feel closer to him.

Amelia sees what I'm looking at, gently picks up the black frame, and turns it to face her, looking down at the photo with a smile.

"You guys were just babies in this picture. What were you, like ten or eleven?" she asks.

"Twelve," I immediately reply, my voice cracking with emotion. "The boys were fifteen."

I can't even bring myself to say their names out loud. It's been nine months since Aiden died. The pain isn't as acute as it once was, but it's still there, hovering under the surface whenever I think of him. It still hurts that he's gone and left me here alone.

Aiden was the one person I could always count on to be here for me, and now he's gone and I'll never have that again.

"Look at that smirk on Aiden's face. Such a cocky little shit, even as a teenager," Amelia laughs.

I laugh along with her, having been the recipient of that smirk many times over the years and knowing exactly what Amelia means. Aiden was always so sure of himself. So sure of his life and the world around him, and he didn't care what anyone thought of him. He thought very highly of himself and that's all that mattered. It came off as snobby and arrogant to most, but to those who really knew him, it was just Aiden. Underneath all that confidence was a guy with a big heart who loved his friends and would do anything for them.

My eyes start to fill with tears when I think about the fact that I'll never see that damn smirk again. I'll never listen to him joke about how good he looked or listen to him brag about how much money he made in commissions that month. He'll never cheer me up by being so much of a pompous idiot that it always made me laugh. He'll never go out of his way to be the best friend he possibly could, always knowing there was something missing and a hole in my heart that nothing could fix, no matter how hard he tried. He did whatever he could to help me forget that one of the Three Musketeers was missing and that made everything feel off and wrong. Since he died, every sad moment has been amplified and made worse because Everett isn't here to talk to about it. Every happy moment has been tinged with the sting of regret that Everett wasn't here to experience it with me.

"Whenever I saw you and Aiden together, I had all sorts of daydreams about the beautiful babies you'd make together. He was such a cutie with that cocky smirk and sense of humor," Amelia says with a shake of her head as she continues to stare at the photo.

"Yeah, well, you never saw Everett in person," I mutter, wanting to take the words back as soon as they leave my mouth.

It feels like a slap in the face to Aiden's memory thinking about how much hotter Everett was to me than Aiden. Where Aiden always felt safe and like coming home whenever I looked at him, Everett always made me feel the exact opposite. Like I needed to fan my face and cross my legs together tightly.

"Jesus, Everett *was* a hottie even at fifteen. I feel really dirty right now. But from what you and Aiden both told me about him over the years, he was too much of a bad boy, too broody, and too much of a jerk. Makes sense since he hasn't given a shit about you or given you a second thought in four years. I know you told me you used to have a crush on Everett back then, but Aiden was clearly the much better choice," Amelia mutters, setting the picture back on top of my desk and turning it back around to face me.

I don't want to look, but I can't help myself. My eyes automatically go to the boy standing on the opposite side of me in the photo. Aiden and Everett both had short brown hair and they both stood around the same height, at least a head taller than me in the photo since I was three years younger than them.

They were similar in looks back then, but where Aiden was always laughing and happy, Everett's smile never quite reached his eyes in all the years I'd known him. It was always a lot of work to even coax a smile from him and almost impossible to pull out a laugh. Amelia's right. He was broody and he was a bad boy, but he wasn't a jerk when we were kids, at least not around me. Maybe that's why I was so drawn to him when we were little. I wanted to fix him. I wanted to make him smile and I wanted to make him laugh. I wanted to be the one to take away the pain of losing his father at such a young age, and having to live with a mother who stopped caring about him and his brother after her husband died. I spent too many years chasing after a dream, and wishing on stars for something that, in the end, was a huge waste of time. Everett never wanted my help. He never wanted to be fixed and he never wanted *me*.

Almost five years he's been gone. All these years without an e-mail or a phone call. Nothing. I've blamed myself all these years because maybe I should've asked him to stay the night before he left for his assignment overseas. Maybe I made it seem that we didn't need him, that we'd be fine without him, that we'd forget about him, so he decided to push us away first. I blamed myself because not only did *I* lose him, but Aiden lost him as well because of what I'd done.

But then I found out he hadn't ignored both of us. I found out a few weeks before Aiden died that he still e-mailed Aiden when he could, and he still called him when he had time. It was just me he left behind. Just me he didn't give a shit about throwing away after twenty-plus years of friendship. Just me he didn't care about.

It pissed me off and it hurt. Aiden's been dead for nine months and I'm sad and I miss him every day. Everett's been out of my life for almost five years and I hate that it hurts *more*. I hate that I miss him *more*. I hate that I feel like I'm tarnishing Aiden's memory by being sadder about a man who just doesn't give a shit about me. A man who I thought was my best friend, who I wished on entirely too many stars that someday he'd be more until I finally had to give up and move on with my life.

"I hate to bring the mood down in here even more, but have you talked to your parents yet?" Amelia asks, pulling me out of my depressing thoughts and my eyes away from that damn photo.

"No, not aside from the usual '*How are things going?*' phone calls every couple of days. I can't tell them the extent of the problems, Amelia, not yet. This camp is their entire life. Their dream. I can't bring myself to tell them we might have to close after this summer session. I can't break their hearts right now when I finally managed to get them out of town two days ago and take a real vacation for the first time in forever," I tell her with a sigh as I start opening the stack of bills in front of me that I've been avoiding for a week.

Camp Rylan has always been free for participants since the doors opened. My parents wouldn't even hear of making people pay for their children to escape real life for a while and be with other children who understood all the struggles they were going through. With generous donations and grants from individuals and corporations, along with the huge charity function I throw here before the start of every summer session, we've never had any problems getting everything we need to make this camp run smoothly. Unfortunately, our biggest benefactor, the one who has almost single-handedly kept Camp Rylan open for twenty-seven years with his yearly donation, recently passed away and his remaining family members are cold-hearted assholes who have cut off all of his charitable donations. Jack Alexander, the founder and CEO of one of the largest car manufacturing plants in the United States, was like family to us. He never had one of his assistants mail in his yearly donation. He'd get in a car and drive himself out here on his own, all the way from New York every summer, to attend the charity function and present us with the check. He would be rolling over in his grave right now if he knew what his family had done.

"I'm hoping I can figure something out before they come home for the charity gala next month. I have a few phone calls out to some companies, and I'm keeping my fingers crossed that I hear something soon. There's one guy who actually replied right away to my e-mail. I've done some research on him, and he's a little weird and has a lot of strict rules about who he gives his money to. My parents would need to be here since he only gives his money to happily married couples who run nonprofit organizations. I'm hoping he'll be my last resort and I won't have to involve them, but just in case, I told him the earliest we could meet would be the weekend of the charity dinner, and I confirmed the date and time with him. I can always cancel if we find something else in the meantime," I explain to Amelia.

If I'm being honest, even with the charity event, the

assistance from the government, and the other miscellaneous donations we get throughout the year, it's not enough to run a camp like this on a plantation this size. All of those things added up would barely cover the cost of electricity and pay for everyone's salary who works here. We've relied on Jack's donation for years and now I need to find someone as amazing and kindhearted as he was, but it's like finding a needle in a haystack at this point. Even the money Aiden left to the camp after he died, every penny he'd ever saved, didn't put a dent in our mounting debt. I've contemplated asking Aiden's parents for help, but I don't want to put them in an uncomfortable position of feeling like they have to do something like this. They moved away after Aiden died, unable to handle the memories here in Charleston, and I don't want to add to their grief by letting them know the money their son left me wasn't enough. I've gone beyond the point of being worried and am now in full-blown panic mode.

I practically begged my parents to transition everything over to me after Aiden died. They were planning on doing it in time, but I needed something else to focus on after he was gone. I needed something else to occupy my thoughts other than missing him. When they finally relented and passed the torch to me, I wouldn't take anything less than total control. Of the camp, of the decisions, and of the money. They know that with Jack dying we're struggling, but I've managed to keep them in the dark about just how much. I refuse to let my parents down. I refuse to let the children and the families who come to this camp down. I grew up here, I met Aiden and Everett here, and all of my best childhood memories are wrapped up in this place. I refuse to let thoughts of Everett Southerland mess with my head and my heart when I have something much more important to worry about. He's a part of my past that I need to let go of, no matter how much it hurts.

No matter how much my heart breaks that I didn't lose just one of my best friends, I lost them both. And I'll never get either one of them back.

Chapter 4

CAMERON

Wishing in the past...
Twelve years old

Wiping my sweaty palms down the skirt of my dress, I take a deep breath as I break through the clearing in the woods that leads to our meeting spot. I lift my chin and pretend like it's not totally weird that I'm wearing a dress. My legs feel naked without the dirty jeans with holes in the knees that I always wear when we hang out, and I force myself not to think about all of the bruises on them from tripping during our basketball game the other day or all the scrapes and scars from years of climbing trees and being one of the boys.

I want to look pretty today. I want him to think of me like an actual girl instead of a tomboy. When I asked my mom if she could take me to the mall yesterday to buy this dress, she couldn't hide the look of shock on her face. She did, however, give me a wink and say something about me wanting to look nice all of a sudden. She's always making comments about how sweet Aiden is and how cute he is. She couldn't be more obvious if she tried. Everyone loves Aiden, but that's only because he lives close by and comes from a good, happy home, just like ours. Everett's home life is anything but good and happy, and my parents just didn't understand him. They think because of the trouble he gets into at home, that he'll be a bad influence on me, but they couldn't be more wrong. He's just as sweet as Aiden when he's here with us in the summer; they just never see it.

I kept my mouth shut and smiled and nodded when my mother droned on and on about how wonderful Aiden is, because at least she didn't laugh at me or tease me about wanting to dress up. I'm so afraid Everett will laugh at me that I almost want to turn around and run back to the house to change into jeans and a T-shirt.

Please, God, don't let him laugh at me.

As soon as I get to the base of the treehouse, where Everett is sitting on a large rock waiting for me, he looks up from the ground and his eyes widen in shock. I paste a smile on my face and try not to let the butterflies flapping around in my stomach force up this morning's breakfast as I continue walking toward him.

I don't even know when I started thinking my best friend was the cutest boy I'd ever seen. It was like one day, I just woke up and started feeling funny whenever we were together. I stuttered over my words when I talked to him and I giggled like all those idiot girls at school who have a crush on a boy. The worst part is that now I can't even stop myself from doing it. After years of having him for a friend, playing with him, and hanging out every summer, not caring what I looked like or acted like in front of him, Everett suddenly made me nervous whenever we were together. I don't know why I'm not nervous around Aiden. He's almost as cute as Everett. But I don't care what Aiden thinks of me and I don't care if I make a fool of myself in front of him. He's just Aiden.

Everett's wide eyes are glued to me without saying a word and I almost wish things could go back to normal. I almost wish Everett could go back to just being Everett.

After a few moments of me standing here awkwardly in front of him, instead of tugging the skirt of my dress down or fiddling with the curls my mom helped me add to my long strawberry blond hair this morning, I put my hands on my hips and glare at the boy in front of me.

"What are you staring at?" I ask in annoyance.

Everett finally blinks and clears his throat.

"You're wearing a dress," he states.

I sigh, wishing he would have said something a little more flattering, but I guess it's better than him pointing and laughing at me.

"Yeah, so?"

"And you don't have hay in your hair," he adds, one corner of his mouth finally tipping up into a smile and forcing one of those totally cute dimples out. "You look really pretty."

The annoying giggle comes out before I can stop it, but I quickly clamp my mouth closed and lick my lips nervously.

"Um, thanks. You know, it's a special occasion and all, so I thought I'd do something different."

Everett finally stands up and I have to tip my head back to look up at him. When he turned fifteen a few months ago, he suddenly shot up in height until he was almost a whole head taller than me.

"It's not every day you turn twelve," he replies, pulling

a six-pack of Grape Crush in glass bottles out from behind his back and holding them up. "I've got our birthday drinks. Hopefully Aiden gets here soon with the food. I'm starving."

Every summer since the three of us became friends, we have a special birthday tradition that I put into place when I found out Aiden and I shared summer birthdays. At the time, Aiden and I only saw Everett when he came to stay with his grandma during the summer and she brought him to camp. It always made me sad that we never got to see him the rest of the year or celebrate his birthday with him, so I made sure we did something extra special to celebrate by appointing July Fourth as Everett's "summer birthday." On each of our birthdays, three separate times every year, we always come out here to the treehouse and have our own birthday celebration separate from the ones we have with our families.

My parents quickly realized a few years after Camp Rylan opened that living in the main plantation house with all of those extra guests sleeping there didn't give them much privacy, so they had a house built just for us. The house is a ten-minute ride in a golf cart from the plantation house. It's close enough that they can get to camp quickly if they need to, but far enough for us to enjoy our privacy and peace and quiet from the camp activities that take place all over the forty acres of land we have. The summer Everett, Aiden, and I became friends, my dad constructed this treehouse for us so we'd have our own place to escape the other campers if we wanted.

"And I've got our birthday tradition ready to go," I tell Everett with a smile, pulling a star-shaped notepad and pen out of the pocket of my dress and holding it up.

Everett shakes his head at me and lets out a soft chuckle that makes my stomach flip-flop.

"We're still doing the wish thing?" he asks.

"Of course we're still doing the wish thing. It's tradition."

Not only do we always come out to the treehouse on our birthdays, we always drink the Grape Crush that Everett brings, and we always eat the entire bag of Fritos that Aiden brings, along with one Little Debbie cupcake. Aiden also provides the candle and swipes one of his dad's lighters from the glove box of his car, where he keeps it hidden from his mom so she doesn't know he smokes cigarettes whenever she's not with him. Last summer, Aiden also swiped three cigarettes from his dad's pack along with the lighter. When I threw up in the garbage can in the treehouse after a few puffs of my cigarette, we decided that was a birthday tradition we wouldn't be continuing.

My contribution to the party is this star-shaped notepad. The boys make fun of me every year, but I don't care. Just because we make a wish when we blow out our candle on the Little Debbie cupcake doesn't mean we shouldn't get another wish. I'm covering all our bases and making sure our wishes come true. I made all three of us special boxes, shoe boxes I stole from my mom's closet, and decorated them with our names in glitter paint and stickers. On our birthday, we get to write down one super-secret wish on one of the pieces of star-shaped paper, something we want more than anything else in this world, and we stick it into our box. Everett pulled up one of the floorboards in the treehouse and we nestle our boxes down inside the secret hiding place, where they wait for the next person's birthday and their next wish on a star.

"What did you write down on your wish star last year?" I ask him.

"I thought those wishes were a secret and we weren't supposed to talk about them?" Everett replies.

Technically, that's true. I even brought a Bible to the treehouse and made Aiden put his hand on it and swear on his mother's life that he'd never look at our boxes. I knew Everett would never do it, but Aiden can't be trusted. He's sneaky and likes to do things to annoy us. But I knew what Everett's wish was. After Aiden left the birthday celebration we had for Everett last year because he had to get home for dinner, the two of us stayed in the treehouse until the sun went down, just talking. Everett had been really quiet and sad that day and it made me sad. No one should be unhappy on their birthday, even if it wasn't really their birthday and just one we made up so we could all celebrate together. Everett told me what his wish was and made me promise never to tell Aiden. A promise I've kept and plan to keep forever. He wished that him and his brother didn't have to live with their mother anymore.

I knew that she wasn't a very good mother, not only from Everett himself, but from a few conversations I'd overheard when my parents didn't know I was in the next room. They talked about how sad it was that Everett's grandmother was the only one in his life who really cared about him, and that someone needed to "get that boy under control." Everett told me about all the fights he got into back at home and how he skipped school all the time and even got in trouble for stealing, and it made me mad that anyone thought he needed control. He just needed love and for someone to care about him.

"Of course they're a secret and we should never talk about them with anyone else, but I know what you wished for last year, Everett Southerland, and I know your wish came true," I remind him.

Right after Christmas this last year, my mom and dad sat me down and told me that I'd be seeing much more of Everett going forward and that him and his brother had officially moved in with his grandma, just a few miles down the road. It made me happy and it made me want to cry all at the same time. If Everett lived with his grandma, I could see him all the time, and not just during the summer. But I didn't want Everett never to see his mom again. Even if she wasn't always nice to him, she was still his mom. I loved mine more than anything else in the world, and I couldn't imagine not seeing her all the time or not living with her.

My happiness won out over the crying. I was so excited, that I called his grandma's house immediately so I could see if Everett really was there, make sure they weren't playing a joke on me. Ever since then, I've seen Everett almost every day. When he's not here just to hang out with me and Aiden, he helps my dad around the plantation in the horse barns and with other work around the camp that needs to be done, and I'm secretly hoping this will go a long way toward proving to my parents that Everett isn't bad. I have never been more grateful for my star wish idea and there's no way I'm stopping this tradition now. Especially with the wish I plan on making this year.

"Yeah, Cam, my wish came true," Everett replies, his voice sounding sad even though he's smiling at me.

I know he misses his mom, and I wish I could take his sadness away. Maybe that's what I should wish for, instead of what I really want.

"I guess the wish thing was a good idea and we should keep doing it, huh? It's kind of nice that I get to see you all the time now and not just in the summer."

The stupid butterflies are back, as well as the dumb nervous giggle, and I decide to stick with my original wish. If it comes true, I'll have plenty of time to figure out how to take Everett's sadness away. I'll have the rest of our lives.

"Who's ready to party?!" Aiden shouts from behind us as he walks into the clearing, holding up a bag of Fritos and a ziplock bag with a Little Debbie cupcake in it.

When he gets up to Everett and me, he stops suddenly and looks me over from head to toe with the same wide-eyed look that Everett had when he first saw me today.

"What the hell are you wearing, kid?" he asks with a laugh, nudging me with his elbow. "And what did you do to your hair?"

I narrow my eyes at him and feel my cheeks heating up with embarrassment, waiting for Everett to join in with Aiden's laughter.

"Shut up, Aiden," Everett scolds him, snatching the Fritos out of his hand and turning to make his way to the ladder that leads up to the treehouse. "It's her birthday and she looks nice."

I stick my tongue out at Aiden and he reaches over and musses up my hair with the palm of his hand. I smack it away with an angry growl and duck out from under his hand, which just makes him laugh harder.

"Fine, fine. I'm sorry. You look good, kid. Let's get this celebration started," he tells me with a smile, grabbing my hand and tugging me toward the ladder. "Do you know what you're going to wish for?"

"That's for me to know, and for you to never find out," I tell him sarcastically as he moves in front of me to start climbing the ladder behind Everett.

"Oh, I'll find out someday, don't you worry. Just don't make a wish that I'll fall madly in love with you and ask you to marry me," he jokes.

It's my turn for my mouth to fall open and my eyes to

widen in shock as I stare after Aiden while he scrambles up the ladder.

If he only knew that's the exact wish I planned on making today.

Just not about him.

Chapter 5

EVERETT

Patting the back pocket of my jeans, I feel the folded piece of paper I put in there this morning when I got dressed and I take a steadying breath. I've become OCD when it comes to that damn piece of paper, always patting my back pocket every couple of minutes just to make sure it's still there.

Six months ago, I wanted to burn that letter. Six months ago, I couldn't stand the pain the words written on it brought me and I tried to drink myself to death, but now I can't stand not having it on me at all times. Now I freak out making sure that it's still there and that I didn't misplace it or forget to put it in my pocket to carry with me everywhere. I've folded and unfolded it so many times, that the creases are about ready to rip in half if I do it one more time. It's not like I need to reread it. Every word has been imprinted on my brain and I don't need to look at it to remember what Aiden said to me, but it brings me comfort now to see his handwriting. It gives me strength to stay away from the booze and wake up each day, wanting to live, wanting to move forward and wanting to be a better man.

I don't know if it was the look on my brother's face and the words he said to me six months ago, when he came home and found me on the floor of the living room, or the sound of Cameron's name that finally woke me up. But whatever it was, it did the trick. I woke the fuck up. I had to accept the fact that there was nothing I could have done to save my best friend, and I had to learn how to live with the pain and the guilt of not being here when he died—without the crutch of alcohol. I was still here, living and breathing and I needed to start acting like it.

"You've traveled around the world, you've saved lives, you've become a goddamn hero to strangers. Now it's time to be a hero back here at home, where you belong."

I can hear Aiden's voice so clearly in my head, the one that was always laced with a hint of sarcasm and a touch of pompous asshole, that it feels like he's standing right next to me. And I smile to myself instead of feeling like I want to curl up in a ball and die. The guilt still stabs into my chest like a knife, and the ache of missing him so much takes my breath away, but the pain of his words makes me stop feeling so goddamn numb.

Leaning across the counter, I pick up the bottle of vodka that's been sitting there next to the sink for the last six months, collecting dust. I unscrew the cap and then twist it back on, over and over again, staring down at the empty bottle. The last one I drank and the one I keep here in my kitchen to remind me how fucked up I was and how I never want to go back to that dark place ever again.

Now that I'm sober, I'm able to process my thoughts and actions a bit more clearly. Finding out Aiden had cancer and I couldn't do a damn thing to help him wasn't exactly a walk in the park. When I was younger, I always wanted to be a doctor like my father. He was a hero who died helping people. When his convoy was pulled over on the side of the road to assist a local who had been shot, a roadside bomb took out his entire unit. I wanted to honor him by helping people in my own way. I thought going off to third world countries would allow me to do this. Little did I know that while I was off being noble, I wasn't there for the one person who really needed me, the one person I should've helped.

I wanted to numb the pain. I wanted to stop feeling. I wanted to stop remembering all the people I couldn't save oversees or the ones I left behind here at home. It worked for a few months. I drank from the minute I woke up in the morning until the minute I passed out at night. I stopped hearing the cries of pain from sick children and I stopped seeing the devastation on family members' faces when I couldn't fix one of their loved ones, and I stopped seeing Aiden's face everywhere I turned. The alcohol worked…until it didn't. Until nothing could keep the memories from breaking in and wreaking havoc on my brain. Until I realized nothing could keep the pain away. And that feeling that pain, even if it hurt like a bitch, was how I knew I was alive.

So I've spent the last six months getting clean and sober, needing to feel the pain, needing to feel alive, needing to be strong enough to be a hero here at home, like Aiden wanted. I may not have been there for him, but I owe it to him and Cameron to be there for her.

I'm still angry he's gone. Not a day goes by that I don't curse him six ways to Sunday for not telling me that he was sick. I understand now that I wouldn't have been able do anything to save him, but he was my best fucking friend. I should have been there with him at the end, and I'm pissed at him for not giving me the chance to say good-bye. But the anger is better than the depression. He was a daredevil, a risk taker, and he always used to joke that he'd die young.

Great job, Aiden. Way to follow through.

Being pissed at him is better than wanting to die right along with him. I can't exactly fix things with Cameron if I'm dead, and fixing things with my remaining best friend is my top priority now. It's the one thing that's kept me from going to the store and stocking up on vodka and from doing nothing but sitting around feeling sorry for myself. It's gonna take a lot for Cameron to forgive me, and I need to be strong enough to push back when she fights me on showing back up in her life, like I know she will. I need to be strong enough to let go of my jealousy and just be content at being her friend again. Because regardless of my feelings in the past, I miss our friendship. I miss *her*, and I hope to God she can let go of her anger and let me back in.

"Do we need to have another intervention? Because I gotta say, the first two were exhausting enough."

I look up from the bottle in my hand to see Jason stroll into the kitchen and right to the fridge, opening it up and grabbing an apple from the drawer. He slams the door closed and takes a huge bite out of it before crossing his arms in front of him.

After I got sober and started going to Alcoholics Anonymous meetings at the local hospital, and when Jason saw I was serious about staying clean this time, he moved out of our grandmother's house and got a place of his own in town. I tried to tell him he didn't need to leave, that this house was as much his as it was mine, and that Grandma had left it to both of us when she moved to Florida to spend her remaining years in the sand and sun, but he reassured me that he'd never really wanted to live here. He just stayed here when

I was gone for all those years so it would be ready for me when I finally decided to come home and stay home. And then when I finally did, there was no way he could leave, out of fear that I'd do something to myself and he wouldn't be here to save me.

Hearing him ask about another intervention and thinking about all the times he took care of me, when it should have been the other way around, almost made me want to pick up the bottle again. I hated that my younger brother was always picking up my pieces. I hated that I made him feel like I was his obligation and that he had no other choice. That hatred with myself and for what I'd done to him is another reason why I'm determined to keep myself on the straight and narrow and not fuck up again.

"Sure, come on in, Jason. Help yourself to whatever you want," I reply sarcastically. "And no, you do not need to have another intervention with me. I got your previous messages loud and clear."

Setting the bottle back down next to the sink, I look back at my brother and we share a look. The last time he saw me with a bottle in my hand, I was one sip away from being hospitalized for alcohol poisoning. Even if the urge to drink is always with me, I'd never do that to him again. Even when I was three sheets to the wind and lying in a pool of my own vomit, I could never forget the look on his face when he snatched the bottle out of my hand and told me that losing our parents was bad enough and I could go fuck myself if I thought I could leave him behind as well.

I shake myself out of that memory, reaching into my back pocket and pulling out the letter. Jason comes up next to me and leans back against the counter to stare down at the piece of paper with me.

"Why do you keep holding on to that thing? It's depressing

as shit," he mutters, taking another loud, crunching bite of his apple.

"It's not depressing. Not now, at least. It gives me something else to focus on other than wanting to drink," I tell him with a shrug.

"You're not Mom."

His softly spoken words pull my eyes away from the letter in my hand as I look at my brother.

"I know," I reply quietly.

"Do you? Because sometimes I think you're still punishing yourself, feeling guilty for something you had no control over. I'm not an idiot. I know you lied to her about what you were doing in college because of me. Because you were afraid she'd turn into a drunk again and ruin everything."

I always told Jason back then that we needed to keep things from her because she never got over our dad's death and knowing that I'd be putting myself into the same kinds of dangerous situations would kill her. I never wanted him to feel like he had any part in that decision. I never wanted *him* to feel guilty. I should have known he'd see right through it. He was my brother after all. He sometimes saw things more clearly than I did.

"You were happy. I couldn't ruin that for you. I didn't want you to have the same childhood I did..." I trail off.

"Newsflash, I *did* have the same childhood as you. I just didn't let it get to me like you did. I knew she was a shitty mother and I also accepted the fact a long time ago that nothing I did would change that. Being a mother didn't keep her sober. You lying to her didn't keep her sober. Nothing worked, Everett. I accepted it and I let it go. It's time for you to do the same."

I look away from him to stare back down at Aiden's letter in my hands, wondering why in the hell I always felt like the weight of our family's happiness rested on my shoulders. If I had talked to Jason about this years ago, maybe I wouldn't have carried around so much guilt for so long.

"Are you gonna do what he wants? Finally get your head out of your ass and go see Cameron?" he asks.

Just like always, the sound of her name wakes up everything dead inside of me. I was too much of a coward to go to her when I got back stateside, too full of guilt that I'd been two weeks too late for Aiden's funeral, and too fucked up for the next few months after that even to think about going anywhere near her. I never deserved having her in my life before I screwed everything up between us, and there was no way in hell I'd go to her when I was at my lowest. I've spent the last six months turning myself around and trying to become a man who deserves her friendship. One who could be strong enough to be there for her, for whatever she needs. I was never a very good friend to her when we were younger, always worrying about my own problems and letting her take care of *me,* and then letting my fucking one-sided feelings for her ruin things even further. Even if all she needs is a shoulder to cry on as she mourns our best friend, the man she fell in love with when I walked away, I'll give it to her. I finally feel strong enough to suck it up and deal with the pain of knowing that I lost my shot a long time ago, and I was never good enough for someone like her. I've moved on, I've grown up, and the only thing I want right now is to be her friend, and to be there for her, like she always was for me.

"Yeah, I'm gonna go see her," I tell him, sliding the letter back into my pocket, patting it a few times to make sure it's secure as I push away from the counter.

"Can I come with you? I really want to be there to see her punch you in the face," Jason laughs, and I shoot him the middle finger when I walk by him and head down the hall to jump in the shower.

It's been over four-and-a-half years since I've seen Cameron James, but not a day has gone by that I haven't thought about her. Haven't wished on a thousand stars that I would have done things differently the last night I saw her. Aiden was right in his letter. I need to stop wishing and start making things happen, by repairing my friendship with her. She's never needed me, always being the strong one in our friendship, always being there for *me*. I don't know if she'll need me now, or even want me anywhere near her after so much time has gone by and after all the ways I've let her down. But I know I can't spend one more day without her in my life.

The Three Musketeers will never be whole again, but maybe the two of us can figure out a way to repair the damage, as long as she lets me try.

Chapter 6

EVERETT

Wishing in the past...
Seventeen years old

My hand stills in midair with a horseshoe pick in it when I hear a girl's voice in the stables, cutting through all the sounds of men talking, cursing, and laughing as they work. The mare's hoof I was holding on to with the other hand slips from my grip as I slowly bring my body upright from its hunched-over position. My eyes are glued to Cameron as she walks into the stable, waving hello to a few of the workers and exchanging greetings with them. She's wearing a short, tattered jean skirt with cowboy boots and a tight tank top that leaves absolutely nothing to the imagination, making me want to grab the nearest horse blanket and throw it around her shoulders, covering up every inch of exposed skin that spills out of her low-cut top, an image that I'm sure more than a few of the men in this barn will be jerking off to later. Myself included.

I am a disgusting human being and I should be put in jail. That's all there is to it. She's fourteen years old and I'm seventeen. Way too old to be getting a damn hard-on for my best friend and wanting to beat the shit out of every other man in this place who has the same problem in his pants.

I have no fucking clue when Cameron suddenly went from gangly teenager with bruises and scrapes on her knees and always covered in dirt to the stunning, "looks older than she really is" girl strutting toward me right now, or when I stopped thinking of her as just one of the guys and started having entirely too many inappropriate thoughts about her. It feels like it happened overnight. One day she was just a tomboy, and the next, she was a damn teenage boy's wet dream. Now that she's in high school with me and Aiden, I feel like all I do is shoot dirty looks to any guy that glances in her general direction and threaten to chop off my friends' dicks when they ask me if she's dating anyone.

I rack my brain, trying to come up with the exact moment I started thinking my best friend was hot, and the memory of her twelfth birthday suddenly pops into my head. The first time I saw her dressed up and wearing makeup. I couldn't stop staring. I couldn't stop thinking about how pretty she looked. I realize now, I pushed that moment in time out of my head because I didn't like how it made me feel. I didn't like having those thoughts about my best friend. And she was twelve! I've spent the last two years pretending that moment never happened, and now I can't ignore it.

Forcing my gaze away from her long, gorgeous legs and the sway of her hips, my eyes finally meet hers when she gets a few feet away. She smiles when she sees me and doesn't stop moving until she's standing so close that I can smell the light, flowery perfume she always wears that smells like magnolia blossoms, that somewhere in the last few months started making my mouth water whenever she was near.

"Aren't you supposed to be helping your mom with her dance class?"

My words come out clipped and filled with annoyance, and I immediately want to take them back when the smile falls from her face. It's not her fault I'm pissed at myself for all the inappropriate thoughts running through my head. Like how I want to wrap my arms around her waist and pull her up against me and how I want to kiss that bottom lip of hers that she's currently running her teeth over.

"My mom and I decided it was best if I avoid her dance classes from now on and help out with a different camp activity. I think she finally realized I will never follow in her footsteps," Cameron replies with an easy shrug.

Cameron's mom was an amazing dancer when she was young, and could have gone on to being one of the best dancers in the world until a car accident ended her career. Thankfully, her love of dance never ended, and she holds hip-hop and other fun classes at camp, and it's one of the most popular activities here. Sadly, Cameron did not inherit her mother's graceful talent, but she refused to give up.

"Who did you send to the nurse this time?" I ask, chuckling when she crosses her arms in front of her with a huff and rolls her eyes.

"Braiden Barber. But it's not my fault. That little snot got in my way on purpose," she complains.

"Braiden is six. I'm pretty sure he didn't do anything on purpose."

"Whatever," she replies with a wave of her hand. "He was showing off and gloating because he picked up a move I couldn't do, and he deserved that kick to the shin for not watching where he was going."

She glares at me when the smile on my face starts to make my cheeks hurt and I hold in my laughter so I don't piss her off even more. No matter how I'm feeling, I can always count on Cameron to make things better. I've been in a shit mood for the last two days, and just listening to her talk makes me forget about my problems for a few minutes.

"I'm going to forgive you for being happy about my morning of misery because I know you've had a rough couple of days, but don't expect this generosity to last," she warns, taking a step toward me and resting her hand on my upper arm, giving it a squeeze.

"I'm fine."

She cocks her head to the side and stares up at me with a knowing look in her gorgeous green eyes that makes me want to unload all of my problems on her and let her take them all away.

"You're lying," she states, knowing me better than anyone, even Aiden.

I don't know why Cameron is always the one I run to with all of my problems. Why she's so much easier to talk to and why I feel more comfortable telling all my shit to her. Sometimes I feel guilty that the two of us have secrets we've never shared with our other best friend, but most of the time, like right now, when she's standing so close and looking up at me like this, prepared to fix everything for me no matter what it is, I don't care that Aiden isn't here and I don't feel guilty that I've kept him in the dark about certain parts of my life.

"I'm not lying. Not exactly. Yesterday was bad, but today is getting better," I reassure her, keeping it to myself that the reason it's getting better is all because of her. Just having her here, regardless of how fucked up my feelings are where she's concerned, always makes me feel better.

"My mom said your mother left already. I'm sorry, Ev."

I shrug, refusing to spend another minute being hurt and pissed off that my mother let me and Jason down again.

"It's okay, I'm fine," I tell her again. "I don't know why I expected this time to be different from any other time she's come out to visit."

"What can I do? Want me to fly to New Jersey and kick her ass?" Cameron asks in complete seriousness, making me smile even though nothing is funny about this situation. "Because you know I'll do it. No one hurts my best friend and gets away with it."

I shake my head at her and take a step back before I do something stupid like bend down and kiss her. She'd probably kick MY ass if I did something like that.

Moving even farther away from her to avoid temptation, I bend over and lift up the mare's leg that I'd abandoned when Cameron first walked into the barn, and busy myself with cleaning out her hoof.

"I'm fine, Cam. I already took my frustrations out on Alan Haynes. Why do you think your dad put me on the shittiest job in the stables, next to shoving actual shit?"

I try to make light of the situation by looking back up at her and smiling, cursing under my breath when I see the ticked-off look on her face and know I need to do something before she races out of here and tells her father off. It's not her dad's fault I keep fucking up, giving him yet another reason to hate me.

"Okay, now I'm going to kick my dad's ass," she grumbles angrily.

"Seriously, Cam, it's fine. Alan pissed me off, I gave him a bloody nose, and your dad had every right to punish me for getting into a fight with another worker."

I don't tell her Alan made some smart-ass comment about

wanting to "tap that ass" when he saw Cameron out by the lake this morning, something I also didn't tell her father when he walked around the corner of the barn and saw me straddling that little bitch, pummeling his smug face. I also didn't say anything when Eli pulled me off of Alan or when Alan starting whining about how I started punching him for no reason. What's the point in defending my self when no one will believe me anyway?

"No ass kicking will be necessary, but thanks for the offer," I add.

I hear her sigh and I dig the pick faster and harder, concentrating on what I'm doing instead of the breathy sound she just made.

"Fine, I'll take ass kicking off of my to-do list, but we're still doing something fun tonight when camp is over. Whatever you want to do, we're doing it. Aiden has a date with some college skank he won't shut up about, so it will be just you and me."

I look back at her over my shoulder and wonder if there will ever come a time when the tables will be turned and I'll be the one doing whatever I can to make Cameron happy and be the better friend in this relationship.

Chapter 7

CAMERON

You sound stressed. Maybe we should come home. *Eli, I think we need to go home,*" my mom says, her voice over the phone growing muffled when she starts talking to my dad instead of me.

I run my hand through my hair, pulling a piece of hay out of the long, tangled strawberry blond strands that I should have pulled up into a ponytail this morning before I started getting knee-deep in problems.

"Mom, everything's fine," I tell her, closing my eyes and wincing at how easily the lie flies right out of my mouth. "You are not coming home from Outer Banks when you just got there. You'll be back for the charity dinner in a month, we made a deal. It's just a few warped boards around the foundation of the dance studio. Nothing I can't handle."

When I convinced my parents to take a vacation and spend some time at their rarely used vacation home on the beach in

Outer Banks, I made light of the money problems with the camp and reassured them that everything would be fixed by the time they came home. I even made them promise they wouldn't set foot back on this land until the dinner. My mom balked at the idea of spending over a month away from here, but my dad reminded her that they'd been letting me take on the running of the camp for almost a year by that point, and if they ever wanted to fully retire, they needed to trust me. It just makes all the lies I've been telling them recently worse, knowing they both *do* trust me to keep this place going. They don't need to know I can count on one hand how many hours of sleep I've gotten since they left, staying up until the crack of dawn almost every night, trying to come up with a solution. They also don't need to know that Amelia has had to yell at me more than once before I realize the entire day has gone by and I haven't eaten anything. Thank God they can't see the dark circles under my eyes or the weight I've lost. They have no clue I'm lying through my teeth when I tell them everything is fine.

Hopefully, by the time they come home, I'll have secured a new donor and they'll forgive me for not being fully honest with them.

"You mean, nothing *Jason* can't handle," my mom laughs over the line and I smile to myself.

"Exactly. Jason will be here any minute now and all will be right with the camp."

I've taken advantage of my friendship with Everett's younger brother, calling on him regularly whenever there's a construction project that I need help with. He's always ready and willing to do whatever he can for me and the camp, but I was a little shocked by how quickly he jumped on my request when I called him earlier today. I know he has a full-time job and usually he stops by at the end of the workday or on the weekend, but he told me he was dropping everything, calling off of work, and heading right out. I tried to tell him it could wait, but he'd already hung up on me. At first, seeing Jason after Everett left was a struggle. He reminded me too much of his older brother, who had written me off and turned his back on me, and it made his disappearance from my life that much more painful. After a while, after Jason learned that mentioning his brother's name did nothing but piss me off and make me sad, it became an unspoken agreement that we'd never discuss him. As much as I wanted to ask Jason a thousand different questions over the years, I didn't want to put him in the middle when he was such a good man and didn't deserve the third degree from me.

"Jason's here."

I turn my head when Seth, a high school student volunteer, walks up next to me and points to the driveway that leads from the main plantation house over here to the dance studio that's attached to the stables. We both watch the swirl of dust kick up around the tires of Jason's truck as it slowly makes its way toward us.

Seth moves around me and down the driveway to meet Jason's truck, and I turn away from his approaching vehicle to stare down at the warped boards that he's coming out here to fix.

"Mom, I gotta go. Jason just got here and I have a hundred other things I need to check on before lunch," I tell her. "I love you. Tell Dad I love him, too, but if either one of you come back here before the charity dinner, I will kick you out. I've got everything under control."

Mom sighs through the line, returns my proclamation of love, and disconnects the call, promising me she'll call back tomorrow to check on things.

I hear the crunch of boots on the gravel driveway and

shove the phone into the back pocket of my jeans, turning around with a smile on my face to greet Jason.

"You didn't have to break speed limit laws to get out here. I told you it was—"

My words cut off and my smile drops, along with my stomach. Tears fill my eyes before I can stop them and all the breath in my body leaves me in a *whoosh* of air past my lips. I have to force myself to remember how to breathe and lock my knees before my legs give out and I drop to the ground.

"Hey, Cam."

The voice I haven't heard in almost five years sounds like it's coming from down a long, dark tunnel, and I realize it's because my heart is pounding so hard it's thundering in my ears. It's the same raspy, deep voice I've heard in my head in the middle of the night, no matter how much I didn't want it there. It's the same soothing sound I spent over twenty years of my life wanting to listen to forever, coming from the same man I wished would *be* my forever. The sound is like music to my ears and I want to beg him to say something else, just so I can hear him again and know that he's really here, and really within touching distance. Even though Jason and I had an unspoken agreement never to mention Everett, he'd still manage to throw in something from time to time, letting me know his brother was at least still among the living, especially when Everett was the first to volunteer to go to the most dangerous places. But it was hard to believe the truth in those words until right this moment, when he's standing in front of me, so real and so perfect and so full of life, his chest rising and falling with every breath he takes, his blue eyes staring right into mine.

I can't stop looking at Everett, standing here a few feet away from me in a pair of tight jeans, black work boots, and a long-sleeved gray Henley, the sleeves pushed up to his elbows and his hands in his front pockets. He's still wearing his dark brown hair shaved short on the sides and a little longer on top, the thick, messy strands falling all over the place on top of his head, making me want to reach up and run my fingers through them to straighten them out and smooth them down. His hair is the only similarity to the Everett I used to know. He'd always been hot, but years abroad, working and volunteering in third world countries, has clearly done wonders for him judging by the muscles I see straining from his forearms, and everywhere else on his upper body for that matter, with how tightly the cotton material of his shirt clings to him.

He'd always kept his face cleanly shaven, and after years of hanging around Aiden, who shaved every day, I started to think I must have a thing for men who had a smooth face. Until now. Everett's facial hair coming down from his sideburns, making a trail down his cheeks and covering his chin and around his mouth, is short and neatly groomed, and dammit if it doesn't make him hotter.

That thought suddenly makes the tears in my eyes dry up and all the emotion I felt at seeing him again for the first time in years vanish in the blink of an eye. How dare he just show up here after all this time after not one word in almost five years. How dare he go from being one of the most important people in my life to someone who threw me away and never looked back. Who couldn't even be bothered to reach out to me when our best fucking friend died.

I resist the urge to close the distance between us and throw myself in his arms, dying to feel the heat from his body and the beat of his heart against my own, reassuring me that he's real.

"What the hell are you doing here?"

His lips twitch with the urge to smile, and my anger that he thinks anything about this is funny pisses me off even more. He has no right to show up out of nowhere, at *my* camp, thinking we can just pick up where we left off.

"It's good to see you, too, Cam. You've got hay in your hair," he tells me in a soft voice, the corner of his mouth tipping up in a half smile when he says the same thing he used to say to me all the time when we were younger. It makes my insides feel all mushy, which makes me want to throw my fist through something.

Like his stupid, hot face.

I hate that his use of my nickname turns me to jelly no matter how mad I am at him, but I refuse to let him see that he has any kind of effect on me. I lock my knees even tighter when he takes a few steps in my direction until he's standing so close to me, I can smell his light, woodsy cologne. Of course he's wearing the same damn cologne he's worn since we were teenagers and I first bought him a bottle of the stuff for Christmas one year, and I liked the way it smelled on him so much, I got him one every year. I'm so flustered and confused with everything I'm feeling right now that I let my anger take over and drive this bus of emotional exhaustion instead of collapsing at his feet in a puddle of tears.

"Jesus, you look good. I missed you so damn much."

That's it. That does it. Any hope of calming myself down and acting like an adult goes right out the window when he says those words.

My hand flies up from down by my side, and before I can stop myself, my palm slaps against his cheek so hard I'll be feeling the sting of it for a week. His head jerks to the side with the force of my smack and he keeps it turned away from me as I slowly lower my hand, panting with furious breaths.

"Don't you *dare* say something like that to me," I tell him through clenched teeth, squeezing my hands into fists down by my side before I hit him again, with a punch to the nose this time. "*You're* the one who decided to ignore me for almost five fucking years. You have no right to come here and say that to me."

He closes his eyes and sighs, turning his head back to face me before opening them again, and it almost takes my breath away. I can see the pain, the sorrow, the hurt, and the misery shining right back at me, mirroring everything I'm feeling inside, but I'm not about to go easy on him now. He hurt me deeper than any person in my life has ever done before. He broke my heart and he left me behind. I will never forgive him for that.

"I know. I know and I'm so fucking sorry. You have no idea how sorry I am."

His eyes plead with me to understand, but I don't. I can't. I've spent all these years wondering what I did wrong and wishing I could fix it. All these damn wasted years where I couldn't let him go and couldn't move on. And I've spent the last nine months mourning our best friend alone, without him.

"I don't give a shit how sorry you are. You should have been here. You and your fancy fucking medical degree, out saving people you didn't even know. Aiden needed you. I needed you and you weren't here. I mourned him alone. I buried him alone. I FUCKING BURIED OUR BEST FRIEND ALONE!" I shout, my voice cracking with tears when I think about Aiden's funeral.

Even being surrounded by friends and family, their arms around me and their tears falling with mine, I'd never felt more alone than I did standing by Aiden's grave and watching them lower his casket into the ground. I wasn't mad at

Everett then, because I knew he was probably in some remote area of the world where he couldn't just drop everything and leave. I forgave him for not being at the funeral and a part of me feels horrible for throwing that at him now, when he had no control over being there, but I can't help it.

Even though he didn't find out until it was too late, I know from Jason that he still found out a few weeks after Aiden died. But he never came home then. He never called me. He never e-mailed. He never did ANYTHING. All those years I spent being his friend and the one time I needed him, he wasn't there. Someone was always with me, day and night for weeks after Aiden's death, but I'd never felt more lost than I had during that time, because Everett wasn't there. My parents and Amelia have done everything they could to pull me out of my funk for the last nine months, but nothing worked because Everett wasn't here. He was the only other person in the world who would have understood what I was feeling, but he wasn't here. And now that he *is* here, I hate him for thinking he can make everything better with an apology. Words can't heal the scars that his actions left behind.

"Cameron, Cameron, are you there?"

The squawk of the radio attached to the waist of my jeans stops me from screaming at Everett again. With my angry eyes still locked on to his sorrowful ones, I snatch the radio from by my hip, bring it up to my mouth, and press the button to talk.

"Amelia, I'm a little busy here. I'll be up to the main house in a few minutes."

Everett moves closer to me as I reattach the radio to my jeans. I'm so wrapped up in my sadness and anger, wanting him to feel all of the hurt that's lived inside of me without him, and distracted by Amelia radioing me, that I don't realize he's touching me until it's too late. His arms are sliding around my waist and my brain wakes up right before he pulls me toward him.

I take a step back from him so quickly that my feet tangle together and I almost trip, steadying myself at the last second before I go down. Everett looks more shocked that I wouldn't let him touch me than he did when I smacked him across the face. What the hell does he expect? Ever since I was thirteen, I dreamed about him wrapping his arms around me and holding me close, pulling me into his chest so I could rest my cheek against it and feel the thudding of his heart against the side of my face. I dreamed about it, fantasized about it, wished for it...and all I ever got were side-armed hugs and the casual fling of his arm around my shoulder if I was lucky. I learned my lesson a long time ago that loving Everett did nothing but cause me pain, and I'll be damned if I get sucked down into that rabbit hole again.

"I'm sorry," Everett says again, sighing in frustration as he runs his fingers through the short hair on top of his head, nervously shifting from one foot to the other.

I'm not sure if he's still apologizing for being a shitty friend, or for his attempt to put his hands on me, and I don't care.

He brings his hand down from his head to rub his palm against the side of his face where I smacked him, and I open my mouth to apologize, but quickly clamp it closed when I remember he deserved it. What the hell is wrong with me? I'm not this person. I don't go around smacking people, and I hate Everett a little bit more that he's turned me into this kind of woman who throws a fit out in the open for all to see.

"Aiden was right. You *have* developed a mean right hook over the years."

His attempt to get me to smile falls flat. Bringing up

Aiden's name and reminding me that the two of them remained in contact over the years he was gone when I was left in the dust makes my heart crack into a thousand pieces.

"Screw you," I whisper, swallowing thickly a few times to stop the burning pain in my throat from the need to cry.

I will not cry in front of this man. I will not let him see just how weak he makes me feel.

"Cam…"

He takes a step in my direction but pauses when my radio crackles to life with Amelia's voice again, high-pitched and screaming this time.

"CAMERON! SOS! YOU HAVE TO—"

With an irritated growl, my hand goes to my hip and I quickly turn the dial for sound until it clicks off. I take a deep, calming breath before addressing Everett for the last time.

"I don't need you here. I don't want you here. Go home, and leave me alone. You had almost five years of practice doing just that. It should be pretty easy for you to pick up where you left off."

Refusing to look at him anymore before I do something stupid like launch myself into his arms and apologize for being such a bitch, I hold my head up high and walk around him.

I was always a sucker when it came to Everett Southerland and I'll be damned if I fall back into the same old patterns just because he's suddenly decided to walk back into my life.

Chapter 8

CAMERON

Wishing in the past…
Fifteen years old

Happy birthday, kid! We still on for seven o'clock tonight?" Aiden asks, mussing up my hair as he rushes by me, turning to walk backward as he makes his way to class.

"Stop messing up my hair! And yes, seven. Don't forget the snacks!" I shout after him as the warning bell rings, kids start moving faster down the hall, and lockers slam closed.

He gives me a salute before turning around and running through the sea of students.

"Is he still dating Michelle Lanford? I heard they broke up. Do you think he'd say yes if I asked him out?"

My head turns to the side as I close my locker to see a girl standing next to me with a dreamy look on her face as she stares after Aiden.

"Yeah, they broke up last week. Doesn't hurt to ask," I

tell her with a shrug, hefting my stack of books up higher in my arms as she thanks me and goes running in Aiden's direction.

Shaking my head, I start walking down the hall to algebra class when my books are suddenly snatched out of my arms. I look up to find a smiling Everett staring down at me, and my stomach flops as he tucks my books under his arms and walks me to class.

"Happy birthday, Cam. How does it feel to be fifteen?" he asks, bumping his shoulder against mine.

I nervously reach up and twirl a lock of my hair between my fingers, forcing myself not to giggle.

"Like I'm too young to drive and too old to play with Barbies."

Jesus, Cameron. Barbies? Really? Way to make him try and see you as a woman instead of a little girl. Real smooth.

Everett just smiles at me, pausing by the algebra room door and handing my books back to me. He puts his arm around my shoulder and pulls me against his side for exactly three seconds before dropping his arm and moving away.

"Have a good day. See you at the treehouse tonight," he tells me with a wave.

I stand in the doorway watching him walk down the hall and let out a long sigh.

"He's so hot. I can't believe you're friends with him," Allison Brantley says, stopping in the doorway next to me to stare after Everett.

Allison Brantley has had a crush on Everett since the beginning of the school year and has flirted shamelessly with him. She lost her virginity a month ago to Alex Conrad, a senior and a football player who's friends with Everett. Ever since then, she thought she was hot shit and she'd upped her flirting game with Everett and it made me want to puke. SHE'D never talked about Barbies in front of him.

"I'm gonna ask him out tonight at lunch."

My head whips in her direction and I can't stop the scowl that takes over my face. I hate Allison Brantley.

"He doesn't date skanks," I inform her, ignoring the pissed-off look on her face as I shoulder past her and into the room to take my seat.

No matter how rude my statement was, Allison would never argue with me or make a scene, because she knows I have the upper hand. Just like every other girl in this school when it comes to my two best friends. Maybe that makes me a total bitch, but I don't care. Every girl here knows if they piss me off, they'll never have a shot with Aiden or Everett. Well, maybe not Aiden. He'd date anything with a vagina, no matter how skanky or pathetic she was. But not Everett. Everett listened to me when I gave my opinion on the girls he dated, even though just the fact that he went on dates with other girls made me sick to my stomach. That thought gives me pause as I set my books on top of my desk, not hearing a word the teacher says when he walks into the room. Why DOES Everett always do what I say, when Aiden always does the exact opposite? Does he really value my opinion? Does he know I have a crush on him and he's just doing it not to embarrass me? Oh, my God, please don't let that be it. I hope he just listens to me because I'm his friend and I'm a girl, therefore I know how other girls think.

Besides I wasn't a complete jerk, even though I wanted to be. I didn't put my foot down with everyone. Just the girls I thought had potential to steal his heart. I learned how to be okay with Everett dating other girls, as long as they weren't "happily ever after" material. It's not like I thought Everett would fall madly in love with Allison and run off and marry her, but it's my birthday, dammit. Nothing is going to ruin this day, especially not Allison Brantley and her giant boobs, skinny waist, long legs, and missing virginity.

* * *

"Stop laughing at me. I am totally your pimp."

Aiden ignores my order, laughing so hard he has to wipe the tears from his eyes.

"The struggle is real. 'Do you think Aiden likes me?' 'Do you think Everett will ask me out?'" I say in a high-pitch, annoying voice. "I am your pimp, letting the female population know when you're free for a new hook-up. It's disgusting. I should start charging both of you."

I bring the bottle of beer up to my mouth and take another drink, realizing quickly how drunk I am when half of it dribbles down my chin instead of going into my mouth.

Everett takes the bottle out of my hand, using the sleeve of his sweatshirt to wipe the beer from my face. I don't even realize I've stopped breathing until he moves his arm away and smiles at me.

Aiden decided Grape Crush wasn't enough for us this year, and brought along a case of beer with his usual provisions. At eighteen, Aiden and Everett have both had plenty of opportunities to drink when they hang out with friends their own age, but I never have. I thought it was the perfect way to show Everett that I'm not a little girl anymore, but somewhere after my third bottle, things got a little hazy and I started slurring my words, talking about pimps like a complete idiot. This is why he's always dating skanks. Because I'm just a little girl who can't hold her liquor, and those skanks are women who probably can.

At least I'm not talking about Barbies anymore, so I have that going for me.

"I think you've had enough," Everett tells me, looking away to set the bottle on the other side of his legs.

Everett and I are sitting side by side, our legs straight out in front of us, and Aiden is sitting cross-legged across from us. I stare at Everett's profile when he leans forward, busying himself collecting all the empties, clinking the bottles together as he pushes them into a cluster on the floor of the treehouse. I want to reach over and rest my palm against the side of his strong jaw, say something to make him smile so one of his dimples pops out and I can lean in and kiss it.

"You're such a buzz kill, Ev," Aiden jokes, finishing off his beer and setting it down next to the empties Everett just collected. "It's her birthday, she can get drunk if she wants to!"

When Everett leans back and puts his hands on the floor behind him, he sprawls his legs out and his thigh brushes up against mine. My heart starts hammering in my chest, and for the first time since I was seven years old, I wish Aiden wasn't here with us.

I hate that that thought is going through my mind. I love Aiden, but right now, I just want to be alone with Everett. I want to move closer to him until our shoulders are touching, I want him to look down at me and smile, I want him to brush my hair over my shoulder like I've seen him do with girls he's dated, I want him to look at me and really see me. As a woman and not as his best friend.

"Good thing you already wrote down your wish and put it in your box; otherwise I might have had to help you and I would have seen what you wished for," Everett says, giving me a wink.

I was kind of grateful for that, too, until just now. If

he'd helped me write my wish, he would know how I feel. It would be out in the open and I wouldn't have to keep pretending anymore. I'm so tired of pretending. I'm so tired of wanting something I feel like I'll never have, no matter how much I wish for it, no matter how hard I try to prove to Everett that I'm not a little girl anymore and I can make him happier than any of those slutty girls at school.

"Aiden! Are you almost done? I'm bored!" a voice shouts from outside, down at the base of the treehouse.

"Oh, my God. Did you seriously bring a date to my birthday party?" I complain, glaring at Aiden while Everett chuckles and shakes his head at him.

"Hey, it's not my fault I'm irresistible and my social calendar is full. And besides, it's not like I brought her up here. I made her wait for me down below, like a gentleman. You can't be pissed at me, kid," Aiden explains with a smirk.

I roll my eyes at him, but the action makes the room spin and I wave my hand at him, concentrating as hard as I can on not throwing up.

"Go. Go be with your skank."

"Are you sure?" Aiden asks, already pushing himself up from the floor.

"Yes. You can make it up to me by sending out a memo that I am done being your pimp. Tell her, to tell all her friends, that I am no longer answering inquiries on the status of your love life."

Aiden laughs, bending forward and giving me a quick kiss on the cheek.

"I'll see what I can do," he smiles, straightening up and pointing at Everett. "You're in charge of holding her hair back when she pukes."

Everett gives him a thumbs-up and I shout after him as he races toward the door.

"I AM NOT GOING TO PUKE!"

He laughs all the way down the ladder, and when silence fills the treehouse, I turn toward Everett.

"I'm not gonna puke," I reassure him quietly, really, really hoping I don't puke.

He bumps his arm into mine and smiles at me.

"But if you do puke, I'll hold your hair back."

It's really sad that that is the most romantic thing I've ever heard in my life. I'm definitely drunk.

His eyes never leave mine and I want to keep my mouth shut so I don't ruin the moment with the word vomit of a beer buzz, but I can't help myself.

"How come you've never brought a girl here?" I ask softly.

Aiden brings a different girl here every week, showing off the fact that he's friends with the people who own the camp, trying to impress them. Everett has never, not once brought a date here, even for the charity dinner my parents throw every year.

He leans closer to me and I tip my head back to look up at him. Our faces are so close, all I'd have to do is lift my chin and our lips would touch. I want him to lift his hand from the floor behind him and curl it around my waist, turn toward me, and pull me closer until we're chest to chest and I can feel his heart beating against mine. I want more than a brush of his shoulder against mine, or a quick side hug. I want him to close the distance. I want him to make the first move. I don't want to be the one to do it and have him pull back and laugh at me.

"This place is special to me," he answers in a quiet voice. "It got me through one of the hardest times in my life. I'd never bring a girl here who wasn't special. Who didn't mean as much to me as this place does."

I wanted him to say he'd never bring a girl here, because

he doesn't need to. Because she's already here. But at least I know I won't have to worry about him bringing a skank who doesn't mean anything to him here every week, like Aiden, and that's good enough for now.

He pulls away from me and gives me another smile, and I immediately feel cold without his arm pressed up against mine.

I think about the wish I wrote down on my star, the same wish I've written down since I turned thirteen. Maybe I should have changed it up and wished that he'd kiss me or, hell, just give me a hug that wasn't brotherly, but it's too late to change it now. It's been put into my box and nestled back down under the floorboard until next year.

Hopefully someday, I'll get my wish, which will lead to a lot more than hugging anyway.

Chapter 9

EVERETT

Jesus, she's beautiful.

That thought is the only thing running through my head right now as Cameron lifts her chin and walks around me. The four-and-a-half years I spent away from her suddenly feel like fifty, and I want to grab on to her and never let go, make up for all the time I stayed away from her, but I know she'd probably smack my face again if I did that.

Judging by the look in her eyes and how quickly she moved away from me when I tried to hug her, I'm thinking I would get a closed fist to my nose instead of her palm. When Jason got a phone call from Cameron earlier while I was in the shower, he decided it was the perfect opportunity for me to come out to the camp and talk to her. My first thought was excitement. I just wanted to see her face and finally hear her voice again. With each mile I drove toward the camp, my trepidation grew, knowing she wasn't going to take me just showing up back in her life like this very well.

I'm realizing I should have thought things through a little more, knowing how pissed off she'd be at me.

My eyes immediately go to her ass as she walks away, and I wonder how it's possible for this woman to have gotten even hotter in four years than I ever imagined. Her skinny jeans cling to her curves and the knee-high boots she wears over them makes her long legs look like they go on for days. The green tank top she has on with the Camp Rylan logo printed over her chest was like a neon sign, flashing in front of my eyes and begging me to stare at how well she filled out the top of that flimsy piece of cotton. Even with a few random pieces of hay stuck in her long, thick blond hair, I still have to fight the urge to reach up and run my fingers through the soft tangles that fall down over her shoulders and halfway down her back.

Cameron James at twenty-six was a woman who didn't even know the power of her own beauty. Cameron James at thirty is full of hurt, anger, and piss and vinegar, and the sway of her hips as she walks is determined and the sexiest damn thing I've ever seen.

"I needed you and you weren't here. I mourned him alone. I buried him alone. I fucking buried our best friend alone!"

Her words had me wishing I'd never quit drinking, but the tears in her eyes almost made me drop to my knees and cry like a fucking baby. I knew staying away had hurt her, but I never realized just how much until I was confronted with her pain. Until I saw her swallow back those tears and show me her anger instead. She has every right to be pissed at me. Every right to throw it in my face how much of a shitty person I'd been to her. I wanted to tell her why I stayed away. I wanted to explain to her about the drinking and the depression and the guilt and how I couldn't let her see me like that. I couldn't let her see me as anything other than the sober man that stood in front of her today.

She spent most of our lives trying to fix me and make things better and I can't let her do that anymore. It's my turn now. The camp still looks as amazing as it always has, and I know from Jason that Cameron is running it now. I don't know how she could possibly need me for anything, but there's no way in hell I'm walking away like she told me to. She's hurting without Aiden, still, after nine months. I don't blame her for that either. He was my best friend and I don't think I'll ever stop hurting. He was the love of her life. That's something you don't get over after nine months, or maybe ever. I wasn't here to help her bury him, but I will be here to do whatever I can to make her hurt a little less.

"Who could that be?"

I look up to see that Cameron has stopped a few feet in front of me, staring down the driveway at a slowly approaching black stretch limo.

"CAMERON! EMERGENCY!"

We both turn toward the direction of the main house, and I see a woman about Cameron's age running toward us at full speed, waving her arms above her head.

"BRAXTON STRATFORD IS COMING! BRAXTON STRATFORD IS COMING!" the woman screams with her arms still flailing around her head.

I watch Cameron slowly turn her head to the approaching limo, wondering what's going on and who the hell Braxton Stratford is.

"Oh, shit. No, no, no. This is not happening right now. Son of a bitch," Cameron whispers, her hands flying up to her hair, picking out pieces of hay and smoothing it down around her shoulders.

She's nervously straightening her tank top, pulling the hem down and brushing dirt off of it as I walk up next to her and the limo stops a few hundred yards away.

"Who is that?"

Her head jerks toward me and she looks at me in shock, like she forgot I was here, before the shock is quickly replaced with anger.

"I thought I told you to leave. Why are you still here?" she growls.

"Who's Braxton Stratford and why are you freaking out?" I try again.

"He's the guy who's going to save Camp Rylan."

The young kid I saw standing next to Cameron when I pulled in a little bit ago walks up next to me.

"Shut up, Seth," Cameron mutters.

"What do you mean, he's going to save the camp?" I ask Seth, since Cameron obviously isn't going to answer me and Seth doesn't seem to care that his boss just told him to shut up.

"We don't have any money. Our main benefactor kicked the bucket and we're out of funds. This guy is our only hope if we want to stay open after this summer session," Seth explains.

"You're fired," Cameron tells him through clenched teeth.

Seth just shrugs and smiles at her. "You don't pay me. I'm a volunteer, so you can't fire me."

Cameron fires off a trail of muttered curses, and I hold back my laughter since I'm standing so close to her and I know she wouldn't hesitate to use that right hook on me again.

The screaming woman running across the yard finally makes it to our group and stops on the other side of Cameron, bending over at the waist with her hand on her chest, trying to catch her breath.

"You...turned...off...radio," she pants. "Stratford... is...here...early."

We turn as a group toward the limo when the front door opens and a man in a black suit gets out, moving to the back door and opening it.

"I can see that," Cameron replies dryly.

"I still don't understand why we're freaking out. This is an amazing camp. You have nothing to be nervous about," I reassure Cameron as we wait for this Braxton guy to get out of the limo.

"*We* are not freaking out. *I'm* freaking out because this is *my* camp, and you can go fuck yourself, Everett," Cameron informs me.

Seth laughs, but I'm too busy thinking about how good my name sounded coming from her lips, even if the sound of it was filled with venom, to pay him any attention.

"Holy shit, you're Everett," the woman on the other side of Cameron says, finally catching her breath and standing upright, grabbing on to Cameron's arm and shaking it. "That's Everett."

"Shut up, Amelia."

"Why are we freaking out if Everett's here? This will work perfectly!" she exclaims, ignoring Cameron's demand to be quiet just like Seth did, clapping her hands together in glee.

I'm not even sad I've been gone so long that Cameron has hired new employees I've never met. I'm too busy liking them a whole hell of a lot even though I just met them.

"What will work perfectly?" I ask, turning to face Seth since I know he'll answer me.

"Braxton Stratford is...um, well, he's kind of an eccentric, weird dude. Totally old school. He only gives his money to family-run businesses, and they have to be run by happily married couples," Seth explains.

"So what's the problem? Eli and Shelby are definitely happily married."

Cameron's parents are the type of couple that fairytales are made of. Every woman in the city of Charleston wanted a love like Shelby James had, and every man cursed the ground Eli James walked on for setting the bar so high.

"The problem is that Cameron convinced them to finally take a vacation, so they aren't here to show him how disgustingly in love they are. They left for Outer Banks a few weeks ago, and she didn't want to worry them about how bad the money problems were and that we only have, like, a month, maybe two left before we run out of funds. Stratford is literally our last hope. He's the only guy that responded to any of her requests so far, but he wasn't supposed to come out to the camp until the charity dinner in a few weeks when Shelby and Eli will be back home," Seth finishes.

"Then, we just tell him that. I'm sure it's not going to be a big deal. Everyone at camp and in this town can vouch for Shelby and Eli, and how perfectly they've run this place for thirty years. You don't have anything to worry about," I tell Cameron softly, wrapping my arm around her shoulder and giving it a squeeze.

"You don't understand, man," Seth sighs. "This guy has a really tight schedule. He's most likely here because of a last-minute cancellation or something. He's not gonna stick around for more than five minutes if he doesn't get to meet the happily married couple who runs this place. I'm telling you, the dude is weird."

Cameron jerks out of my hold and shoots me *and* Seth a look that could kill, just as Braxton exits the vehicle and starts walking toward us.

Seth was right. The guy is definitely eccentric, judging by his outfit alone. Wearing a purple suit with a bright yellow button-down underneath, he makes his way toward us using a cane sparkling with rhinestones.

"Jesus. He looks like Liberace on crack," I mutter.

Seth snorts and Amelia laughs, which earns her a smack in the arm from Cameron, before she squares her shoulders and pastes a huge smile on her face when Braxton stops a few feet in front of her.

"Shelby James?" he questions.

Cameron steps forward and holds out her hand. "No, but I'm her daughter, Cameron James. It's a pleasure to meet you, Mr. Stratford. We weren't expecting you until the charity dinner."

He doesn't even glance at her outstretched hand, just pulls a yellow pocket square out of the breast pocket of his suit coat and dabs his forehead and cheeks with it.

"I don't shake hands. Too many germs," Stratford states.

Cameron's hand slowly falls back down to her side, and I have to resist the urge to walk around her and punch this asshole in the face, money or no money.

"I was under the impression I'd be meeting with the married owners of this camp. Are they not here?" he asks with a sigh, looking around the plantation instead of at Cameron when he speaks.

I can practically hear the panic swirling through Cameron as she clears her throat and tries to come up with something to say. Amelia's happy proclamation a few minutes ago about me being here and how it will work perfectly suddenly makes sense. The idea takes root before I even have a chance to let it fully form and think about the repercussions, only thinking about the fact that this is it. This is the moment where Cameron needs me. I quickly wrap my arm around Cameron's waist, turn her to face me, and yank her roughly against my body. The only thought in my head right now is

Seth's explanation that this guy will only give his money to happily married couples, and not about how good it feels to have Cameron pressed up against me.

Cameron's body is molded to mine from chest to thigh and I tighten my arm around her when she tries to pull away, sliding my hand down to cup her ass and pull her lower body closer to mine. My brain momentarily forgets everything I've stored there for thirty-three years, even my own fucking name, as she looks up at me with those gorgeous green eyes and her teeth bite down on her full bottom lip. All I can think about is how long I've wanted to have her pressed this close to me. How long I've wanted to feel her breasts flattened against my chest, have my hand on her ass and have the freedom to do all of this without consequences. I quickly push those thoughts away because they have no business being in my head. I gave up on those desires a long time ago, and the only thing I want right now is to be her friend again.

"Well, you're in luck, Mr. Braxton!" Amelia announces, her voice pulling me out of my lust-filled thoughts.

I give Cameron a look that hopefully tells her it wouldn't be a good idea for her to punch me in the face right now.

"This is Everett Southerland, Cameron's husband, and they've recently taken over running Camp Rylan in preparation for Mr. and Mrs. James's retirement," Amelia finishes, proving that she is, in fact, a very smart woman.

Cameron lets out a little squeak and I can tell she's three seconds away from freaking out and completely losing her shit. Sure, I probably could have come up with a hundred different solutions to this problem if I'd had more time, but I didn't. It was a spur-of-the-moment decision brought on by wanting to do whatever I could to help Cameron. One look at her panic-stricken face when she realized Stratford was here and I acted without thinking. I'm sure this idiotic decision will come back to bite me in the ass, and will bring on even more problems when Cameron's parents come home or, I don't know, Stratford does a little digging and finds out we're not really married, but I'll cross that bridge when I come to it. Or more than likely, Cameron will shove me off of that bridge.

I give Stratford a smile before looking back down at her. Keeping one hand still clutched tightly to her ass, I bring the other one up and brush her hair over her shoulder before wrapping it around her neck. Leaning my head down, I press my forehead to hers and smile, winking at her with my left eye so Stratford doesn't see it.

"Everything's gonna be okay, Cam," I whisper softly, lifting my head and pressing my lips to her forehead.

Not only does Cameron need me to help her get over losing the man she loved, but it looks like she also needs me to help her convince a rich asshole that Camp Rylan is more than deserving of his money. I refuse to let this camp down when it saved me. And I refuse to let Cameron down when she did the same.

It's about damn time the tables are turned. I'll do whatever it takes to convince Cameron to forgive me for what I did to her, even if it means pretending to be her husband.

I spent the last six months fighting to stay sober and fighting to want to live again. Being in poverty-stricken countries with no clean water didn't kill me, going to the most dangerous places around the world didn't kill me, the booze didn't kill me, and drowning in guilt didn't kill me.

Going by how hard I am right now just holding Cameron close, I have a feeling *this* is the thing that will kill me. I know I'm only feeling like this right now because all of my memories of Cameron are wrapped up in the past, during a time when I'd wished for something more, and being here with her again is muddling everything.

I just need to get my head on straight and remember why I came back. To restore our friendship, nothing else. I owe it to her and Aiden.

Chapter 10

EVERETT

Wishing in the past…
Twenty-one years old

Damn, there are a lot of hot chicks here tonight," Aiden says, clinking his bottle of beer with mine.

"Uh-huh," I mumble distractedly, scanning the crowd under the tent in search of Cameron, trying not to make it too obvious that I'm looking for her.

"I just had sex with one on the dance floor. In front of God and everyone. I got a standing ovation."

"Yep," I reply, craning my neck when I see a blond head in between the sea of people milling around, drinking and talking.

Aiden punches me in the arm right when I lose sight of the blonde I thought was Cameron. I turn to look at him with a glare.

"What the fuck?"

Aiden laughs and shakes his head at me.

"I just told you I had sex with a girl on the dance floor and you didn't even blink. Earth to Everett. Are you still thinking about finals? I'm sure you aced them," he states, taking a sip of his beer.

There's no way in hell I'm going to tell him what has me so distracted tonight, so I keep my mouth shut and just let him assume it's because of finals. While Aiden has been away studying at Clemson University, I've been enrolled at the College of Charleston right downtown for the last three years, telling my mother I was enrolled in business classes when I was really earning my undergrad degree in premed. Even though I'm going to school locally and not a few hours away like Aiden, I've been so busy studying for finals the last couple of months that I haven't seen Cameron at all. It's the longest we've gone without talking and I hate it. I finished my last final today, on the day of the annual charity dinner her parents throw at the camp that they combined with a high school graduation party for her this year, and I've been anxious all week knowing I'd finally have some free time and I'd finally get to see her. Finally get to talk to her about something important that scares the shit out of me.

"Damn. Our little girl is all grown up."

Aiden's quietly muttered comment makes my eyes shoot through the crowd to where he's staring and the sight in front of me almost makes me drop my bottle of beer.

Cameron. Talking to a small group of people, looking more beautiful than I've ever seen her. She's wearing a short, strapless white dress that molds to her curves and shows off her long, toned legs, with a black satin ribbon around her small waist and matching black heels that make her legs look even hotter. Her wavy blond hair has been pulled up and pinned all over her head with a few strands hanging down over her bare shoulders and her bangs falling down over one eye. I watch as she reaches up and brushes them out of her face, smiling at something someone says to her, and it takes everything in me not to walk over to her and pull her away. I want that smile aimed at me. I've missed that smile the last few months. I've missed her the last few months.

"Seriously. When the hell did the kid get so hot? I think I'm gonna ask her out. I mean, she just graduated from high school. She'll be legal in a month. It wouldn't be creepy or anything, right?" Aiden asks, his eyes still glued to Cameron.

I have to resist the urge to punch my best friend in the face and tell him to stop staring at her. Especially since I can't stop staring at her either, and have been thinking the exact same thing he just said for months.

"Fuck off. You're not asking Cameron out," I tell him, wincing when it comes out as a growl and I can't hide how pissed off I am that he'd say something like that.

"You're right. It would be creepy. I mean, she's one of my best friends. And she can still kick my ass in basketball. If word got out my girlfriend could kick my ass in anything, I'd never live it down," Aiden laughs. "Besides, I think she's in love, and I probably shouldn't get in the middle of that."

Aiden nods in Cameron's direction and I look back out at the dance floor to see a guy I don't know walk up next to her and wrap his arm around her waist. She looks up at him and smiles, then says something to the group of people she was talking to before he grabs her hand and leads her to the middle of the floor.

The two beers I had tonight start churning in my stomach when I watch her turn to face him and he pulls her up against him, his arms holding her tightly to him and his hands resting right above her ass. I want to walk out there on the dance floor, rip his arms from his body, and beat him with them.

"Who the fuck is that?" I mutter, unable to take my eyes off of the train wreck in front of me.

The way she's pressing her palms against his chest, the way he leans down and nuzzles his face into the side of her neck, then kisses his way up to her ear, whispering something that makes her tip her head back and laugh, makes me want to start throwing punches at anyone in my general vicinity.

I hate him and I want to kill him. Who the hell is this guy she's letting touch her? Kiss her? Make her laugh?

"That's Grady Stevens. He graduated with her, and they've been dating for, like, three months. How the hell did you not know this? You talk to Cameron more than I do," Aiden states.

It's true, I do talk to Cameron more than Aiden does, aside from the last three fucking months when I was buried in schoolwork, doing whatever I could to distract myself from tonight, knowing I was finally going to pull my head out of my ass and talk to Cameron about how I felt.

"Anyway," Aiden continues, not paying any attention to me losing my shit next to him as we both stare across the room at Cameron and the asshole whose hands keep inching closer and closer to her ass. "He's a good guy from what I hear. Valedictorian of their class, full scholarship to Clemson for football. His dad owns one of the biggest champion horse breeding farms in the country on the other side of town, and plans on turning the whole thing over to Grady as soon as he graduates college. Nice kid. Has a good head on his shoulders and Cameron seems to like him."

The song ends and I watch as Cameron and Grady stay locked together staring at each other, not even realizing the music isn't playing anymore.

"Oh, yeah. Our little girl is definitely all grown up," Aiden laughs. "Pretty sure she's going to be giving up the V to that guy tonight. Lucky bastard."

I'm squeezing the bottle of beer in my hand so hard, I'm surprised it doesn't shatter into a thousand pieces, the pain in my chest so acute that I'm pretty sure my heart shattered in its place. Aiden continues rambling and I want to tell him to shut the hell up, but I can't. All I can do is stare at what should have been mine.

"I tried offering my services for taking her virtue, but she punched me in the stomach. At least Grady is a nice guy and has a good future ahead of him. And Shelby and Eli adore the guy. She could do worse."

She could definitely do worse. Like ME worse. Now I'm sure a lot of parents would want their daughter to date a doctor. Unless you're Cameron's parents, who still see me as the loser kid from a broken home who couldn't stay out of trouble, no matter how much I've busted my ass over the last few years to show them I was trying to change. Aiden's right. Grady has a good future ahead of him if he's going to be running his dad's farm after college. I lost my shot, biding my time until she turned eighteen and it didn't seem weird as fuck that I was lusting after my best friend three years younger than me. I could have sworn I'd seen something in her eyes in the last year. Something that said she wanted the same thing I did, but was too afraid to say it, just like I'd been. Obviously I was wrong. She's looking at Grady the way I thought she'd been looking at me. And going by the murderous thoughts running through my head just by looking at the two of them together, Cameron's parents are right to still not trust me. I'm still fucked up, I'm just better at hiding it now.

That guy is definitely the better choice. He knows what

he wants in life, and even though I do, too, I have so much on my plate right now trying to make sure I get into medical school, and lying to my mother to keep her from breaking down. I was all set to tell her about what I planned on studying as soon as I found out I'd gotten accepted to the College of Charleston, figuring she was already at the lowest point in her life and there's no way my news could possibly make things worse for her than they already were. I'd always said I'd never do something as risky as my father, but when one of my professors came back from a year in another country, showed us photos, and explained how much help these people needed, I knew it was what I had to do. And I could never tell my mother how important this was for me, because all she would care about is that I would be doing the exact same thing that took my father from us. I couldn't do that to my brother. Not when he was happier than I'd ever seen him having her back in our lives with a clear head and a loving heart. I couldn't be the one to ruin that for him, so I continued lying to her. I hated every minute of it, but I did it, and I'll continue doing it until I'm sure our mother is strong enough and has been sober enough to handle the news.

I have no idea what my future will bring. No idea where I'll be sent if I get accepted to that international program. And that kid, the one who can't keep his hands off of Cameron and the one she can't stop smiling at, he has his whole life mapped out right here in Charleston. His dreams won't take him all over the world into dangerous situations and away from her. His plans won't make her choose between staying here at this camp that she loves so much, or leaving with him if he gets assigned somewhere else. And dating him definitely won't piss off her parents.

It was all just a stupid dream. A silly fantasy. Idiotic wishes I'd been making on my birthday the last few years and never had the courage to verbalize until tonight, and now it was too late.

"Ev, you're here!" Cameron's voice pulls me out of my depressing thoughts and I realize she's walked over to us, her hand still firmly held in Grady's as he stands next to her, looking down at her with an adoring smile.

Grady slides his arm around her waist and pulls her to his side, holding his hand out to me.

"I've heard a lot about you, man. I'm Grady, nice to meet you."

I take his hand and shake it, squeezing it a little harder than I should have, narrowing my eyes at the guy and hoping he understands my nonverbal communication that if he hurts Cameron in any way, I will end him.

Cameron looks back and forth between us with a smile, oblivious to the stare down we're giving each other before I drop his hand and take a drink of my beer.

The four of us stand here for a few minutes, Aiden, Grady, and Cameron talking easily among themselves while I drink my beer and feel like a third wheel, wishing I had the guts to pull her away from Grady. Just say "to hell with it" and lay my cards on the table.

She's happy. So fucking happy. I can see it written all over her face each time Grady says something and she can't keep her eyes off of him. I can't be "that" guy. The one who fucks up her happiness and ruins our friendship. The one who finally gets what I've always wanted and then leaves her behind, makes her constantly put her life on hold, waiting for me to come home. Aiden would do it. Aiden would give zero fucks about putting her in an uncomfortable position. Telling her how he felt and not caring if she felt the same way, not even thinking about her feelings or how much it might tear her in half. But I'm not Aiden. I couldn't do that to her no matter how much I wanted to. We were friends first and I don't want to screw that up and lose her completely. I don't want to make things awkward and not have her in my life, even if I have to spend the rest of my years knowing I lost my shot.

I just want her to be happy, and if Grady makes her happy, I need to learn how to deal with it. So much for making all those wishes on all those fucking stars. I was an idiot for thinking they'd ever come true.

Chapter 11

CAMERON

As you can see, at Camp Rylan, we offer the complete summer camp experience year round, from horseback riding and dance classes, to nature hikes and swimming, even during the nonsummer months when we're only open on weekends. But we keep in mind that this camp is for children who have family members either currently deployed, home and trying to adjust to civilian life, or who have passed away, and we also provide individual and group counseling for anyone who needs it. After dinner we can..."

My eyes almost roll into the back of my head and I have to struggle to pay attention to what Everett is saying when he moves to stand behind me, rests his hands on my shoulders, and starts gently massaging my neck with his thumbs.

I let him take the lead on the tour of the plantation for Mr. Stratford, mostly because he knows this camp as well as I do after growing up and working here when he was a teenager. And also because I was so pissed at him that I was afraid if I started talking, all that would come out would be curse words.

I'm angry he didn't leave when I told him to. I'm angry he thought I needed his help. I'm angry he decided he could just waltz back in here and fix everything. And I'm angry he so easily went along with Amelia's lie, telling Mr. Stratford we're married. I was still too frazzled at seeing him again, and too shocked when he wrapped his arm around me and tugged me against him to say anything at the time, and now I have to go along with his stupid idea if I want any chance of saving this camp and not looking like a fool in front of Mr. Stratford.

He knew I wouldn't fight him on this. He knew I wouldn't make a scene in front of a man who held the future of Camp Rylan in his hands, no matter how much I want to move away from him so I can remember how to breathe again. What he doesn't know is that his stupid, spur-of-the-moment decision just brought on a whole new set of problems. If Mr. Stratford *does* decide to give us the money before he leaves, what's going to happen next year? Or the year after that? It's not like Everett and I can just pretend to be married for the rest of our lives, every time Mr. Stratford decides to come for a visit. I also don't expect my parents to agree to this ruse once they get home and find out what happened. Before Amelia and Everett opened their big mouths, I was just getting ready to tell Mr. Stratford where my parents were, swallow my pride, and call them to tell them to get home as fast as possible, hoping Stratford would wait around long enough to meet them.

"How many campers do you usually get during the summer months?" Mr. Stratford asks.

I open my mouth to answer, figuring I should probably start talking at some point since this is *my* camp, even though

Everett is putting on a good show, but the words get stuck in my throat.

Everett's hands slide off my shoulders, down my back, and circle around my waist, pulling me back against him as he locks his hands together over my stomach. He rests his chin on top of my head like it's the most natural thing in the world. Like he touches me this way and holds me this close all the time. I can feel the beat of his heart through his chest as it presses up against my back and it makes me want to turn around in his arms, press my face to his chest, and feel the strength of it against my cheek. I can't stop fighting this internal battle of wanting to throttle him for showing up out of the blue after almost five years, or holding on to him and never letting him go. I want to scream at him for inserting himself back into my life, but at the same time, I just want to stay here in his arms, reassuring myself that he's really here and safe and alive.

"We're always at full capacity during the summer, and we actually have a waiting list," Everett explains, telling Mr. Stratford our process for picking who gets to attend Camp Rylan while I stand here like a mute, growing angrier by the second as his voice vibrates through my body since he's holding me so tightly against him.

I hold on to my anger and let it flourish. Being pissed off is much better than the alternative. What I really want to do is run across the camp to the guest house, where I live, lock myself in my bedroom, curl up on my bed and cry. I want to let it all out, all of the anger and fear and confusion. I just want to be left alone so I can get my head back on straight, and I can't do that when Everett is here, standing so close to me that I can't think. I can't concentrate on anything but how good it feels to be this close to him, how *right* it feels to pretend like we're something more than we are. Jesus, we're not even really friends at this point, and now we're pretending to be husband and wife.

I just wanted him to leave and give me time to get my emotions under control. Time to be sad and hurt and cry and scream and let it out all out. I can't handle standing here in his arms pretending. It hurts too much that I'm being forced to fake something I wished for and dreamed about for most of my life. It makes me angry that it hurts so much and all I can think about is how much time we lost that we'll never get back, and how he can so easily walk back into my life and put on this act.

"Thank you for taking the time to show me around," Mr. Stratford says, his voice pulling me out of my thoughts. "I know you weren't expecting me for another month, but a few things changed in my schedule involving other charities I'm looking to possibly invest in, and I needed to push this meeting up a little sooner. My accountant needs a decision sooner than I expected, so I don't have a lot of time to waste. I appreciate your cooperation. I don't usually say anything until after a decision has been made, but Camp Rylan is at the very top of my list, as long as all of my requirements are met. If you don't mind, I think I'll walk back to the main house, talk to a few of the staff, and do some sightseeing alone."

I give him a smile I don't feel and Everett lets him know to have the staff radio me if he needs anything, telling him we'll see him at dinner.

We both watch Mr. Stratford turn and walk away, neither one of us moving or saying a word as he makes his way around the pond, an acre away from the main house, that the campers use for fishing and canoeing. I wait until Mr. Stratford is far enough away, and see him meet up with Seth and Amelia, who just walked out of the stables, before I move.

Jerking out of his arms, I whirl around to face Everett,

shoving all of my sadness as far down as it will go and pulling up my anger to give me strength.

"You're not staying for dinner."

Everett sighs, running his hand through his hair in frustration.

"Cam, he thinks we're married. Don't you think it would be a little weird if I didn't show up for dinner? You have, what? A month, maybe two tops, before this place shuts down completely? And you heard him just now. Camp Rylan is at the top of his list, as long as we meet all of his requirements, the most important one being that this charity is run by a happily married couple. You need me right now. It's not that big of a deal," he tells me softly.

My mouth drops open and I have to resist the urge to smack my hands against his chest and shove him. I don't want to touch any part of him. Having his hands on me was bad enough. If I put my hands on his chest and feel the muscles beneath his cotton shirt, my brain will turn to mush.

"Not that big of a deal? Are you fucking kidding me right now?!" I shout. "I haven't seen you in *years!* You don't know one damn thing about me, and the only reason I need you right now is because you didn't give me any other choice! I could have easily called my parents and explained things to Mr. Stratford, but no. You made a decision for me and now I'm stuck with it, or I'll risk looking like an idiot who lies and doesn't know how to run things around here!"

He steps toward me, and I immediately take a step back. It's one thing for him to be all touchy-feely in front of Mr. Stratford, but he's not coming anywhere near me when we're alone.

"I'm sorry. You're right, I made a hasty decision, but I don't regret it. Stratford doesn't seem like a man who would have waited around for your parents to get here if we'd told him the truth right from the start. He would have gotten back in his limo and moved on to the next place on his list. We can worry about my stupid decision down the road, *after* Stratford gives you his money. I know you need to save this camp. It's your parent's dream and your legacy. Stop being so fucking stubborn, Cam. Let me help you," he pleads.

Of course he knows exactly the right words to say to make me come off as an ungrateful bitch for being so angry about a situation that he's probably right about. I should thank him like a normal person, even though pretending to be married to someone is nowhere near normal. But I've never been a normal person when it comes to Everett. I've been a lovesick fool who put her trust in the wrong man and it came back to bite me, leaving me lost and alone and confused for too many years.

I knew from a young age that I wanted nothing more out of life than living on this plantation and working at the camp my parents sacrificed everything for. I spent every free minute I had here, following my parents around and learning everything I could about what goes into running a place like this. I moved out of the home I shared with my parents when I graduated high school and into the plantation's old guest house, close to the main house. I never went away to college like all of my friends from school did because I couldn't imagine spending one day, let alone four years away, from Camp Rylan and the kids I'd come to know and love and looked forward to seeing every time they set foot on this forty acres of land, in search of understanding and something to take their mind off of things.

Most people didn't understand why my parents never forced me to go to college and get an education, but they didn't understand the type of people Shelby and Eli James are. All they cared about was my happiness. My mom spent most of her life doing exactly what her mother demanded, never living her own dreams or having anything for herself, and she refused to do that to me. All my parents wanted was to see me happy, doing whatever it was that got me there, and I loved them more than anything for it.

Which is why I kept my mouth shut when Everett put his arms around me and pretended we were married. And it's why I'm going to continue going along with it, even though everything inside of me is screaming that it's a bad idea. The more time I spend with Everett, letting him get inside my head and my heart, the more it's going to hurt when he pushes me away again. I couldn't handle it the first time. I won't survive it a second time. At least he's right about one thing. We can worry about the consequences of his stupid decision later on, when I'm not sleep-deprived from worrying about the camp and still in shock about him being home.

"Don't pretend like this fixes *anything* just because you happened to waltz back into my life today of all days," I remind him. "We aren't friends anymore, you made sure of that. Just because you know this camp and you know how much it means to me doesn't mean you get a free pass for being an asshole."

Everett doesn't say anything else as I brush past him. I walk away and I keep right on walking, not stopping to talk to any of the workers as I go. I keep my head down and my tears in check until I get to the guest house. I move quickly through the living room and down the hall, refusing to let anything out until I'm in the safety of my bedroom. I don't even make it to the bed. Closing the door behind me, I lean back against it and slide down to the floor, hugging my knees to my chest as the tears start to fall.

I hate that I've missed Everett so much, that a part of me wants to forgive him for everything. I hate that seeing him again gave me butterflies and made me remember all of the feelings I used to have for him. I hate that he'll never understand how much his disappearance from my life broke my heart, because I can never tell him. I can never tell him that he always had my heart, and he took it with him when he left, because it will just make me look like a fool. A fool who waited around for years, hoping her best friend would someday fall in love with her. Hoping she'd get an e-mail or a phone call. Hoping for *something*. I refuse to let him know just how sad and pathetic I've been. How I've kept men at arm's length since he left, building up a protective wall around me over the years because I refuse ever to be hurt like that again or allow anyone to get that close again. I've always been the strong, independent one in our friendship, and I don't need the embarrassment of him seeing me as anything less than that. I refuse to be that girl.

My tears fall so fast that everything around me becomes a blur. I rest my head on my knees and don't even try to stop them. I miss Aiden right now more than I have in nine months. If he were here right now, and we had to pretend to be married, we'd be laughing our asses off at the ridiculousness of it. He'd be making jokes about how he hit the jackpot with such a "hot" wife and he'd be demanding we consummate our fake marriage on every inch of the camp just to make it authentic.

My body shakes with sobs and I'm filled with so much guilt I think I might drown in it. I look down at the ring Aiden gave me, hold my hand up in front of me, twisting it until it catches on the overhead light in the room and sparkles. I picture Aiden's smiling, happy face the day he gave me that ring and my heart hurts so much with missing him I feel like I can't breathe. Pulling the ring off of my right hand, I switch it over to the left, sliding it on my ring finger. The pressure in my chest hurts so much I have to press my hand there to keep it inside, knowing I'm going to use this piece of jewelry now as a prop in this stupid farce with Stratford.

Even though I'd give anything to have Aiden back, I can't stop that small flutter of joy in my heart that Everett is the one who came back to me, no matter how much damage he did to us. It feels like I'm being disloyal to Aiden. He never broke my heart. He never let me down. He never pushed me away. And yet, I know if someone had asked me, "Who do you wish had gotten out of Jason's truck earlier?"— and if wishes really did come true and the impossible could happen, like someone coming back from the dead—I still would have wished for Everett. It would always be Everett who I wished for. I was always drawn to him because he was lost, and I wanted to help him find his way. Now that our situations are reversed, I'm scared to death to let him help me. Without Aiden, who's going to help *me* find my way when Everett lets me down again?

Chapter 12

CAMERON

Wishing in the past...
Twenty-three years old

I watch Allison Brantley stomp her foot like a toddler and storm away from Everett. If he didn't look so miserable watching her walk away, I'd be smiling right now.

"Looks like he finally cut that clinger loose," Aiden states, flopping down next to me on the couch. "See? It was a great idea to throw a party at my place. Now Everett can get piss-drunk and pass out in the spare bedroom."

I just nod my head, unable to take my eyes off of Everett standing across the room in the doorway of the kitchen, still staring at the front door, where Allison disappeared. He came to Aiden's place right from his clinical rotation at the hospital, not bothering to change out of his blue scrubs. Everett looks hot no matter what he's wearing, but there's just something about seeing him in those things that raises my body temperature and makes me want to fan my face.

Everett had protested Aiden's idea of a party, but I knew he needed it. He'd just buried his mother two weeks ago and needed something to take his mind off of things. We both told him to wait a little longer before he made any big decisions, but he'd gone and accepted an offer with some international medical organization an hour after the ceremony and signed the papers. He'd complete a year or two stateside, learning all he could about internal medicine, and then he'd complete his residency abroad, giving him firsthand experience around the world.

"How about I get you a fresh drink? Feel free to pass out in MY bedroom tonight."

I pull my eyes away from Everett to see Aiden wagging his eyebrows at me as he throws his arm over the back of the couch behind me, and I can't help but laugh at his attempt to flirt with me. Something he's started doing more and more ever since I turned twenty-one.

"Never gonna happen, Aiden," I inform him, patting his thigh as I push myself up from the couch.

"Never say never, kid. One of these days you're going to find my charms irresistible."

I roll my eyes at him, which just makes him laugh.

"You have three dates here tonight. I don't think you need a fourth."

Aiden waves his hand at me, taking a drink of his beer.

"They won't mind. And besides, I wasn't talking about a date. I was talking about a few hours of sweaty, enjoyable, meaningless sex," he informs me with a smirk.

"I think you meant to say a few minutes."

Aiden's hand comes up over his heart and his eyes widen.

"You wound me, kid. You really wound me."

"I'm sure your ego will recover," I reply dryly. "Go find one of your skanks to keep you occupied. I'm going to go check on Everett."

"Uh-huh. Sure. 'Check on Everett,'" he replies, complete with air quotes, making me pause from getting off the couch.

"What the hell does that mean?"

Aiden just laughs. "You two are so cute and stupid."

Shaking my head at him as he continues chuckling, I push up from the couch and leave Aiden behind, ignoring whatever the hell he was implying as I head in Everett's direction. Moving opposite him in the doorway, I slide my hands behind my back and lean against the inside frame of the entrance to the kitchen.

For a few minutes, we just stare at each other silently and I call myself all kinds of fool when my heart stutters inside my chest. I've tried so hard for so many years to let go of my feelings for him, but nothing works. Right when I think I have the perfect opportunity to finally admit everything to him, something gets in the way. As soon as I start dating someone, he's single. As soon as I find myself without someone, he's signing up to save the world. That old saying about two ships passing in the night…nothing could describe Everett and me better. One of us is always passing the other by.

"So I guess Allison didn't take the news very well. Are you okay?" I ask him softly.

Everett sighs, shoving his hands into the front pockets of his scrubs.

"I kind of saw it coming. She didn't think I was serious about leaving the country to finish my residency, and when she realized I was, she thought the threat of breaking up with me if I leave would make me change her mind. So I told her not to let the door hit her in the ass on the way out."

Even though I shouldn't laugh, I can't help it. Everett lets out a deep chuckle right along with me, and it's the best sound in the world. I live for his smiles and his laughs, since they're so few and far between. Especially lately.

"She was a bitch in high school and she was a bitch as a grown-ass adult. Good riddance!" I tell him.

He holds his smile for a few minutes and I watch as it slowly falls and his face grows serious.

"Is it wrong that I'm happy? That I feel...free?" he whispers.

I immediately know that he's talking about his mother without even having to ask him to clarify. It breaks my heart that he's leaving and I'm losing yet another shot at what I want, but nothing else matters to me more than Everett's happiness. Besides, he won't be gone forever.

"No. It's not wrong. I know you're not happy she's gone, but you carried a lot on your shoulders your entire life. All because of her. You SHOULD feel free. You don't have to pretend to be something you're not anymore. You don't have to pretend just to keep her from falling apart. You can do what you really want to do now. You can still be sad she's gone and be happy that your dreams are going to come true. You deserve this, Everett. You deserve to finally do what makes you happy," I tell him with a reassuring smile.

The last few years haven't been easy on Everett. He had to create a web of lies and deception because his mother suddenly decided to get sober and be a mother, and it wore him down. I know he didn't want to rock the boat with her sobriety and I hated that for him. That he felt so much pressure to keep their family together when she'd never cared. It turned out that being sober wasn't something she was very good at, and even though she kept it in check when she came out here to visit, back home in New Jersey, she made up for lost time. She died in her sleep from acute pancreatitis and liver failure.

Everett pushes away from the doorway and moves closer to me until only a few inches are separating us. My palms start to sweat as they clutch tightly to the wood frame behind my back and I stare up into his eyes, the blue color in them magnified and more vivid with the blue scrubs he's wearing.

"Are you happy, Cameron?" he asks softly.

His eyes search my face and I wish I knew what he was looking for. I wish he could see how much it's killing me not to blurt out how much it hurts that he's leaving. That I'm scared to death it will change everything between us.

I swallow thickly and nod my head, afraid to open my mouth and tell him the truth. He's finally free. I can't be the one to stand in the way of his dreams.

"Can you give me any reason why I shouldn't go? Why I shouldn't go through with this crazy plan?" he asks quietly, leaning even closer to me until I can feel his breath on my face and the heat from his body.

I don't know why he's asking me this. I don't know what he wants me to say. Is he having second thoughts about going? He's always wanted to be a doctor and help people. He deserves this. Does he have second thoughts about leaving me behind? I'm imagining things, I know I am. I want it so much that I'm starting to see things that aren't there. He's only standing this close because he doesn't want the other people at the party to hear what we're talking about. He's only looking at me like this because he's scared about the steps he's taking to make his dreams come true. There's nothing else there and I'm an idiot for pretending otherwise. I know he needs to do this. It's what he's always dreamed of. If I asked him to stay, he would. I don't want him to resent me for getting in the way of his dreams.

"You need to go, Everett. This is everything you've ever wanted and it's an amazing opportunity. Besides, it's only your residency. Once the next three years are done, you can come back home."

He stares into my eyes for a few more seconds before letting out a deep breath, moving away from me, and muttering something under his breath that sounds like "Not everything."

He turns away from me, and before I can get a chance to ask him what he just said and what it meant, Aiden comes up to him with a beer. My head thumps back against the wall, and I close my eyes as they clink their bottles together.

Everett's dreams are coming true and I just need to focus on being happy for him, being a good friend, and making sure he knows he's not making a mistake.

He's passing me by and there's nothing I can do about it. I want to grab on to him and never let go, but that would be selfish.

Why does doing the right thing have to hurt so much?

Chapter 13

Everett

Walking up the steps to the main house, seeing the gas lanterns attached to either side of the front door flickering, I can almost pretend I haven't been gone for so long. I've walked through these doors a thousand times; felt the heat from the lanterns as I walked by; heard the hustle and bustle of staff on the other side of the door; eaten dinner here almost every night with Cameron, her parents, and their extended family of volunteers and campers; and sat out on the sprawling front porch in wicker chairs with Cameron and Aiden after dinner and watched the sun go down off in the distance.

I felt like a stranger wandering around the camp alone today after Cameron walked away from me, even though I knew where everything was like the back of my hand and still knew most of the workers and volunteers here. But for the first time since I was three years old, I felt like I didn't belong, because Cameron obviously didn't want me here. I always felt like an outsider with Cameron's parents. I always knew they didn't like me. It never mattered to me when I was a young, dumb punk, always getting into fights and causing trouble, because Cameron's opinion of me was the only one I cared about. It didn't matter if her parents didn't like me because they were just background noise. Cameron was always my main focus.

As soon as I push open the front door, I'm hit with a wave of nostalgia that makes me regret every day I spent away from this place. When Cameron's parents remodeled the old plantation house that her mother grew up in, she littered the walls with hundreds of photos of campers and staff. I slowly make my way through the foyer, feeling a knot form in my chest when I see Cameron has hung up newer photos. Some with her in them, with kids I don't recognize. Some with a few of the new employees I met when I wandered around the camp, introducing myself and making sure everyone understood what was going on with Stratford and the little lie we'd told him. No one even batted an eye when I told them about the ruse they'd all have to keep up when he was around. They were so in love with Cameron and her parents and proud to be part of this camp, they'd do just about anything for them.

I pause in front of a candid photo of Cameron squatting down, speaking to a child around the age of five. She has her hands on the little girl's hips and her head is dipped low so she can make eye contact with her. There's a soft smile on Cameron's face, and I'm sure she was probably reassuring the little girl that she didn't need to be scared and she would have a ton of fun at camp. Cameron was always good at easing people's fears. Making them feel special, and even though there were a hundred other children begging for her attention, when she focused on you, the whole world melted away. She always knew exactly what to say to make you feel like you were on top of the world.

"We aren't friends anymore, you made sure of that. Just because you know this camp and you know how much it means to me doesn't mean you get a free pass for being an asshole."

I think about the words she said to me before she walked away this afternoon and realize she also knows exactly what to say to cut you to the quick, too. I fucked up thinking I could just show up out of the blue like this. But I'm here now, and I'm not going anywhere. She needs my help whether she wants to admit it or not. I know doing this isn't going to fix our problems, but it will give me a chance to spend time with her and show her I can still be a good friend to her.

"Mr. Everett, you're home!"

I turn when I hear my name, smiling when I see an older woman coming out of the kitchen with a huge covered pot in her hand, her full head of white hair pulled back in its usual bun at the nape of her neck, wearing the same blue and white checkered apron she's worn since we were kids.

Walking quickly over to her, I try to take the pot out of her hand to help her, but she moves out of my reach.

"You've been gone too long. You seemed to have forgotten I don't let anyone help me serve dinner."

I laugh, nodding my head at the woman who has been cooking for Camp Rylan since it opened.

"Oh, I remember, Mrs. Michaels. I just thought you might have gotten softer in the last few years," I joke.

She glares at me, something that used to scare the shit out of Cameron, Aiden, and me when we were younger.

"The day I become soft...the kids in this place would walk all over me," she complains, even though everyone knows she actually does have a soft spot for the kids that come to this camp, even if she puts up a good front of being stern. "Now, go make yourself useful. That odd Stratford fellow is already in the dining hall and I'm just finishing up serving the food. Go find Cameron and tell her it's time to eat. I think I saw her go into the office a little while ago."

Mrs. Michaels hustles away from me, down the main hall, and into the dining hall, while I follow behind her in search of Cameron. I find her right where Mrs. Michaels said she was, in the office right across the hall from the dining area. I pause in the doorway when I see her on the other side of the room, with her back to me, staring at the wall.

She's exchanged her jeans, boots, and tank top for a dark teal wrap dress, her bare legs on full display beneath the short skirt, with a pair of nude-colored heels making them look a mile long. Her hair has been pulled up into a ponytail and the long blond strands hang down between her shoulders, swaying when she shifts to the side as I watch her bring a hand up to her face and swipe her fingers against her cheek, hearing a soft sniffle from all the way over here.

I saw her eyes fill with tears a few times today when she was confronting me, but she blinked them away and replaced them with anger. I can handle her anger. I can handle her yelling and cursing at me, but I can't handle seeing her sad. I can't handle knowing I'm the one who put those tears in her eyes.

Clearing my throat so she knows I'm here, I move across the room, watching her swipe at her cheeks a few more times before she turns to face me. My feet come to a stuttering stop when I get a better look at her in that dress. The deep vee in the front where the dress wraps around her body shows off a mouthwatering amount of cleavage, and the dress ties together at her side, molding the material to all of her curves.

My eyes move up to her face and I immediately feel like the asshole she thinks I am when I see her eyes are bloodshot from the tears she tried to hide from me.

"Cam…" I whisper, taking another step in her direction, wanting to say something, anything, to make her forgive me.

She holds up her hand and I stop moving. My eyes zero in on the ring on the third finger of her left hand, which she starts to fiddle with when she drops her hand. The huge emerald square-cut stone in the center, the same deep, brilliant color as her eyes, sparkling along with the diamonds that surround it as the light hits the jewels each time she spins it around on her finger.

It looks like something Aiden would have bought her. Bright, flashy, and worth a shit ton of money. I wonder if it's her engagement ring and I wonder why she still wears it at all now that he's gone, and that thought makes me feel like the biggest dick in the world.

"I can't do this with you right now. We need to go in there and play nice with Stratford. That's all I care about and all I have the energy to think about right now."

"Did Aiden give you that ring?" I ask suddenly, my eyes still staring down at her hand as her fingers continue to worry the ring on her finger, twisting and twisting and twisting it around.

I know there are a thousand more important things we should be talking about right now, but my curiosity is killing me.

I want to hear the words, feel the sharp sting they'll bring, even though I already know the answer.

"Uh…yes," she states in confusion, probably wondering why I'm asking about a ring when she assumes I'm going to pick a fight with her.

Two words. That's all it takes to confirm what I thought

and for the pain in my chest to magnify tenfold. It's one thing when Aiden was sending me e-mails from halfway around the world, bragging about the ring he bought. It's another form of torture to be standing in the same room as Cameron, watching her fingers continue touching the piece of jewelry he gave to her when he stole her heart.

"It's the only good piece of jewelry I have. And since we're supposed to be married, I figured…"

She figured using the ring Aiden gave her as a symbol of their love would be a great way to symbolize our *fake* love. That thought pisses me off more than the fact that Aiden even gave her a ring in the first place.

I nod as she walks around me, closing my eyes when I get a whiff of her soft magnolia-blossom-scented perfume. That smell is like home to me, reminding me of all the things I missed while I was gone. I wish I could just grab her and pull her into my arms, bury my face into the side of her neck, and breathe her in.

When her heels clicking on the floor fade away and out of the room, I finally open my eyes and look up. Now that Cameron is no longer standing in front of me, I have a clear view of what she'd been staring at when I walked into the room, and the cause for her tears, and it's like someone just shoved a knife through my heart.

Hanging on the wall is a framed picture of Aiden and Cameron, taken within the last few years. They're standing on the makeshift wooden stage out in the main area of camp where kids put on plays and volunteers host sing-alongs and other fun activities. They're standing shoulder-to-shoulder, holding up one of the props used for the plays—a large empty picture frame. Cameron is looking right at the camera and Aiden is looking at her, both of them with huge smiles on their faces, like someone caught them mid-laugh.

I feel his absence more strongly now than I ever have, and I hate myself for being jealous of him. For being here for Cameron when I wasn't. For stepping in and loving her and making her happy. For being the cause for her tears. For giving her a piece of jewelry she won't take off, and touches when she's upset.

With one last look at the picture, I turn and leave the room before I'm tempted to rip the frame from the wall and send it crashing across the room, behaving like the stupid, young punk Cameron's parents always thought I was.

* * *

"So tell me how the two of you met and fell in love."

Cameron immediately starts choking on a piece of food in her seat next to me when Stratford speaks, and I quickly reach over and gently pat her on the back while she grabs her glass of water and drinks half of it.

While Cameron spent the day avoiding me, I spent the day making sure everything still ran the same at camp, studying up and making sure I'd be able to answer any of Stratford's questions at dinner without hesitation or pausing awkwardly so Cameron could answer for me. Unfortunately, it was a waste of time. As soon as the first course was served, Stratford did nothing but ask personal questions about Cameron and me. Luckily, the questions were fairly simple, Stratford wanting to know about our individual families and what kind of lives we had growing up. I should have known, with how obsessed he is with only giving money to happily married couples who run businesses that this would come up. When Seth said this guy was eccentric, he wasn't kidding. What kind of a businessman cares more about the personal lives of people he's thinking about investing in than about their actual business?

Cameron hasn't looked at me once during dinner, but at least she didn't pull away from me when I moved my seat closer to her and rested my hand on the back of her chair in between courses. She turns her head in my direction now with a look of panic on her face. I give her a reassuring smile, rubbing small circles against her back to let her know I can handle this question.

"As you know, Cameron and I have been friends almost all of our lives," I begin, my eyes remaining locked on Cameron's as I speak. "Around the time when I was ten and she was seven, we became best friends. She was my rock, the one person I told everything to, and the most important person in my life."

I watch Cameron's throat bob as she swallows nervously, but her beautiful green eyes never leave mine, and Stratford suddenly disappears from the room. I speak from the heart, saying everything I wanted to say to her years ago, but never had the guts to. I know she thinks I'm putting on an act, and I guess I sort of am, considering the most I could ever hope for is her genuine friendship, but I don't care. I've needed to say these things out loud since I was seventeen years old, and now is my chance to say them, let them have life for a few minutes, and then finally put them to rest once and for all so I can concentrate on being her friend without the past clouding everything in my mind.

"I remember the exact day I knew I was falling in love with her. She was fourteen and I was working in the horse stables. She walked in and I forgot how to breathe. For the first time since we met, I *saw* her. Really saw how beautiful she was, inside and out, and I couldn't breathe. But I was a few years older than her and I was too much of a chicken to say anything. Not for a long time. I was afraid she didn't feel the same and I was scared to death to lose her as a friend." I speak softly, still scared to death that she's going to see the truth in the words I'm saying to her right now and I'll lose her again before I've even gotten her back. "It wasn't until the week before I started my residency that I realized I was so damn tired of hiding what I felt for her. I asked her if she could give me a reason why I shouldn't go. I held my breath and prayed to God she'd tell me not to leave her and that she was in love with me, but she didn't."

Cameron's eyes fill with tears, but she doesn't blink them away. I just watch them pool in her eyes as I continue speaking, unable to stop telling the story the way I wished to God it would have gone, but never did.

"She knew I needed to go. She knew it was my dream to be a doctor and be able to help people around the world and she was the type of friend who would never do anything to stop me from achieving my dreams. She told me I had to go, that it was everything I'd ever wanted, and I *needed* to go."

Cameron's body leans toward mine, until we're so close that I can see the flecks of gold in her eyes, and it takes everything in me not to close the distance and kiss her. Make her really believe the words I'm saying, and how I wished things would have turned out the way I'm explaining it.

Being around her again is messing with my head a lot more than I thought it would. And talking about the past, remembering the feelings I used to have for her, is just making things more confusing instead of clearer, but I'm too far into this walk down memory lane to stop now.

"But before my heart could break in half, she told me she'd wait for me. For however long it took for me to come home. She stuck it out with me for my residency and for the three years I spent away from her working for Doctors Without Borders. She forgave me for leaving her, she forgave me for not being there for her when she needed me most. She forgave me for hurting her, and making mistakes, and she knew I would do anything to take them back," I whisper, lifting my hand off the table in front of us and brushing her bangs out of her eyes. "*Anything.*"

I rest my palm against the side of her cheek, rubbing my thumb back and forth under her eyes, leaning my head forward until our foreheads are pressed together, keeping my voice low and just for her.

"I never deserved to have her in my life. I still don't. But there's nothing I won't do for her. Nothing I won't do to show her that I have always loved her, and always will."

Jesus, where the hell did that come from? I could have just said I'll always be her friend and that would have been good enough for her *and* the man hanging on my every word across the table.

I close my eyes, my heart beating so fast in my chest, I'm sure she can hear it. I hear her let out a small sigh and I pull back so I can see her face, Stratford's voice interrupting the little bubble I'd created where it was just the two of us in this room.

"How long have you been home?"

"Nine months."

I'm so busy staring into Cameron's eyes that I speak without thinking. It just comes out before I realize what I've said. I didn't even realize Cameron still held a fork in her hand during my speech until it slips from her grasp and clatters to the plate in front of her. She jerks her face out of my hand, turning away from me and giving a nervous smile to Stratford as she picks up the fork and places it next to her plate.

"Sorry. Talking about him being away in such dangerous places always makes me a little jittery," Cameron tells Stratford, her voice coming out forced.

Shit. Son of a bitch.

I didn't mean to blurt that out. I knew she'd be pissed when she found out how long I'd been home without coming to see her. I just wanted more time with her. Time for her to forgive me for being gone before I got into the messiness of how I fucked up my life was when I got home and was too ashamed to go to her. I hate that it had to come out like this, but I'm glad I don't have to hide it from her now.

I'm so busy staring at Cameron's profile, wishing she'd turn and look at me again, that I barely pay attention to Stratford when he speaks.

"What a beautiful story. It's nice to see a young couple like yourselves who are so clearly meant to be together, and refusing to let anything get in the way of that," he says, wiping his mouth with his napkin as he pushes back his chair and gets up from the table. "Thank you for the lovely meal and conversation. It's been a long day, so I'm going to retire upstairs to my room. I'll meet you both tomorrow morning around nine by the stables so you can show me more about how you two handle being married and working together."

Stratford gives us a nod and a smile, whistling to himself as he leaves the dining hall and heads upstairs to his room to turn in for the night. As soon as he's gone and we hear his footsteps disappear upstairs, Cameron pushes her chair back from the table so quickly, the scraping of the chair legs echoes around the huge room.

"Cameron, wait!" I yell after her, yanking my napkin off my lap and smacking it down on the table, jumping up out of my chair, and racing after her as she runs from the room.

I don't catch up to her until we get outside the front door and down the porch stairs, my hand wrapping around her arm and pulling her to a stop.

She yanks her arm out of my hold and whirls around to

face me, the tears that were shining in her eyes just moments ago making trails down her cheeks.

"Cam, please. I'm sorry..." I beg, not even sure what I'm pleading for at this point. I just want her to stop and listen to me, let me explain.

"No, don't even try to apologize," she fires back. "Your apologies mean *nothing* to me anymore. God, I'm such an idiot. Nice work in there, by the way, with that whole falling in love bullshit story. It was actually pretty believable that you give a shit about me."

I grab on to both of her arms this time and pull her closer, but she wiggles and jerks herself away from me until I have nothing to do with my hands but drop them down to my sides.

"Goddammit, I do care about you! Just let me explain—"

"I DON'T CARE!" she shouts, her body shaking with anger. "Nine months? Nine fucking months you've been right down the road?"

Her voice cracks with emotion and it makes me want to drop down on my knees, it hurts so much. It kills me that I've hurt her like this.

"I know, God, I know. Please, Cameron. Let me explain."

She crosses her arms in front of her and shakes her head.

"I'm so tired, Everett. So tired of being sad and confused. Go home. Just please, if you really care about me like you claim to, just *go home*. I can't do this. I thought I could, I thought I could suck it up for the camp, but I can't. It hurts too much. It hurts so fucking much," she cries, turning and walking away from me.

I stand here in the yard and watch her walk away, knowing there's nothing I can say right now to make her understand. Nothing I can do to take her pain away, and no amount of wishes I could make that will change the past and make what I said inside the truth, instead of just a dream.

Chapter 14

EVERETT

Wishing in the past…
Twenty-eight years old

My eyes meet Cameron's across the room and she gives me a small smile. Even though my nerves are shot and the dinner she made for me tonight is threatening to come right back up, I return her smile. I should be nervous that I'm getting on a plane tomorrow and being flown halfway across the world, but that's the last thing on my mind right now. I just spent the last two years in an intense program—cramming three years of training into essentially two. Now I'm heading for my last official year of residency, but it'll be in Ethiopia. It's supposed to only be a year, but I know this is what I'm meant to do, and I started researching what I could do after I was finished with the program, and discovered Doctors Without Borders. I haven't told Aiden or Cameron about this yet, though, since I don't know if I could leave Cameron any longer than a year.

I'm ready to do this. I'm confident in my abilities and my training. What I'm not confident about right now is Cameron's reaction to what I'm going to say to her.

I've pissed away every opportunity I've had to tell Cameron how I feel about her, even all the times over the last two years that I was able to come home and visit, and I know I'm the biggest asshole in the world for attempting it one more time, the day before I leave again. Am I really going to ask her to wait for me? To tell her I've loved her for as long as I can remember and I need to know she feels the same?

I am. Jesus Christ, I am.

She laughs at something Aiden says and the sound of her laughter hits me right in the gut like someone took a sledgehammer to it. He's been particularly annoying lately with his flirting with Cameron, and I wonder if he knows how I feel about her and he's doing it just to piss me off. Well, it's working. After years of watching her date guys I didn't know, didn't give two shits about, and knew wouldn't last, the thought of her being with Aiden makes me want to throw my fist through a wall.

Cameron filled the main house with all of my friends and the people I've met and become close to working part-time at the farm over the years, to give me a proper send-off tomorrow. I've been mingling and talking to everyone all evening, just biding my time until I can get Cameron alone. Knowing it's going to be a while before that happens, I make my way out of the dining hall and toward the kitchen to see if her parents need any help cleaning up since I know they weren't exactly thrilled about Cameron throwing this party for me tonight. Her mother has taken every opportunity she could to bring up other guys who are interested in Cameron and other guys she went out on dates with recently, like she knows what I'm about to do and is trying to remind me to keep my distance, but I'm not going to let it get to me. I need to do something to keep my mind busy so I stop thinking about what I'll say to her and how she'll react.

As I pass by all the pictures hanging on the wall, showing happy scenes of years past, I smile to myself even though it makes me sad knowing I'm going to miss out on making memories with everyone here at camp. But I know this next year will go by fast, and hopefully, I'll have Cameron here waiting for me when I get home.

When I get to the kitchen, I hear Cameron's parents talking and pause right outside the doorway.

"If Aiden doesn't stop flirting with her, I'm going to put my fist through his face."

I chuckle under my breath when I hear Cameron's dad complain, voicing the same thoughts I'd just had.

"Honey, Cameron is twenty-two and an adult. You can't threaten to beat up every man who wants her. And besides, Aiden is a wonderful young man who we already love like he's our son," her mother tells him.

"Shit. I know that. If I had to handpick anyone for our daughter, it would be Aiden. But that doesn't mean I have to like it. She's my little girl..." Eli trails off.

"Well, I don't think Aiden is the one you have to worry about anyway," Shelby muses.

I know I should walk through the door and make my presence known, but something keeps my feet rooted in place.

"What are you talking about?"

"I'm talking about Everett. You'd have to be blind not to see how he's always looking at her."

"Bullshit."

"I love you, Eli, but sometimes you are really clueless. That boy has been in love with her for a long time."

"He's not good enough for her. Would it kill the guy to smile every once in a while? If Cameron's going to be with anyone, it should be someone who makes her happy, not someone she exhausts herself trying to fix."

"I know, but Eli..."

"Don't even start, Shelby. I don't want to hear it. He's not good enough, and he never will be. End of story."

I start moving backward, away from the kitchen, not wanting to hear anything else. All of my fears and doubts and the main reason why I've waited so long to tell Cameron how I felt about her have just been thrown back in my face, by a man I've always looked up to and respected. I always suspected he felt this way, and most times I was able to brush it off, but hearing the words right from his mouth...I feel like a fool. I feel like an idiot, knowing just how right he is. Who the hell am I to think I'm good enough for someone like Cameron? A man from a broken home, who's getting ready to go to a third world country, with nothing to offer her but a life of worry and waiting and wondering when I'll come back home to her. It's not good enough for someone like Cameron. Eli is right, I'M not good enough for someone like Cameron, so beautiful and sweet and perfect. I would do nothing but taint that beauty and perfection.

I'm still backing away, lost in my thoughts, when I bump into something. I hear Cameron's soft laughter as I turn around to find her smiling up at me.

She's standing so close to me that I can feel the heat from her skin and it warms everything cold inside of me. I want to stand here forever, wrap my arms around her, pull her close, and let her chase away all of my doubts, but I can't.

"Hey. You okay?" she asks softly, cocking her head to the side as she continues looking up at me.

I take a step back from her before I lose whatever will I have left to keep my hands off of her.

"I'm good. Fine. Just thinking about tomorrow."

The lie comes easily and I immediately feel bad about it when her smile falls and her face fills with worry.

"Come on. Let's go for a walk."

She grabs my hand and I force myself not to pull away. Her fingers intertwine with mine as she tugs me toward the door and I let myself enjoy the feel of her small, soft hand inside of mine for the few minutes it takes us to walk down the hall and outside onto the porch.

She drops my hand when we get to the railing that overlooks the property, turning away from me to rest her palms on top of the wood as she stares out over the yard. I stare at her profile, memorizing every detail, wishing I could be a different man. A man with a better past who had a better family. A man who could make her happy. Someone worthy of this amazing woman standing in front of me.

"Everything's going to be fine. YOU'RE going to be fine. You're going to go over there, learn as much as you can, help as many people as you can, and come home safely."

I listen to the quiet cadence of her voice, knowing she's saying these things to convince herself of their truth more than me, and it reaffirms my decision to forget about everything I planned on saying to her tonight. She doesn't deserve this. Even if by some miracle she feels the same about me, I can't do this to her. I can't make her put her life on hold for me.

She suddenly turns back to face me and catches me staring at her. Our eyes meet, and as much as I want to look away, I can't.

"Aiden asked me out."

Her words are like a knife to the heart, but they don't surprise me.

She laughs and rolls her eyes.

"I mean, he's joked about it for years, but he was serious this time. Dead serious. Can you believe that?"

I'm afraid to open my mouth, so I just quietly nod. I hate everything about this moment and I want to pretend like it's not really happening, but I can't. As much as I want to curl up and die, Aiden is still my best friend, and I'd never stop him from getting what he wants, even if it's the same thing I've been wanting for as long as I can remember. I don't know why I've never told Aiden how I felt about Cameron. Maybe a part of me thought if I said it out loud, if I admitted to someone else how I felt, it would make it more real. And if it's real, it can be taken away from you. It was a stupid way to think, especially knowing that Aiden would have never asked her out if he knew how I felt. And now it's being taken away from me anyway, even before it was truly mine to have.

Aiden is clearly the better choice. He's here, he has a stable, well-paying job, he's not going to disappear for months at a time, Cameron's parents love him...and he's good enough for her. Better than good enough. He'll make her happy and she'll never exhaust herself trying to fix him.

I slide my hands into the front pockets of my jeans so that I can't grab on to Cameron's arms and pull her against me, beg her to wait for me, and try to convince her I'm worth it, when I know I'm not.

She pushes away from the railing and moves right up to me until we're toe to toe. I watch her throat bob as she swallows, mesmerized by the way her tongue darts out to lick her lips nervously.

"Can you give me any reason why I shouldn't say yes to him?" she whispers.

She throws almost the same words back at me that I

said to her two years ago when I was starting my residency, trying to feel her out and see if there was something there between us, or if it was just my imagination. And like an idiot, I start to second-guess everything I'm thinking. I start to wonder if she's asking me this because she feels something more than friendship between us, but I know it's not true. She's just nervous. She's just scared because things are going to change. I'm not always going to be here, following her around like a puppy, wishing on stars that she'll someday feel the same.

I want to hold her in my arms and kiss her. I want to show her all of the reasons why she shouldn't say yes to Aiden, but I can't. The only reason I can give her is because I'm so desperately in love with her I can't think straight. But it's not good enough, and it never will be.

"Nope. Not one reason why you shouldn't say yes. Aiden is perfect for you. I'm sure you two will be very happy together. If not, it sounds like you've got a long line of men your mother approves of to take up where he left off."

I have to fight to put a smile on my face even though the words coming out of my mouth are complete bullshit and I want to take them back as soon as I see the hurt and sadness in her eyes. I shouldn't have been so cold. I shouldn't have been such a prick, and I know all I'm doing right now is proving her dad right, even though I've tried so hard to change.

If you love something, set it free. Isn't that what they always say?

Cameron will never come back to me, though, because she was never meant to be mine. She was just a stupid wish on a handful of stupid stars, and as she turns away from me and walks back into the house without another word, I let her go, and watch the dream of her disappear right in front of my eyes.

Chapter 15

CAMERON

Swiping away the tears that won't seem to stop falling, I lean down and rest my elbows on the wooden fence in front of me. After I stormed away from Everett a few hours ago, I kept walking and crying, hurting and feeling so lost that I didn't even realize how far I'd walked until I found myself a few acres away, at the far end of the fenced-off grazing area for the horses. For the first time in my life, I didn't put the needs of this camp first and that just makes me cry even harder. I might have just screwed up everything my parents built by sending Everett away, but I couldn't be around him for another minute, keeping up with this stupid farce, without losing myself completely in the process.

Who am I kidding? I lost myself a long time ago, and having Everett here again just highlighted that fact. Being around the campers didn't make me happy, organizing the charity dinner didn't make me happy, being in charge of something I'm so incredibly proud to be a part of didn't make me happy. All the things that used to give me purpose and used to make me feel alive just felt stagnant and flat. I attributed this to Aiden's death, but standing here now, looking out at the plantation I grew up on and thinking about all of the memories I've made here, I realize I've felt this way for a lot longer. Four-and-a-half years, to be exact. I haven't felt like myself and I haven't been able to figure out how to be happy again since Everett left.

I hate him for ruining all of this for me.

I hate him for making it impossible for me to forgive him.

I hate him for tainting every good memory I have of this place, replacing it with sadness that he wasn't here the last few years with me to make new memories.

I hate that I can't just let go of my hurt and anger and let him help me save the camp.

I hate that I can't pretend as easily as he can.

"I just left Everett at home, slamming cupboards and muttering a whole bunch of fun curse words. How mad are you at me right now?"

The voice behind me makes me jump and whirl around.

"Like, throw a punch at me mad, or just scream at me and call me horrible names mad?"

I laugh through my tears even though nothing about my situation right now is funny, staring at a man who can always make me smile.

"I'm not going to punch you, Jason."

He lets out a deep sigh of relief, moving to stand next to me as he slides one hand through his hair on top of his head, just like his brother does when he's nervous or frustrated.

Why couldn't I have fallen in love with THIS brother? It would have been so much easier.

No matter how much or how little time we spend together, we've always been able to laugh easily with each other. It never feels like a job trying to make Jason smile. He's never let me down or disappointed me, unlike his brother.

"I really, really want to punch you, but I like you too much to ruin that pretty face of yours," I reassure him with a smile as we both turn to stare at the horses, which have been let out into the pasture for one last time before they get locked up into the stables for the night.

Jason laughs, removing one hand from his pocket to reach up and give my shoulder a squeeze.

"I do have a really pretty face. Especially since I own a razor, unlike my brother."

I close my eyes at his mention of Everett, his face floating through my mind and the destroyed look on it when I told him to go home. Along with the look in his eyes when he was spouting all that bullshit for Stratford's benefit. Bullshit that I fed into and allowed myself to pretend for a few minutes was real, allowed myself to be transported back in time when I was so crazy in love with him that hearing those words would have had me kicking Stratford out of the room and climbing onto his lap. And then he had to go and ruin it all with his announcement of how long he's been home. Just like always, I'm reminded of how loving that man brought me nothing but pain. And obviously being friends with him again would produce the same result.

"You should have told me he was home," I whisper, my throat tightening and my eyes stinging with tears all over again. "Nine months, Jason. He's been home for nine months and you didn't say anything. Why?"

I look away from the horses to stare at his profile. A muscle ticks in his jaw as he grinds his teeth together, probably trying to come up with a plausible excuse for keeping something like this from me. Strong jaw, full lips, a mess of unruly hair on top of his head, the same dark brown color as

Everett's. That's where the similarities end. Jason is always in a good mood, always smiling and happy no matter what he's doing. He was never affected by his childhood the way Everett was. He never needed someone to fix him, because he was never broken.

"How many years have you worked here?" he suddenly asks, finally turning to look at me.

"Um, since I was a teenager, which you already know."

It's a stupid question, and one that confuses me. Even though Jason and I have never been super close—like Everett, Aiden, and I were—we were still friends. He never needed the comfort of this camp growing up like Everett did, but he still hung out here from time to time, and he stops by all the time when I need his help fixing things, or just to hang out with me, or other people here at camp that he's become friends with over the years. He knows everything about my life and what I do here. He knows exactly how long I've worked here.

"Technically, all your life, since you live here," he adds.

"Yes," I tell him, trying to keep the annoyance out of my voice.

He turns to face me, crossing his arms over his chest and tilting his head to the side.

"And in all that time, you've spent countless hours working with families and helping children cope, when their loved one came home from deployment and couldn't quite get a handle on the reality of not being in a war zone anymore," he states, his voice growing softer.

My shoulders start to drop and all the tightness in my body from my irritation with him beating around the bush rushes out of me so quickly that I almost feel light-headed.

"You've seen firsthand what PTSD can do to someone. You know how it can break a person, make their entire personality change, and make it really fucking hard for them to remember how to wake up each day and want to take another breath. He might not have fought in a war, but he still struggles with his own form of PTSD. Everett saw things no one should have to see. He saw people he knew die right in front of him with their blood on his hands, he held parents as they cried in his arms because he couldn't save their child, and then he dealt with the guilt of not knowing his best friend was dying, not being able to save him either."

My head starts shaking back and forth with the reality of what he's saying to me. I don't want it to be true, but I know it is. I can see it written all over his face. He wouldn't be saying something like this if it wasn't the God's honest truth, and I feel like an idiot. I've been so wrapped up in my anger that Everett would just show up here out of the blue after almost five long years, and then overwhelmed with hurt when I found out he'd been here for nine months before he came to me, that I didn't even stop to think *why*. I just assumed. I never once thought about what all that time overseas would have done to him, or what he would have seen and lived through. I never looked at him and saw anything other than the old Everett. The man who, as an adult, was always strong and sure and confident. The man who wouldn't let anything get in the way of his dreams. I didn't look at him and see someone hurting and vulnerable. I didn't want to think of him as someone who couldn't handle anything, but I should have known. Jason is right. I've seen firsthand what PTSD can do to a person, and sometimes, it isn't pretty.

"It also didn't help that he learned one of his best friends had died after being diagnosed with pancreatic cancer and that best friend forbade anyone from telling Everett that he was sick since he wanted him to come back for the 'right' reasons, and not just to watch him die, and so he couldn't get back for the funeral and he never got a chance to say good-bye. It just got to be too much for him, and it broke him," Jason tells me softly, turning away to look out at the horses. "I'm sorry I didn't tell you he was here, but I couldn't. I wanted him to come to you, believe me. I begged him to get his shit together and go to you. I knew you of all people would have been able to get through to him, but he was lost. For a while there, I didn't think I'd ever get him back, Cameron, and it scared the hell out of me."

Just when I think I don't have any tears left, they come pouring out of me so quickly that Jason's face becomes a blur. I should never have agreed to Aiden's demand not to track down Everett as soon as we found out he was sick. Aiden knew he didn't have much time left, and he was adamant that he didn't want Everett to see him that way, so weak and frail and confined to a bed. As angry as I was with Everett at the time, it killed me that he wasn't here to say good-bye, and I can only imagine the guilt he felt about not being by Aiden's bedside right along with me.

"I'm such a bitch," I mutter, wrapping my arms around my waist to hold myself together. "I smacked him across the face. I screamed at him. I told him I didn't care and I told him to go home."

Jason chuckles under his breath and glances over at me.

"He probably deserved a little bit of that. I even warned him that you'd probably punch him in the face when he showed up here."

He wraps his arm around my shoulder and pulls me against his side, rubbing his hand comfortingly up and down my arm.

"I didn't tell you this to make you feel guilty, Cam. I just wanted you to understand that he didn't stay away these last nine months because he was an asshole and didn't care about you. If anything, his problem is that he cares *too* much, and he didn't want you to see him like that."

We stay like this for a few quiet minutes until I'm finally able to speak.

"How bad was it?" I whisper, resting my cheek against the side of his chest.

"Really bad. Do you remember a few months ago when I was here fixing the porch railing and Amelia's ex-husband showed up?" he asks softly.

I nod against his chest. I'll never forget that day. Amelia had been doing so well and had been so happy for so long, that I almost forgot she had a husband who wouldn't get help for his PTSD and almost ruined her and their son, right along with him. He was so drunk he could barely stand up, stumbling around the camp with a bottle of whiskey in his hand, screaming for her and cursing at the top of his lungs. She'd recently filed for divorce, and the papers had been delivered to him that day. It took three men, including Jason, to get him under control and get him away from her. Amelia handled it better than I thought she would, and I had never been prouder of her for standing her ground, telling him he needed to get help, and that she didn't want to see him or speak to him again until he did.

"Multiply that by about a thousand, and that's what Everett was like the first couple of months after he got home," Jason tells me.

I squeeze my eyes closed, not wanting to have that picture of Everett in my mind. Not wanting to know how badly he struggled when he came home, how hard he must have fought to get better, and how much it must have hurt him when he showed up here today and I threw it in his face and made him feel guilty.

I should have known better. All these years, all of my

training working with soldiers, and I couldn't separate from my own pain long enough even to consider that Everett might have been hurting just as badly, even if he wasn't a soldier. He must've seen so many horrible things when all he wanted to do was save lives. He lost people right in front of his eyes, and then he came home and had to deal with losing one of the most important people in his life. Knowing that he couldn't do anything to help him.

"I'm a horrible person."

Jason laughs again, pulling away and grabbing my arms, turning me to face him. He bends his knees and looks directly into my eyes.

"You're not a horrible person. You've got a lot on your plate right now and it's my fault for convincing Everett it would be a super idea to just show up here without giving you some kind of warning or explanation first. I'm not excusing him for being a complete asshole for signing up with Doctors Without Borders when he was supposed to come back here and refusing to come home even for one weekend. Don't get all sappy on me now and let him off easy for that shit. Just give him a break for the last nine months; that's all I'm asking."

Jason kisses the top of my head and walks away, leaving me alone again with my thoughts…a place I really don't want to be right now.

Chapter 16

EVERETT

My body jerks upright in bed with a scream dying in my throat as I pant heavily and try to get my bearings.

It was just a dream, just a dream, just a dream…

Scrubbing my palms over my face, I try to rub away the images that won't leave my head, knowing it wasn't *just a dream*. It was memories. Nightmares of my own personal hell that will never go away.

The four-year-old boy with chocolate brown eyes, who taught me how to play soccer, taking his last breath while I furiously pressed up and down on his chest after the infection in his body spread to his brain.

The pregnant mother who always brought me a small trinket when I examined her, who had the translator teach her how to say "handsome doctor," who bled out right in front of me when I didn't have the tools I needed to repair her torn uterus.

The self-appointed grandmother of a village I visited, who

could never have children of her own and, therefore, "adopted" everyone else's children, spending every cent she had to buy them special treats. The sound her lungs made when they filled with blood after being shot by an insurgent, and the feel of her heart against my palm, taking its final beat as I held my hands against her chest to try to stop the bleeding.

I wish I could forget their faces, all of them blurring into a hundred other faces of everyone I couldn't save. I wish I could forget the way they looked at me, so sure that I would save them, with so much trust in me that I didn't deserve.

Flinging my sweat-soaked sheet off of my body, I get out of bed and pad across the floor of my dark bedroom, knowing I'll never be able to get back to sleep now.

I don't even bother turning on the light in the bathroom when I enter it. The soft pinkish-purple glow of dawn from the sun just beginning to rise off in the horizon peeks through the window next to the sink and gives me enough light to see what I'm doing as I reach into the shower and turn the handle to the coldest setting. I don't need to turn on the bright, overhead light to know what I look like in the mirror. I've seen it too many times since I came back home and another nightmare wreaked havoc on me. The bloodshot eyes, the ashen skin, the misery, the guilt...

Yanking my boxer briefs off, I step under the shower, hissing when the icy water hits my skin. Pressing my hands against the wall under the showerhead, I drop my head down between my shoulders, willing the cold spray that rains down over my head and drips into my eyes to freeze away my memories or wash them down the drain, but it doesn't work. It never works.

The dream is still fresh in my mind when I finally give up an hour later. I turn the water off, grab a towel from the shelf above the toilet, and with my teeth chattering and my body aching with the tremor of shivers, I wrap the towel around my waist and make my way back into the bedroom.

It's been a while since I had one of those dreams. They still show up randomly, usually when I'm overly stressed or upset about something. My interaction with Cameron last night was definitely stressful and upsetting.

"You're out of milk."

"JESUS CHRIST!" I shout, spinning around from my dresser to find Jason lounging against the door frame to my bedroom.

With an irritated huff, I secure the towel from my recent shower more tightly around my waist.

"What the hell are you doing here so early?" I complain, turning away from him to grab a pair of boxer briefs and jeans out of my dresser drawer.

"I got hungry," he shrugs, as I glare at his reflection in the mirror above my dresser. "And I didn't really feel like I was at the top of my game with my pep talk last night. I want a do-over."

Jason's "pep talk," if you can call it that, was just him stopping by the house the previous night and calling me an asshole for an hour. I tossed and turned all night and got maybe a total of two hours sleep, and then those two hours were interrupted by a damn nightmare. I was in no mood for his pep talk *then*, and I'm definitely in no mood for another one now. Last night over coffee, I stupidly told him everything that happened with Cameron, hoping he'd maybe side with me and tell me I had every right to be feeling the way I am now, but that didn't happen.

"I already know I was an asshole, I don't need a recap," I mutter, stepping into my boxers and sliding them up under my towel, repeating the process with my jeans before unwinding the towel from around my waist.

I felt like shit when Cameron walked away from me last

night, and like a fool, I obeyed her wishes and went home, where I spent the last twelve hours getting pissed off instead of being sad about the way things went down. She has every right to be mad at me, but she didn't even give me a chance to explain. It hasn't exactly been a walk in the park for me to gather up the courage to tell her what I did to myself when I got home. I haven't been looking forward to her staring at me in pity or having her feel like she needs to walk on eggshells around me, but I was going to suck it up because I knew she needed an explanation. I knew she *deserved* an explanation as to why I didn't come to her sooner.

But she didn't give me a chance. And that pissed me off the more I thought about it. I know I haven't been the best friend to her lately, and I pretty much cut her out of my life, but I'm back now and I'm trying. I'm fucking *trying* to push aside my hurt and my jealousy because I know I have a lot of making up to do with her. Being her friend trumps everything else right now. I need to help her heal from losing Aiden, and do whatever I can to help her save the camp. Those things have to come before my bullshit hang-ups and insecurities, and before her stubbornness and anger, and she's just going to have to deal with it.

Yanking a T-shirt out of my drawer, I slam it closed harder than necessary.

"You're in a bad mood. I'm thinking that going back to the camp and telling Cameron you're not going anywhere isn't the best idea right now," Jason states.

"I really don't give a shit what you think," I tell him, tossing my shirt on top of the dresser and turning around to face him.

Jason shrugs, backing out of the doorway.

"Don't say I didn't warn you. That woman is going to chew you up and spit you out once she stops being sad."

His boots thump against the floor as he disappears around the corner and down the stairs. I wait until I hear the front door slam closed before I let out the breath I was holding. I refuse to think about the picture he painted for me during his "pep talk," how he went to the camp last night to fix whatever Cameron needed help with, and found her crying out in the back pasture. It was bad enough watching her cry and fall apart right in front of me, I didn't need that image of her being all alone with her sadness, knowing someone else was there to comfort her when I'd walked away. Again.

That shit stops right now. I'm done walking away from her, whether she likes it or not.

As soon as I turn to grab my discarded T-shirt, I hear a knock at the door.

Cursing under my breath, I leave my bedroom and head downstairs, calling Jason every name I can think of. He waltzes in my house any other time, but of course he chooses now to be a fucking gentleman and make me open the door for him.

"What the fuck do you want now?" I growl when I fling open the front door, shock replacing my irritation when I see Cameron standing right in front of me.

My tongue gets stuck to the roof of my mouth, and every thought in my mind flies right out of my head as I stand here staring at her. She's wearing a pair of tiny jean shorts that show off every inch of her gorgeous legs, and a form-fitting Camp Rylan T-shirt with a wide neck that hangs off one bare shoulder. Her hands are shoved into the back pockets of her shorts, and the position pushes her breasts out and makes my eyes want to do nothing but stare at them all day and my hands itch to feel the weight of them in my palms. The sun rising in the distance is partially blocked by her body, making the bright rays surround her like a halo.

Fucking hell. Does she ever have a bad day, or does she always roll out of bed looking like a goddamn Disney princess? A hot Disney princess that I want to pull into the house and shove up against the wall next to me.

"Can I come in?"

Her voice penetrates my lust-filled thoughts and I realize I'm still standing here in the doorway with my tongue practically hanging out of my mouth. With an irritated sigh, I push the door open wider and step out of the way to let her inside. Closing it behind her, I turn and lean against the wood, crossing my arms in front of me while I make myself remember why I was mad at her just a few minutes ago, instead of thinking about stripping her out of those damn shorts.

She pulls her hands out of her back pockets and starts wringing them together nervously in front of her, twisting that damn ring around her finger, looking down at her feet instead of at me. I should say something and break the tension floating around the room right now, but *she* came to *me*, and I need to let her do the talking. After a few minutes, she finally looks up and lets out a huff of annoyance, flapping one of her hands in my direction.

"Can you go put on a shirt or something?" she complains, still refusing to look right at me as she stares at a spot over my shoulder.

I can't stop the smirk that tips up the corner of my mouth when the first thing she says is something I least expected. I'm not gonna lie—the fact that me without my shirt on is making Cameron uncomfortable is more than a little surprising, but a great boost to the ego. Sure, I know I'm not a bad-looking guy, and the years overseas, hefting around medical equipment, lifting heavy boxes of supplies when we got deliveries, and having to carrying everything I needed to work on a patient with me no matter where I went gave me a pretty damn good fit and muscular physique, but after years of having all those one-sided feelings for the woman standing in front of me who is doing everything she can to avoid looking at my shirtless torso, it makes me more than a little cocky.

Dropping my arms to my sides, I push away from the door until I'm standing right in front of her.

"What's wrong? You look a little flushed," I tell her, my concern laced with more than a little amusement.

She steps back away from me, crossing her arms in front of her with another huff of annoyance when she finally looks up at me. "You're an asshole."

"Did you come all the way out here to tell me that?"

The glare she's giving me turns arctic and it's almost powerful enough to throw a layer of ice around the room, making me *want* to go put a shirt on instead of ignoring her request.

"Yes, I drove all the way out here to remind you, just in case you forgot," she fires back.

So much for thinking she was going to look at me with pity in her eyes.

I almost tossed my brother through the wall last night when he told me he said something to Cameron so she wouldn't be so angry with me about staying away the last nine months. He swore he didn't go into detail, but felt like he needed to say *something* so she'd know I wasn't exactly a fully functioning member of society who just didn't give a shit about her when I got home. He knew I wanted to be the one to tell her everything, but I couldn't stay mad at him for not being able to keep his mouth shut when she was so angry at me and didn't know at least some of the truth.

Standing here now, watching her irritation with my

cockiness grow, I'm more than a little happy Jason was the one to say something to her first. It looks like he made it possible for me to skip right over the pity party and move on to pissing her off in more fun ways.

"You're gonna have to do better than that weak little right hook of yours," I inform her with a wink, blatantly lying right to her face.

That shit *hurt*. And I've been punched in the face by grown men twice my size before.

But watching her chest rise and fall with annoyance is the most fun I've had in years. Much better than picturing her eyes filled with tears or thinking about all the ways I've let her down.

"Oh, screw you," she mutters. "I can't believe I came out here to apologize and ask you to come back to camp."

"There's no need for you to apologize, *or* ask me to come back. I was coming back whether you wanted me to or not. Also, I packed a bag. Since we're husband and wife, I'll be shacking up with you going forward."

"Oh, really? And you didn't bother to think I might want to have a say in this decision?"

"You don't get to have a say in this decision. You need me, end of story."

"*I* don't need you, the camp needs you, there's a difference. And I definitely don't need you *shacking up with me*," she argues.

"No, there isn't a difference. You and the camp are a package deal, I'm coming back, and I'm staying with you in the guest house so Stratford sees nothing but a happy little couple, coming out of their happy little home together first thing in the morning. I'm not waking up at the ass crack of dawn to drive all the way over there before he wakes up every damn morning."

"I changed my mind. You're too annoying and you can't even follow simple instructions like PUTTING ON A GOD-DAMN SHIRT!" she shouts, throwing her hands up in the air and stalking around me as she heads to the door.

Jesus, this woman is infuriating. And she makes my dick hard. Which is also infuriating.

"Sorry, sweetheart. You can't change your mind now."

I chuckle under my breath when she pulls the door open so hard it bounces off the wall behind it and almost comes back to smack her in the ass.

"Too bad!" she shouts over her shoulder as she stomps down the front steps.

I move to the doorway and watch her walk over to the driveway, where she parked her car.

"So I'll meet you in about fifteen minutes? I'll see if I can find a shirt by then," I yell over to her.

I can see her talking to herself as she gets in the car and slams the door closed, and I keep right on smiling to myself as she starts up the car and peels out of the driveway. I can only imagine all the names she's currently calling me as she drives back to the plantation.

Yep, getting under Cameron's skin is much better than the alternative. I'd much rather annoy her than have her hate me. I know it's going to take a hell of a lot of work for her to forgive me and want to be my friend again, but at least it's a step in the right direction. At least she didn't treat me any differently now that Jason gave her some of my truths.

I can handle a Cameron who's annoyed with me. I'm no longer the angry punk kid Cameron always worried about and felt like she needed to fix. It's my turn to fix things, and she's just going to have to learn how to deal with it.

Chapter 17

CAMERON

You're gonna have to do better than that weak little right hook of yours," I mumble, mimicking Everett's stupid low, raspy voice as I open drawers in my desk and slam them closed when I don't find what I'm looking for.

"I'll show you a weak right hook when I punch you in your stupid, smug neck, attached to your stupid shirtless body," I complain to myself, slamming yet another desk drawer closed in frustration.

Holy hell, that shirtless body…

I went over to Everett's house this morning with every intention of apologizing to him for not being more under-standing or sympathetic toward him, and I forgot everything I wanted to say as soon as he opened the door. His hair was still damp from the shower and droplets of water that he must have missed when he dried off were still pebbled on his chest. Sweet Lord, that chest…I had seen Everett without a shirt plenty of times over our twenty-plus years of friendship since we spent a lot of time in the summer swimming in the lake at the camp. He was always good-looking, even as a teenager, playing sports to keep himself in shape, and working out whenever he could.

Praise be to Doctors Without Borders and whatever the hell they did to him. Who would've thought a doctor could look that good? That man is more ripped than anything my fantasies have ever conjured about him. I could wash my laundry on his abs and use the indents in his narrow waist to hold my cup of afternoon tea.

My sleepless night worrying about him and how hurt he must have been by the things I said was quickly forgotten when he smirked at me and took way too much joy in my discomfort at being that close to him when he was half naked. I couldn't even look at him. All I could do was picture what he looked like *fully* naked. Instead of apologizing and asking him to tell me the full story of what happened when he came home, something I needed to hear and dreaded hearing both at the same time, he riled me up and pissed me off.

"Who the hell does he think he is? Cocky, stupid asshole..."

"I hope you're not talking about me."

I jump when I hear a voice in the doorway of the office, trying not to groan when I see Grady standing there, leaning against the doorjamb with his hands in the front pockets of his jeans, smiling at me.

Grady Stevens, the guy I lost my virginity to the summer I graduated high school, who I broke up with a few months later when he started talking about marriage and moving in together after college and I realized I was the biggest bitch in the world for making him think we'd ever have a future together. I only went out with him back then to make Everett jealous. I only gave him my virginity because I was hurt and pissed that it didn't work. He was a good guy. A sweet guy. But he wasn't the man of my dreams.

I ran into Grady again right after Aiden died. I was sad and vulnerable and I just wanted to feel something other than numb and angry all the time and I found myself right back where I started with him. Using him just to stop feeling so sad.

Over the last couple of months, Grady has been my on-again/off-again…I don't even know what he is. According to Amelia, he's my "special friend." Is he just a casual date when I have an event to attend and need a plus one? Random hook-up every once in a while when I'm feeling particularly lonely? I definitely wouldn't call him a friend, even though he's one of the nicest guys I've ever met and I'm sure I could easily turn whatever this is into something more if I had the ability to knock down the walls I've built and let him in. But that's never going to happen. I made sure this time that he knew the score before I ever agreed to go out with him or let him into my bed. That he understood I'd closed myself off from love, and what he got from me every so often would be all he'd ever get from me. He was a kind, understanding man who never pressured me for anything more. He was perfectly fine letting me drive the bus and letting me always be the one who reached out to him instead of the other way around. He had his own life away from me running his family's championship horse racing farm and dating other women since we've never been exclusive, so it's not like he was sitting around, pining away for me or anything. What we had worked.

Until now, when I completely forgot that I sent him a text and invited him out to the camp today so I could release some tension after all my sleepless nights and worry. I sent him a text before Everett showed back up into my life, and after everything that happened yesterday, I forgot to cancel.

"I'm so sorry, Grady. Now isn't really a good time," I tell him as I stand up behind the desk.

Grady pushes off the doorjamb and moves into the room. I watch him saunter toward me and I wonder why he's never given me butterflies. He was good-looking as a teenager, and has grown into a very handsome man. His blond hair is short and spiky on top with the sides and back shaved in a tapered fashion. He's a few inches taller than my five foot seven frame, and his body is full of lean muscle, which he keeps in shape by paying a ridiculous amount of money to one of those meat market gyms he goes to every single morning.

I think again about Everett with his shirt off, with his ripped body, and how I have to crane my neck to look up at him, and the butterflies start swarming around in my stomach, pissing me off.

Leaning his hip against the edge of my desk, Grady wraps his hands around my upper arms and pulls me closer to him. He smells like soap, a smell I used to enjoy because it was clean and fresh, but now the smell is foreign and all I crave is Everett's woodsy, manly smell.

"I saw Amelia outside when I pulled in. She told me something about your best friend coming home and how you two are pretending to be married. What in the hell is going on?"

He smiles at me, showing me his question isn't one filled with anger, but amused confusion, proving yet again what a good man he is. Any other guy would be losing his shit right now, regardless of whether or not our relationship was serious.

"It's a long, very annoying story that I don't want to bore you with that involves needing funds for the camp as soon as possible and not really having any other option at the time. I'm really sorry that I need to cancel today. I've just...got a lot on my plate right now," I explain as he rubs his hands up and down the sides of my arms.

We've never really been touchy-feely together. We don't snuggle, we don't hold hands, we don't kiss in public, all of our physical contact is reserved for the bedroom, and his attempt at soothing me makes me a little uncomfortable.

I take a step back from him until his hands drop down to his sides.

"I don't understand why you didn't just call me. I have to say, I don't really like the idea of you doing something like this with another guy, even if you *are* pretending. You know I would have gladly helped you out. It would have been fun to play house," he tells me softly, reaching out and brushing my bangs out of my eyes.

Okay, now it's just getting weird. Is he trying to mark his territory or something? Does he feel threatened by a man he doesn't even know, I've never even mentioned, and met only once twelve years ago? We aren't this couple. We aren't these people, getting jealous of others.

"Look, Grady—"

"It's fine," he cuts me off. "Although I thought that guy was a real dick the one time I met him right after graduation. Since you've never mentioned him all this time, I thought he was out of your life, and then to find out he's here and pretending to be your husband…it was just a little shocking. We'll be fine."

His words confuse me even more and now I'm the one standing here in shock, unable to move or say anything in reply when he leans in and kisses the side of my cheek. Of course I've never mentioned Everett to Grady. I don't talk about Everett with anyone really, and especially not with him. We don't talk about our lives when we're together. We don't talk at all when we're together.

"I'll give you a call later in the week when things have calmed down," he tells me.

I can do nothing but stand here behind my desk and watch him go as he gives me a wave over his shoulder and disappears around the corner.

I've always liked Grady because he was easygoing, no fuss, no muss, and didn't care what I did when I was away from him. Having him show up here and act completely different throws me for a loop. I know if Everett hadn't shown up and tipped my world upside down, things would have gone just like they always have with Grady. He wouldn't have felt the need to mark his territory, and he wouldn't have said something so utterly ridiculous about us playing house together, which made me uncomfortable and unlikely ever to call him again. We would have locked ourselves in my office and partaken in thirty minutes of stress relief.

Now I'm full of tension and annoyance, and it's not even nine in the morning.

I resume what I was doing before Grady interrupted, turning away from the door. I go back to opening and closing drawers in the metal filing cabinet behind my desk, cursing under my breath in annoyance.

"Am I interrupting? Did that desk do something to tick you off?"

I slam another drawer closed, looking back over my shoulder at Amelia.

"I'm fine. Everything is fine. F. I. N. E. Fine," I mutter, yanking open another drawer and cursing at the top of my lungs when I still can't find what I need.

"I'm sensing a little hostility and I'm pretty sure you're anything *but* fine."

When she comes around the desk and stands behind me, I wordlessly reach back over my shoulder and hand her the two letters I've been holding on to since I opened them, and the reason for my desk drawer anger. Sort of.

"I hate you. You will pay," Amelia says, reading the two letters and the short, simple threat that each one had printed on it. "Creepy, but not unusual and definitely not the reason you're beating the shit out of your desk."

She pushes me out of the way and leans down, calmly sliding open the bottom drawer and pulling out the file folder where I keep all the previous letters I've received, standing up and handing it to me with a smile.

"I looked in that drawer three times. Also, I hate you," I tell her, snatching the file and the letters out of her hands, shoving them inside and putting everything back in the drawer, kicking it closed with my foot just to make myself feel better.

"Does your cheerful personality this morning have anything to do with the booty call that just drove away? Sex shouldn't piss you off. Did he do it wrong? He sure wasn't here very long for it to have been any good. Or does this have to do with the hot piece of ass that just pulled up outside?" Amelia asks as I flop down onto my chair and she perches her hip on the edge of the desk next to me.

My traitorous heart starts to beat faster and butterflies swarm around my stomach as I glance out the window and see Jason's truck in the drive. Everett came back, even after I gave him hell and stomped away from him like a two-year-old throwing a temper tantrum.

Why couldn't I have gotten this excited when Grady walked into the room?

I push Grady from my mind, only having enough energy at this point to concentrate on one problem at a time.

"Is he actually wearing a shirt this time?" I snap.

Amelia's eyes widen and she whistles softly, reaching down to pat the top of my thigh.

"Yes, the man is fully clothed; you can retract your claws. But now I'm gonna need more details. I really feel like seeing Everett without his shirt on would have put you in a much better mood. I don't care if he is an asshole and we don't like him; that man is hot. Wait. We don't like him, right? That hasn't changed?"

Leaning forward, I rest my arms on the desk and smack my head down on top of them with a groan.

"What am I going to do, Amelia? I can't go out there and pretend like we're married. This is the dumbest idea in the world. I can't even handle standing in his hallway and seeing him with his shirt off. I will spontaneously combust if he puts his hands on me today. And on top of all that, I don't know whether I want to cry or scream whenever I'm around him. He makes me feel so damn confused."

Amelia's hand comes under my chin and she lifts my face up from my arms.

"When you saw him yesterday, what was your first thought? Don't think about what happened after. Don't think about how you're feeling right now. Think about what you felt when you first turned around and saw him standing there," she tells me softly.

"That I was just happy he was here. That he was close enough for me to touch and reassure myself he was real and he was okay," I whisper.

She smiles at me and brushes my hair out of my eyes.

"Then stop worrying about everything else and just stick to that for now. I know you guys have a lot to talk about, and he has a lot of apologizing to do and explanations to give, but just hold on to that feeling. That he's here, and he's alive and he's okay. And he is determined to not let you down again."

I let out a huge sigh and push away from the top of the

desk, leaning against the back of my chair to look up at my friend.

"How did you get so wise?" I ask.

"I wasn't always this awesome, but I have a pretty amazing friend who gave me some great advice over the years."

We share a smile and I thank God, not for the first time, that this woman walked into my life when she did.

"Enough about my shit. How are you? How's Brandon?" I ask, inquiring about her son, whom I haven't seen around camp in a few weeks.

When Jason brought up Amelia's husband last night to give me some sort of comparison to what Everett was like when he got home from deployment, it made me realize I'd been so wrapped up in trying to find money for the camp, and then distracted by Everett coming back, that I hadn't checked in with her lately.

"Brandon is good. He's been wanting to spend more time with Rob's parents lately. Since he doesn't get to see his father, I guess it's the next best thing."

It's my turn to reach out and give her a comforting pat on the leg.

"And before you even ask, I'm fine. And not *your* kind of fine. I'm actually *really* fine," she tells me with a laugh. "Rob has surprisingly stuck it out with rehab this time and he seems to be doing really good. He's not happy I won't take Brandon to see him, but he understands. Eight is just too young to have to explain to him what that place is and why Daddy has to stay there. Telling him his dad is out of town for work is just easier right now, and Rob calls Brandon almost every day, which makes things a little better."

"Wow, I can't believe he actually stayed in rehab for more than a few days," I tell her.

"I know, no one is more shocked than me. As scary as

it was to draw up those divorce papers, and then see what it did to him after he got them, I know I made the right decision. I think it might have scared him straight. Or at least scared him enough to know he couldn't keep going on the way he was."

Amelia tells me a little more about her most recent phone calls with Rob and how clear-headed he sounds, and how he's told her on more than one occasion that he's thankful she and Brandon have this camp for support. It makes me forget about the newest letters I received and remember that the good always outweighs the bad.

She leaves me alone in the office and heads out to a worker and volunteer meeting as everyone starts readying the camp for the kids that will be arriving in the next hour to kick off this weekend's session. Staring down at today's calendar printout that Amelia left for me, I make a mental note of all the activities that Mr. Stratford would be attending to check things out, knowing I'm going to have to be right there with him to explain things, along with my "husband."

Amelia's right. We have a lot to talk about. I can't keep letting my emotions get the best of me, especially not in front of Stratford. Seeing that archery is the first activity on the agenda, I force myself to do what Amelia suggested, and just think about the way I felt when I first saw Everett again, instead of how easy it is for him to push my buttons.

Chapter 18

EVERETT

Leaning my elbows against the fence railing, I watch Cameron help one of the campers down from the horse he just rode, Cameron walking next to him the entire time with one of her hands on his leg so he wouldn't be scared. I smile to myself when she and the boy start jumping up and down, cheering and giving each other high fives.

"She's very good with the children," Stratford states, walking up next to me and looking out into the pasture as Cameron shows the boy how to hold the reins and lead the horse back to the stables.

"She is. She's amazing," I agree.

As much as I wanted to continue needling Cameron all day just to get a reaction out of her, I realized as soon as we met out at the archery station that it wouldn't be a good idea. And not just because she feigned ignorance on how to use a bow and arrow, and when I stood behind her with my hands on her hips, she stepped forward, turned, and aimed the damn thing right at my face. Which in turn prompted all of the kids to recite the camp rule that you never point an arrow or any kind of weapon at someone's face. Cameron claimed she only did that to make sure the kids were paying attention, but the smirk on her face when she said that to me proved otherwise. Even though she put on a brave, confident attitude for Stratford's benefit, I knew her better than that. I knew she was nervous and scared about the future of this camp. Every time I spoke and her eyes darted in Stratford's direction, every time I touched her and she tensed up, then quickly forced herself to relax, I knew I needed to go easy on her.

It kills me that she's so worried about the future of the camp. It makes me feel so damn ashamed of myself that I wasn't here earlier to help her. I should have been here. I hate how weak and pathetic I was that I couldn't see past my own misery and grief to put her first.

"It's quite a big undertaking, running a camp this size."

I tear my eyes away from Cameron to look over at Stratford.

"It is, but as you can see, Cameron handles this place beautifully. It's a well-oiled machine with amazing workers and volunteers. There is nothing more important to her than this camp and these kids."

I have to clamp my mouth closed and take a few deep breaths before I let my anger start speaking for me. I hate that Cameron has to impress this man, prove herself and the worth of this camp to someone like him who has more money than God and, with one wrong move, could shut this place down for good. I don't understand how even after only two days he hasn't seen what everyone else has. That this place helps people. This place gives people something to be happy about when they feel like life has failed them.

"I can't imagine what my life would have been like if I didn't have Camp Rylan to come to," I continue, turning away from the pasture to stare out over the land.

From the outside, the forty-acre land that was once a cotton plantation before the Civil War has a pecan grove, saltwater marshes, two lakes, orchards, and a thirty-five-thousand-square-foot stable with an attached dance studio. It's the most beautiful piece of land I've ever been on, but that's not all it is. It's a home. It's a safety net. It's hope that not everything has to be about war and death and sadness.

"When those kids are at home, everywhere they look, there are reminders of how hard life can be. Whether they've lost one parent to war and they're left behind with a parent who doesn't know how to move on, or they've spent months away from one, never knowing if they're coming home again, they can't escape the worry or the fear or the grief. It eats away at them until it's all they can think about. Camp Rylan gives them a place to escape. It gives them a place to be with people who know exactly what they're going through. And it's not just the kids this place helps. Cameron has become an amazing counselor over the years. Her sessions with the vets are remarkable, and no one walks out of there without feeling like they can conquer anything. This place has to continue existing. You can't let the hope and the happiness be erased from their lives because of rules you have about happily married couples running a camp. This place would still be amazing, and it would still change people's lives if I wasn't here."

Stratford stares at me without saying a word, and I wonder if I crossed a line talking to him like this, but I don't care. What I said was true, even if he doesn't know it. This place thrived while I was gone. Maybe it's because Shelby and Eli *are* a happily married couple, but I don't think so. It's because of their hearts and because of Cameron's heart and everyone else who works here that has a hand in helping these people. Stratford has followed us around all day watching Cameron and me interact with the kids; he's seen the smiles on their faces and heard the laughter in their voices. He's listened to Cameron tell him the personal stories of each and every child he came in contact with, because she knows them. All of them. She knows their names, she knows their ages, she knows their birthdates, she knows their favorite flavor of ice cream, and she knows which camp activity is their favorite. She knows what personal demons each one is struggling with, and she does whatever she can to fight them off and be their champion. If Stratford can't see within an hour, let alone two days, that this place is worth fighting for, I don't know what the hell he's still doing here, or why he needs to spend the next few weeks wasting everyone's time.

"I know you think I'm strange and that my requests are even stranger," Stratford replies, turning away from me to continue watching Cameron out in the horse pasture. "I loved my wife to distraction. She was with me when I didn't have two nickels to rub together. She loved me when we couldn't even afford hot dogs for dinner, and she was with me every step of the way when I built my fortune, even through the long days, late nights, and ridiculous amount of travel. She loved me when I was at my lowest, and she brought me down a peg or two when I was at my highest and a cocky son of a bitch."

Stratford pauses with a soft chuckle before sadness washes over his face as he continues with his story.

"I lost her ten years ago, very suddenly. I just woke up one morning and she was gone. Like I blinked and she no longer existed. She was no longer there to pick out my tie before I left for work, stop by the office with lunch because she knew I'd be too busy to grab something on my own, or stay up to ask me how my day was, no matter what time I came home. I buy suits in every color of the rainbow because she loved color. My world became dark as night when she died, and it makes me feel close to her wearing one of her favorite colors."

I think about all the ways Cameron used to add color to my life growing up, just by smiling at me and making me feel loved and important. I think about how I lost her suddenly, and even though it was by my own doing, it changed me. It made me more sullen and less excited about my future. My life more…beige and boring. I suddenly don't think Stratford's demands are all that strange now. I can understand how losing someone changes your whole view on life and the way you behave.

He smooths his hands down the lapels of his bright purple suit coat and straightens his purple and yellow tie before turning to look at me.

"I have insane rules about who I give my money to, because losing my wife probably made me go a little insane," he says with a soft smile. "I miss being in love. I miss having that one person in my life who knew everything about me, and still loved me anyway. I miss the way it felt to be having a bad day, and just the touch of her lips would make everything better. I miss not having someone to talk about my business with, who would still love me whether I made a good decision, or a horrible one. Seeing other people experience that, it makes me happy. Seeing a couple who love each other so much that they refuse to keep it to themselves and want to spread the love around makes me happy. Life's too short to do something that doesn't make you happy, and to spend your time with someone who isn't your entire world."

Stratford slides his hands into the pockets of his purple dress pants, giving me a nod.

"I'll take everything you've said into consideration. If you'll excuse me, I think I'll go rest before dinner," he says before turning and walking away.

Shaking my head as I watch him walk away, Cameron comes up next to me and looks back and forth between Stratford's retreating form and myself.

"Well, that went well. At least now I know why he's so strange."

I hate seeing the look of worry on her face as her eyes continue to dart over to Stratford, probably wondering if I screwed things up, so I quickly try to lighten the situation, saying the first thing I can think of to try to get a smile out of her.

"I can't believe I put on a shirt for this," I mutter with a smirk.

"I don't want to fight with you, Everett," she sighs, still looking off into the distance, where Stratford has met up with a worker who is walking him back to the main house.

"I'm not trying to pick a fight, I swear," I tell her, feeling like a dick for the way I egged her on this morning, no matter how fun it was at the time. "I shouldn't have been such a jerk this morning. But you know, the way you just couldn't stop *staring* at me..."

She smacks me on the arm and laughs, a smile lighting up her face and erasing all the worry.

There it is. That's what I was waiting for.

"I was only staring because you're so hideous."

I smile back at her and we both turn to rest our arms on the fence railing with our shoulders touching.

"Seriously. I'm surprised no one has told you before now. You really shouldn't even go out in public. You're going to start scaring small children and possibly make them cry," she adds, bumping her shoulder against mine.

Cameron looks up at me and the smile slowly falls from her face when I don't look away.

"I'm sorry for the way I acted last night. And this morning. You're right, I do need your help and I shouldn't have been such a bitch about it," she tells me softly.

My eyes move away from hers and down to her lips when she licks them nervously. Almost five years away from this woman and I still want her even though I know I shouldn't.

"I just want to know why," she suddenly whispers.

My forehead creases in confusion as she continues looking up at me.

"Why Aiden and not me?"

She asks me the same question I've asked myself a thousand times over the last few years, but I know it means something different to her, and my heart beats faster, knowing I'm going to have to cut myself open and bleed out in front of her if I want to give her the truth.

"Why did you still keep in touch with him, and not me? Why did you push me away?"

There's nothing I want to do more than get lost in her eyes and keep pretending things had been different, that I'd made different choices and I had every right to be here with her right now instead of forcing myself back into her life and taking advantage of her when she was at her lowest. I wish I could tell her everything, but it's too late now. She doesn't need the burden of knowing about my unrequited love from the past, on top of everything else.

"Because Aiden never made me want to forget about my dreams. He never made me want to stay," I tell her, giving her as much truth as I can right now.

Her eyes fill with tears and I want to take the words back, but I know I can't. She deserves answers and she deserves an explanation, no matter how much it hurts for me to say, as much as it hurts for her to hear.

"I never would have asked you to stay. I never would have made you give up your dreams."

"I know," I reassure her with a nod. "And I know it was selfish of me to think like that. To push you away, but it's the only thing I could do to survive over there. If I heard your voice, if I saw your face and saw how happy you were, I would have dropped everything and come home so I didn't have to miss one second of it."

If I saw how happy Aiden made you, when it should have been me, I wouldn't be standing here right now. I would have been distracted and I would have fucked up, getting myself killed in one of the many dangerous countries I lived in.

It was bad enough getting updates every couple of months from Aiden. It was hard enough hearing how happy *he* was in every e-mail and every phone call.

"I'm in love, can you believe it?!"

"I'm still in love, in case you were wondering. And it's amazing. Why didn't someone tell me how amazing it is to stick it out with one woman?"

"I bought a ring."

"I'm gonna do it, man. I'm gonna propose. Tell me how deliriously happy you are for me. Women all over Charleston will be crying themselves to sleep tonight knowing I'm off the market."

Without communicating with Cameron, I could almost pretend like none of it was really happening. That Aiden was making someone *else* happy, instead of her.

"Everett..."

She breathes my name instead of speaking it, and a tear falls down her cheek.

Turning to face her, I bring my hand up and press it against her face, swiping the wetness away with my thumb.

"Tell me it was worth it, Cam. Tell me I did the right thing. Were you happy?"

Chapter 19

CAMERON

*W*ere you happy?"

Everett's question makes my palms sweat and my heart drop down to my toes. I want to blurt everything out. Tell him I couldn't possibly be happy without him here. I couldn't find joy in anything without him here to share it with me. I couldn't figure out a way to mend my broken heart when he told me he couldn't give me any reason why I shouldn't go out with Aiden and then made that shitty comment about guys my mother approved of lining up for me. He shattered every dream and every wish I'd ever made with just a handful of words, and I continued to break apart year after year without him, until there was nothing left. Until I looked in the mirror and didn't even recognize the woman staring back at me. Until I almost screwed up my relationship with Aiden because of my hang-ups, and continued to make mistakes with Grady, because I just wanted to feel something again.

I wrapped myself up in him so completely that I didn't know how to live without him in my life. I hurt Aiden every time he could see the misery written all over my face, when I couldn't be happy with just him. A piece of me was missing and I couldn't breathe without it.

Everett's here, he's home, he's safe, and he's alive. He's close enough for me to reach out and touch, but every time that happens, I feel myself falling right back into the same old patterns. Getting sucked right back into dreams and wishes I know will never come true.

He gave me the explanation I needed, but it came with a price. After everything he's gone through, I can't be the one to tell him he didn't do the right thing. I can't tell him it wasn't worth it. Not even close.

I close my eyes and turn my face into his palm, wishing we could just stay like this forever. That I wouldn't have to lie to him right now when he gave me the truth I asked for. Refusing to look like a fool in front of him and watch him laugh when I tell him I've always been in love with him, and as much as I want to deny it, I feel some of the walls I've built around me start to crack. Tell him that I couldn't possibly have been happy without that love being returned.

I open my eyes and look up at him, swallowing back my sadness and blinking the tears out of my eyes.

"Yes. I was happy," I whisper with a smile. "I had my family, my friends, this camp, and Aiden. Of course I was happy."

His hand drops from my face and he returns my smile.

"Good. That's good. That's all I ever wanted, you know that, right?"

I nod, clearing my throat and taking a step back from him before I'm tempted to wrap my arms around his waist, bury my face in the side of his neck, and take it all back.

"Will you do something for me?" Everett suddenly asks with a hopeful look on his face.

"Of course."

He pulls his phone out of his back pocket and glances down at it before looking back up at me.

"We have about two hours before we need to sit through another dinner with Stratford. Will you meet me somewhere in about thirty minutes?"

* * *

I'm climbing the ladder up into the treehouse exactly thirty minutes after Everett left me out by the stables, saying he needed to do something really quick before he met me. Even though coming back here brings back so many memories of Aiden, I can't help but smile remembering all the times we climbed this ladder, and the fun we had in this treehouse. When I walk through the door, my smile grows even bigger when I see Everett sitting on one of the old bean bag chairs in the middle of the small room, and the glow of the white Christmas lights we hung all over the ceiling when we were teenagers shining down on him.

"I can't believe those things still work," I muse, looking up at the lights and turning slowly around in a circle before looking back down at him. "And I can't believe you're sitting in a sparkly pink bean bag chair. I should take a picture and send it to all your buddies and knock your street cred down a few notches."

Everett laughs, leaning forward to grab my hand and yank me down next to him in the matching purple bean bag chair, a cloud of dust puffing out around me and making me cough when I land.

"If you even think about doing that, I'll tell all your

friends about the time you drank your weight in beer and almost threw up on me."

"Hey, I *didn't* throw up on you; that's all that really matters."

"You were looking pretty green. It was touch and go there for a while."

If you only knew it wasn't the beer making me nauseous, but the thought that I might die from wanting you to kiss me so badly that night.

"Did you bring me up here just to talk about all of my bad decisions as a teenager?" I ask.

He shakes his head at me and pushes himself off the bean bag chair. I watch in silence as he pulls up the loose floorboard between his legs and my heart starts beating so fast I'm afraid it might jump right out of my chest.

"What are you doing?" I ask nervously, hoping to God he doesn't think it's time for us to open up our boxes and look at all the wishes we made over the years. "We promised we wouldn't look at those things until we were old and gray. I am neither old, nor gray, thank you very much, and I don't think this is a good idea."

I'm rambling like an idiot, but I can't help it. He *cannot* open up my box of wishes. I will be completely mortified. Even more than the night I almost threw up on him.

"Don't worry, I remember the pact we made when we were kids, the three of us sitting in a circle and linking our pinky fingers together, swearing that we'd never look at another person's wishes or open another person's box, until we were all old people, to find out if any of them came true," Everett says with his back still to me.

I hold my breath until he reaches into the hole in the floor and pulls out just his box, resting it on his thighs as he moves back to his chair.

"Were you ever tempted to come up here by yourself and

read through our wishes?" Everett asks, shaking his box, all the little paper wishes rattling around inside.

"Nope, never. Pinky swears are binding and punishable by death," I tell him, hoping to God he doesn't start reading his wishes and expect me to do the same.

"This is probably going to sound stupid, but this is one of the things I missed when I was gone," he tells me with a shrug, running his hands over all the glittery puff paint and stickers I used to decorate the thing back when we were kids. "Even though the other doctors I was with always made a big deal out of birthdays no matter where we were stationed, it just felt like any other day. It never felt like my birthday without our annual summer tradition."

He looks up and gives me a sheepish smile, and dammit if I don't want to start crying all over again. I'm touched that he missed this, something he and Aiden used to always tease me about, and I always assumed they only did just to humor me. And I'm brokenhearted that Everett never got to make any wishes the four years he was gone.

"I know you and Aiden still got to do this every year, and there's probably some kind of wish law about making up for lost time and doing four wishes at once, but I don't care. It's tradition, and I'd like to make my wishes now," he tells me, reaching to the other side of where he's sitting.

I hear the sound of plastic crinkling and glasses clinking together, and when he turns back to face me, he's holding up a six-pack of Grape Crush in bottles and a bag of Fritos.

Getting up quickly from my chair, I move to the other side of the treehouse, where there's a small end table in the corner with a lamp on top of it. Pulling open the drawer in the front, I grab the star-shaped notepad and pen and move back over to Everett, kneeling down next to him and handing them to him.

Setting the snacks down, he wraps his hands around the

items, his fingers resting on top of mine, but I don't let go right away.

"We didn't," I tell him quietly as we both continue to hold the notepad and pen. "Do this every year, I mean."

His eyes stay locked on mine, and his thumb starts rubbing back and forth over my knuckles as I continue.

"We tried that first summer after you left, but it didn't feel right making our wishes without you here, so we never came back again."

And it killed me. God, it killed me to be here without you and try to pretend like everything was okay.

I finally drop my hand and let Everett have the notepad and pen when the way his thumb kept moving over my knuckles started to distract me and I almost said my thoughts out loud.

Looking away from him, my eyes move around the room as I remember the night of my first birthday after Everett left, when Aiden and I thought it would be easy to come up here and do what we'd always done. As soon as we sat down in the middle of the room, neither one of us could bring ourselves to even pull up the floorboard and take my box out. I'd never been more thankful that Aiden could read me like a book, and made up an excuse for us to leave before I broke down in tears and made a fool of myself. It was a flimsy excuse, but it worked.

"Shit. I forgot the snacks. We can't do this without our tasty treats or your wish won't come true. And then THAT wish would taint all the other wishes when you put it in the box, and it would be complete wish anarchy. We can't have wish anarchy, kid. Let's blow this Popsicle stand, find a bar, and get completely wasted instead."

I laugh softly when I think about how Aiden dragged me to not one, but four different bars in Charleston and, true to his word, got me completely wasted.

Everett looks at me questioningly. "What's so funny?"

"Nothing. I was just thinking about Aiden. You'll be happy to know that he was the recipient of my puke that night. I threw up in his lap," I tell him, my smile faltering when pain flashes across Everett's face and he quickly looks down at his lap and starts tapping the pen against the notepad.

"I'm sorry. I should have realized bringing you up here would be hard. We don't have to do this."

I quickly shuffle around on my knees until I'm in between his legs, and I rest my hands on top of his thighs.

"No, I want to do this. Aiden would want us to. In fact, he'd probably be a little pissed if we didn't."

Everett doesn't look up at me, and I realize he's staring at my hands on his thighs. I feel them flex under my palms and I quickly snatch them away and scramble over to my bean bag chair. I know we're pretending to be husband and wife and have to constantly touch for Stratford's benefit, but he's not here right now. Touching Everett in any way when we're alone is too much for my heart and my head to handle. My heart is instantly thrown back into the past, back to a time where I would have given anything to be able to touch him whenever I wanted. But my head is constantly reminding me this is all an act, and imagining it's anything other than that will break me. I'm not that foolish young girl anymore. I'm an adult with responsibilities and I don't have time to waste on wishing things could be different.

"I miss him. I miss him every day, but he'd want us to do this," I reassure Everett again.

He closes his eyes and I watch a muscle tick in his jaw as he remains quiet for a few minutes, and I wish there was something I could do to make him feel less sad and less guilty about not being here when Aiden died. I got to say good-bye to him at the end of his illness, and at the funeral, but Everett never got that closure, and I can't imagine what that must be doing to him.

Everett finally opens his eyes, and I silently watch him flip through the notepad, quickly scribbling four wishes, on four different star-shaped pieces of paper. He rips them off the top of the pad, lifts the lid on his box, and tosses them inside before securing the lid back on top. Leaning forward, he places his box back inside the hole, nestled between mine and Aiden's boxes, and then replaces the floorboard on top of them.

He grabs the bag of Fritos, tears it open, and sets it down on the floor between us, then reaches into the cardboard container and grabs two bottles of Crush, twisting off both of the caps before handing one over to me.

Turning to face me, he tips his bottle toward me and I clink mine against it.

"Happy four years of belated birthday wishes, Everett. I hope they come true," I tell him.

"Doubtful, but thank you."

As I bring the bottle up to my mouth and take a sip of the cold, grape-flavored soda, I want to ask him why he would say something like that. Why he'd want to come up here and continue with this tradition if he doesn't really believe in it, but I'm too busy silently apologizing to Aiden, hoping that wherever he is, he can hear me and forgive me for the thoughts running through my head, brought on by Everett.

I'm sorry I made you miss out on four years of wishes, even if you were only humoring me.

I'm sorry if I ever made you feel like you were never enough.

And I'm sorry . . . so sorry, that being here without you right now isn't half as hard as being here without Everett was.

Chapter 20

EVERETT

The glow from the crackling fire shines on Cameron's face as she stares into the burning logs and embers. She's so damn beautiful no matter what she's doing, but I know this picture of her, so comfortable and relaxed after a long, stressful weekend, is going to be burned into my brain for a long time.

Before Stratford went back to the main house an hour ago when all the campers left to go home, he'd been sitting right across the fire pit, looking through the flames at us while we conducted the camp's usual end-of-the-weekend bonfire. The workers told stories, sang songs with the kids, and set up a table filled with s'mores fixings and helped them make as many as they could stuff in their mouths. Knowing Stratford's eyes were on us, remembering every-thing he told me about how watching another couple in love makes him happy, and knowing how exhausted Cameron was after the long weekend, I leaned down and grabbed her feet, pulling her legs up onto my lap. I tossed her flip-flops onto the ground and gave her a much-needed foot massage.

Even though the time for putting on a show has passed since Stratford is long gone and probably tucked away in his bed by now, I don't want to move from this position. She's sitting sideways in her chair, staring at the fire, and her legs are still in my lap, my hands now resting on her shins. I know I'm supposed to be concentrating on trying to be her best friend again and nothing else, but I can't stop wanting to touch her.

Taking her up to the treehouse the other day was a good idea at the time. I wanted to do something we always did as friends, but I quickly realized how stupid that idea was when it made her think of Aiden and the ring on her hand sparkled when she placed it on my thigh, reminding me what he was to her.

I've spent so much time thinking about him and allowing myself to grieve him since I got sober. I've spent months making myself remember all the good times and what a great friend he was and letting go of the guilt that I wasn't here, knowing he'd want me to be happy and stop being so sad all the time. It wasn't until I saw the sorrow on Cameron's face and the sparkle from that fucking ring that remembering him started to make me feel like it did when I was drunk all the time—spiteful, pissed off, and angry. And then I felt like an asshole for being jealous of how much she missed him and how happy she looked when she spoke of him. I tried my hardest to hide it, but she knew something was wrong when I couldn't even speak, let alone look at her. I couldn't stand to see the misery on her face, thinking about the man she loved. It hurts twice as much that he was my best friend, and I feel like I'm dishonoring his memory by being pissed at him all the time. It makes me feel like the shittiest friend in the world because I know, if given the choice between Aiden being back here right now, alive and well and full of life, or Cameron sitting next to me, still unsure of our friendship and keeping me at a safe distance, I'd pick Cameron every time. I'd pick these few quiet moments, this small handful of days faking it with her, over a lifetime of friendship with Aiden.

I need to get this shit in check before I fuck everything up with her again. But sometimes, the way she looks at me…Jesus, it confuses the hell out of me. Especially when I'm sitting here wondering if she sat here by the fire like this with Aiden. If he ever rubbed her feet after a long weekend, kept his hands on her at all times because he couldn't stand *not* touching her. I'm so sick of everything always coming back to my own insecurities and jealousy that I'm starting to annoy myself.

"I'm so tired, even my hair hurts," Cameron says with a sigh, turning her head away from the fire to look over at me with a smile. "You don't look as exhausted as I feel. How is that possible?"

Because you keep me so on edge, I feel like I'll never sleep again.

"You get used to feeling tired all the time sleeping on cots in the middle of rain forests, and figuring out how to work through it since no one gives a shit about how exhausted you are when there's people who are sick and dying and need you to help them."

My fingers start gently massaging into her calves, and the little moan of pleasure that comes out of her mouth shoots right to my dick, making me want to shove her legs off my lap, jump up, and run the fuck away to try to get my head back on straight.

"I know you missed our annual birthday tradition while you were gone, but what else did you miss?" she asks, opening her eyes to look at me again while I continue working the kinks out of her legs, because I'm a glutton for punishment.

"Color," I immediately reply.

She laughs, lifting her head up from the back of her chair to look at me quizzically.

"I have to say, Stratford's weird outfit choices are growing on me," I tell her.

I gave her a condensed version of what he told me about why he has so many strange rules about where his money goes during a few minutes we had alone earlier while he was talking to Seth.

"You have no idea how *beige* being in those medical tents all the time is, especially when we were in the desert. The sand is beige, the tents are beige, our scrubs were beige…even half of the food is beige. I missed reds and purples and especially bright green," I explain with a shrug.

Especially bright green because it's the color of your eyes. Goddammit I missed looking into those eyes.

"Okay. What else?"

I take a minute to think about all the things I missed when I was overseas, knowing Cameron was at the top of that list, but I'm not about to tell her that. She knows I regret pushing her away and why, even if it wasn't the full truth. If I don't keep things light and easy right now, I'll be tempted to spit out a whole bunch of shit I shouldn't.

Like how I forced myself to stop being in love with her a long time ago, but there's no way in hell I could ever stop wanting her.

"The brisket from Lewis Barbecue. I used to dream about that shit."

"They do have really good barbecue. That's a good one. What else?" she asks.

I rub my palms gently up and down her legs while we talk, knowing I'm just torturing myself, but I can't help it. It feels good to be sitting here with her talking like friends. Friends do things like this, right? I can touch her legs without it getting weird, and it's not like she's doing anything to move away or getting pissed at me for touching her. I'm reestablishing our friendship, that's it. I'm showing her she can still talk to me like she used to and she can trust me to be a good friend to her.

"Magnolia blossoms. And don't laugh at me because it sounds girly as shit, but I missed the smell of those things. I even missed how everyone in this town decorates every damn table with those stupid mason jars filled with magnolia blossoms," I state.

"I'm not going to laugh at you. The smell of magnolia blossoms is my favorite smell in the world."

I already know this, since she wears perfume that smells like them. Not only did I used to dream about brisket from Lewis Barbecue, but I used to dream about that damned scent. It would wake me up out of a dead sleep, and even in the middle of a war-torn country, I could swear Cameron was right there next to me.

Knowing I need to move things away from the dangerous territory they're heading, I think of something I know will make her laugh.

I rest my head on the back of the chair, staring up at the night sky, and let out a sigh.

"But the one thing I missed most of all, the one thing I couldn't stop dreaming about . . . was Guns and Posers."

Cameron's laughter echoes around the clearing in the woods, and I turn my head, giving her an outraged look.

"Don't laugh at my misery, Cameron. It was torture going four years without them in my life. You have no idea the struggle."

"I should have known you'd miss that stupid eighties cover band most of all. How many times did you drag us to every bar in Charleston to hear them play?" she asks.

"Clearly not enough since you still haven't learned to appreciate their brilliance."

"You're insane. Just for that, I'm going to look up their schedule and take you to their next performance immediately. Maybe now that you're older and wiser, you'll realize how much they actually suck. I might have to break into my savings account so we have enough money to get completely trashed. You can't listen to them sing unless you're drunk."

I start to laugh, but watch as her eyes widen in shock and she brings a hand up to cover her mouth. I realize what she just said, and know that after whatever Jason told her about me, she thinks she said something wrong, and I know it's time to give her more truths.

"Cam, it's fine," I reassure her.

"I'm sorry. That was a stupid thing to say," she whispers, dropping her hand from her mouth.

"I'm telling you, it's fine. I'm fine. I wasn't for a while, but I am now."

I keep my eyes on her so she can see the truth in them and watch the worry slowly disappear from her face.

"Are you mad at Jason for telling me?" she asks softly.

"I was at first, but I'm not anymore. It needed to be said. I'm just sorry *I* wasn't the one to tell you. I had every intention of explaining things to you, but when I got here, everything with Stratford just happened so fast and I didn't get a chance."

The sounds of the fire crackling, frogs croaking from

the nearby pond, and crickets chirping all around us fill the silence between us as I watch Cameron get her thoughts in order.

"It's okay. You can ask me anything. Whatever you want to know," I tell her.

She thinks for a few seconds, then rests the side of her head against the back of her chair as she looks over at me.

"I know it's selfish of me, but I almost don't want to know. I hate thinking about you like that. I hate knowing you were struggling when you came home. And I hate that I got so mad at you and didn't even stop to think about why you didn't come here right when you got home. This is what I do for a living, and I failed one of the most important people in my life," she whispers.

"You didn't fail anyone, Cameron, especially me. *I* failed. It's all on me, not you. I didn't know how to deal when I got home. I just wanted the pain to go away, and alcohol was the only thing that worked. Until it didn't. Until the pain still worked its way under my skin and into my head and not even being drunk twenty-four/seven could make it go away," I explain.

"What made you stop?"

You. Knowing I needed to go to you and I could never let you see me like that.

I can feel Aiden's letter in my back pocket, tucked securely away where I still carry it around everywhere I go. I wish I could pull the letter out and show it to her, but there are too many things written in there that I can't explain to her right now.

"It was a mixture of things, but seeing the look on Jason's face every time he came home and found me drunk or passed out was what finally made me get my head out of my ass. He made a comment about losing me, just like we lost our mom, and it woke me the fuck up. I never wanted to be like her. I didn't want to turn into someone who was so weak that they stopped caring about everything in their life," I explain.

"I'm proud of you. I can't even imagine how hard it must have been. How hard it *still* is."

"I've had a lot of help. I went to an in-patient, ninety-day rehab facility that dried me out. And I still go back every week for meetings. I made some good friends there. Other people I can talk to if things get hard or I feel like I'm struggling."

Cameron leans forward and places her hands on top of mine, which are still resting on her legs.

"You can always talk to me. I know things are a little weird right now with everything going on here at the camp and with us, but I am always here if you need someone. Promise me you won't push me away again. I can't go another four years without you..."

She trails off, looking quickly away from me to fiddle with a loose thread on her jean shorts, and her words start fucking with my head.

I want them to mean something else, which is completely ridiculous. I want to stop feeling so confused and tied up in knots when I'm with this woman, but I don't know if that will ever be possible.

Chapter 21

CAMERON

The sound of shouting pulls me out of a dead sleep and has me jerking up in bed. My heart is beating out of my chest as I glance over at the clock on my nightstand and realize it's three in the morning. Taking a few deep breaths to slow down my heart, I remain completely still, listening for another sound and wondering if I imagined it or it was part of whatever dream I'd been having.

After a few minutes of silence and realizing it must have been in my head, I start to lie back down when another shout from the living room has me flinging off the covers and racing out of the room, not even bothering to throw on something over the tank top and underwear I wore to bed.

Everett has been sleeping on the living room couch in the guest house ever since the day after Stratford arrived. To say it's been a challenge is putting it mildly. It's not like we spend a lot of time here alone since our days are long, and by the time we come back here, we're too exhausted to do anything other than go to our respective beds, face-plant on them, and pass out for the night. But I'm just not used to sharing my space with someone else, and having it be Everett is even worse. He's constantly walking around every morning in a pair of jogging pants that hang low on his hips, without wearing a shirt. Since the last time I mentioned how he needed to put on a damn shirt, he got entirely too much pleasure out of teasing me, I've had to keep my mouth shut and pretend like it doesn't bother me. I also have to pretend like it doesn't bother me that I can smell him in every room of my house, and everywhere I turn, I see something of his. A pair of jeans crumpled up on the bathroom floor, his wallet and keys on the kitchen counter, a shirt flung over the back of the couch that I will never admit to anyone I brought up to my face and smelled while he was taking a shower…He's invaded my space and he's invaded my senses and it's slowly driving me insane.

As I round the corner of the hallway that leads into the living room, the light from the full moon shining through the huge picture window right above the couch silhouettes his form on the couch. His body thrashes and jerks around on the cushions, his limbs getting twisted around the thin sheet he covered up with.

"I'm sorry! I'm so sorry! I tried to save her!" Everett shouts as I slide across the hardwood floor and drop down to my knee next to the couch.

Even with just a sliver of moonlight shining through the window, I can see the agony on his face as he throws his head back onto his pillow, a soft, pain-filled keening sound coming from him now that breaks my heart.

"Everett, wake up," I say softly, not wanting to scare him awake from this nightmare that he's having.

His head shakes back and forth and his eyes remain

squeezed closed as he battles with whatever demons are in his mind.

"I did everything I could…I did everything…"

Lifting myself up from the floor, I quickly perch next to him on the couch, leaning over his chest as I softly run my fingers through his hair and down the side of his face, the scruff on his cheeks tickling my palm.

"Shhh, it's okay, Everett. Wake up. It's okay, I'm here," I whisper quietly as I continue touching him and trying to bring him back to me.

All of a sudden, his eyes fly open and my hand stills on his cheek, our faces inches apart since I'm still leaning over him.

His chest rises and falls rapidly and he pants, blinking his eyes into focus as he continues looking up at me.

I don't move, I don't make a sound, I just start running my palm softly over his cheek again, whispering quietly to him to ground him and remind him where he is and who I am. I've counseled enough vets and listened to their spouses talk about waking them up from PTSD dreams, and I saw my mother do this with my father enough over the years that I know what to do in theory. I've never experienced it myself before, and having to witness it happening to Everett is enough to crack my heart wide open.

"I'm sorry I woke you," he finally says, his voice raspy with sleep and from shouting, his face still clouded with sadness from the remnants of whatever he was dreaming about.

"It's fine. Are you okay? Do you want to talk about it?"

He closes his eyes for a few seconds and takes a couple of deep breaths. When he opens his eyes again, he shakes his head no.

"I'm good now."

I want to ask him more. I want to ask him what he was

dreaming about and how often he has these dreams, but I don't want to push him.

As I drop my hand from his cheek and start to pull away, his hand darts out and wraps around my wrist.

"Stay with me? Just for a little while."

Now I know why he didn't want me to see him when he came home after Aiden died and struggled with drinking. Seeing him like this, so torn apart and full of misery, makes me want to cry like a baby, curse God, and do everything I can to make it better.

As he pulls back the sheet, I twist around and slide onto the couch next to him, pushing my body back against his, wishing I would have taken the time to throw on leggings and a sweatshirt, or maybe even a suit of armor. Being pressed back against Everett's strong, muscular body when I'm only wearing a tank top and he's only wearing a pair of sweatpants and I can feel every contour of his naked chest against my back makes me forget that we're just friends.

Everett silently throws the sheet back over both of us and his arms come around my waist, holding me tightly to him.

He nestles his face into the back of my neck, and a few minutes later, I feel the even sounds of his breathing as it puffs against my neck and his chest moves slowly up and down against my back. I mentally will away the goose bumps that I feel all over my body.

Not only has Everett invaded my home, he's quickly starting to invade my heart again, and that scares the hell out of me. As soon as I feel like I've taken ten steps forward, he does something that takes me a million steps back. Back into the past, back where I let him hurt me and break me apart, piece by piece. If I'm not careful, he'll shatter me all over again.

* * *

"Thank you so much for doing this last minute. You have no idea how much it means to me. Okay. Thanks again. See you next week."

Hanging up the phone in my office, I let out a huge sigh of relief and lean back in my chair, wanting nothing more than to take a nap.

For once, I didn't spend last night restlessly tossing and turning because of worries about the camp. I spent it with my eyes wide open, staring off into the darkness of my living room, doing everything I could not to move in Everett's arms. I told myself it was because he was finally sleeping peacefully after the nightmare he had and I didn't want to interrupt that, but it's a lie. I didn't want to move because I was afraid to leave the warm confines of his arms and the feel of his body pressed up against mine. I was afraid to close my eyes because I didn't want to wake up and find out it had been a dream, or watch him pull back and pretend like it hadn't happened. That he hadn't needed me and he hadn't held me so tightly all night long, like he couldn't bear to let me go.

They were stupid thoughts to have, making me feel like that young, foolish girl who wanted nothing more than for the boy she loved to love her back. We're becoming friends again, and that's all I want. It's all I can afford and I need to stop letting my thoughts get away from me.

No sooner do I close my eyes and start to enjoy some peace and quiet, when Amelia rushes into my office, smacking a pile of papers in front of me.

"Updated menu from the caterers you need to sign, updated decorations order that you need to initial, contract from the band you need to sign *and* initial, and a copy of the linens order, which you don't have to do anything with but make sure it's correct."

Leaning forward, I grab a pen from next to the stack of papers and start flipping through them.

"You're insane, have I told you that lately? I can't believe you decided to change almost everything about the charity dinner a week before the damn thing," Amelia states, sitting down in the chair across from me.

For as long as I can remember, this charity dinner has always had the same theme—white and classy. White linens, white decorations, white table service, soft jazz music.

"I know. But I just felt like this year needed to be different. It could be our last dinner, and if it is, I want to go out with a bang," I tell her, signing the last piece of paper and sliding them across the desk to her so she can fax them over to the appropriate companies.

"And it has absolutely nothing to do with the conversation you had with Everett last week. Uh-huh. Sure," she laughs.

Not only did I tell Amelia about the conversation Everett and I had out by the fire, I also came clean with her about a few other things. Namely, the fact that I didn't just have a "crush" on Everett when I was younger. I told her how desperately in love with him I'd been, I told her about all the wishes I'd made over the years, and I told her how confused I'd been feeling now that he's home. She was shocked, to say the least. She'd been Team Aiden ever since the first day she met him, and now she's suddenly changing her allegiance, much to my annoyance.

So maybe I decided to change a few things up with the charity dinner after we talked out at the fire pit. Whatever. It's not insane to want to do something special for your friend who just came home and who you haven't seen in four years.

"Shit. It's totally insane," I groan, resting my elbows on the desk and my head in my hands. "Like I don't already have enough on my plate right now, I had to go and change everything we've ever done for this dinner. It's crazy. *I'm* crazy. I have officially lost my mind."

Everett has been back in my life for one week. Seven days were all it took for me to completely lose myself in him. Again.

"You aren't crazy," Amelia reassures me.

"The definition of insanity is doing the same thing over and over again and expecting different results. How is that not exactly what I'm doing? He walks back into my life after four years and suddenly I'm a teenager again, wishing on stars and hoping he'll love me back. Why is everything so easy with him, and so confusing at the same time?" I complain.

"How is it confusing? You're learning to trust him again. He's opening up to you. You're rebuilding your friendship, and going by what I've seen the last week, it's going amazingly well."

"And that's the problem. He's been gone for so long and he's missed so much. We're two different people than we were years ago, but it feels like no time has passed. He just *fits*. He fits into my life, he fits into this camp..." I trail off.

"Still don't see the problem."

"He shouldn't fit! That's the problem!" I argue. "And it makes me angry that he does. It pisses me off that I spent all of this time trying to move on, and in one week, he messes all of that up. In one week and a handful of apologies, I'm right back where I started. Wanting something I'll never have."

And in one week, I've spent more time analyzing every touch he's given me, every look he's thrown my way, and every move he's made around me, until he's the only thing that occupies my thoughts.

"I think the problem is that you only *tried* to move on, Cam. You tried with Aiden and you tried with Grady, but you never actually succeeded. And what makes you think you'll never have what you want? What makes you think if you marched your ass over to the stables right now where he is, and told him everything you just said to me, that he wouldn't prove you wrong?" she asks.

And that's just another thing to add to my list of distractions. So many what-ifs that my head is spinning.

What if I told him how I've felt since I was thirteen years old?

What if I told him I couldn't erase those feelings, no matter how hard I tried or how much distance he put between us?

What if all those touches and looks I've been overanalyzing actually meant something other than being just for show?

I'm so afraid to ruin the fragile ground we've started to build into being friends again.

What if I tell him and he thinks it's a joke?

What if I tell him and he walks away again?

What if I tell him and it ruins everything we've started to rebuild?

"You need a distraction," Amelia states, pulling me out of my thoughts.

"Have you not been listening to a word I said? I'm already distracted enough."

She scoffs and rolls her eyes at me.

"I'm talking about a *fun* distraction. Use this fake marriage to Everett to your advantage. You don't want to spill the beans to him? Fine. Turn up the heat a little and see how he handles it."

"I'm not screwing things up by making him uncomfortable," I argue, even though the idea of things getting hot with Everett makes my brain take a nosedive right into the gutter.

I haven't been able to stop thinking about that night we spent by the fire and his hands on my legs, wondering what I would have done if he slid them up higher. I haven't been able to stop thinking about this morning, when I finally managed to fall asleep for an hour, and woke up when Everett did, stretching behind me. How I scrambled off the couch, wondering how awkward things were going to be, and they weren't awkward in the least. He smiled at me, apologized again for waking me up last night, and casually got up from the couch and put on a pot of coffee. I wondered what would have happened if I hadn't gotten off the couch, and just rolled over to face him, hooking my leg over his hip and snuggling up against him.

"I can almost guarantee you that man will not be the least bit uncomfortable with anything you do to him. I've seen the way he looks at you and the way he touches you," she informs me.

"You've seen the way he *fake* looks at me and *fake* touches me when Stratford is around," I remind her, keeping my mouth shut about the many times I've caught him looking at me when Stratford wasn't around and how natural it felt to have him hold me last night.

"Whatever helps you sleep at night," she laughs, pushing herself up from the desk. "I'm going to fax these over and then I'll meet you out at the dance studio."

She pauses by the door when she sees the look of confusion on my face.

"We're meeting out there with Stratford to go over some of the new physical activity ideas we have for fully utilizing the dance studio, remember? Everett is taking him around the stables now until we get there."

I groan and shake my head.

"See? Too many distractions already. I'm not adding another one by turning up any stupid heat," I tell her, standing up from the desk and moving around to the front of it to follow her out of the room.

I pause when she remains in the doorway, looking me up and down.

"What?" I ask, glancing down at my jeans and T-shirt to make sure I don't have a huge stain anywhere.

"You're not going to wear that, are you? I'm sure Stratford is going to want us to demonstrate some of these things. Especially you and Everett, since he wants to see the happy couple in action. Put on those tiny little gray shorts that make your ass look fantastic, with the matching teal and gray sports bra that shows off your abs and makes your boobs look bigger. You can show Everett how bendy you are in your yoga poses. Go Team Everett!"

I glare at her when she gives me a cheeky wink, turns, and walks out of the room.

"I'm not heating things up, Amelia! What I'm wearing is just fine!" I shout after her.

I hear her laughter echo down the hall.

"What I'm wearing is just fine," I repeat, muttering to myself as I look back down at my Camp Rylan T-shirt that is two sizes too big and does indeed have some kind of mystery stain over the stomach.

Glancing over at the corner of the room where I keep a stack of clean workout clothes in case I'm here at the main house and need to quickly change for an activity, I see the gray shorts and sports bra Amelia just mentioned at the bottom of the pile. And picture myself bending over in front of Everett while I do Downward Facing Dog. There's no way I'm even contemplating falling for the guy again, but who says we can't have a little fun? We're both attractive, single people and he seems to get a huge thrill out of making me uncomfortable with his shirt off and his little teasing comments about how I can't stop looking at him.

Plus, it's his fault I no longer have a tension reliever in the form of Grady.

"Son of a bitch," I whisper, rushing over to the clothing and yanking what I need out of the stack.

Chapter 22

EVERETT

Hi, Jason!"

I watch as my brother turns around, his elbow hitting the box of nails he left on the windowsill and sending them crashing to the ground, scattering everywhere. The spilled nails cause a chain of events that has Jason juggling the wrench and hammer he has in his hands, until he drops both of those as well.

"Oh, hey, Amelia!" Jason replies a little too loudly.

His eyes never leave hers when he bends over to start picking up what he dropped, gravity making another hammer and two screwdrivers fall out of the utility belt around his waist, everything clamoring to the hardwood floor and echoing around the huge dance studio.

Biting down on my bottom lip, I keep my laughter locked up tight, nodding a greeting to Amelia as she waves and then turns to walk over to the other side of the room with a few other workers. When she's out of earshot, I bend down to help Jason, letting my laughter burst out of me.

"You are so pathetic," I chuckle, lifting up one of the hammers as Jason mutters curses under his breath while he scoops up nails and puts them back into the box.

"Fuck off," he grumbles.

Jason has always come out to the camp to help Cameron with things that need to be fixed, but I found out recently that he's been stopping by a lot more frequently since Amelia started working here. When Cameron told him yesterday the new window they had installed in the dance studio had started leaking when it rained, and informed him Amelia would be using the studio for most of the day and he could stop by another time so they wouldn't be a distraction, he quickly told her it was no trouble and he'd be there first thing in the morning.

"I think it's kind of cute you're all shy and nervous around a girl. You could probably put an end to your misery by actually talking to her and asking her out," I tell him with another laugh.

"I don't need dating advice, especially from you," he informs me, snatching the hammer out of my hand as I pick up a screwdriver.

"What the hell does that mean?"

Jason looks up at me and opens his mouth, but he's cut off when Cameron walks in and we hear her call a greeting from behind us. As I turn my head to look back over my shoulder and give her a wave, my jaw drops open and the screwdriver slips from my hand, thumping to the floor.

Jesus Christ, what is she wearing?

I don't know whether I should run in search of the nearest blanket and cover her up, or drag her out of here and toss her into another room where we can be alone and I can stare at her without anyone else noticing.

My head moves with her, following her as she walks down the middle of the room to the front, where Amelia and a few other workers have gathered for the demonstration. The minuscule gray shorts she's wearing hug her perfect ass and that half-tank-top-looking thing shows off every inch of her tightly toned stomach. It's been years since I've seen Cameron in something this revealing, the last time being when she was in her early twenties and we went swimming out at one of the lakes. She looked good in a bathing suit then, so good I had fantasies about her in it for months after. But this…sweet Christ, she's so fucking hot it takes my breath away and fills my head with much dirtier thoughts than when we were younger.

"Who's the pathetic one now, asshole?" Jason chuckles, making me turn my head away from her guiltily and scowl at him.

"I don't know what you're talking about," I mutter, shoving the screwdriver in his hand as we both stand up.

"You're so transparent you're practically clear. How's that hard-on you've got hiding in your pants? Also, you've got a little drool on your chin," he laughs again.

"So she looks good? Whatever. She's my best friend. I don't get hard-ons for my best friend," I lie, shoving my hands into the front pockets of my pants and pulling them away from my body to hide the fucking hard-on I do, in fact, have for my best friend right now.

"I think it's kind of cute you're all shy and nervous around your best friend. You could probably put an end to your misery by actually talking to her and asking her out," Jason states, repeating the words I said to him, but with a huge smile on his face. "Carrying a torch for her all these years must be exhausting."

Jesus, am I really that obvious? I've never told anyone

how I felt about Cameron, especially not my brother. He never would have let me live it down, and he most definitely would have kicked my ass for being such a chicken shit all these years.

"Shut the hell up and go fix your window," I grumble, turning and walking away from him to go stand in the back of the room, where I put Stratford in a chair, and as far away from Cameron as possible.

Chapter 23

CAMERON

And those are just a few of the more advanced poses we'll teach once the beginners get the hang of things," I finish explaining to Stratford, helping Amelia and a few of the other workers up from their mats on the floor where we did a quick yoga demonstration.

For years, this dance studio has only been used for fun, hip-hop dance classes for campers. Amelia had the idea a few months ago that we should start offering a few classes geared just toward the parents whose children attend the camp. For the weekend sessions, to give them something to do if they want to give their kids some alone time with other children, and during the summer months when they come out for visits if their kids are staying for several weeks. After e-mailing all of our parents with a survey to see what they would most be interested in, we'd decided on yoga, kickboxing, and meditation. We had a certified trainer for each of these classes, but she's on vacation, and since I've taken all of these types of classes for years at the local gym, I felt confident enough to lead our demonstration.

Clearing my throat, I wipe my sweaty palms on my gray shorts and give Stratford a nervous smile. He hasn't said one word since Everett brought him in here and pulled up a chair for him in the back of the room. I think I'd much rather he tell us it's a stupid idea than just sit there not saying anything. At least give me *some* sort of indication this was a good idea and something that would convince him to give his money to this camp.

It's also not helping that Everett has done nothing but stand at the back of the room a few feet away from Stratford, leaning against the wall with his arms crossed in front of him. He wouldn't even make eye contact with me each time I looked over at him for silent encouragement, or even some sort of hint that he appreciated the way I looked. So much for Amelia's bright idea that I wear this dumb outfit to get a rise out of him. I just feel stupid and practically naked with all this skin showing. He leans against the wall looking almost bored. And in a pair of black track pants and a tight white T-shirt stretched across the muscles of his chest and arms, with a backward black baseball cap on his head, he looks bored and hot.

"I'm assuming you have more to offer the parents than just exercise classes," Stratford finally says, not looking up from the phone that he's furiously typing away on.

"I, um, we actually—"

"You've done a nice job today, Cameron, but I'd like to hear from your husband this time. He's been unusually quiet today," Stratford says, interrupting my stuttering as he looks up from his phone and over to Everett.

Shit. Shit, shit, shit.

Out of all the things Everett and I have discussed over the

last week, we never talked much about future plans for the camp. It didn't seem necessary. Like I told Amelia earlier, he fit back into this place perfectly. He remembered everything from when he used to work here, he knew the history of the place and everything about the back office, and there wasn't much of a point.

Everett's eyes finally meet my panicked ones, and he pushes away from the wall with a nod.

"Actually, sir, I've been contemplating the idea of adding a self-defense class to the list. It's not only something I think adults need to learn, but even the older kids who attend the camp. It would be a great way to build their confidence. Make them feel like warriors, when most of them are feeling so scared and weak," Everett explains, walking across the room to stand next to me.

"Hmmm, I like the sound of this. Show me a few things," Stratford orders, waving his hand between Everett and me.

Without a word, Everett moves behind me, the front of his body pressed against my back. I can feel his heat and smell his skin and my heart stutters in my chest when he reaches around me and grabs my arms, pulling them up until they're pressed in close to my chest.

He leans his head down until his mouth is right by my ear.

"Just follow my lead and do what I say. Keep your arms up where they are," he whispers, his warm breath floating over my ear and making goose bumps break out over my skin even though I'm still hot and sweaty from the yoga demonstration.

I can't speak. I can't even nod that I understand. Before I can take my next breath, Everett's strong arms band around me and he yanks me back against his chest, squeezing me tightly to him.

"This is called the Bear Hug. A very common strategy for

an attacker sneaking up on someone from behind," Everett explains. "Hard to get out of if your attacker is larger than you, but not impossible."

Blah, blah, blah. That's all I hear right now. I can't pay attention to anything when I can feel every inch of Everett's body against mine. I can feel the muscles of his chest against my back and the beat of his heart. My ass is nestled into his groin and it takes every ounce of control I have not to wiggle against him.

"Now, raise your hands, keeping your elbows bent at a ninety-degree angle, with your palms straight up."

My eyes start to close, when I suddenly hear my name.

"Cam. Raise your hands," Everett whispers in my ear.

I shake my head to clear it, trying to remember the instructions he just gave without asking him to repeat himself, and I admit I have no idea what's going on right now because he's distracting me with all this touching and breathing in my ear.

"This won't break you free, but it will allow you some freedom of movement," Everett states as I raise my hands, making sure to keep my elbows bent like he instructed.

"Next, take your right foot, and move it back until it's between my legs and behind *my* right foot."

I do as he says, pushing my ass even farther into his groin as I move my leg into position, and that's when I feel it, and I have to swallow back a groan. He's hard. And there is no way he can hide it in those track pants he's wearing. I want to smile and let out a *whoop,* but he just goes right on with his instruction. No stuttering of his words, no labored breathing, no shaking hands or arms, no forgetting where he is or what he's doing—all things I've been struggling with. *Nothing* to indicate this has any effect on him whatsoever. Here I am, a ball of nervous, lust-filled, can barely remember my own name ridiculousness, and he's calm as a cucumber. He's a guy. I'm a woman. Replace me with *any* damn woman and he'd probably have the same reaction.

"You'll then lift your leg that's behind mine, jamming it into my knee and making it give out, throwing your attacker off balance and loosening his hold on you so you can get away."

I'm so ticked off by his calmness that he's already moved away before I can do what he says, slam my knee into his, and then maybe even turn and bring it up into his crotch for good measure. He crosses his arms in front of him, his face showing no emotion at all as he starts to tell Stratford about a few other moves. He clearly thinks I'm out of my element because I've been letting him take the lead.

Little does Everett know, I've been taking self-defense classes with Amelia for two years.

Game on.

Chapter 24

EVERETT

She did all this to torture me. I swear to God, every time she bent over, I could almost hear her laughing under her breath, knowing I was standing in the back of the room, barely holding on to my sanity. I'd been clenching my jaw so hard, watching her bend into every yoga pose known to man, that before I knew it, my temples were pounding with a headache and my dick hurt from being hard for so long that I'd need an ice pack soon.

For a week, I've been helping out here at the camp, doing all of the things I used to do back before I joined Doctors Without Borders, fitting back into the fold seamlessly and helping out wherever I'm needed. It felt good that Cameron would leave me alone from time to time to go back up to the main house and get things ready for the charity dinner, trusting me enough to know I wouldn't screw anything up for her, letting me take care of Stratford on my own, and having faith in me to do right by her and the camp and make up for lost time.

She's asked me on more than one occasion if I'm going to apply for a position at a local hospital and I brushed off her questions with a joke about being too busy helping her in her time of need. I've received several requests from some of the most well-renowned hospitals in the area, in desperate need of a doctor to run their trauma department, and they know I'm one of the best because of my experience overseas. I've ignored all of them, tossing the letters in the trash can and deleting e-mails as soon as I scan through them. I can't tell Cameron the truth right now. That I'm scared to death to be a doctor again. That I'm petrified to be alone with a patient, making split-second decisions about them that could save their life or end it.

It's been easy to push aside all these lingering feelings for her with both of us being so busy, and just concentrate on being a good friend and helping her however she needs it. It also helps that she's never given me any indication that there could be something more. I'm always the one instigating the hand-holding, the touches, and the cutesy little pet names when Stratford is around, and she always just goes along with whatever I do, even though I can feel her nerves and tension every time I touch her. And last night doesn't count. Waking up with her in my arms this morning and how right it felt had nothing to do with trying to make this into something more and everything to do with just needing not to be alone after that damn dream I had. If she gave me any kind of a sign that what I was doing affected her, there would be no way I could stick to my guns and focus only on being her friend.

Until now.

Until she waltzed in here in that outfit, bent over, and stuck her ass up in the air, or sat on the ground with her legs spread and leaned all the way forward until her chest was pressed to the ground.

It suddenly got really fucking hot in this room, and I could feel beads of sweat gathering under the baseball hat I'd thrown on this morning.

When Stratford looked at me, inquiring about other plans we have aside from exercise classes, I saw the panic written all over Cameron's face, and I pushed away from the wall to come to her rescue, coming up with the first thing that popped into my head.

When I got behind her and wrapped my arms around her body, I realized self-defense wasn't the brightest idea of activities to demonstrate. As soon as I pulled her against me and her ass nestled into my groin, my dick roared to life inside my pants. It took all the control I had to continue speaking in a calm and clear voice. It took every ounce of willpower I possessed to pretend like holding her in my arms, smelling her skin, and feeling the heat of her body didn't make me want to throw her to the floor, slide between her legs, and ease some of the pain between mine. When she pushed her leg back between mine and hooked it around my foot, her ass rubbed right up against my cock and my eyes almost rolled into the back of my head.

As soon as I finish demonstrating the Bear Hug, I drop my hold on her and move away as quickly as possible before I come in my pants like a damn teenager. I continue explaining different moves to Stratford to try to clear my head of everything Cameron.

"We could even pair up teenagers with their parents to give them some time together for certain classes," I finish, letting out a slow breath as I mentally count to ten and will my dick to forget all about the half-dressed woman I just had in my arms.

Right when my brain finally gets back on track, something slams into my ankles. It takes me by such surprise that my feet come out from under me and I feel myself falling, my arms windmilling until my back smacks against the ground and all the air gets knocked out of my lungs as my baseball hat flies off my head. Before I can even catch my breath or figure out what the fuck just happened, my eyes widen in shock when Cameron is suddenly on top of me, straddling my thighs.

She grabs tightly to my wrists and yanks my arms up, smacking them against the floor above my head. The position forces her body up until all that mouthwatering cleavage the top she's wearing gave her is hovering right over my mouth and I can't stop staring at it. The temptation to lift my head and slide my tongue right down the center of it is so strong that I immediately bite down on it until I taste blood.

Cameron turns her head to the side with my wrists still firmly in her grasp and my eyes move up to her profile as she smiles out at the audience.

"And that's what we call a Leg Sweep. A little more advanced than the Bear Hug, but a lot of fun to practice," she states.

The room erupts into a roar of applause, and I see out of the corner of my eye that Amelia and a few other workers crowd around Stratford and start talking to him in more depth about self-defense and how good it would be for the camp.

Cameron's head slowly turns back and she looks down at me, her chest heaving with a few lingering, labored breaths from the exertion she needed to use to take me down.

I want to ask her where the fuck she learned a move like that. I'm six foot two and weigh two hundred pounds, and she just took me down like I weighed no more than a feather. I should be pissed she got the drop on me, but I'm too busy thinking it's the hottest fucking thing I've ever seen.

But most of all, I want to yank my arms out from

under her hands, slide my palms up her thighs, which are still straddling me, grab on to her hips, and pull her tighter against me. I want her to feel how hot she makes me and know it's always been her, and it always will be.

Her hold on my wrists slowly eases and she slides her hands down the underside of my arms, and over my chest, pushing herself up as she goes until she's sitting astride me, filling my head with new fantasies, like what she would look like doing this completely naked.

For the first time, her eyes stay locked on to mine instead of glancing away nervously. Her tongue darts out and slides across her bottom lip before her teeth bite down on the pink, wet fullness of it. There's a challenge in those beautiful green eyes that I've never seen before. Never imagined in my wildest dreams I'd *ever* see, and it makes my heart beat faster inside my chest.

Without saying a word, she pushes down harder on my chest and swings her leg over mine, pulling her body off of me and quickly getting up from the ground.

"I've got some work to do. See you at dinner, honey," she says from above me, loud enough for Stratford's benefit, before turning and walking away.

I stare at her as she goes, watching her ass move and her high ponytail sway back and forth across her shoulders, until something suddenly blocks my view.

Looking up in irritation, I see Jason standing above me with his hand out and an amused smile on his face. I smack away his hand in annoyance, rolling over onto my stomach and pushing myself up from the ground, wiping off imaginary dirt from my pants just to give myself something to do other than look at my brother's smug face.

"Oh, how the mighty have fallen," Jason laughs.

"Fuck off," I mutter, slamming my shoulder into his as I

walk past him and out of the room to find somewhere I can hide until dinner to get my fucking thoughts in order.

So much for Cameron never giving me any indication that she wants more. If a challenge is what she wants, and going by the way she stared at me while she licked her lip and took her time getting off of me, I'm assuming it is, a challenge is what she'll get.

Game fucking on.

Chapter 25

CAMERON

Amelia was right.

Everett is the best distraction there is. The stress I've been living with for months about the camp possibly closing hasn't even entered my mind the last few days. I haven't been prone to random bouts of crying, and I've been sleeping better than I ever have, even with Everett down the hall and out in the living room, still invading my space. The sharp, stabbing pain of missing Aiden hasn't woken me up in the middle of the night either. All I can think about, all I can concentrate on, is trying to figure my best friend out.

Ever since the self-defense lesson when I took Amelia's words to heart and decided to turn up the heat a little and see how Everett would react, he's done the exact opposite of what I thought he'd do. He didn't laugh, he didn't ask me what the hell I was doing, and he didn't look at me like I was insane. Instead, he gave as good as he got until my head was swimming with possibilities and the need for more.

We rode four-wheelers out to a hiking area two days ago to check and make sure the path was still clear for campers. I stupidly forgot to make sure mine had enough gas and it stalled out halfway back to the barn next to the stables, where we keep the ATVs and golf carts for traveling quickly around the camp. My only option was to ride on the back of Everett's, straddling the seat behind him with the front of my legs molded to the back of his, my chest pressed against him, and my arms held tightly around his waist. I closed my eyes and rested my cheek against his back, letting my palms flatten, one hand pressed against the muscles of his chest and the other sitting dangerously low on his stomach. I could feel his muscles tighten when that hand started sliding down the front of him and felt his quick intake of breath as my hand went down.

He paid me back by teaching me how to drive a stick yesterday. Something I'd been meaning to do for years since we have a truck with a manual transmission here at camp we use for emergencies, but I never got around to doing. I lost track of how many times I stalled the damn thing, and not because I wasn't able to understand his instruction. It all had to do with how closely he sat next to me on the bench seat, with one of his arms resting around me on the back of the seat. I could smell the soap on his skin from his recent shower, feel his breath against the side of my neck as he patiently told me what to do. When he set his free hand on top of mine on the gear shift to help me move it, I stalled. When he placed his palm on my bare thigh, then slowly slid it down to my knee while telling me how much gas to give the truck as I took my foot off the clutch, I stalled.

Something in Everett has changed. When he looks at me, the glances are more intense, his stare holding mine until I'm the one who breaks it and looks away, because it's too much and not enough all at once.

I want to ask him what the hell is going on, but I don't. I want to ask him why he's looking at me like he wants me, and it's taking everything in him to hold himself back, but I can't. Whatever is going on between the two of us, I'm afraid to say it out loud. I feel like I'm floating up to the sky on a bubble filled with wanting and need, and if I speak, it will be like someone stuck a pin in my bubble and I'll come crashing back down to earth.

I'm not ready to crash. I'm not ready to find out why Everett suddenly looks at me like he can't get enough of me, can't stop touching me, and is one second away from pulling me against him and finally letting me feel his mouth on mine.

I don't want to know if he's only doing it for Stratford, because the charity dinner is fast approaching and our deadline for convincing him we're a happily married couple who runs this camp is almost upon us. It doesn't even matter that half of the things he's doing that are driving me crazy are when we're alone and Stratford is nowhere to be found. Maybe he thinks he has to keep up with the charade when we're alone, to make it more believable when we're not. I don't want to know that maybe he's using me as his own distraction. His way of forgetting about being overseas and what he saw and did there, like he did the night he asked me to curl up with him on the couch after his nightmare, and his way of forgetting about not being here for Aiden's funeral...using flirting and playing with my emotions without realizing he's even doing it, so he's not tempted to pick up a bottle and take a drink.

The sad thing is, I'd understand if that's what he's doing. I'd understand and I'd let him keep right on doing whatever he needed to take away his pain and his guilt, no matter what it did to me.

I'm not ready for my bubble to burst. I'm not ready for the pain of crashing. He's happier than I've ever seen him. He smiles easier, laughs harder, his face isn't filled with worry lines, and he doesn't stare off into the distance, lost in his own memories and pain. He flirts and he teases and he throws my sass right back at me without hesitation.

I want that for him. I've *always* wanted that for him. I want to be the one who makes him happy, no matter the cost, and now that it seems like I've succeeded, I'm in no hurry to ruin everything by opening my mouth and letting my insecurities out.

"If he takes his shirt off and dives into the water, I might fight you for him," Amelia whispers, coming up next to me on the dock to stare over at the small beach surrounding the lake.

Everett stands in the sand with his arms crossed in front of him, nodding his head at something the lifeguard says. His board-short-style swim trunks show off his amazing ass, and the Camp Rylan T-shirt he wears is stretched across the muscles of his chest and back, making my hands tingle remembering how it felt to have my arms around his body and my hands pressed against that chest.

Even though it's Friday and we don't usually have campers here during the week until the summer session starts, once a month, we open up the camp for a day so kids who have never been here before can give it a try and test it out to see if it's something they might like to do. We don't offer all camp activities on testing day, but enough to give them a good idea of what it's like to attend Camp Rylan. I probably should have rescheduled this month's testing day, since it fell the day before the charity dinner, but by the time I realized the date, it was too late. I've got a million and one things I need to be doing to get ready for the dinner on top of trying not to panic that there isn't much time left to make Stratford believe we love each other, but instead, I'm standing on the dock, ogling Everett and quietly wishing he'd take his shirt off, like Amelia stated.

Going even further with his idea about empowering the kids, Everett thought we should try hosting a class on CPR and teach the older kids how to save someone who's drowning. Stratford is sitting in a chair a few feet from Everett, the lifeguard, and the twenty kids who wanted to attend today's lesson, holding an umbrella over his head as he watches the class. I've seen him almost crack a smile twice, so it seems to have been a good idea.

"What the hell are we doing?" I mutter, unable to take my eyes off of Everett when he turns away from the group and starts walking across the sand toward the dock, where we're standing.

"I don't know about you, but I'm dreaming about that man taking his shirt off," Amelia says.

"I don't mean me and you, I mean me and *him*," I tell her, nodding in Everett's direction.

"You're finally acting on something you should have done a long time ago. I can't believe that for all these years I thought you and Aiden were meant to be. One look at you and Everett together and I realize how wrong I was. How did no one else see this?"

"It's never okay to want your best friend. It's messy and it's complicated," I state, even though I know it's a lie.

Maybe what I had with Aiden was more comfortable and safe than the electric charge of want and need running through my veins all the time with Everett, but it was never messy or complicated.

"No, it's how it's supposed to be. As your best friend, he knows you better than anyone. He knows your faults and he still wants to be around you anyway. He's the person who believes in you and supports you and always has your back. There's no learning curve getting to know each other, because you already know everything there is to know. You just have to stop being afraid."

Amelia gives my arm a squeeze as she walks away from me and down the dock, saluting Everett as she moves past him and he moves toward me. I have to bite back a laugh when she turns around behind him and makes grabby hands toward his ass then fans herself.

Everett sees me trying to hide my smile and looks back over his shoulder.

"What's so funny?"

Amelia quickly drops her hands, gives him a serious nod, then turns and walks away.

"Just my friend being an idiot. You ready to do this?" I ask, looking up at his face when he turns back around to face me.

"Am I ready to save a drowning damsel in distress and show those kids how it's done? Absolutely," he grins down at me.

Putting my hands on my hips, I glare up at him.

"I have never been, nor will I ever be, a damsel in distress. *Your* ass is going in the water and *I'm* going to save *you*," I inform him.

"ANYTIME YOU GUYS ARE READY OVER THERE!"

Everett and I both turn when our lifeguard on staff shouts from the beach, lifting his hand to give us a wave.

"You better hurry up and get in the water so I can save you. It's almost time for lunch and those teenagers are going to revolt if we don't feed them," Everett says, looking back at me with a smirk.

"No, *you* better hurry up in the water so I can save *you*."

"Will you stop being so stubborn," he says with a shake of his head.

"I'm not being stubborn, *you're* being stubborn. Get in the water."

"You have five seconds or I'm going to toss you in," he threatens, taking a step toward me as he begins his count-down. "Five, four—"

"You wouldn't dare! You can't throw me in when I still have my clothes on," I argue.

"Three…you have your bathing suit on under your shorts and tank top. It's a shame I'm already at three. It would have been nice to see you take your clothes off all nice and slow."

The heat in his eyes as they trail up and down my body almost makes me forget he's ticking me off.

"Everett…"

I try to growl his name in warning, but it comes out as a pathetic squeak because now his hands have grabbed ahold of the hem of my tank top. The tips of his fingers graze across my stomach as he slowly starts to lift it.

"Two," he whispers, his eyes never leaving mine, making me forget all about the campers a few hundred yards away, watching and waiting.

My heart thunders in my chest when his hands flatten against my sides, moving them up and bringing my tank top with them. He pauses with his palms resting on my rib cage, his thumbs moving back and forth along the underside of my breasts.

I hold my breath as I stare up at him, and watch his eyes trail down my face until he's staring at my lips. I can feel myself leaning toward him, pushing up on my toes until my mouth is hovering right over his. I want his mouth on mine. I want his hands to keep moving higher until he's cupping my breasts in them.

My eyes flutter closed as all the things I want and need are swirling around in my head, making my body ache for more.

"One."

I don't even have time to open my eyes. Everett's hands on me suddenly shove me away, and before I know it, I'm tumbling backward, splashing into the cold water of the lake. My shock and surprise is short-lived, and I immediately start kicking my legs and slicing my arms through the water to bring myself up to the surface, every curse word I've ever heard before on the tip of my tongue, ready to be screamed to the heavens as soon as my head comes up out of the water.

I hear a loud splash, and a second later, Everett's arm suddenly wraps around my waist from behind, pulling me up to the surface. At this point, my fight or flight has kicked in, and coupled with my anger that he just pushed me into the lake, I start struggling against him, clawing at his arm and kicking my legs back, trying to find some part of him to connect with.

My head comes up out of the water and I take in a huge lungful of air, removing my nails from the skin of his forearm long enough to swipe my wet hair out of my eyes.

"I *cannot* believe you pushed me in!" I shout, trying to kick and squirm out of his hold.

Everett doesn't say a word, just tightens his arm around my waist and continues swimming us both through the water toward the shore. He grunts and curses under his breath when my elbow makes contact with his chest. Out of the corner of my eye, I see the campers all gathered around on the beach, watching Everett pull me in, and I realize I'm making it extremely hard on him by struggling and flailing all around, and not acting like I should to make this demonstration accurate.

For the good of the camp, I give up fighting and let my body go limp, making myself feel better by calling Everett every name I can think of quietly in my head as he finally gets us to shore and I'm placed on my back on the sand.

Closing my eyes so I won't be tempted to reach up and punch him when I see his face, I hear him splash the rest of the way out of the water and move up by my head. His hands grab me under my arms and he quickly pulls me a few feet away from the water's edge.

"After your drowning victim is safely out of the water, you'll kneel down by their side, placing your ear by their mouth and nose to check for breathing," our lifeguard explains.

Drops of water from Everett splash down on me when he leans over me, doing as instructed.

"If the person is not breathing, check for a pulse by placing two fingers under their chin right at the pressure point."

Behind my eyes, I see the shadow of Everett move away and feel his fingers pressing against my throat, where my heartbeat is strong and steady.

"If there is no pulse, start CPR," the lifeguard states, listing the steps as Everett follows along.

I feel his palms press gently against my chest between my breasts, his fingers resting so close to my nipples that I'm glad he's no longer feeling for a pulse, or he'd know just how fast my heart is beating right now.

As the lifeguard tells everyone how to tip the victim's head back, pinch their nose closed, and cover the victim's mouth with your own to create an airtight seal, I hold my breath, waiting to feel Everett's mouth on mine.

I crack my eyes open, staring up to see Everett looming over me, his eyes glued to my mouth and his head slowly lowering to mine. My lips part when his are a centimeter from mine. His fingers are still resting against my chin, tipping it back as his mouth gets closer and closer to me. I can feel his breath on my face, the anticipation making my stomach flip-flop and my skin tingle. His lips are hovering right above mine. All I have to do is tilt my head back a little farther and I'll finally have his mouth on me. I've never wanted anything more. I've never *needed* anything more.

"And that's how CPR is done!" the lifeguard suddenly announces, making my eyes fly the rest of the way open.

I watch Everett quickly lean back away from me, running one hand through his wet hair as he smiles at the group of kids, who are now clapping and cheering.

He pushes himself up from the sand and starts helping the lifeguard put the kids into pairs so they can practice pulling each other out of the water and going through the CPR motions. My heart is still thumping wildly in my chest, and my lips still tingle with the need to feel Everett's against them. I can't make myself move from lying flat on my back on the sand, watching him give the kids instructions like it's no big deal. Like he didn't just almost put his mouth on mine.

"Is it hot out here, or is it just me?" Amelia asks, squatting down next to me in the sand. "I thought for a second there you were going to wrap your hand around his neck and yank him down to you. I almost came up behind him and shoved his head down for you."

She grabs my arm and hauls me up to sitting.

"See? Messy and complicated," I mutter, pushing myself up from the ground as Amelia stands up with me. "I almost forgot there were other people here. I almost forgot there were *kids* here."

I swipe my hands angrily against my arms and legs to try to brush off the sand, more than a little irritated that

Everett can make me lose my mind just by doing a CPR demonstration.

"Sorry, try again. The only thing messy right now is your ass, covered in sand. And relationships are always complicated. You don't get a free pass. It's how you handle the complications that matter. So how are you going to handle it, Cameron?" Amelia asks.

I look back over my shoulder at Everett, all of my irritation melting away when I see him talking and joking with a few of the kids, and the cracks in the wall around my heart start to splinter off in a thousand different directions.

He's always been a complication worth fighting for; I just never had the guts to do it. I don't know if this fight will be worth it in the end, but I'll never know if I don't try.

Chapter 26

EVERETT

I've never been so tied up in knots or on the verge of practically coming out of my skin as I have been this week. Every time Cameron looks at me, every time she touches me, every time she's close to me, I want to cross every line I've ever drawn with her.

I almost kissed her in front of everyone out on that dock earlier. I didn't plan on pushing her in the water. As stubborn as she was being, I was just teasing her, wanting to get a rise out of her. Wanting to watch her chest heave with angry breaths and her cheeks flush with irritation. I had every intention of diving into that water and letting her rescue me. Then I put my hands on her and made a comment about watching her take her clothes off, and she leaned into me, closed her eyes, and tilted her chin up, and I almost forgot where we were. I almost slammed my lips against hers and finally tasted her. I came to my senses with my mouth hovering over hers and shoved her in the water before I did something stupid.

And now I'm paying for it. She's been avoiding me since the CPR demonstration out on the beach. I want to tell her I'm sorry for shoving her in the water and pissing her off, but a part of me isn't sorry. Jumping into the cold water after her cooled me off enough that I was able to concentrate on something other than kissing her.

Sitting at one of the round tables under the tent that was set up earlier this morning for the charity dinner, I stare across the room at Cameron as she talks to one of the workers in charge of getting everything ready for tomorrow night. She's so goddamn beautiful I want to stalk across the room and wrap my arms around her, tell her that all of this teasing and touching the last couple of days is driving me insane. I don't know what's happening between us, but something has changed. Something has shifted. It thrills me and it scares the shit out of me at the same time. We've stopped putting on a show for Stratford and everything has suddenly become real. I can see it in her eyes and I can feel it when she's close to me. I want to tell her how I feel. How I've always felt. I want to throw caution to the wind and make her see that it's always been her, and always will be, but I don't even know what I'm feeling right now to try to articulate it. I shut off my feelings for her and buried my love for her so far down so long ago, that I knew I'd never be able to reach it again and be tempted by it again. Spending all this time with her, getting closer to her, seeing something similar in her eyes when she looks at me...all of those old feelings are slowly starting to work their way to the surface no matter how hard I try to keep them down.

I continue staring at Cameron across the tent as she points around and tells the worker where to put things. After our dip in the lake, she went back to the guest house and changed into dry clothes. In a casual strapless light blue cotton sundress that hugs her curves and falls down around her legs to the floor, her long blond hair full of waves from air-drying, and not a stitch of makeup on, she's stunning. Looking at her makes my chest feel tight. It makes me wonder why in the hell I've waited so long to say something to her. She's the most important person in my life and I never wanted to risk our friendship, but I can't keep going on like this. I can't keep pretending like the flirting and the teasing are just fun and games.

Cameron finally turns away from the worker, and our eyes meet across the tent. I see her take a deep breath and slowly rise from my chair as she moves toward me. I force my feet to move, meeting her halfway until we're standing toe to toe.

"Things look like they're coming along nicely," I say, seeing the anxiety and nervousness written all over her face as her eyes dart around under the tent, watching workers move about, setting up tables and chairs, not wanting to do anything right now to add to her stress.

"There's still so much to do that my head is spinning," she says with a sigh, her face finally coming back to mine. "I got an e-mail from Stratford while I was changing. He wants to meet us here in a little bit. I think he made his decision. And I think I might throw up."

I smile down at her, placing my hands against either side of her neck and using my thumbs to tilt her chin up higher so I can see her eyes.

"Everything will be fine. I promise. If he decides not to give the camp his money, we'll find another way. I'm not gonna let you lose this place," I reassure her softy.

"Everett."

She whispers my name and closes her eyes for a few seconds before opening them again, locking them right on to mine. She opens her mouth to say something else, but is quickly cut off by the appearance of Amelia at our sides.

"All right, you two, the sound system is all hooked up and I've wirelessly connected my phone to it so I can play some music and test it out, which will require your assistance," she announces.

I keep my eyes on Cameron as she turns her head to look at Amelia.

"I need to call the caterer. I don't think you need my assistance to listen to music," Cameron tells her as I drop my hands from the soft skin of her neck.

"Oh, I don't need your help with that. I need your help testing out the dance floor you're currently standing on," Amelia states with a smile.

Cameron and I both look down and I realize we are indeed standing in the middle of the hardwood floor that I watched the workers snap together like puzzle pieces over the last hour.

Amelia pulls her phone out of the pocket of her shorts, presses a few buttons, and within seconds, the straining sounds of a guitar echo around the room, along with the voice of Niall Horan singing "This Town."

She couldn't have picked a more appropriate song, and going by the wink Amelia gives me before she turns and walks away, she knows it. Cameron still makes me nervous when she walks in the room, just like when we were teenagers. I want to tell her everything I never said when we were younger. Just like the song says, I know it's wrong, but I can't move on. Everything always comes back to her.

Holding my hand out between us, Cameron looks down at it quickly, then back up at me. Her small, soft hand slides against my palm and I pull her against me, bringing our joined hands up and pressing them against my chest. Her free hand goes up to my shoulder and I wrap my arm around her waist.

She fits so perfectly in my arms, her body sliding against mine as she pushes herself up on her toes and her face nestles into the crook of my neck. I feel her warm breath puffing out against my skin as I slowly start swaying us to the music, never wanting to let her go.

"I haven't been happy here," she suddenly blurts out, her cheek sliding against mine as she pulls her head back to look at me.

She closes her eyes for a few seconds as I stare down at her in confusion. When she opens them again, they dart between my own eyes and my mouth, and I watch her wet her lips with the tip of her tongue before she continues speaking.

"I love this camp, more than anything else in the world, but it stopped making me happy," she whispers. "I started to wonder if this is what I was really supposed to do with my life. I started to question everything I always thought I wanted."

Her hand slides across my shoulder to the back of my neck, and my arm tightens around her waist, holding her as close to me as possible, our bodies barely moving now, as the song continues to play and every word this guy sings is like he's reaching into my chest and pulling them right out of my heart.

"I realized something since you've been back here," she continues, moving her head to the side of mine until her lips are right by my ear. "Everything was wrong when you were gone. Nothing made sense without you here. I didn't know how to be happy without you. I didn't know how to *live* without you."

I flatten the hand that's still holding hers between us against my chest, moving it to rest right over my heart. I want her to feel how fast it's beating. I want her to know it's beating for *her* and the things she's saying to me.

She turns her face into the side of mine, her nose brushing against my cheek as she pulls back until she's looking up at me. Her eyes are shining with the truth of her words. They sparkle with wanting and a hint of worry. I don't know if she's worried about what I'm thinking after what she just said, or if she's worried because she knows we're crossing a line we can never turn back from, and I don't care. All I care about is the desire I see shining underneath all of that worry, how tightly she's clinging to me, and how everything around us seems to fade away. There aren't any workers milling about; there isn't the chaos of a party being set up. There's just the two of us, standing here in the middle of this dance floor.

It makes me feel alive and scared at the same time. I don't know if I'm ready to dig up all of those old feelings again, examine them and let them loose, give them a chance to grow back into what they once were, but I think it's already too late for that. At this point, it's pretty clear that those feelings never really went away. I just don't know if I'm strong enough to walk away from her a second time if she changes her mind or realizes this could be a huge mistake.

We both start leaning in closer to each other, her eyes trailing down to my mouth, to where her lips are heading straight for, and I forget how to breathe. I forget all the hundred and one things I should be saying to her right now and all the reasons I'm afraid; all I can think about is kissing her. Finally doing what I've been dreaming about and aching for, for years.

A loud banging sound from the far side of the tent makes both of us jump and our faces pull apart. I come crashing back down to earth as she pulls away from me and quickly turns to see what happened. My arms feel empty without her in them and I remember where we are and what's happening around us.

"Sorry, I have to go see what the hell that was," Cameron says. "Can we continue this later?"

I forget how to speak and just nod my head instead. I thought for sure she would pretend like we didn't just have a moment and we weren't about to kiss, but the smile she gives me proves me wrong. Watching her quickly walk away from me, picking up the skirt of her sundress so she doesn't trip over it as she moves, I smile to myself and shove my hands into the front pockets of my shorts.

We're definitely going to continue this later. I'm done hiding how I feel about her, and it's time she knew the truth about all those wishes I've been making for all these years.

Chapter 27

CAMERON

Stratford, Everett, and I are all standing on the wraparound porch of the main house as the sun starts to set. He and Everett have been chatting casually about the weather and a few of the campers Stratford met during his time here, and I want to scream at both of them to stop talking so we can get on with this.

My palms are sweating and my foot hasn't stopped tapping against the wood floor ever since Stratford met us here twenty minutes ago. He holds the fate of this camp and my future in his hands, and he won't stop talking about the damn clouds in the sky.

Everett has been holding my hand through this entire conversation, giving it a squeeze every few minutes to try to calm me down since he knows I'm about ready to come out of my skin wanting to know what Stratford's decision is. It works for a few seconds, feeling his warm, strong hand wrapped around mine as well as leaning against the side of his body. And then I start second-guessing everything we did while Stratford was here. Were we convincing enough as husband and wife? Does he think we're madly in love? Have all of the confusing thoughts and emotions I've been having thrown a wrench into everything? Could he see that every time I looked at Everett, I was equal parts scared to death and excited about what might be happening between us?

"So I'm sure you'd like to know what my decision is since I know you have a million other things you need to do to get ready for the charity dinner tomorrow. I'm sorry to say something has come up and I won't be able to attend," Stratford says, finally looking away from Everett to give me a regretful smile.

"Oh, I'm so sorry you won't be here," I tell him, even though I want to let out a relieved breath that we'll no longer be under a microscope.

Not to mention that my parents will be back from vacation and that will bring on a whole other list of problems I wouldn't be able to deal with if Stratford were still around.

He reaches into the inside pocket of his bright orange suit coat and pulls out an envelope, handing it over to me.

With one hand still clinging tightly to Everett, the other one reaches out, shaking like a leaf as I take the envelope from him.

"No need to open that now. I had my accountant crunch some numbers after I went through your books, and that should be more than enough to keep you up and running for the next five years. We can meet again at that time to reevaluate things, but I'm sure I won't have a problem writing another check for you."

My eyes immediately fill with tears, and I can't stop my chin and my lips from quivering with emotion as I stare down at my future, the future of this camp and everyone who works here and everyone who attends it, held in between my fingers. I want to thank him, but a simple thank-you just doesn't seem like enough.

"I applaud what you're doing here, Cameron. It's selfless and it's amazing, and like your husband said to me one day, this place has to continue existing," Stratford tells me. "You two remind me so much of my wife and me, that some days, it was almost hard to watch the two of you together. But something tells me you're holding back. Not giving each other everything you could. Don't make that mistake because, one day, it might be too late. Love each other with everything you have. Trust each other with everything inside of you. And never, ever let the other one go. I wish every day that things were different. That my wife was still here by my side and I could tell her everything I should have said when she was still alive. Don't leave things unsaid. Don't waste one minute of the time you have together. I hope the two of you, as well as Camp Rylan, have a very long and happy life together."

With that, Stratford tips his head to us and heads down the front steps to his waiting limo. We watch his driver open the back door, and he gives us a wave before he disappears inside. As soon as the limo starts to take off down the driveway, I finally look up at Everett as the tears I've been holding back fall down my cheeks.

"We did it," I whisper, still unable to believe what just happened.

"No, *you* did it. I just showed up at the right time and made things interesting." Everett smiles.

We stare at each other silently for a few seconds when Everett suddenly lets out a whoop, scoops me up into his arms, and spins me around. I cry, I laugh, and I cling to Everett, never wanting this feeling to end. I feel relief, I feel excitement, and I let every word Stratford said to us sink into my soul and take it to heart. I don't want to leave things unsaid. I don't want to waste another minute with Everett. I thought I could let him back into my life and be his friend again, while keeping the walls up around me and protecting my heart, but I was a fool. He tore through those walls the minute he walked back into my life and smiled at me.

A ding from Everett's phone has him cutting our celebration short as he sets me back on my feet and pulls it out of his back pocket. The smile on his face quickly drops as he reads a text.

"What's wrong?"

He shakes his head and, with a sigh, shoves his phone back in his pocket.

"It's nothing. It's fine. Just a friend who needs me. I don't want to leave you right now..." He trails off, cupping my face in his hand as he stares down at me.

"Is it someone from your meetings?"

Everett told me that during his recovery, he still attended weekly meetings at the local hospital and he's left camp a small handful of times since he's been here to talk to a few people who needed his help when they were having a bad day. I'm so proud of him that he was able to get better, and doesn't hesitate to drop everything to help someone else who struggled like he did.

"I swear I won't be gone that long. This guy has been doing great lately so I'm sure he'll only need me for a little bit," Everett reassures me as he drops his hand from my face and starts backing away.

"It's fine. Go work your magic and I'll be here, waiting for you when you get back."

As I say the words, Everett pauses on the top step, giving me a wistful smile, I suddenly remember everything he said to Stratford during our first dinner together. How he changed our past and made it into a fairytale of me sticking it out with him during his residency and all his time overseas, and how I forgave him for not being here and we fell in love. As he stands on that top step with his eyes staring into mine, my heart flutters in my chest wondering if everything he said that night wasn't a fairytale, but was exactly the way he wished things would have gone between us.

"I'll be back soon," Everett says softly, hustling down the stairs as I watch him go, knowing that as soon as he comes back, we're going to have a serious talk.

After Everett gets in the truck and takes off down the driveway, I start wandering around the camp, looking at it with new eyes. Everything makes me smile and everything makes me happy again, because of him. I'm finally excited again about what the future will hold, and it feels so good.

As I make my way along the trail that leads back to my parents' house, I feel the vibration of my phone in my back pocket. Pulling it out, I groan when I see the name on the display.

"Grady, hi. I've been meaning to call you…" I trail off, wondering what the best way is to tell someone you are no longer in need of their services.

It sounds so cold, but that's all he ever was. The way he behaved when he stopped by the camp a few weeks ago only proved that point. He provided a service. A quick, emotionless way for me to stop feeling so alone until the next time I was overwhelmed with misery and loneliness. His possessiveness that day made me realize that all I was doing was hurting him. He agreed to my demands in the beginning, but I should have known it wouldn't be that easy. There was never another man in my life that threatened what we had together, no matter how little that was. As soon as he heard about Everett, even though Amelia didn't give him much information other than the fact we used to be friends and now we were playing husband and wife, it was enough for him to forget about our arrangement and turn into a jealous boyfriend.

Something I didn't want or need, especially now.

Especially when everything I've ever wanted is right within my grasp, and all I have to do is reach out and take it.

"I stopped by the camp the other day," Grady interrupts. "I saw you and your *husband* and decided it wasn't the best time for us to talk."

I'm shocked that no one noticed Grady had stopped by, or thought to tell me. But I'm more shocked by the way he says the word *husband*. Full of thinly veiled anger and a whole lot of that jealousy he has no right to feel.

"Grady, I'm sorry. This just…like I said before, now isn't a good time. I think it's best if we both just move on. You deserve so much better."

"You're right, I deserve better than a quick fuck every couple of months," he barks through the phone.

I wince at the harshness of his words. I should feel badly that I've hurt him, but I don't. He knew the score; he just chose not to believe it.

"I know you're angry, and I'm sorry. I wish things could have been different. You are a wonderful man."

"Save it. I didn't stick around long the other day, but it was long enough to see the way you looked at that guy. Pretending, my ass. I actually thought if I called, if you heard my voice, you'd remember what we had together. You'd invite me to the charity dinner tomorrow night and prove you aren't as cold as I thought you were. Thanks for ruining my life."

He ends the call before I can get another word in. Before

I can apologize again, even though he's clearly delusional and only saw what he wanted to see between us. He saw a future, and all I saw was a way to bide my time until my future finally came home.

I don't realize I continued walking during our short phone call, and before I know it, I find myself at the base of our treehouse. I look up at the ten-foot-in-diameter, hexagon-shaped wooden house with faded yellow curtains in the window and suddenly, every memory I've ever had in that thing flashes through my mind, as well as every moment I've spent with Everett since he came back. I can't keep holding on to the past if I want to move forward with my future. It's time for me to let go of Aiden, let go of the pain of losing him, and stop trying to hold on to him so tightly. I can't pursue something real with Everett until I shed all of the things still holding me back, Aiden being the biggest thing of all right now.

With a deep breath and a pounding heart, I quickly climb the ladder.

Grabbing the star-shaped notepad and pen that Everett and I left in the middle of the floor the last time we were here, I sit down cross-legged and close my eyes. I sit in the middle of the small room high up in a tree and let the memories wash over me. I let them fill me with joy that I was able to experience such happiness in my life, instead of the usual heart-breaking feeling that I'll never have moments with Aiden like that again, finally letting go of the pain of losing him. Opening my eyes, I quickly scribble down the four years of wishes I missed, and I let everything out. All of the tears, all of the sadness and all of the loneliness without him here. I let it all go and finally let myself feel hopeful that what I've always wanted might finally be coming true.

"I miss you so much, Aiden," I whisper through my tears

as I pull my box out of its hiding spot and put my wishes inside with all the others.

Nestling my box back down next to Aiden's and Everett's, I run my palm over the top of Aiden's box. "I will always miss you, no matter how much time goes by."

As I replace the wooden floorboard to hide our boxes, I hope that, wherever he is, he hears me, and he understands that it's time for me to let him go.

Chapter 28

EVERETT

I feel like I'm coming outta my skin, man. I need a drink so bad it hurts."

I stare at Bobby across the table of the small coffeehouse in town where I met him, wondering where in the hell the guy went that I met at my first Alcoholics Anonymous meeting over six months ago. Out of everyone I've met at those meetings, Bobby was the last person I thought would call me needing help.

At my first meeting, he'd been the leader of the small group since he'd been sober the longest and had been coming to the meetings the longest. He was a natural leader and helpful person with a clear head and mind and a charismatic personality. In those meetings, we learned a lot about one another and our reasons for turning to alcohol to numb the pain, but Bobby was never very forthcoming about his past, always letting others do the talking because he said they needed help more than him.

I wonder now if there were signs that he was slipping during my last couple of meetings, but I was too wrapped up in Cameron and what was happening at the camp to notice them. I'd never blame her for distracting me. She was the best kind of distraction there was. It's my own damn fault for not being able to focus on what I was supposed to at the time.

"When was the last time you had a drink? Or maybe something stronger?" I ask, taking in his disheveled appearance, unkempt hair, dirty and wrinkled clothes, and the way he keeps scratching at his arms and scrubbing his face with his hands.

This guy is withdrawing from a lot more than booze.

"I don't know. What does it matter? I'm sober now and I called you. I did what I was supposed to. I just can't take it anymore. I can't believe Milly did this to us. I can't believe she fucked me over and took everything from me."

I've been listening to Bobby talk about his wife for the last hour, saying more to me in sixty minutes than he's said in the six months I've known him. His emotions are all over the place. One minute he's sad and quiet, and the next he's pissed off and cursing her name.

"She moved on. She found someone else. It sucks and it hurts, but you can't change it. You can't change her. All you can do is worry about yourself and change *you*. Say it with me."

I give him a pointed look and he finally stops maniacally scratching his arms. He drops his hands into his lap as he recites the prayer with me that we start every meeting with.

"God, grant me the serenity to accept the things I cannot change, courage to change the things I can, and wisdom to know the difference," we say in unison.

We share a moment of silence and it looks like Bobby has calmed down some. He's no longer fidgeting in his chair or getting distracted, his eyes shifting and his head jerking all around the coffee shop every time the espresso machine fires up or there's a loud clanging of coffee cups being dumped into the sink.

He's breathing easier and his face is smooth and calm and no longer scrunched up in anger.

"You good now?" I ask, glancing down at my watch when he brings his folded hands up to the table and stares down at them.

I don't want to leave if he still needs me, but I'm anxious to get back to Cameron. As soon as she said she'd be right there, waiting for me when I got back, all I could think about was how many times I wished she'd said those words to me over the years. I need to get back to her. We need to celebrate Camp Rylan and we need to talk. I still don't know what's happening between us, but I'm sick and tired of waiting. Exhausted from trying to keep everything buried when it's screaming to get out.

"I'm good, man. Thanks for coming and thanks for the talk," Bobby tells me, reaching across the table with his hand outstretched.

I shake his hand, squeezing it a little harder before I let it go.

"You call me anytime you need to talk, okay? You don't need a crutch to get through this. You're strong and you're gonna be fine. Just take it one day at a time."

With a promise from Bobby that he'll call me tomorrow and let me know how he is, I race out of the coffee shop and try not to break any speed limits getting back to the camp.

* * *

By the time I finished with Bobby and felt good about leaving him alone, the sun had gone down and most of the staff had gone home for the night. It takes me a while of wandering around the camp before I finally find someone who knows where Cameron is, and I can't wipe the sappy grin off my face as I race toward our treehouse.

I can't stop thinking about the words she whispered in my ear; I can't stop thinking about the look in her eyes right before my lips touched hers and we got interrupted. I can't stop thinking about everything I want to say to her that I've kept locked up inside for so long. I climb the ladder faster than I ever have before, but my feet turn into blocks of cement when I get to the top and stop in the doorway.

Cameron's back is to me as she sits cross-legged on the floor in the middle of the room, but I hear her sniffle and watch her hand come up to wipe the tears off her cheeks. I hear them in her voice when she speaks out loud, telling Aiden she misses him, and will always miss him. The pain in my chest explodes, and I'm surprised I don't stumble backward and fall off the damn ledge around the edge of the treehouse.

I should let her know I'm here. I should move into the room and wrap her in my arms and say something to take away her pain, but I can't. I'm too busy trying to remember how to breathe through my own agony.

All this time, I thought something was happening between us, but maybe I was just seeing what I wanted to see, instead of what was really there. She's still hurting, she's still mourning, and I was a good distraction from all of that. I made her forget about her broken heart. She said my being back here made her happy again, but maybe all it did was make her forget about what she lost.

Leaving Cameron to be alone with her grief, I back out of the treehouse quietly and take the ladder down slowly, calling myself all kinds of a fool for thinking it was a good idea to dig something up that should have stayed buried.

Chapter 29

CAMERON

"Wow."

Standing at the edge of the tent, I look away from all the people smiling, drinking, eating, and having a good time, when my mom comes up next to me and wraps her arm around my waist.

"It's not too much?"

She shakes her head with wide eyes, searching the room and taking in everything.

"It's perfect. Absolutely perfect. I'm so proud of you."

I smile wider when her eyes, the same shape and color as mine, turn toward me. When I found out last night that Stratford decided to give us the money, I wanted to call my parents immediately, but I refrained. I waited until she and my dad got back home this morning from Outer Banks to tell them. I wanted to see their faces when I told them their dream and their legacy would continue to go on. I didn't, however, tell them about what I decided to do for the charity dinner. I wanted to keep that part a secret until they walked under the tent, and I'm glad I did. The look on her face tells me everything I need to know. That I didn't go overboard changing everything up, and even though it's shocking, she loves it.

The giant tent is white, and the tablecloths are white, but that's where everything we've done in years past ends. Red, purple, and green fabrics are draped along the ceiling, meeting in the middle of the tent, where a huge chandelier hangs. Huge clusters of red and purple magnolia blossoms are bunched together in mason jars in the center of each table, with a bright green ribbon tied around the glass holders. All around the giant tent is color. Lots and lots of color, and nothing boring or beige of any kind, exactly what Everett missed while he was deployed.

As much as it pained me, I placed a call to Guns and Posers, Everett's favorite 1980s cover band, and they are currently playing a few soft rock ballads on a stage off to the back of the tent, while people finish their dinner. A dinner of the best brisket in town from Lewis Barbecue. I had to give a lot of apologies to our usual caterer who has fed everyone at this charity dinner for over twenty years, promising we would throw another party soon to make up for it, but it was worth it. I know as soon as Everett gets here, he's going to take one look around and know what I've done and why. Not even the light rain that has been falling all night could put a damper on my good mood and my excitement about what's to come. I know that this charity dinner is for the camp, not for Everett, but I'm killing two birds with one stone. I'm making this camp mine, taking on my parents' legacy but with my own personal touch instead of theirs. And I'm showing Everett what he means to me and how important it is to me that he's happy.

"I'm going to assume these changes have a little something to do with the reappearance of a certain man in your life, that you can't stop looking around for?" my mom asks, laughing softly when my jaw drops.

During all of our phone calls the last few weeks, I glossed over the issue of Everett being back home and how I was handling it. I told her I was fine, that it was no big deal, that we were reestablishing our friendship and that was it. I wasn't ready to open up to one of the most important people in my life, whose opinion I value above all others, and have her tell me what a fool I was. Whether she thought I was a fool for never saying anything to Everett, or a fool for thinking we could cross this line of friendship and not ruin everything. Either way, I wasn't ready to hear it, but now I need to hear it. I need to know I'm doing the right thing.

After what happened here in the tent yesterday, I haven't been able to stop thinking about what's going to happen next. I haven't been able to stop thinking about the way Everett held me, the way he looked at me, and the way I was seconds away from kissing him before we were interrupted. I'd never wanted anything more in my life, and I was scared to death about what he would do after I opened up to him and told him how I couldn't live without him, and hadn't been happy here at the camp with him gone.

I haven't seen Everett since we parted ways on the porch yesterday, but I finally got a text from him this morning, telling me he had things to take care of and he'd see me at the dinner. I hate that we didn't get our alone time last night, and I didn't get to share the excitement of this whole Stratford charade finally being over, but I knew it would all be worth it when he finally gets here.

"I thought for sure you and Grady would be out on the dance floor, wrapped up in each other by now," my mother says, pulling me from my thoughts and making me look over at her like she's crazy.

"Grady? Why in the hell would Grady be here?"

"Oh, my bad. I mean, the two of you have been dancing around each other for months. After Aiden died, I just thought... I really liked him from the few times I met him when he stopped by to pick you up, and he comes from a very nice family. I thought you really liked him, too, but you were just afraid to let yourself fall in love again," she explains.

"I *was* afraid to let myself fall in love again, but not with him. With Everett," I whisper.

The shock on her face couldn't be more evident. Her mouth drops open and her eyes widen as she shakes her head at me.

"But... Everett? Really? I mean, I always wondered if he had a thing for you, but I never thought you felt the same. He was always such a troubled young man and then he leaves and doesn't even come home for Aiden's funeral. I'm sorry, Cameron, I just don't trust him."

It takes everything in me not to yell at my mother and cause a scene in front of everyone. I take a step closer to her and speak with barely concealed anger and disappointment.

"Didn't your own mother hate Dad so much that she had him sent off to war, where he was tortured for five years and almost killed? You should understand what it's like to be unfairly judged. Please, don't fault him for the things he did when he was younger. You don't know anything about him now. You don't know how much he went through helping all those people overseas or the kinds of horrors he saw. You don't know how much he struggles every day not to break down from those memories," I tell her, taking a minute to swallow back my tears before I continue.

My mother and I look so much alike that we're often

confused for sisters instead of mother and daughter. She has the same long, strawberry blond hair, the same piercing green eyes with thick lashes, the same slim build and long legs. Suddenly, I don't feel like I'm looking in a mirror when I look at her. I see sadness and regret on her face when I know mine is filled with anger and indignation on Everett's behalf.

"This camp is still able to stay open because of *him* and what he did for me. He put his life on hold for *me*. He spent every waking moment of the last few weeks doing whatever he could so that the dream you and Dad started could keep going. I've been in love with him since I was thirteen years old. I thought I had it under control, I thought I had grown up and moved on, and then suddenly he's back, and all of those same feelings, all of those same wants and needs, are screaming at me to do something about it. To finally tell him how I feel, how I've *always* felt, and hope to God he feels the same way, because I can't do this without him. I can't breathe without him." I choke on a sob as my mother quickly closes the distance and wraps her arms around me.

She rocks me back and forth in her arms as I swipe the tears from my cheeks and get myself under control.

"I'm sorry. Oh, baby girl, I'm so sorry. You're right. You're absolutely right. I'm an idiot and a hypocrite and you have every right to be pissed at me," she says, pulling back to help me wipe a stray tear off my cheek. "My mother kept me away from your father and it was one of the darkest times in my life. I swore I'd never do that to you. I swore I'd never judge anyone who wanted to love you and cherish you. I guess I'm just in shock. I always saw the way *he* looked at *you*, but never the other way around. You are my whole world, Cameron. You are a piece of my heart, living and breathing outside of my body, and I just don't want you to get hurt. I saw what his leaving did to you all those years ago, and I just don't want you to ever hurt like that again."

Her explanation makes me feel better. At least now I know that she doesn't actually hate Everett; she's just worried for me.

"I know. I don't want to get hurt like that again either, and you just have to trust that I know what I'm doing. Sort of," I tell her with a small laugh and a deep breath. "I was good at hiding the way I felt about Everett for a long time, but I'm tired of hiding. The camp is going to be fine, I just don't know if I am. Were you afraid to tell Dad how you felt when you were younger?" I ask her, staring out at the sea of people laughing and enjoying the food and music all around us.

"Terrified," she laughs. "Telling him gave him power. The power to love me back more fiercely than I'd ever known, or the power to break me harder than anything I'd ever suffered before."

She turns back to face me, pressing her hands against either side of my face.

"No one gets anywhere in life without taking risks, baby girl. What scares you more? Telling him how you feel and getting rejected, or keeping it to yourself and spending the rest of your life wondering?"

"I'm tired of wondering. I can't do it anymore," I whisper, staring up at the soft smile on her face.

"Then you have your answer. Telling your dad I was in love with him was like jumping off a cliff. Scary and exciting all at the same time. Take the leap. From everything you've said about him, I have a feeling he'll be there to catch you when you land."

She leans toward me and gives me a kiss on the cheek, then walks away in search of my father. There's a crowd of people, but some of them are moving to the dance floor, and

I have a clear view of the opposite side of the tent, where the main doorway is leading into the dinner. My heart stutters in my chest when I see Everett walk inside the tent.

It's been a long time since I've seen him in something other than jeans or shorts and a T-shirt, and I'd almost forgotten how breathtakingly handsome he is dressed up. Since this year's event has a more relaxed dress code, I made sure everyone invited knew that tuxedos and ball gowns were not necessary like in previous years. As much as I would have liked to see Everett in a tuxedo again, watching him walk into the room in a pair of straight-leg black pants, white button-down with the sleeves pushed up to his elbows, and a pair of black and white striped suspenders was enough to keep my jaw permanently dropped open and my mouth watering. All of the facial hair I'd been fantasizing about feeling against my skin has been groomed neatly and I can't wait to feel it against my body.

My feet automatically start moving, taking me in his direction, needing to be close to him, needing to put my hands on him and needing to feel his arms around me. I come to a stuttering stop when all of a sudden the fantasy standing across the room starts to fade away.

"Uh-oh. You were looking all dreamy there for a second, and now you look like someone killed your dog. What happened?" Amelia asks, coming up next to me.

I shake my head back and forth as tears fill my eyes and everything in my line of sight gets blurry. I know I should look away, but I can't.

Amelia's head turns in the direction I'm staring and she lets out a string of curses that under normal circumstances would make me laugh. But nothing about this is funny at all. Nothing about what I'm looking at is amusing.

"Who in the hell is *that* skank, and why is she draped all

over Everett?" she asks, watching the train wreck happening right in front of our eyes.

I want to pretend like this isn't really happening. Like Everett didn't just walk into this charity dinner with a tall redhead who has her arms wrapped around his shoulders, and her mouth pressed against his ear as she whispers something in it. Maybe she's just a guest, saw how good he looks, and thought she'd give it a shot. Any minute now he'll politely turn her down and untangle himself from her, meeting my eyes and giving me a sheepish smile as he walks toward me.

But that doesn't happen. One of his arms slides around her slim waist, holding her against his side as they continue moving through the crowd of people, stopping every few feet to say hello to someone.

My sleeveless satin rockabilly dress in emerald green to match my eyes, with a plunging V-neck to show off my ample cleavage and a black satin belt around the waist, which I picked out specifically with Everett in mind, suddenly seems silly and hideous compared to the skin-tight white tube top dress the woman on Everett's arm is wearing, which shows off every curve. My long blond hair, which I took two hours to put soft curls in, with a few pieces in front pulled back into tiny braids and woven through the curls, suddenly feels childish and nowhere near as sexy as the poker-straight fire-engine red locks that hang down the woman's back.

"Okay, so he brought a date. I mean, it's not exactly the end of the world. It's not like you looked him right in the eye and told him you were in love with him. We can fix this," Amelia reassures me.

The tears in my eyes start to spill out onto my cheeks, and I shake my head back and forth when I remember the words Everett said to me back when we were teenagers.

The one thing I held on to all these years and always gave me hope.

"This place is special to me. It got me through one of the hardest times in my life. I'd never bring a girl here who wasn't special. Who didn't mean as much to me as this place does."

Either he lied to me back then, or he's had someone special in his life all this time, and I was just too stupid to realize it. Too wrapped up in my own problems and my own fantasies to even ask him if he had someone. I want to be angry. I want to storm over there and scream at him. Ask him what the hell he's been doing with me the last few weeks if this was going to be the final result. Why flirt with me, why look at me like he wanted me and needed me and touch me like he meant it?

"It's too late," I tell Amelia in a small, broken voice. "He said he'd never bring someone here who wasn't special to him. I always wished, all these years, that the reason why he never brought a girl here was because the one who was the most special to him was already here."

I laugh, but the sound comes out cracked and not at all filled with humor.

"God, I'm such an idiot," I mutter, the tears falling fast and hard now as I start to back away from Amelia, unable to take my eyes off of Everett and the woman he's holding close to his side, no matter how much it hurts.

"Cameron, wait. Don't leave," Amelia begs.

I don't listen to her. I can't stay here. I turn with my head down so none of the people standing around us can see the misery on my face, and make my way out of the tent into the steadily falling rain.

I took the leap.

I jumped.

But he wasn't there to catch me.

Chapter 30

EVERETT

Everything is a mess.

Starting with having someone who isn't Cameron, with her body pressed up against me and her arms around my shoulders. It makes me cringe and it takes everything in me not to shove her off of me. She doesn't feel the same, she doesn't smell the same, and her hot breath in my ear giggling and whispering how drunk she is solidifies that fact. I have to wrap my arm around her waist as we move into the room just so she doesn't stumble and fall in those fucking six-inch heels she's wearing and make a fool out of herself.

I'm going to kill my brother for saddling me with his date because he was tied up at work. Why he decided to tell her to meet him at my house is beyond me, and I had no choice but to agree to his pathetic begging on the phone when he called to say he was running late. It was either bring her to the dinner so he could meet us here later, or stand in my kitchen half the night and continue watching her drink herself into a coma with the bottle of tequila she pulled out of her purse after I let her in the door.

Right now, I'm wishing I would have let her continue drinking and left her passed out on my couch. I have too much on my mind to worry about making sure this woman doesn't throw up on someone's shoes or fall down in the middle of the dance floor.

In the span of twenty-four hours, my life went to shit and I have no one to blame but myself. I'm an idiot. Such a fucking idiot.

After getting that text from Bobby, hightailing it out of camp and getting him off the ledge of wanting to take a drink, I wanted nothing more than to get back to Cameron and pick up where we'd left off, hating that I had to walk away from her when we were right on the edge of something, but I couldn't let that guy down, and I knew she'd understand. Then I got back to camp, I saw her crying over Aiden, and it all blew up in my face.

"Hey, asshole. Who's the skank?"

My head jerks to the side to find Amelia standing next to me, shooting daggers at the woman still plastered to my side.

"I'm Bethany!" she chirps, holding her hand out toward Amelia, too drunk to realize she was just insulted.

"Don't care," Amelia tells her in a bored voice, ignoring Bethany's outstretched hand and turning her angry eyes to mine.

"Sorry I'm late. What did I miss?"

Jason appears on the other side of Bethany, and she immediately unwraps her arms from around my shoulders and throws herself at my brother, causing him to stumble backward a few steps before bracing himself and the woman teetering on her heels of death by placing his hands on her hips to steady her swaying body.

"You missed about a gallon of tequila shooters," I tell him. "You owe me so big right now it's not even funny."

Jason laughs, but the smile on his face quickly dies when he notices Amelia standing on the other side of me.

"Wait. This is *your* date?" she asks him, putting her hands on her hips and glaring at him.

"I…um…well…" Jason stutters, trying to untangle himself from Bethany, who isn't so much holding on to him because she wants to, but because she has to.

"Would it have killed you to ask *me* if I wanted to be your date?" Amelia asks in annoyance as Jason continues standing here staring at her with his mouth wide open. "Forget it. I'll deal with *you* later."

She looks away from my brother and his drunk date to point at me.

"You. Come with me."

She whirls around and stomps off, and I decide to follow her when I hear gagging noises coming from Bethany. Leaving my brother to deal with his own mess, I quickly move through the crowd of people until I catch up with Amelia standing by the opening of the tent opposite the main door I just came through.

"You are so lucky right now that woman was not really your date," Amelia tells me as soon as I get to her. "You're going to have to do a lot of groveling with Cameron, but I've got your back."

I have no idea what she's talking about, but the more she speaks, the angrier I get.

"I don't need you to have my back. I'm sure Cameron is fine."

Amelia's eyes narrow as she stares at me.

"You're sure Cameron's fine? Are you kidding me right now? I have never seen her so devastated as when you walked in that damn door with another woman on your arm. What the hell has gotten into you?" she asks.

"Maybe I finally realized I wasn't in the mood to be her fucking rebound from Aiden!" I fire back, clenching my hands into fists when the truth of the words I just said hit me like a ton of bricks.

I feel sick to my stomach saying something like that out loud, but now that it's out, I can't take it back. I hate myself for being so damn jealous of my best friend, but I can't help it. It hurts everything inside of me that he got what I'd always wanted, and will never have.

Her mouth opens and closes like a fish out of water and I angrily shove my hands into the front pockets of my pants. I don't want to have this discussion right now, especially with Amelia. She has no idea what's going on and she'd never understand.

"You're a goddamn idiot," she finally mutters, shaking her head at me.

"Excuse me?"

"You heard me. You, are a goddamn *idiot!*" she tells me, her voice rising, not giving a shit if people in our general vicinity can hear her.

"You could never, in a million years, be Cameron's rebound from Aiden."

"Really?" I scoff. "And why is that?"

She takes a step closer to me and lowers her voice, the anger suddenly gone from it and replaced with sincerity.

"Because Aiden was always her rebound from *you*. You goddamn idiot," she says again with a sigh. "And really, you can't even call what she had with him a rebound. Three dates in the span of two weeks right after you left, each one more awkward and weird than the last, until they finally realized it was a dumb idea. And don't even get me started on the guy she dated in high school that she ran into after Aiden died. She keeps that guy so far at arm's length it's a wonder he can even hear her when she speaks. Jesus, do you two *ever* talk about anything even remotely important?"

What the hell is happening right now? There's no way what she's saying is true. No fucking way.

"They were in love. He was getting ready to propose. Aiden told me that himself and she still wears his fucking ring on her finger," I reply lamely, my heart beating faster and my body breaking out into a cold sweat.

"Uh, they definitely were *not* in love," Amelia laughs. "Cameron was heartbroken and lonely after you left, and Aiden wanted to get laid. The farthest he got was trying to hold her hand at dinner at a fancy restaurant and she freaked out and yanked it away, knocking over an entire bottle of wine, which spilled onto his lap. Two weeks later, she introduced him to a single mother here at camp, and he fell head over heels in love with her and her daughter. He proposed to *her* a few months before he died. Yeah, that ring she wears was from Aiden. It was a birthday present from him."

No, no, no. This is not happening. This can't be happening. Why in the hell didn't he tell me? Why didn't he come right out and say he was in love with someone other than Cameron and that he was going to marry someone other than Cameron?

I'm pissed at Aiden for all of thirty seconds. Half a minute is all it takes for my anger to morph into guilt. He never told me, because I never asked. I never once asked him for more details. I never once asked him to tell me all about the woman he was in love with, because I assumed it was Cameron. I knew he'd asked her out right after I left, and I couldn't handle knowing anything about it. I couldn't stand hearing all of the details about what was happening between them. Imagining everything they were doing together was bad enough; I was the worst friend in the world, all because I couldn't see anything through my jealousy. I stayed away for four years because I couldn't handle coming home and seeing Cameron happy with someone who wasn't me, even if he was my best friend.

"And if you're still doubting things, take a look around you, my friend. Anything look familiar?" Amelia asks.

I finally take the time to look around the tent and all the air in my lungs rushes out of me like someone punched me in the stomach.

Red, purple, and green decorations brighten every inch of the tent, magnolia blossoms sit on every table, people walk by with plates heaping with barbecued brisket, and going by the mouthwatering smell alone, I know it's from Lewis's. The band that's been playing at the far end of the tent suddenly catches my eye, and my hands start to shake when I realize who it is that's playing.

"Like I said, you've got a lot of groveling to do," Amelia reminds me. "The last thing Cameron said before she walked out of here was something about how you once told her you'd never bring a girl here who wasn't as special to you as this camp was. I've forgiven you now that I know she wasn't *your* date, but Cameron is going to be a whole other story. I'm not kidding you when I say I've never seen that woman so devastated."

She filled this place with everything I told her I'd missed when I was overseas. She did this for me, and I devastated her.

Jesus, I'm a fucking idiot.

"She went that way, heading towards the stables," Amelia tells me, pointing behind her to the opening of the tent.

I don't even take the time to thank her. I take off running out into the rain, splashing through puddles, moving as quickly as I can across the lawn until I get to the stables. Shaking the rain off of me as I walk inside, my eyes roam around the dimly lit area in search of Cameron. The main overhead lights have been shut off for the night, and the only lights to see by are the strands of large lightbulbs hung from the rafters above my head.

Moving quickly down the long hallway, I pass by all of the horse stalls until the hallway opens up into a large tack room. My feet come to a stop when I see Cameron. Her back is to me and she's leaning her elbows on the railing of the gate that leads into the indoor arena, staring at the huge, empty room.

I watch her head drop forward and I hear her let out a sigh before she turns around to face me, and I realize she must have heard my footsteps pounding against the concrete as I made my way to her.

Nothing prepares me for what I see when she turns around. The green dress she's wearing is the most stunning thing I've ever seen, even though it's wet from the rain and the skirt is clinging to her thighs. Wet pieces of her long blond hair are stuck to her neck and her shoulders, and even though she's so beautiful standing here fresh from the rain, that's not what makes it so hard for me to breathe right now. Seeing the devastation Amelia told me about written all over her face, and the tears streaming down her cheeks, mixing with the splatters of rain that fell down on her, is what stabs a knife right through my heart.

Neither one of us says a word as I continue walking toward her and then stop again a few feet away.

"You were never in love with Aiden," I state in a low voice.

She looks at me like I'm insane before angrily swiping the tears off her cheeks.

"What? No. Of course I was never in love with Aiden. Are you serious right now?"

I nod, taking another step forward.

"Did you really mean it when you said you didn't know how to be happy without me here? That you didn't know how to live without me?" I ask.

Her eyes narrow and she crosses her arms in irritation in front of her.

"You're an asshole. I can't believe you're asking me this. I can't believe what an *idiot* I was," she complains.

"Just answer the question. Did you mean it?"

She just shakes her head at me and I watch her cheeks flush with anger.

"Cameron, did you mean it?"

"OF COURSE I MEANT IT!" she finally shouts, throwing her hands up in the air.

I take another step toward her.

"But it doesn't matter, does it? None of it matters," she continues, the anger in her voice quickly replaced with a small sob that breaks my heart. "I asked you to give me a reason. Four years ago, I asked you to give me a reason and you didn't. You pushed me away and you left. And here we are, back where we started, and it's happening all over again. I'm making a fool of myself and making wishes that will never come true. You took yourself out of the game five years ago and now you're doing it again. I can't do this anymore, Everett. I can't play these games anymore."

I stare into her eyes. I watch the tears fall down her cheeks, and I know after this moment, there will never be any going back. I can't do this anymore either.

"It was never a game for me. Ever."

With one final step, I close the distance between us. In one quick move, I grab her face in my hands, pull her toward me, and slam my mouth against hers.

Chapter 31

CAMERON

I've seen my share of romantic movies. Read my fill of romantic books. I've heard the phrase *He devoured me* at least a hundred times, and I never understood it.

Until now.

Until the moment Everett grabs my face and crashes his lips against mine.

Until I open my mouth on a gasp and his tongue immediately pushes inside.

He completely devours me, pushing his tongue harder against mine, forcing my head to change position so he can deepen the kiss. He breathes me in and I let him. I give him everything I have because this moment...this moment is everything. This kiss is everything.

I clutch the front of his shirt in my fists and pull his body closer, needing more. Needing the heat of him to warm me from the outside in. I know I should push him away. I know I should question why the hell he suddenly decided to kiss me and I know I should ask him about the woman he brought with him tonight. I've been cold for so long, I've been wanting this for so long, it almost feels like a dream, and right now, I just don't care about anything else. I don't have space in my head to think about anything else but finally feeling Everett's mouth on mine.

When he drops one hand from the side of my face and wraps it around my waist, yanking me roughly against him, I stop thinking altogether. His arm tightens around me and my feet suddenly leave the ground. I throw my arms over his shoulders and cling to him as I feel myself being turned, my tongue swirling around his. My back hits the wall next to us and he pushes his body against mine until I can feel every inch of him from chest to stomach to thigh, pressing into me as he continues punishing me with his lips and tongue.

I wrap one of my legs around the back of his, using the muscles in my thigh to pull him closer. He bends his knees and pushes up, and I tighten my arms around his shoulders to bring my other leg up around his waist. I moan around his tongue when I feel him between my thighs, so hard and full of need for me. Both of his hands move to my bare thighs, sliding up under the damp skirt of my dress until he's clutching my ass in his hands, pulling me harder against his cock straining inside his pants. I move my hips, sliding myself against him, needing to feel more...so much more.

He suddenly tears his mouth away from mine, and I let out a little whimper, not ready for this to be over. I don't want him to stop. I don't want him to think about all the reasons why this could be a bad idea. I don't want to give him one second to regret what's happening between us.

Everett pulls his head back from mine just far enough to look into my eyes. I'm panting and out of breath, my heart is beating out of my chest, and I just want more. I don't care about breathing. I don't care about anything but having his lips back on mine.

One of his hands lets go of my ass and he brings it up between us, brushing away a few strands of wet hair that got stuck on my cheek during our kissing. He cups the side of my face in his warm palm, his thumb sliding back and forth over my cheek.

"She wasn't my date, she was Jason's," he says in a low voice, his eyes never leaving mine. "There has never, nor will there *ever* be, any other woman in this world more special to me than you."

The breath I was holding, waiting to see if he'd tell me this was a mistake, comes out in a flutter of air.

"I have never wanted any woman more than you. I have never *needed* any woman more than you. If you don't want this, if you don't feel the same, tell me right now and I'll walk away. Nothing will change between us, I promise. I don't want to lose you, Cameron, no matter what." He swallows thickly, his voice lowering to a whisper. "I can't lose you. Not again."

I just nod at him, afraid that if I open my mouth and speak, all of the emotions I'm feeling will turn me into a crying mess. Instead, I give him my answer by wrapping my hands around the back of his head and yanking his lips back to mine.

He groans into my mouth, and I can tell it's one filled with relief. I tighten my legs around his waist when he wraps both of his arms around me, lifting me up higher to walk us into a smaller tack room right next to the wall where we were leaning.

As soon as we get into the room, he kicks the door closed and my back is pressed up against hard wood once again. Our hands are everywhere all at once. With the lower half of his body pinning me to the door, his hands are free to roam. He pulls his mouth away from mine to watch himself touch me. He runs his hands over my bare shoulders and down over my breasts, cupping them in his hands and pushing them up, molding them his palms. I grab his suspenders and yank them off of his shoulders, before clutching the front of his white dress shirt and ripping it open, buttons popping off and pinging to the floor all around us.

I run my palms down the sides of his neck and shoulders, pushing his shirt off and down his arms until it falls to the floor. I move my hands over his pecs, feeling his heart thundering under my hand against the heat from his skin. His hands slide off my breasts and around to the back of my shoulders, clutching the thick straps of my dress in his fists.

"Are you attached to this dress?" he asks.

"Not at all."

The words barely leave my mouth when I hear a *rip*, and he tears the dress off me, splitting it right down the back until the straps fall off my shoulders and it drops down to my waist, leaving me completely bare to him from the waist up.

He quickly grabs the demolished dress, yanks it out from between us, and tosses it to the side.

"Jesus, Cameron. You're so fucking beautiful," he whispers as his eyes trail over my naked breasts and back up to my face.

He rests one of his hands flat against the door next to my head, and I watch his eyes, staring down as his other hand presses against my chest bone. He slowly drags it down until he's cupping the weight of my naked breast in his hand, rubbing his thumb back and forth over my nipple.

A low moan escapes me as I continue watching him stare

at what he's doing to me. His eyes darken and his lips part with a sigh and I feel pulsing, wet heat between my thighs as he gently rubs his thumb over my hardened nipple.

I've never felt need this strong. I've never wanted to come with just a man's hand on my breast, but I know it has everything to do with Everett. With the way he's looking at me and the way I've dreamed about this moment almost my entire life.

Reaching between our bodies, I quickly unbuckle his belt and unzip his pants, needing more. Needing to touch him and feel him in my hand. Needing *everything* this man can give me.

"Bed," he mutters, looking away from me long enough to glance over his shoulder at the small, twin-sized bed in the corner of the room, used for stable hands in case of an emergency with a sick horse or a mare about ready to give birth.

I push my hand inside the elastic waistband of his boxer briefs and wrap my fingers around his hardness, squeezing it before sliding my palm up and down his length.

"Fuck," he groans, his forehead dropping forward against mine and his hips jerking as I continue pumping my hand up and down him.

Moving my head to the side, I press my cheek against his and my lips by his ear.

"I don't need a bed. I just need you. Right here, right now," I whisper, rubbing my thumb over the wetness that has gathered on the tip of him.

His hands drop from the door and my breast, and his slides his fingers into the edge of my lace thong at my hip. Another *rip* sounds in the room as he tears them off of me, chucking them to the side to land on top of my ruined dress.

We stare into each other's eyes as we work together to

push his pants and boxers down just far enough for him to pull his cock out, wrap his hand around the base, and line it up with my entrance.

He slides the tip of himself through my wetness, rubbing it against me until my eyelids flutter closed and my head thumps back against the door. I'm so wet for him, so full of anticipation and need that I feel crazy with it. My hands go back behind his head and I clutch a handful of his short hair. I rock my hips against him, the muscles in my thighs burning as I cling to him tighter and pull him in closer.

I feel his mouth close to mine, just a butterfly kiss of his lips barely touching mine.

"Open your eyes and look at me," he demands, his warm breath skating over my lips.

I comply, and as soon as I do, as soon as I look into his eyes, he pulls his hips back and slams inside of me.

A strangled cry of pleasure flies from my mouth when I finally feel him inside of me, so hard and full, filling me so completely that I don't know how I survived without him like this for so long.

His hands go back to my ass, clutching it tightly, pulling me against him as he starts to move, thrusting roughly in and out of me. I lock my ankles behind his back and rock my body with him, pulling him in deeper. His lips are still just a featherlight touch against my own, and it makes everything hotter that he's not kissing me. That he's just looking into my eyes as he takes me against the door. The deep thrusting of him in and out of me, and the way his groin smacks against me each time he pushes inside, makes my legs start to shake and my hips move erratically as I race toward the release that's teetering right on the edge.

All of the blood in my body feels like it's rushing

through my veins and gathering between my legs. My clit pulses and throbs and aches with each slam of Everett's body against mine. He fucks me like he can't get enough of me, and I love that he doesn't feel the need to be gentle with me. After years of buildup and weeks of sexual tension, neither one of us needs to take it slow. We've been taking it slow for over twenty years. I need fast and hard. I need the smacking sounds of our sweaty bodies coming together echoing in my ears. I need to hear his muttered curses as he pushes as deep inside me as he can and holds himself still.

"Everett," I moan, my orgasm quickly working its way through me.

One of his hands moves from my ass and he cups my face in his palm as he starts moving again, making tight circles with his hips.

"Say it again. I need to hear you say my name when you come."

His words and the rubbing of his groin against my clit make my release explode out of me so quickly it almost takes my breath away.

"Everett, Everett, Everett," I pant with each breath I take as my body clenches around him, wave after wave of the most intense pleasure I've ever felt making me want to cling to him forever and never let go.

He growls against my mouth and starts moving again, thrusting and pumping roughly into me, chanting my name against my lips as he follows right behind me, slamming deep one last time as he comes.

I tighten my arms and legs around him as his body jerks against mine with the force of his release, until his body stills and he drops his head down to the crook of my neck. We stay like this for a long time, wrapped around each other, our chests pressed together as we try to catch our breath and slow down our racing hearts.

Everett was wrong when he said nothing will change between us.

This moment, right here . . . it changes everything.

And it's about damn time.

Chapter 32

EVERETT

The morning sun starts to shine through the small window above the bed, and I realize I've been awake for hours, just lying on my side with my elbow on the mattress and my head in my hand, staring at the woman next to me.

After everything that happened between us last night, I wanted nothing more than to lock Cameron in this tack room and never leave, but I knew she had responsibilities. Sneaking back to the guest house under the cover of night in the rain might have been the most fun I've had in a while. Listening to her curse at me as we dodged puddles and ran between trees and bushes so no one would see us while she unsuccessfully tried to keep her ripped dress around her body had me laughing at her expense more than once.

After she threw on a clean dress that wasn't ripped to shreds, fixed her hair, and reapplied her makeup, we went back to the charity dinner, where we spent the night on opposite sides of the room, much to my disappointment. I wanted to drag her into a corner and make out with her or pull her out into the middle of the dance floor, wrap my arms around her as we swayed to the music and feel her body pressed up to mine, and reassure myself that this was real and not a dream.

Watching her walk around the room all night, smiling and talking to people, thanking them for their donations and for attending the dinner was almost as good. And she made it up to me as soon as the night was over by dragging me back here to this room and letting me rip the second dress of the night off of her in record time.

With my eyes still on Cameron as she sleeps, I wonder how in the hell I got here, and how I got so fucking lucky.

She's on her stomach with her arms above her head, turned away from me, her blond hair spilling all around the pillow. I run the tips of my fingers gently down her spine, staring at the skin of her bare back as I move my fingers all the way down to her lower back, where the sheet pools around her waist.

I've been running everything that happened between us last night through my mind, and I still can't believe it's real. I can't believe she didn't push me away when I kissed her, I can't believe she let me put my hands on her, I can't believe she let me inside of her body, and I can't believe I didn't feel like I was finally home until she did.

Jesus, we wasted so much time. *I* wasted so much time with my head up my ass and jealousy coursing through me, when I should have just been honest with her from the very beginning.

Cameron lets out a soft moan and I flatten my hand against her lower back as she arches her body and stretches her arms out straight before turning her head on the pillow to face me.

Sliding my hand up her back, I move the tangles of her hair off her shoulder.

"How long have you been awake?" she asks, her voice raspy and still full of sleep.

I trail the tips of my fingers over her forehead, tracing over one perfectly sculpted eyebrow and down her cheek, before running my thumb over her full bottom lip.

"Long enough to know you talk in your sleep," I reply, chuckling softly when she rolls her eyes at me.

"I do not talk in my sleep."

"Then it must have been one of the horses whispering, '*Everett, Everett, oh, Everett!*'" I say, laughing again when she smacks my hand away from her mouth.

I watch her cheeks heat with embarrassment, and I scoot my body closer to her on the bed, resting my hand on her hip and pushing gently so she rolls to her side to face me.

"Hottest thing I've ever heard," I whisper, staring at her mouth when her tongue darts out to wet her bottom lip.

"No regrets now that the sun is up?" she asks.

I can see the worry written all over her face, and I hate it. I hate that after what happened between us last night, she still has doubts about me and how I feel, but it's my own fault. I was too stubborn for so long that I couldn't even see what was right in front of me. I couldn't even fathom that she might feel the same, and I was too fucking scared to say anything, worried that I might lose her. And yet I lost her anyway. I pushed her away, and I have no idea how she could have ever forgiven me.

"I have a million regrets when it comes to you, but not one of them has anything to do with what happened last night," I reassure her.

Her hand comes up from resting on the bed between us, and she presses her palm against the side of my face.

"Why didn't you ever say anything?" she whispers.

"Which time?" I ask with a small smile. "When you were fourteen and I was seventeen and you came waltzing into the stables while I was working and gave me the worst case of blue balls I'd ever experienced? Or when you were fifteen and I was eighteen and you got drunk up in the treehouse and I came up with a hundred different reasons why I couldn't kiss you? Or how about when you were eighteen and I was twenty-one and you were dating that douche bag Grady Stevens and I wanted to rip his arm from his socket and beat the shit out of him with it when he put his hands on you? Or last night, when Amelia told me you ran into him a few months ago and started seeing him again, and I wanted to hunt him down, rip his arm from his socket, and beat the shit out of him with it all over again?"

Her eyes widen in shock, and I inch my body even closer to hers on the mattress, sliding my hand over her hip and around her back to tug her toward me.

"I was an idiot for a long time, Cameron. Longer than I'd like to admit. I regret every minute I spent with you that I never told you how I felt. I regret every time I was close enough to kiss you and never had the guts to do it," I tell her, making sure she knows without a shadow of a doubt that I'm serious about this. About us. About everything that's happening now and everything that will happen going forward.

I watch her eyes fill with tears, and she quickly squeezes them closed, letting out a small, shaky sigh before opening them again to look at me.

"You're not the only idiot in the room right now. I should have said something, too, but I was scared."

Moving my hand off her waist, I bring it between us and press my palm against the side of her cheek.

"What were you scared of?" I ask softly.

"That you wouldn't feel the same and it would ruin our friendship. That you'd laugh at me and think I was pathetic for having feelings for you all these years. Maybe if I had said something sooner, you wouldn't have thought all this time that I was in love with Aiden. It kills me that you stayed away because of that."

With a sigh, I drop my hand from her cheek, slide it back around her waist, and pull her closer.

"We both made mistakes. You can't take all of the blame. I should have asked Aiden more questions every time he bragged about being in love. I should have told him a long time ago I had feelings for you, but I was afraid if I ever said it out loud, my wishes would never come true, and you're the only thing I've ever wished for," I tell her.

"That was the cheesiest thing you've ever said," she replies, lightening the deep mood I just threw us in by smiling up at me. "If you'd said that eleven years ago, I probably wouldn't have given my virginity to Grady Stevens, or made the poor guy my booty call the last few months when I was lonely and sad because I still wished it had been you."

A low growl rumbles through my chest, and my arm gets even tighter around her body. I had a feeling she lost her virginity to that asshole, but now that I know for sure, I want to kill him. That thought pisses me off more than knowing she'd been sleeping with him again. It's not like I'd exactly been a saint myself while I was away from her all these years.

"You're going to pay for that," I mutter.

She rolls away from me onto her back, sliding her hands behind her head, and gives me a mischievous smile.

"And how exactly do you plan on punishing me?" she asks in a low, seductive voice.

Jesus Christ she's beautiful.

With her hands behind her head, her tits are on full display for my eyes. Her gorgeous pink nipples are hard and begging for my mouth.

Pulling my arm out from under her body, I trail my hand over her hip, and stomach, inching it down beneath the sheet until I'm cupping her. The tip of my middle finger teases her opening and I stare down at her in awe that she's already wet for me. In awe that she's naked in bed next to me. Completely amazed that I can touch her like this after so many years of dreaming about it.

"Last night was too fast. I want to take my time now."

I don't give her a chance to respond; I just slowly inch one finger inside of her tight, wet heat until I'm as deep as I can go.

"It wasn't too fast. It was . . . perfect," she sighs, her words stuttering out of her when I curl my finger inside her and press my thumb against her clit. "Both times were perfect."

I leisurely drag my finger in and out of her, and her hips start to rock against my hand. I torture her by not going any faster, doing exactly what I told her I wanted to do by taking my time. I stare down at her, refusing to look anywhere else. I want to take my time and memorize everything. I don't want to miss one single second of this moment.

I never want to forget how she looks with her back arched and her head thrown back on the pillow, her hands clenching the sheets down by her sides when I push a second finger inside of her. I never want to forget the flush blossoming over her chest and brightening her cheeks as I rub my thumb over her clit each time I thrust my fingers between her parted thighs. I never want to forget the way she bites down on her bottom lip as I work my hand between her legs.

Last night was hurried and amazing, taking her up against

the door the first time and on the floor the second time because we couldn't even get two steps inside the room without ripping each other's clothes off again, but I missed all of this. I missed the beauty of watching her come apart slowly in my hands.

Her hips start moving faster, pulling my fingers inside her harder and deeper. I watch her lips part and my cock feels like it's going to explode when she moans my name as I drag my fingers out of her, pulling her wetness up to circle the pads of my fingers around her clit.

"Oh, God. Don't stop. Don't stop," she begs, her hips jerking against my hand.

How in the hell did I ever live so long without experiencing this?

How the fuck will I ever be able to function going forward now that I have?

One of her hands lets go of its hold on the sheet and she brings it up to wrap it around the back of my head, pulling me down toward her until our foreheads are touching.

I listen to every whimper she makes, pay attention to every jerk of her hips, and learn everything I can about her body and what makes her feel good. I alternate between pumping my fingers in and out of her, slow and deep, and bringing them back up to circle around her clit, soft and gentle.

I take my time.

I memorize the feel of her clenching around me.

I memorize her swollen clit as it pulses under my fingertips.

I memorize the breathy way she says my name and begs for more, not afraid or embarrassed about her wants and needs.

I pull my head back so I can watch her better, memorizing everything about this moment.

"Everett...Everett," she pants, her hips thrusting harder as I pick up the speed, circling my fingers faster.

"Let go, baby," I whisper, pushing my fingers inside of her and holding them deep, using my thumb to continue the soft friction against her clit.

She arches her back harder, her body suspended above the bed, as she does what I told her and lets go. Her hands are clutching so tightly to the hair at the back of my head that I'm sure she's pulling out a few strands, but it's worth the pain as I watch her orgasm wash over her and she screams my name.

The flush across her chest gets darker and I feel her clench tightly around my fingers, her clit throbbing with her release as I keep lightly brushing my thumb back and forth, pulling every ounce of pleasure out of her body.

She finally collapses back against the mattress, her chest heaving with quick puffs of breath, and I slowly pull my fingers from her body.

I memorize the way her eyes flutter open and she stares up at me.

I memorize the way she gives me a lazy smile, and starts sliding her fingers through the hair on top of my head as I position myself between her legs.

I memorize the way she smells and the feel of the heat from her body as I slowly push inside of her.

I memorize it all, knowing that everything has changed between us, knowing that there's no going back to being just friends, as her legs wrap around my waist and her arms drape over my shoulders, pulling me closer.

And cursing myself a thousand times for not doing this sooner.

Chapter 33

CAMERON

You need to have a talk with him. He can't keep stomping around here, muttering to himself and glaring at Everett every time they're in the same room," I tell my mom with a frustrated sigh.

She laughs, pushing her toe against the floor of the porch and gently rocking the porch swing we're seated on that hangs in front of the main house.

"Baby girl, he's your father. And he saw his daughter half dressed, walking out of a room with a man not wearing a shirt. Give him some time to not have that image burned in his brain."

Okay, so walking out of the tack room in the stables last week and coming face-to-face with my dad wasn't my finest moment. Wearing my second dress from the previous night that was ripped to shreds all the way down the back just like the first one, and Everett standing behind me shirtless, because I'd been wearing his white dress shirt at the time to cover myself as best as possible, on top of my hair being a tangled mess and my makeup smudged under my eyes, it was more than obvious what the two of us had been doing in that room the night before. And the following morning.

But I'm thirty years old. Too old for my dad to be looking at Everett like he wants to kill him all the time.

Regardless of that, I can't stop the smile that takes over my face as I look out over the grounds and think about the last week with Everett.

I was irritated when he first showed back up in my life because he fit so perfectly in it. And now we fit so perfectly *together*, it's hard to believe it's only been a week.

"It's good to see you happy again and to have you prove me wrong about Everett. He's a good man and he cares about you a great deal," my mom says softly. "Your dad is going to see it for himself soon enough, don't worry," she reassures me.

"I'm not worried. Is that weird? I mean, Everett and I crossed a huge line. We went from being best friends all of our lives, to not speaking for four years, to sort-of-friends, to this. It all happened so fast that my head should be spinning, but it's not," I tell her.

"I think thirty years of knowing someone is the exact opposite of going fast," she laughs. "You took the long way to get here, but it was the right way. You had to experience all of it—the longing, the pain, the heartbreak, the confusion, and the anger to appreciate what you have now. I don't think the two of you would be where you are now if either one of you had admitted your feelings sooner. You had to experience being apart to realize you're better together."

I let her words sink in, knowing everything she says is true, even though I can't stop wondering what would have happened if we hadn't been so afraid to say something about how we felt to each other sooner. Everett might not have stayed away for four years, repeatedly signing back up for Doctors Without Borders just to stay away from me and what he thought was happening between Aiden and me, and beat himself up with guilt about not being here when Aiden died. We might not have wasted so many years apart, when we could have been spending them together, where we fit so perfectly.

I hear the crunch of tires and look up to see a cloud of dust surrounding Everett's truck as he pulls down the driveway and parks in the turnaround in front of the house. My mom pushes herself off the swing, leans down, and gives me a kiss on the cheek before pulling back to stare down at me.

"I can see the wheels turning. Stop running all the what-ifs through that pretty head of yours. You can't change the past, baby girl. You can only move forward and make different choices."

I watch her turn and walk toward the front door, greeting Everett with a smile and a wave as he pounds up the front steps. My eyes lock on to his and my heart flutters in my chest when he stalks across the porch and, without hesitation, grabs my face in his hands and bends down, pressing his lips to mine.

"You can't change the past... You can only move forward and make different choices."

My mom's words play on a loop in my head as Everett kisses me softly, his tongue sliding past my lips and swirling with mine.

I don't know if I'll ever stop being sad about the choices we made in the past, but I can't help being deliriously happy about the ones we've made now that have gotten us to this point.

Everett ends the kiss, pulling his head back from mine to smile down at me.

"Hey."

"Hey, yourself," I reply, returning his smile as he sits down next to me on the swing and throws his arm over the back of it behind my shoulders. "How was lunch with your friend?"

Everett continues to go to weekly Alcoholics Anonymous meetings, and he got a phone call earlier from of the same guy who needed his help the night before the charity dinner. Everett took off immediately to meet him in person and convince him again not to take a drink to deal with his problems.

He spends all of his free time here at camp, either just being with me, or helping out wherever he's needed, and I know going to his meetings and hanging out with the friends he's made there gives him something to do and a sense of purpose, but it can't possibly be fulfilling enough for a man who traveled around the world, saving people's lives. I've mentioned to him a few times that he should apply for a position at the hospital downtown, and he'll smile and nod and tell me it's a good idea, but he's never done anything about it. I don't want him to get bored. I don't want him to regret coming home and leaving his work behind.

"Stressful. Exhausting. He was in a good place when I left him, but it took a while to get him there. I just want to take a shower and pass out facedown in bed."

Wrapping my arms around his waist, I curl up into his side, resting my cheek on his shoulder.

"Poor baby. I was going to suggest I hop in the shower with you, but if you're too tired..." I trail off.

I almost topple over on the swing when Everett jumps up, grabbing my hands and pulling me up with him.

"Did I say exhausted? I meant exhilarated. Hurry up, let's go before your dad realizes I'm here and silently threatens to kill me," Everett jokes.

He laughs, but the smile on his face doesn't quite reach his eyes. I know my dad's behavior has been bothering him, and it pisses me off. Everett has been a part of this family since he was three years old. If anything, my dad should be happy that I'm with someone I've been around all my life instead of someone I just met that he doesn't know. My mom accepted the idea of the two of us together in the blink of an eye once she started getting to know Everett again, and I don't understand why my dad isn't giving him the same chance.

I open my mouth to give him reassurance that I'm going to have a talk with my dad, when a car pulls up the drive and stops right in front of the house, turning my attention away from Everett to watch a woman exit the vehicle, grabbing a box out of the backseat before heading in our direction.

"Oh, my God," I mutter, butterflies flapping around in my stomach when I see who it is, happy to see her again, but knowing immediately she doesn't feel the same going by the scowl on her face, aimed right at me as she stops at the base of the stairs.

Everett immediately moves closer to me, wrapping his arm around my waist in a protective manner.

"Michelle," I whisper. "It's so good to see you. Everett, this is Michelle. Aiden's fiancée."

The tight hold Everett has on me slowly eases as he leans forward and holds out his hand to her.

Michelle ignores it, her angry eyes never leaving mine.

"I'm not here for a social visit. I just stopped by to give you your things. I found them at Aiden's place when I was cleaning it out."

She thrusts the box roughly into my chest, and I quickly wrap my arms around it when she lets go and takes a step back, crossing her own arms in front of her as I glance down and see one of my old sweatshirts, a coat, a pair of flip-flops, and a few other random things I'd left behind at Aiden's whenever we hung out.

"Why don't you come inside. We can have some iced tea and talk. I've missed you, and Abby," I tell her, thinking about her ten-year-old daughter, whom I fell in love with when she started attending camp a few years ago, and haven't seen at all since Aiden's funeral.

"Oh, save it, Cameron. Like you ever gave a shit about either one of us," she says with a roll of her eyes. "I don't even know why you introduced me to Aiden when you just wanted him for yourself."

It's the same thing she accused me of after Aiden's funeral, and the reason we haven't talked since then, but her words are still like a knife to the heart. She was my friend. There was no one happier than me when I got to watch her and my best friend fall in love, and it broke my heart that Michelle finally found happiness after her husband was killed overseas, only to have it ripped away from her again.

"Michelle, you know that's not true. Aiden was my friend. I never wanted anything but for you guys to be happy. I'm so sorry you and Abby lost him."

Everett doesn't say anything, but his hand slides up my spine and cups the back of my neck, massaging it gently, silently giving me his comfort and support.

"Aiden was my second chance. I was finally able to be happy again after I lost my husband and you couldn't even let me have that. Do you have any idea how much it hurts to always come in second in your own fiancé's life, even when he was dying? I gave him everything, and it was never enough because I wasn't you. Perfect little Cameron, with her perfect little life. He worshipped you and you just ate it up. He followed you around like a puppy, even more so after you started getting those stupid letters. Canceling plans with me and Abby just to make sure nothing happened to pathetic little Cameron," she sneers, venom filling her voice.

"What letters?" Everett finally asks.

Michelle looks away from me to smile unkindly at Everett.

"Oh, didn't you know? Poor Cameron was being threatened. My fiancé gave up time with me and my daughter for *her*. Because *she* always came first. *Her* safety was all that mattered. Even in the end, he didn't want me by his bedside, he wanted *her*," she states through clenched teeth, turning her murderous look in my direction. "You didn't even try to help. You didn't even care that it should have been *me* holding his hand when he died, telling him I loved him and giving him comfort."

Setting the box on the porch railing next to me, I take a step away from Everett toward Michelle, tears clouding my vision as I move down the stairs, wanting to wrap her in my arms and make her believe that none of what she's saying is true. I tried explaining to her several times why Aiden didn't want her there at the end, but she never believed me. She never understood that Aiden didn't want her last memories to be of the frail, weak patient he'd become, and not the strong, handsome man she fell in love with. It was one of the only arguments Aiden and I ever had when he was sick. Michelle deserved to be there, but he wouldn't hear of it. Just like he didn't want Everett to see him like that.

I pause halfway down the steps when she holds up her hands to stop me.

"Dry your tears, sweetheart. I don't need them, and I don't need any of your bullshit explanations. I just wanted to give you your stuff and tell you to stop trying to contact me. I don't want your phone calls, I don't want your texts, and I don't want you anywhere near me or my daughter."

With that, she turns and walks away, gets into her car, and peels down the driveway.

"Jesus, and I thought I was the jealous one," Everett mutters, making me smile through my tears like he always does.

"I thought she was my friend. I thought if I just kept trying to reach out to her, she'd be able to push aside her anger and grief enough to listen to me," I tell him.

He moves down a few steps to stand behind me, resting his hands on my shoulders and kissing the top of my head. He doesn't even need to say anything; just having him here is comfort enough.

Everett and I stand quietly on the porch, watching her drive away, until Amelia interrupts the moment, jogging across the front lawn and stopping at the base of the steps. She looks back over her shoulder at Michelle's car as it disappears down the driveway.

"Was that Michelle? Is she finally ready to talk to you?" Amelia asks, turning back around to face me and noticing the tears in my eyes. "I take it that's a no. I'm sorry, honey. She just needs more time."

I nod, swiping the tears off my cheeks, knowing that no amount of time will ever heal the pain and anger in Michelle's heart.

"Sorry to ruin your day even more, but another piece of fan mail came today," Amelia tells me sarcastically. "I was going to just put it in the file with the rest, but I wasn't sure if you wanted to look at it first."

With a sigh, I take the envelope she's holding in her outstretched hand, ripping it open and pulling the folded piece of paper out of it.

"What the fuck?" Everett mutters, leaning against my side to read over my shoulder.

You will regret ruining my life.

"It's nothing," I tell him, refolding the paper and shoving it back in the envelope before handing it back to Amelia. "Go ahead and file it with the others."

Amelia starts to take the envelop, but Everett quickly snatches it away.

"This isn't nothing, Cameron. This is serious. Is this what Michelle was talking about?"

The light, teasing voice and bright, shining eyes from just moments ago when he was joking about us showering together are long gone, as well as the silent comfort he gave me during Michelle's visit. Everett is clutching the envelope so hard in his fist that his knuckles are turning white.

"Everett, it's fine. We get letters like this all the time," I tell him, deciding to keep it to myself that we've never received ones quite this threatening before, considering how pissed off he is right now.

"What the hell do you mean you get letters like this all the time? Why the fuck didn't you tell me?" he growls through clenched teeth.

My need to keep him calm vanishes in a flash, I forget all about my hurt and sadness over Michelle's accusations, and I cross my arms angrily in front of me as I stare him down.

"Maybe because I knew you'd react just like this," I fire back, annoyed that he's making such a big deal about nothing.

"How the fuck do you expect me to react when I'm just now finding out that you've been getting threatened?!" he shouts.

"*Aaaaand* that's my cue to leave," Amelia mutters, slowly backing away from us. "Jason and I have dinner plans, so you two kids try and manage not to kill each other while I'm gone."

I don't even say good-bye to her, I'm too busy staring Everett down. And I'm too angry even to acknowledge the fact that Jason finally grew some balls and asked Amelia out. They've been joined at the hip since the day after the charity dinner, when Amelia gave him hell after helping him put his drunk date in a cab and sending her home.

I'll have plenty of time to be happy for my friend after I give Everett a piece of my mind.

"I need to go to the police with these. Make some calls and see what the fuck is going on. I can't believe you didn't tell me about this," he mutters, shaking his head and looking down at the letter still clutched tightly in his fist.

"Stop acting like a Neanderthal and like I don't know what I'm doing," I argue. "I didn't tell you about this because it's not that big of a deal. My parents had been getting letters like this long before I took over the camp. And in case you didn't notice, things have been a little crazy around here lately and it wasn't exactly at the top of my list of things we should discuss."

"Clearly you don't know what you're doing since the letters haven't stopped coming!" he shouts.

Before I say something I might regret, I turn and walk away from him, stomping down the steps as I go.

"Cameron!" Everett yells after me.

"Screw you!" I shout back as I keep walking.

It was bad enough that Aiden got overly protective of me when the notes became increasingly threatening, making Michelle hate me and think he loved me more. I can't change the past, but I can damn sure make different choices going forward. Like not letting Everett turn all alpha male and think I can't take care of myself.

Chapter 34

EVERETT

I find Cameron sitting on the end of the dock by the lake an hour later, with her legs dangling over the edge. Shoving my hands into the front pockets of my jeans, I start walking down the wooden planks toward her.

I probably shouldn't have let her walk away earlier, but I knew we both needed some time to cool off. I felt like a dick for losing it with her, but I couldn't help it. Something didn't sit right with me when I read that letter. Something tugged at the back of my mind when I read those words, but I couldn't figure out why. I reacted first without thinking. All I could imagine was something horrible happening to Cameron and it scared the shit out of me.

I walk right up to Cameron's side, pull my hands out of my pockets, and ease myself down next to her, hanging my legs down over the edge with her.

"I'm sorry. I was an asshole."

I stare at her profile, a light breeze kicking up a few pieces of her hair and blowing them around her face. Reaching over, I push them away and tuck them behind her ear so I can see her better.

She finally turns to look at me and lets out a long sigh.

"I didn't keep the letters from you on purpose. I honestly forgot about them until that moment."

"I know," I tell her with a nod. "And I'm sorry."

"I'm not an idiot. I know they're serious, even though the camp has been getting letters like that for years and nothing has ever happened. I would never, ever put the kids that come here in that kind of danger. The police get a copy of every one we get, and we keep the originals in a file in the office," she explains.

"I know," I repeat. "But it's not just the kids I was worried about. If anything ever happens to you—"

She cuts me off by pressing her fingers to my lips.

"I was going to tell you, I promise. And I'm also sorry for acting like a bitch. I shouldn't have yelled at you and walked away. Michelle showing up and saying those things rattled me, and then Amelia giving me another letter at the worst possible time…" she apologizes, trailing off.

Wrapping my hand around her wrist, I pull her fingers away from my mouth and kiss the palm of her hand before lacing my fingers through hers. I tug on our joined hands to get her to move closer to me, resting them in my lap.

"You're kind of hot when you're pissed off."

She rolls her eyes at me, and I feel some of the pressure in my chest ease. As much as I like fighting with her, I don't like it when she's mad at me because I was acting like an asshole.

We sit at the edge of the dock, looking out at the lake in front of us in silence for a few minutes, before Cameron speaks again.

"Aiden was really pissed off when he found out about the letters, too, which you already sort of know now," she says quietly.

A knot forms in my chest when she says his name, but not like it used to. Not because of jealousy or guilt. This time, it's because I know I've been an asshole for never really talking about our best friend since I've been home. Not even in the last week after I found out Aiden and Cameron were never in love.

I should have asked. I should have learned my lesson last time about not asking the right questions, but obviously I didn't. I've been too busy getting Cameron naked as often as possible in the last seven days, but as fun as that has been, we have to be able to communicate with each other to make this work. We spent too many years not talking about important things, and I don't want to fuck this up now that we're in a good place.

"God, he'd be making so much fun of us right now," she says with a small smile, shaking her head.

"He'd still try to get in your pants, and then ask me to rate you on a scale of one to ten," I add with my own smile.

"He was a horrible date. I can't believe I repeated it two more times after the first disaster," she complains. "I blame you for that, by the way."

I can actually laugh about this now. It feels good to think about Aiden and not hate him, and then hate myself for feeling that way.

"You have every right to blame me. I take full responsibility. I already heard about how he tried to grab your hand and you spilled wine all over him," I tell her.

She looks at me questioningly.

"Amelia," I add.

"Of course," she replies with a roll of her eyes. "That

was the last straw. Although the last straw should have come after the first date when he took me to the movies and kept leaving to go out in the lobby and take calls from a bunch of his skanks that kept calling."

"He didn't!"

"Oh, he did," she nods with a laugh. "But I mean, that's Aiden. It's who he was and why I loved him, because he was so ridiculous and full of life, never wanting to miss an opportunity to have fun. I knew damn well I wasn't going to be the person who made him change, and I didn't want that job anyway, which is why I quickly realized dating him was the dumbest idea ever."

She's quiet for a few minutes, lost in thought as she looks out at the lake again.

"God, you should have seen him with Michelle and Abby. They were his game changers," she says wistfully.

"I still don't believe it. Even seeing Michelle and hearing her say they were engaged. I cannot believe *our* Aiden fell in love with a woman who had a kid. He hated kids. Every time he was at camp, he would cringe when they came up to him, afraid they'd get his fancy suits dirty."

"He was so different with her. With both of them. The first time he looked at Michelle, I just knew. I could see it in his eyes. He never spoke to another skank, and he loved Abby like she was his own," Cameron explains.

Sadness blankets her face and tears fill her eyes.

"Today was the first time I've seen her since the funeral. As you heard her say, I've tried calling her and texting her, but she doesn't respond. She took it really hard. I mean, obviously she did, and I tried to help her as much as I could, but her stages of grief were all screwed up. She went right into anger and everything I did made it worse. She started blaming me for all the time she lost with him because he was with me instead of her and Abby. It was just too painful for her to be here and be around me because it reminded her of him. And all this time, she's been jealous and letting it fester and grow into hatred. It sucks. We were friends and now she doesn't want anything to do with me."

I wrap my arm around her shoulder and pull her against my side. I wish for the hundredth time that I had pulled my head out of my ass sooner after I got home from overseas. Cameron went through so much, and I wasn't here to help her, and I hate that.

"I don't really want to ask this, but I have to. Do you think Michelle is the one sending the letters?"

Cameron pulls her head back and shakes it quickly.

"No. No way."

I can hear the doubt in her voice that doesn't match her words, especially with how angry and hateful Michelle was toward her earlier, but I don't want to argue with her. I know it will piss her off, but I'm still going to place my own call to the police about those letters. I don't like knowing it could be someone who knows Cameron and everything about her, and could use that to their advantage to scare her. I also plan on doing some digging into that asshole, Grady Stevens. Cameron told me the other day how weird and possessive he got as soon as I showed up here, and I don't like some of the things she told me he said to her. Especially the part about how she ruined his life. It's pretty much word for word what was written on that damn letter I saw a little while ago.

"It's hard for people to move on. To let go of the hurt and sadness and fear and just learn to live again and be happy," I tell her.

"Is this why you haven't taken a job at a hospital? Are you afraid? Do you miss traveling the world?" she asks softly.

After four years abroad, I still have some time before I

need to make the decision about signing back up for another assignment with Doctors Without Borders, but I already know what I'm going to do. I knew it as soon as I got back on U.S. soil ten months ago.

"I do miss it. I just..." I trail off, trying to get my thoughts in order.

I haven't told anyone about my decision or the reasons behind it, but Cameron deserves to know. We've spent weeks reestablishing our friendship, and another week developing more, but we haven't really discussed anything important. She needs to know everything about me and the things I've done before this can go any further.

I've tried to act like her dad's sudden dislike of me is no big deal and doesn't bother me, but it does. It hurts. And every time he glares at me or walks out of the room when I enter it, it brings up that shitty, stupid memory from the night before my first deployment. The reason why I pushed her to date Aiden. The reason why I spent four years away from her.

"He's not good enough for her. Would it kill the guy to smile every once in a while? If Cameron's going to be with anyone, it should be someone who makes her happy, not someone she exhausts herself trying to fix."

Those words Mr. James spoke to Cameron's mom that night have never left me. They planted themselves deep inside my brain and I let them fester for years. It's only gotten worse in the last week. Every time I touch her, every time I kiss her, I hear his voice in my head saying I'm not good enough, and a part of me knows he's right. A part of me is scared shitless that when she knows everything about me, she's going to realize it, too.

"There's a line between good and evil. Right and wrong. I spent all of my life making sure I never crossed that line.

Not with you, not with anyone," I tell her, looking out at the lake so I don't have to see her face and possibly see the same thing I see in her dad's eyes when he looks at me. "I always made the right choices. I always did what was good and I always did what was right and I never thought I'd ever have to make a decision that would change that. Then I went overseas."

I stop for a minute and remember how to breathe. Push aside the memories that try to make their way into the forefront of my mind. The screaming, the crying, the pain on people's faces, the loss and the anger…everything that has haunted my dreams since the first time I went to a third world country.

"You don't have to talk about this if you don't want to," Cameron says, her hand moving to my back, making small, soothing circles against it with her palm.

"I know, but I need to. I spent too much time keeping things like this locked up inside, and it kept me away from you for months staring at the bottom of a bottle, when I should have been here."

She nods in understanding and doesn't say anything else, waiting quietly for me to continue.

"I dreamed all my life of being a doctor. Helping people and being a hero. I thought it was the best thing I could do with my life, and for a while, it was," I continue. "Until it suddenly became really easy to stick my toe over that line. To play God with people's lives. I know I did what I had to do, what I was trained to do. I know there's only a split second to make a decision when someone is dying right in front of you, and you damn well better make it count. I know I couldn't save everyone, but I made choices about who I saved. Who I thought deserved it more. Someone's son, someone's daughter, someone's father. I played God, knowing I only had enough vaccinations and medicine for half of the village I was in, picking and choosing the people I thought were worthy. I turned away mothers I thought weren't good enough, I turned away fathers I thought were already too sick to benefit from medication. I didn't know these people. I didn't know their lives or their struggles or what they'd been through. I waltzed into their villages and judged them, and I don't know how to forgive myself for that. I don't know how to get back over that line where I'm supposed to be. I don't even know if I can at this point."

I let out a shaky breath, closing my eyes and running my hand through my hair, knowing if I wasn't here right now, if I hadn't finally gotten my head out of my ass months ago, I'd be going in search of the closest liquor store and drinking myself into a coma.

My eyes open back up when I feel Cameron's hands press to either side of my face and she turns my head toward her.

"I don't care what you say, you never crossed that line, Everett," she whispers, staring into my eyes. "I know you lost people, but the things you did saved so many others. You are the bravest, strongest man I've ever met. Never, for one minute, think you are anything less than that."

Her words are like a soothing balm to my soul, and for the first time, I actually start to believe what she's saying. I did things I'll never be able to forget. I made decisions that will haunt me for the rest of my life, but with this woman by my side, giving me more than I ever deserved, I might be able to stop doubting whether or not I'm good enough for her.

I might finally be able to let go, and do whatever I can to prove her dad wrong.

Chapter 35

CAMERON

I cradle Everett's body between my thighs, tilting my hips to meet him as he slowly pushes inside me. He groans my name and I cling tightly to his shoulders, still unable to believe that this is us. That this is where we are right now.

Even after two weeks, having him inside me still feels like a dream. I'll never get used to how good he feels. How *perfectly* we fit.

He kisses his way down the side of my neck, and I rock my hips against him, locking my ankles behind his back. He slides both of his hands behind me, grabbing my ass and pulling me tighter against him, moving inside me deeper with slow, shallow thrusts until his fullness is stretching me in the most delicious way.

Grabbing fistfuls of his hair, I pull his face away from where he's gently biting the skin of my neck and bring his mouth to mine. His tongue slides past my lips and leisurely moves in and out of my mouth in the same unhurried rhythm as his hips pumping in and out of me, fanning the flames of the fire that's been burning inside of me since he woke me up this morning with his hand between my legs.

"Jesus, you feel so good. So fucking perfect," Everett mutters, pulling his mouth away from mine long enough to speak against my lips.

I open my eyes and look up at him, bringing my hand away from the back of his head to run the tips of my fingers across his lips as he holds himself deep inside of me and churns his hips, hitting a spot that sends tingles up my spine and makes my toes curl.

These lips are mine. This man is mine. After all this time, he's finally mine. He came home to me because he needed me, even if it took him a while to admit it. I've always loved him, even when I denied it. Always knew I'd never be able to escape him no matter how hard I tried, and now he's mine.

"I love you," I whisper against his lips, knowing it's the most clichéd time to tell someone you love them, and not caring.

It's not the first time I've said these words to him anyway. I blurted them out for the first time last week when I was feeling particularly melancholy after a counseling session with a family, and he said something to make me laugh. After I said them, he quickly kissed me and pulled me to him, not giving me even a second to be embarrassed that I just let something like that slip.

I've whispered those words to him when we've been wrapped up together late at night, just about ready to fall asleep, and I've muttered a distracted "love you" to him in the mornings when I'm grabbing my coffee and rushing out the door before him to get to work, never really paying attention to the fact that he hasn't returned the words because I've been too deliriously happy and busy with the camp.

Everett growls deep in his chest, slamming his mouth to mine as he thrusts faster, pushing inside me in long, hard strokes until I can't hold back any longer.

My hips move faster against him, straining, reaching, needing to feel the sweet oblivion of falling and having him finally here to catch me.

Pleasure bursts out of me, and I scream into Everett's mouth, where he swallows my cries, his fingers clutching harder to my ass as he pistons his hips, slamming into me, making the bed creak and groan with the force of his thrusts. My body is still clenching and pulsing around him with a release that feels like it will never end, until he rips his mouth away from mine, buries his face into the side of my neck, and curses, moaning my name as he comes inside of me.

My arms fall out to the sides of the bed as he collapses on top of me, our breaths coming out fast and hard as we lie here tangled up in each other until our hearts start beating normally again.

After a few minutes, Everett pushes himself up on his elbows and looks down at me, reaching up to brush my hair off my forehead.

"Good morning," he says with a smile.

"Good morning to you, too. You're better than an alarm clock."

He laughs and rolls off of me. Pulling the sheet up to cover me, I rest my elbow on the pillow and prop my head in my hands, staring at his naked body as he gets out of bed, grabs his boxer briefs from the floor, and pulls them on, keeping a smile plastered on my face and trying not to let my emotions ruin what has started off as a great day.

I don't want to be one of those women who tell a man she loves him and then feel insecure because he didn't say it back, but he's starting to make me self-conscious. He's shown me, in more ways than one that he does, but sometimes, a woman just needs to hear the words before she can believe them. After everything we've gone through to get to this point, I don't want to let doubt start clouding things, but it's impossible to push it away when it's rooted itself into my brain and won't let go.

"Busy day today. Want to share a shower with me to save time?" he asks, turning around and pressing his palms to the mattress to lean toward me, peppering kisses along my cheek.

"If I share a shower with you, that will definitely *not* save time," I tell him, pushing on his chest until he moves away and stands back up.

Tomorrow is the official start day of the summer session. Knowing things are about to get incredibly hectic, Everett convinced me to take a night off last night and brought me back to his house so we could enjoy some peace and quiet away from the camp and the demands that seem to always find a way to interrupt us. He cooked me dinner, we talked, we made love, we made plans for the rest of the week and the things he'll be helping with at camp in between his construction job, then we woke up this morning and made love again.

It was perfect. It was easy. It was natural. Crossing the line from friendship to this was seamless, but I can't help feeling like I've given him everything, and he's given me only small pieces in return.

I give Everett another small smile when he turns away from me and closes himself in the bathroom attached to his bedroom. When I hear the shower turn on, I let my smile fall and I sigh, throwing the sheet off me and getting out of bed.

I'm being a stupid girl, and it's starting to annoy me. Everett has been through a lot and I don't want to rush him. I have no reason to doubt how he feels about me. He told me the first time we had sex in the stables about all the times over the years he wanted me. Too bad my brain and my heart can't seem to get on the same page, and I know that wanting someone and being in love with them are two totally different things.

Grabbing my bra and underwear from the floor, where they were tossed aside last night, I put them on, doing the same with my sundress, pulling it down over my head and trying to smooth some of the wrinkles out.

I start walking around Everett's bedroom, picking up his discarded clothes from last night and laying them on the end of the bed. Reaching for his jeans, I shake them out, pausing when a piece of paper flies out of the back pocket.

Tossing the jeans onto the bed, I bend down and pick up the small square of folded paper, opening it up as I move over to the window and slide my feet into my flip-flops.

My heart stutters in my chest when I get the paper unfolded and see the familiar handwriting across the page. My stomach drops down to my toes and my knees give out when I skim the letter, my body dropping into the chair next to the window, my hands shaking so hard I'm surprised I don't accidentally rip the letter in half, since it looks like it's been folded and unfolded, read and reread, a million times before.

Every doubt and insecurity that I forced myself to push back just a few minutes ago flares back to life and starts eating away at everything inside of me. My eyes blur with tears until the words on the page in my hand can no longer be seen.

"Do we have time for breakfast before you need to leave?"

I don't even look over at Everett when he walks out of the bathroom. I know if I look at him, if I see the smile on his face, look at the lips that were just on me, stare at the hands that just touched me so perfectly, I'll be tempted to hide my tears and pretend like everything is fine. I'm a stupid, stupid girl and everything is not fine.

"Did you come back because you wanted me, or because you felt guilty?" I whisper, still staring down at the letter in my hand, my voice coming out cracked and full of emotion that I wish I could just turn off.

"What are you—"

Everett's question is abruptly cut off and I finally turn my head to look at him, and see him staring at the letter that I hold in my hand.

"Cameron..." he whispers, looking away from the letter, his face filled with anguish when he sees a tear fall down my cheek.

"I know it shouldn't matter, especially now, but it does," I continue, clearing my throat around the knot that has started to form as I try to hold back my tears. "Did you come back because you were in love with me, just like I've always been in love with you, or because Aiden made you feel guilty for being gone and he told you to come back and take care of me?"

I slowly push myself up from the chair as Everett moves farther into the room, until he's standing right in front of me.

"It wasn't like that. Not exactly..." He trails off. "I mean, of course I felt guilty. Jesus, Cameron. I pushed you away and kept myself out of your life because I was jealous of my best fucking friend, and for no reason. I let you mourn him alone because I was an asshole. Yes, the guilt was eating me alive, but you know how I feel about you. You know how I've *always* felt about you."

He takes another step toward me and reaches his hands out to me, but I step to the side. I know if I let him put his arms around me, I'll push aside everything I'm feeling right now. I'll let him fill my head and my heart with explanations and promises, bury my worries down deep, and they will eat me alive. I did that for too many years and I'm not doing it again. I won't.

"Do I? Do I know how you feel about me? I know you wanted me. I know you *still* want me, that's something you can't exactly hide," I tell him. "I'm *in love* with you, Everett. I've been in love with you for almost all my life, hiding it away and pretending like I wasn't. Do you know how exhausting it is being in love with your best friend for as long as you can remember? Always wondering if you're staring too long, standing too close, laughing too loudly at his jokes. Scared to death about telling him how you feel and finding out he doesn't feel the same. Jesus, I feel like I'm in high school again and it pisses me off!"

I hate that I feel so insecure. I hate that I'm questioning everything right now, but I can't help it. Seeing Aiden's letter—knowing Everett has been carrying it around all this time, reading those words, and possibly doing everything he has with me out of some sort of misplaced guilt—has broken apart something inside of me.

"How can you even question what I feel for you? After everything that has happened between us. After everything we've done together," Everett mutters with a shake of his head, running his hand through his hair in frustration. "Goddammit, Cameron! What more do you want from me? Tell me, and I'll give it to you. I'll do anything. Say anything. Just tell me what you need."

I back away from him again when he tries to get closer, shaking my head and holding my hand up between us. I can't think with him standing this close.

"I wished for you, every fucking year, I wished for you. You are everything I've ever wanted, everything I've ever needed. Don't do this, Cameron, please. Tell me what to do."

Handing Aiden's letter to him, he takes it from my hand and tosses it to the ground. I swipe away at the tears on my cheeks and continue moving backward until I'm standing in the doorway.

"Tell me you love me, too," I whisper. "Tell me you've been in love with me for as long as you can remember, and you love me so much that sometimes it hurts to breathe with how overwhelming it is. Because that's how I feel about you. That's how I've *always* felt about you."

Everett doesn't move and doesn't say anything, just continues to stand there across the room, staring at me with the same sad look of regret on his face.

"Then I guess you can't do anything," I tell him.

Turning away from him, I walk out of the room, hurry down the stairs and out the front door, not giving him a chance to come after me. I just need to be away from him right now so I can think more clearly. I know I'm behaving like a child. I know I should trust him and believe in the things he's saying to me, trust all the ways he's shown me how much he cares about me, but I can't. Aiden's letter screwed everything up in my head and my heart, and nothing makes sense anymore.

Chapter 36

EVERETT

You're being a pussy, you know that?" Jason asks, tossing the two boxes I asked him to get for me onto my kitchen table.

I quickly grab them and remove the lids, dumping the contents onto the table top.

"I'm not being a pussy. I'm giving her some space. Giving her time to think and realize she has no reason to doubt how I feel about her," I tell him, flipping over all the little pieces, my heart feeling like someone stuck a knife in it when I see Cameron's handwriting, which hasn't really changed much over the years.

Each star has the date written on it, and each one of her stars from the time she was twelve has the exact same wish scribbled on it. I want to laugh when I start flipping my own stars over, but I'm not exactly in a laughing mood right now.

Why in the hell didn't I just tell her I'm in love with her?

"Besides," I continue, standing up from the chair and organizing everything I need on the table. "Three days is long enough. I'm going over there today and I'm not leaving until she talks to me."

Three days without Cameron have been more than long enough. Too long. Each night I've gone to bed without her in my arms has been torture. Each text message and voice mail I've left her without a response has pushed me past my limit. My limit should have been the other morning in my bedroom when I let her walk away from me, but I honestly thought she'd come to her senses and realize none of what she was accusing me of is true.

That I didn't love her.

That I only came back here and stayed and poured my heart out to her out of guilt.

That I hadn't also been exhausted after years of being in love with my best friend and not doing anything about it because I was afraid.

"Are you actually going to tell her you love her this time?" Jason asks me, flopping down on the chair and picking up one of the pieces of paper.

I smack it out of his hand, glare at him, and go back to work with my project.

"I told her I love her."

Jason laughs, the sound grating on my already frayed nerves.

"So you took her face in your hands, looked her right in the eyes, and said, 'Cameron, I'm in love with you. I've been in love with you forever. I. Love. You.'?"

"It was implied," I growl.

"Sweet Christ, you're an idiot. Have you learned nothing over the last few weeks? Hell, over the last thirty-three years?" he criticizes.

"I thought the whole *show, don't tell* thing was what women liked. Romantic gestures, and all that shit," I mumble.

"Not in this case. Tell me, how did you feel when Cameron actually said the words to you?"

I sigh, dropping the bottle of glue, resting my hands on top of the table, and letting my head drop as I take a minute to think about what he's asking.

"Relief," I finally whisper.

"And why is that?"

"Because no matter what was happening between us, I don't think I actually believed it until she said the words."

Son of a bitch.

"Bingo! And we have a winner!" Jason proclaims.

Why the hell didn't I just say the words? Why did I think my actions would speak for themselves? More than anything else in the world, I wanted to look her in the eyes and tell her I loved her, but I was scared. I'd never said those words to another person in my life. I felt them for Cameron, deep down in my soul I felt them, but they just wouldn't come out of my mouth when she needed to hear them. I spent so much time pretending like I hadn't been in love with her all those years I spent away from her, that having everything I ever wished for right within my grasp scared the hell out of me. Saying something out loud makes it real. And when it's real, it can be taken away from you. I didn't want to lose her again, but I knew if I didn't tell her what I should have the other morning, she'd slip right out of my grasp and no amount of apologizing would bring her back this time.

"This is probably a really stupid idea now, isn't it?" I ask my brother, setting my creation into a glass frame and reattaching the wooden edges.

Jason stands up from his chair next to me and looks down, smacking me on the back.

"It's pretty girly and shit, but I think she'll like it. Are you taking it over there now?"

My phone dings with an incoming text message, and I quickly pull it out of my back pocket, my hope falling when I see it's not from Cameron.

"Shit. Fucking hell," I mutter, sending off a quick reply before putting my phone back in my pocket.

"You're going out to the camp now, right?" I ask Jason, walking over to the kitchen counter and grabbing the keys to the truck.

"Yeah. Amelia is running some errands and she's gonna meet me there for lunch."

Grabbing the huge frame from the table, I hand it to him.

"Good, take this with you and give it to Cameron. I need to go meet up with someone really quick. And honestly, it might be better if someone else gives this to her and butters her up before I get there," I tell him.

"Who are you meeting with?" Jason calls after me as I rush toward the front door.

"Just a friend from rehab. He's having a bad day. I shouldn't be too long."

Chapter 37

CAMERON

Yஂou can't ignore the man forever. Jason told me he's going crazy," Amelia tells me as we lean against the fence around the pasture and watch some of the new campers get their first lesson on riding horses.

I'd like to say that having the camp open for the summer session, and having kids here twenty-four/seven has kept my mind off of Everett, but that would be a lie. He's all I think about. He's all I worry about. And it's all I can do not to return his text messages and voice mails, telling him I'm sorry and I was an idiot.

Each message has been the same, and each one has made me want to get in my car and drive to his house as fast as possible.

Please talk to me.

I want to talk to him, but I don't know what to say. I know I was an idiot and I know I shouldn't have ignored him the last three days, but I needed something from him and he didn't give it to me. What if I go to him now, and he says those three magic words that I need so badly? How will I know if he really means them, or he's just saying them to get me to come back?

I'm saved from having to answer Amelia when we hear a vehicle pull into the driveway. We both turn around and watch Jason get out of his truck, carrying what looks like a huge picture frame in his hands as he walks over to us.

"Did you bring me a present?" Amelia asks him when he gets to us and leans down to kiss her cheek.

"Not this time, Milly girl."

Amelia makes an annoyed sound and Jason laughs.

"Sorry, I can't help it. You should never have told me that was your nickname."

"It was a nickname my ex gave me. It's weird you think it's cute," she argues with a roll of her eyes.

"I am comfortable enough in my manhood to not be threatened by another man, thank you very much."

I stand to the side, watching the two of them go back and forth, and it's so damn sweet and cute that my heart physically aches inside of my chest. I miss Everett. I miss him so much and I know Amelia is right. I can't ignore him forever. I have to talk to him. I have to stop being so afraid. I have everything I've ever wanted, and I'm ruining it on a stupid technicality.

"This is for you," Jason says, pulling me out of my thoughts as he hands the large frame over to me.

I look at him in confusion as I take it from his hands and glance down at it.

My head slowly shakes with disbelief when I see what's under the glass of the frame.

I choke back a sob and my chin quivers as my eyes fill with tears over what I'm looking at. What Everett has done. What Everett has given me.

"Is that…wow. Holy shit…He was doing the same thing as you, all these years," Amelia mutters, looking over my shoulder and down at the frame.

My heart cracks wide open and I have to clutch one hand to my stomach, trying to stop myself from falling completely apart as the tears fall fast and hard down my face.

Glued to the cardboard backing of the frame under the glass, neatly spaced out across the entire thing, is every single one of my star wishes from the year I turned twelve, including the most recent four wishes I made the night before the charity dinner when I went up to the treehouse by myself. All of them written in my curly handwriting with the date I made the wish, each one of them saying the exact same thing: *I wish Everett would love me back.*

Seeing these stars brings back so many memories and feelings, remembering exactly how I felt each year when I made that same wish, worried and terrified that I'd go my whole life never finding the courage to tell him how I felt.

But it's not seeing my star wishes that completely ruins me. It's seeing all the ones Everett has glued right next to mine. All of *his* wishes over the years from the time he was seventeen, until the last four he did after he first came home and he asked me to meet him up in the treehouse. They sit neatly next to each one of mine, like an answer to the wishes I made. His small, messy handwriting on each star says the exact same thing, just like mine do, just worded differently: *I wish I was good enough for Cameron to love me back.*

I run my palm over the glass, my fingers tracing over each one of his stars as I sob.

"I think that's Everett's way of saying he loves you. And that he's always loved you," Amelia whispers next to me.

I hear her sniffle and look up to find her crying just as hard as I am.

"Seriously? You're *both* crying? God help me," Jason mutters.

He pulls his phone out of his pocket and walks away. I look away from him and back down at the frame, staring at it in awe for a few minutes before handing it over to Amelia.

"Can you take this into the main house and put it in the office for now? I've got a man to see and some groveling to do."

We both swipe away our tears and laugh as she takes the frame from my hands and starts walking back to the house. I watch her walk away, smiling to myself when I see her cradling the frame to her chest, holding on to it like it's the most precious thing she's ever held.

Chapter 38

EVERETT

I pull into Bobby's apartment and park right in front of his unit, getting out of the truck and pocketing my keys as I walk up to his door.

The cryptic message I got from him just said that he couldn't do it anymore. That he was getting his family back today one way or another. I told him to stay put until I got here and could talk him down from whatever ledge he was currently standing on.

After our last two meetings, he seemed to be doing so much better. As soon as I sat down with him, his hatred would come pouring out, but after an hour or two of conversation, he'd calm down and be okay. Even though he teetered back and forth between sobriety and not giving a shit about anything, I really believed he was on the road to recovery since he had a lot more good days than bad ones recently.

Lifting my hand, I knock on his door and as soon as my

fist connects with the wood, I hear a *click* and the door slowly creaks open. Pushing it open wider, I take a tentative step into the small living room of his one-bedroom apartment.

"Bobby? You in here?" I call out.

When he doesn't answer, I move the rest of the way inside, closing the door behind me.

The room is dark and smells like old, rotting food. Covering my nose with my hand, I feel against the wall and flip on the switch, cringing when I see the mess of his living room.

I had just been here talking to him a few weeks ago and it looked nothing like this. It was a small room, but he kept it neat and orderly, everything in its place, just like your typical career military man.

Fast-food containers and bags litter every available surface, stacks of dirty plates with moldy food are piled all over the coffee table and end tables, and I kick aside empty beer bottles that are scattered all around the floor, tipped on their sides.

"Son of a bitch, Bobby," I mutter with a shake of my head as I move farther into the room.

I feel the vibration of my phone in my back pocket and pull it out, checking the display to see that Jason is calling as I bring it up to my ear, and continue making my way through the mess of the living room until I get to the hallway.

"Well, your plan worked," Jason says into my ear.

I move slowly down the dark hallway and come to a stop outside of the closed bedroom door, scared to death of what I'm going to find on the other side. Plenty of men, ones stronger than Bobby, have made the decision to end their lives when they couldn't cope after coming home from a deployment. I can't lose someone else in my life. Not someone I tried to help.

Please, God, don't let me find him on the other side of this door.

"Did you hear me? I said your plan worked," Jason says again.

I'm barely listening to my brother rambling in my ear, telling me about how he gave Cameron the gift I made her and she loved it, going into great detail about what she said and what she did when she saw it.

"Uh-huh," I reply distractedly, my hand shaking as I reach for the handle of the door.

"It was crazy. You even made Milly cry," Jason laughs.

My body jerks and my hand stills on the handle of the bedroom door, a hundred memories and conversations flying through my head, scrambling around in my brain.

"What did you call her?" I whisper, turning the handle and pushing open the door to the bedroom, my feet not making any sound as I walk slowly over the carpet.

"What? Oh, I meant Amelia. Milly. It's a nickname, but she hates it. I like to use it just to piss her off sometimes, and because it's kind of cute."

All I hear is a buzzing in my ear and the rapid pounding of my heart against my chest when some of the things Bobby has said to me during our last few conversations come rushing back to me.

"I'm gonna do whatever it takes to get my Milly back."

"That bitch is going to pay for taking my family away."

"She will regret ruining my life."

"Jason, what was Amelia's husband's name?" I ask, reaching for a framed photo that sits on the nightstand next to the bed.

"Uh, Rob? Or Robert, I guess. But I think they called him Bobby in the military, why?"

My blood runs cold as soon as I turn the frame around.

The 8-by-10 glossy photo is a picture of Amelia in a wedding dress, smiling and happy, looking up at the man in a tuxedo next to her. Looking up at her husband, Rob/Robert/Bobby.

I think about all those letters someone sent to Cameron out at the camp. After our fight, I snuck into the office, found the file, and looked through all of them. At the time, I couldn't shake the feeling that something seemed familiar about them. I even wasted time calling around about Aiden's fiancée, Michelle. I had a buddy run a background check on her and even follow her around for a few days. All this time, I was looking at the wrong person.

All this time, the person threatening Cameron was one of my own fucking friends. Someone I helped and someone I thought had been getting better.

"Have Seth and whatever workers you can find get all the campers locked inside the main house, then put Cameron and Amelia in your truck and get them the fuck away from camp, right now!" I shout into the phone, racing out of the bedroom and down the hall.

I fling open the front door so hard it slams against the opposite wall, not even bothering to close it behind me as I run to the truck.

"What the hell are you talking about?" Jason asks as I hop inside the vehicle.

"JUST DO IT!" I scream into the phone as I put the truck in reverse and peel out of the parking lot as fast as I can.

"Okay, okay, Jesus," Jason mutters as I ignore the blare of car horns and the slamming of brakes when I pull out of the apartment complex and onto the main road.

"Oh, shit. Oh fuck," I hear on the other end of the line when I cut someone else off in traffic.

"Jason, what's going on?"

I hear nothing but a rustling sound coming from his end, followed quickly by shouting, and then the unmistakable sounds of women screaming.

"JASON!" I shout into the phone as I press harder on the gas.

The screams are quickly cut off when the line goes dead. I throw my phone across the cab of the truck until it smashes into the passenger side window, cursing at the top of my lungs as I slam my fist down on the steering wheel.

Chapter 39

CAMERON

I hear a group of workers on the other side of the fence behind me, and I turn around to let them know I need to leave the camp for a little while and I ask them to keep an eye on things until I get back.

"Who's that? He's driving like an asshole," one of the women says.

I look back over my shoulder to where she's pointing and see a small black car come flying down the driveway, veering off at the fork in it and heading right this way.

"I have no idea," I mutter, turning fully around and walking in that direction.

We don't have any scheduled deliveries today, and there are signs all along the main driveway that tell visitors to pull up to the turnaround at the main house so they can check in and get a visitor badge. There are also signs along *this* driveway that say it's for camp workers only. This driveway leads right to the stables, and there's no reason for any visitors to be on it.

The car kicks up even more dust than before when it slams to a stop and I cross my arms in front of me, watching a man get out from behind the wheel. He looks familiar, but something about him doesn't seem right.

He doesn't bother closing the car door behind him, and he stumbles a little as he walks in my direction, not noticing me standing here as his eyes search the grounds to his left. He's wearing a white T-shirt with stains all over the front of it, and a pair of dirty jeans that have seen better days. His short, dark blond hair is sticking up in all directions on top of his head, and his face looks like it hasn't seen a razor in weeks.

The closer he gets, the more nervous I start to become. Glancing quickly around, I find Jason standing a few hundred yards away, still talking on his phone with his back to me.

"Sir, can I help you?" I finally call out loudly, taking a few steps forward.

He doesn't answer me as he continues walking in my direction, but my voice causes his head to come up and he looks right at me. Even from this far away I can see anger written all over his face.

"Get the kids off the horses and lock everyone inside the stables—now," I say softly over my shoulder to the handful of workers who are still standing behind me on the other side of the fence. "Radio out to everyone in the middle of activities and tell them Code 10."

We have several secret codes in place for security at the camp, and Code 10 is the most important one. It means there is a threat at the camp and everyone should get to safety and stay put until further notice.

Maybe I'm making a big deal about nothing, and this is just some guy who's lost and needs direction, but I won't take any chances with my workers or these kids.

All of a sudden, the man still walking toward me lifts his

arm, and a few of the workers who haven't left yet and are talking on their radios start to scream.

My stomach flops when I see the gun in his hand, pointed right at my chest as he continues stalking toward me and then suddenly comes to a stop about twenty yards away.

His eyes are cold, hard, and bloodshot, and they're locked right on mine. I try not to show fear, I try to remain as calm as possible, but my heart is beating so fast I'm afraid he might hear it. My hands are shaking so badly as I lift them in the air in a sign of peace that I know he sees it.

"Are you Cameron James?" he asks in a low, angry voice, his upper lip curling with disgust when he says my name.

"Sir, please put the gun down. We have children here. If you can just—"

"ARE YOU CAMERON JAMES?!" he screams, cutting me off, spittle flying from his mouth as he takes another step toward me, the gun in his hand starting to shake as he continues aiming it right at me.

My body starts shaking from head to toe and my mouth opens and closes several times as I try to think about what I should say.

"Please put the gun down," I whisper brokenly, my throat cracking through my words.

"You're the one who ruined my life. I know it's you, so just admit it. Admit what you did," he says, a muscle ticking in his jaw when he speaks through clenched teeth.

"Sir, please," I beg, wanting to turn and run, but knowing there's nowhere I can go.

I can't outrun a gun.

"I told you. I TOLD YOU that you'd regret what you did."

His words make the hair on the back of my neck stand up, and I realize I'm standing in front of the man responsible for sending those letters.

My eyes dart to the side of him when I see a familiar truck come barreling down the main driveway, but he quickly moves and blocks my line of sight.

"I'm sorry. I don't—"

"SHUT THE FUCK UP!" he screams, taking another step toward me. "It's too late for apologies. You ruined everything, and now you need to pay."

A million thoughts run through my head in a split second. Things I should say to him to get him to put the gun down, but I don't have time to say any of them.

There's a blur of movement out of the corner of my eye. The man and I both glance that way, and before I can process what's happening, before I can even open my mouth and scream, the explosive sound of the gun going off rings through my ears.

Chapter 40

EVERETT

I don't bother turning off the engine, and I barely get the truck in Park next to Bobby's car, before I'm flinging my door open and take off running. I see the back of Bobby and a few workers huddled together in the pasture beyond him, but I don't see Cameron.

I pump my legs faster and harder, needing to get to him before he does something stupid, but my brother gets to him first.

My feet falter when I see Jason come flying from the left of Bobby. I hear the blast of a gun and my body jerks as Jason tackles Bobby and takes him to the ground. I hear screaming as I run faster, and realize it's coming from me, and it's coming from the workers as they all start jumping the fence and racing toward the spot where Bobby and my brother are struggling.

I finally catch a glimpse of Cameron by the fence and realize Bobby was blocking her from my view. I see her hunched forward with her hands covering her head and I finally let out a thankful breath of air as I get to Bobby and Jason. Two of the workers and I all dive on top of them at the same time, helping to subdue a screaming, flailing, and cursing Bobby.

Someone knocks the gun out of his hand and another worker comes running up to us and kicks it out of the way as we all get Bobby on his stomach with his arms behind his back.

"SHE NEEDS TO PAY! THAT FUCKING BITCH NEEDS TO PAY!" Bobby screams.

I hear sirens in the distance, thanking God that the police understood the frantic call I made on the way here, thankful my phone still worked after I shattered the glass.

"We got him. Go check on Cameron," Jason tells me in a winded voice, kneeling on Bobby's back to keep him down.

I feel like I should say something to this man. Ask him what the hell he was doing, but I can't think about anything right now but getting to Cameron, putting my arms around her, and making sure she's okay.

Standing up from the ground, I hear shouting and see Amelia and a few volunteers racing out of the main house and over to where we are.

Letting out a heavy sigh, I run my hand through my hair and finally look back over at Cameron. Her eyes meet mine as she slowly starts to stand up, and I move my feet toward her, seeing the fear in her eyes and noticing the ashen color of her face. I give her a small smile to reassure her that everything is okay now, but she looks away from me and down.

My smile falters and my feet start moving faster as my eyes move down her body to where she's looking. Her hands are folded over her stomach and my heart stutters when she suddenly drops to her knees.

"CAMERON!" I shout, bursting into a run, making it to her right before she tips to the side.

I skid through the grass on my knees and my arms fly around her, easing her down to the ground. Her body shakes against mine, and I set her down on her back, kneeling next to her as my eyes dart down to where her hands are still folded over her stomach.

"Oh, God," I mutter, my hands flying over the top of hers, which are now covered in blood.

"Everett," she sobs, my eyes moving back to her face. "It hurts."

Pain hits the back of my throat, and my eyes burn with tears as I look down at her, taking one of my hands off of hers to smooth some hair off her forehead.

"I know, baby," I whisper, leaning down and pressing my lips to her forehead. "It's gonna be okay. You're gonna be okay."

Her feet slide up and she bends her knees, her legs rocking back and forth as she moans in pain through her tears, and it breaks me apart.

"SOMEONE CALL A FUCKING AMBULANCE!" I scream, gathering her in my arms and pulling her head onto my lap.

All of my training, everything I know about bullet wounds and what needs to be done, flies from my mind. All I can think about is Cameron dying right in front of my eyes. All I can do is hold on to her and pray that she's not taken from me.

Someone is suddenly next to me and I see Jason kneel down, ripping off his shirt and balling it up. He gently pulls Cameron's hands away from her stomach, and the blood starts pouring out of her faster until Jason quickly presses his shirt over the wound.

I can hear people shouting and people crying, I can see out of the corner of my eye that people are racing all around and calling orders. I can hear Amelia screaming at Bobby, but it's all just noise. I don't know what they're doing, I don't know what they're saying, and I don't care.

I stare down at Cameron's face and her eyes start to flutter closed.

"No. No, no, no. Open your eyes, baby," I demand, bringing my hand up to the side of her fast and pressing my palm against her cheek.

Her eyes slowly open back up and tears leak out of the corners, trailing down into her hair as she looks up at me.

"I love you. I love you so much. Stay with me, okay? Just stay with me," I sob, running my hand through her hair, over and over, as I speak.

"I just had to get shot for you to finally say it."

She tries to smile, but her face scrunches up in pain and then misery as the tears start falling faster.

"I'm sorry," she chokes out through her tears.

"You have nothing to be sorry for. Okay? Nothing. Just stay with me. Help will be here soon."

She nods, but I can see her struggling to keep her eyes open, struggling to keep looking at me. I need to smile down at her, give her some reassurance that I believe what I'm saying, but I'm sitting here watching her fucking bleed out right in front of me. I know what a bullet to the stomach can do to someone. I've seen it a hundred times and it's not pretty.

"I can't lose you. Do you hear me? You stay with me, Cameron!" I shout down at her when her eyes close and don't open back up.

I pull her body tighter to mine, rocking us back and forth,

refusing to believe this is happening right now. Refusing to believe I waited all this time for her and it's just going to end like this.

I kiss her forehead, I kiss her lips, I kiss her cheek, and I continue rocking us while I speak in her ear, chanting over and over until my voice grows hoarse.

"Don't you dare leave me. I love you. Please don't leave me."

* * *

The hospital waiting room is packed wall to wall with workers, volunteers, and kids from camp with their families. Everyone talks in hushed voices, drinking coffee and waiting.

So much fucking waiting I want to scream and claw at my skin. I can't handle being around anyone right now. I can't listen to another person tell me she's going to be fine, when not one person in this fucking hospital has come out to give us any kind of update in the fifteen hours that we've been here, other than she's in surgery.

I feel a hand come down on my shoulder and I jump, turning away from the window where I'd been staring to see Cameron's dad.

He looks as bad as I feel. His eyes are bloodshot and there are dark shadows under them. Cameron's parents were in town having lunch when everything went down, and someone called them and had them meet us in the hospital. I'd been avoiding them since they got here. Eli already disliked me, and now I was giving him a reason to outright hate me.

I didn't keep his daughter safe. I knew the person who'd been sending her those letters and I never put two and two together. If I had, none of this would have happened. I wouldn't be standing here right now with Cameron's blood covering the front of my shirt. She wouldn't be somewhere in this hospital, fighting for her life. She bled out in my arms because I couldn't remember anything I needed to do to save her. I should have done something more than hold Jason's balled-up shirt against her stomach until the ambulance got there, but it's not like I could have performed surgery in the middle of the lawn at camp. I failed her. I failed everyone who loves her.

Eli eases down on the window seat, and motions for me to sit down next to him.

My eyes dart around the room, but no one is looking over here. No one knows this man is probably two seconds away from screaming at me, blaming me, and probably gearing up to punch me in the face, but they will soon enough.

I take a seat next to him with our backs to the window. He leans forward and rests his elbows on his knees, and I do the same, folding my hands together between my legs.

"I'm sorry," I tell him quietly, staring down at my hands.

"What the hell for?" Eli asks.

My head jerks to the side to look at him.

"This wasn't your fault. It wasn't anyone's fault. He was a troubled man. That's all there is to it."

I shake my head in disagreement, looking back down at my hands.

"I'm not good enough for her," I whisper. "You were right, and I just fucking proved it."

"What are you talking about? Who said you aren't good enough for her?" Eli asks.

I scoff, sitting up to look at him again in disbelief.

"*You* did. The night before I left four years ago. I heard you say that to Cameron's mom."

He frowns, narrowing his eyes at me, and I watch as he

tries to pull up that memory. His mouth drops open and he groans when it finally comes to him.

"Jesus Christ, son," Eli mutters, shaking his head at me.

"You were right," I tell him again.

"Yes. I was. Of course I was fucking right."

My hands start to sweat and I have to wipe my palms on the thighs of my pants. I mean, it's one thing to overhear the guy saying it years ago, but it's fucking painful to hear him admit.

"Wipe that hurt look off your face," Eli scolds me. "Let me tell you something, and make sure you open your ears and listen this time. If you had stuck around longer when you were spying on the conversation I had with my wife back then, you would have heard everything else I told her."

He leans back so he's sitting upright and we're eye to eye before he continues.

"No, you aren't good enough for my daughter. And you never will be no matter how hard you try. But you know what? *No* man will ever be good enough for her. Because she's my fucking *daughter*," he tells me, sighing as he brings one of his hands up to rub the back of his neck. "When you have a little girl of your own someday, when you watch her say her first words, take her first steps, when you send her off to her first day of school, watch her grow into a beautiful, smart, strong, amazing woman, you'll understand what I'm saying. But until then, this is something you're just going to have to deal with. When I look at you, I see myself. It's like looking in a fucking mirror. Struggling through the PTSD, struggling to keep my head above water, doing everything I could to not let the guilt and the regret and the memories drag me under. Letting the woman I love fix everything, put me before everything else in her life, even her own happiness. When I look at you and Cameron together, I see her mother and me. And as much as I adore Shelby, as much as I could never imagine my life without her, and as much as I know she loves me more than I've ever deserved, I never wanted that for my own daughter. I never wanted her to put anything before herself and her own happiness, I never wanted her to deal with the heartache and pain of loving a man who was broken. I know you're not that same troubled, punk kid who used to get in fights all over my stables. I know you've battled your demons and come out of it stronger than you were before. And I know you've done a damn good job with all the medical work you did around the country all those years and you should be proud of that. But I don't have to like one thing about the fact that you're sleeping with my daughter."

I can't help it—after all of the emotions raging through me, I let out a small laugh.

"I'm not just sleeping with her. I'm in love with her. I've been in love with her for a very long time, and she loves me right back," I tell him, my voice cracking when I picture her lying on that grass, covered in blood, and watching her slip away from me.

"Well then, let me give you some advice. The worst thing you can do is think you're not good enough for a woman who loves you, when that thought hasn't even entered her mind," he says. "Forget about the fact that I don't like you and probably never will. Do you honestly think that daughter of mine would love someone who wasn't good enough for her? Who didn't love her as much as she deserved? She loves you because she knows you. Better than you know yourself, obviously. Trust her to know when she's giving her heart to the right person. Trust yourself to be worthy of that heart and don't you ever, *ever* break it. You hold on to that thing with both hands, you worship it, and you never let it go. And that right there is how you become good enough for her."

Eli rests his hand on my shoulder and gives it a squeeze before standing up from the window seat and walking away. I watch him move over to where Cameron's mom is sitting next to Amelia, both of them clinging to each other and offering words of comfort through their tears.

The double doors leading to the hallway of operating rooms suddenly burst open, and I quickly stand up, while everyone else in the room stops talking.

"I need to see the family of Cameron James," the doctor says loudly.

Chapter 41

CAMERON

My eyes slowly open, and then I quickly close them again when so much bright light shines into them that it makes my head pound.

I try to move, but everything hurts, and I let out a groan of pain.

"Baby. Come on, baby. Open your eyes."

I know that voice, and the sound of it almost makes me forget about the pain. I feel my hands being squeezed, and I try again to open my eyes, taking my time and getting used to the light.

I blink rapidly, staring up at a white ceiling, trying to remember where I am.

A warm palm presses against the side of my face and turns my head to the side. Everett's T-shirt is full of wrinkles, his hair is an absolute mess, and he looks like he hasn't slept in days.

It takes me a few tries to speak. I clear my throat, swallow a few times, and slide my tongue over my dry lips.

"You look like shit," I croak out.

A smile lights up Everett's face and he laughs softly before pulling my hand up to his mouth and holding the top of it against his lips. He turns his cheek to the side, keeping my hand against his warm skin.

"I feel like shit. How do *you* feel?" he asks, rubbing his thumb back and forth against my cheek.

Everything suddenly comes back to me in a rush of memories. Standing by the fence at camp. Pleading with the man holding the gun. The sound of it going off ringing through my ears. Everett catching me before I fell to the ground. The look in his eyes and the things he said to me.

And the pain...so much pain.

"Like I was shot," I mutter, which makes Everett wince.

His hand moves off my face and he rests it gently over the blanket that's covering my stomach.

"Are you in pain? Do you want me to call the nurse?" he asks.

I'm definitely in pain. I'm in a shitload of pain, but I just want to be alone with Everett for a few more minutes.

"You love me," I whisper.

His face softens and he nods, holding on to my hand with both of his, still keeping it up by his cheek with his elbows resting on the edge of my bed.

"You've loved me for a long time."

He nods again, and something on the wall behind him catches my eye. I look away from him, smiling when I see what it is. As I turn my head and look around the room, my smile falls and my eyes fill with tears.

"How long was I out?" I ask.

"Three-and-a-half days. Technically, eighty-seven hours. I altered the rules a little and decided to make a wish once an hour."

Stuck to the walls all around the hospital room, are little paper stars, each one with the words *Come back to me* written on them in Everett's handwriting.

"I seem to be on a roll with my wishes coming true," he adds when my eyes finally come back to his.

"You've always been good enough for me to love you back," I whisper, thinking about all those wishes he made ever since he was seventeen.

"I know. At least, I do now."

Everett stands up and leans down over me, pressing his forehead against mine.

"I'm never letting you go," he tells me softly.

I close my eyes with a smile.

"I wouldn't let you, even if you tried."

Epilogue

EVERETT

Two years later...

Standing in the back of the room, I stare in wonder at Cameron as she laughs and talks to a group of kids in the class who have surrounded her.

Not a day goes by that I don't appreciate what I have. That I don't run my hand over the scar left behind on Cameron's stomach and thank God she's still here with me.

After a grueling fifteen-hour surgery two years ago, the bullet fired from Bobby Sparks's gun that day at camp didn't end up doing as much damage as it could have. It missed her stomach completely, and lodged itself in her kidney. She's minus that kidney now, but she likes to joke that it was a great way to lose a couple of pounds.

Bobby Sparks, my friend, and the man I tried to help, was convicted of aggravated assault with a deadly weapon, and sentenced to twenty-five years in prison. Cameron was

more than a little upset about the outcome of the case, and
not because she thought he should get a worse punishment.
Not only was the guilt eating *me* alive that I somehow could
have prevented what happened that day, but it ate away
at Cameron, too. She knew about Bobby's struggles with
Amelia and their son. She felt like she should have tried
harder to get in touch with him and get him to attend family
counseling sessions at the camp.

It took a lot of time, and a lot of reassurance from everyone
in Cameron's life, including Amelia, that there was nothing
anyone could have done. Cameron and I are both amazed
that after the initial shock, anger, and pain, knowing that
her ex-husband was the one responsible for sending those
threatening letters to Cameron, and then tried to exact his
revenge by shooting her, Amelia has shown just how strong
she is by moving forward and refusing to look back.

She and my brother have been going strong for the last
two years, and I know he's the reason she's doing so well. He
took to the role of father figure to Amelia's son immediately,
and Cameron and I are both getting impatient waiting for
him to finally pop the question and get that woman to marry
him before she comes to her senses.

I thought I could be content just working here at the
camp, being a handyman, helping out wherever I was needed
and spending the rest of my life doing just that, but after a
few months, I grew restless and I didn't know why. I had
Cameron and that should have been enough, and I hated that
I couldn't put a finger on what was making me so anxious
and unsettled. Thankfully, Cameron knew me better than I
knew myself. After a lot of prodding and a few arguments,
she made me realize that even though I was scared, I missed
being a doctor. She reminded me that the good always outweighs the bad. For every one patient I lost, I saved ten

others. I immediately went back to work part-time at one of the local hospitals, and spent the rest of my time being the on-call doctor here at camp.

I shake my head and laugh at the sight before me, pushing off the wall to move farther into the room.

"If you keep moving like that, you're going to send another kid to the nurse!" I shout to my wife as she tries to dance to the rhythm of the music playing over the sound system, and failing miserably.

Cameron glares at me through the reflection in the floor-to-ceiling windows before turning around and marching over to me, dodging all of the campers who are in the middle of a dance lesson.

"How many times do I have to tell you, it's not my fault I kicked Jack Alexander in the shin. He got in my way," she complains.

"Yeah, well, I'll forgive you this time. I saw him looking at Olivia funny the other day. I don't like that kid."

Our five-month-old daughter, Olivia Aiden Southerland, lets out a happy squeal from the front of Cameron's body where she's nestled in a baby carrier. I grab on to her pudgy little hands and start clapping them together.

"We don't like that kid, do we, Olivia? He's bad news," I tell her in a singsong voice.

"He's four, Everett. I don't think he's a threat to our daughter just yet," Cameron laughs.

"He's a boy. That's threat enough."

I hear a loud bark of laughter, and Cameron and I both turn to find her mom and dad standing behind us, Eli holding his hand to his stomach as he continues laughing.

"You'll have to forgive your father-in-law. He's most definitely laughing *at* you," Shelby tells me, smacking her husband on the arm.

"How can you not find the humor in this right now?" Eli chuckles. "Thirty-two years ago, in this very room, I caught you staring at *our* seven-month-old baby girl, and I wanted to kill you."

Cameron and I watch as her mom wraps her arms around her dad's waist and looks up at him.

"Full circle, baby. Full circle."

I look away from them to stare down at my little girl. My blond-haired, green-eyed little girl, who looks exactly like her mother, and suddenly, everything Eli said to me that day in the hospital two years ago makes perfect sense.

"Son of a bitch," I mutter.

"You okay?" Cameron asks, resting her hands on my shoulders.

I wrap my arms around her and pull her in closer, careful not to squish the little lady between us as she sticks her fist in her mouth and makes babbling sounds.

"I'm definitely okay."

"Two years, and you still haven't let me go," Cameron whispers.

"Of course I haven't. It was meant to be. I wished for you and it was written on the stars."

She throws her head back and laughs, bringing it back up to shake it at me.

"That was so cheesy."

"But you still love me," I remind her.

She pushes up on her toes and presses a quick kiss to my lips.

"I do. You're my wish come true."

I lean down and kiss her again, never more thankful than right this moment that Cameron decided on her tenth birthday we should start making wishes on star-shaped pieces of paper.

We might have gone about it the wrong way, and it took us a while to get here, but at least all of our wishes finally came true.

"Hey, Grandma and Grandpa, would you mind watching your granddaughter for a little while?"

Shelby immediately moves forward to take Olivia, and I help Cameron remove the carrier from off her shoulders, tossing it to Eli. Lacing my fingers through hers, I pull her out of the studio and over to a golf cart parked right outside.

"Where are you taking me?" Cameron asks as I pull away from the studio, keeping one hand on the wheel and resting the other on her thigh.

"You'll see," I tell her with a smile.

A few minutes later, I pull up in front of our treehouse and park at the base of the ladder.

"My birthday isn't for another couple of weeks," Cameron muses as we get out of the golf cart and I gesture with my hand for her to go ahead of me up the ladder.

We still honor our wish tradition every year, even if we have other plans on our birthdays, and even if we have to sneak away from the parties her parents throw for us. Since I emptied both of our boxes of wishes two years ago, we've started refilling them again, but now, we tell each other what our wishes are after we put them in our boxes. We learned our lesson about not being honest with each other, and we won't make that same mistake again.

Once we get up into the treehouse, I plug in the white Christmas lights as Cameron sits in the beanbag chair in the middle of the small room. Dropping down to my knees next to her, I pull up the loose floorboard and grab Aiden's box from our hiding spot, where it's still nestled down inside next to ours, wiping off the layer of dust on top of it.

"I think enough time has passed, and it's only fair that we

read his wishes now," I inform Cameron, sliding the lid off of his box, my throat clogging with tears when I look down into the box and see the pile of stars with his handwriting on them.

"I mean, he *did* invade your privacy and read all your wishes," Cameron agrees as I hand the box over to her.

She laughs to herself, pulling the top star out of the box and reading it out loud.

"I want to be the richest man in the world."

I laugh right along with her and shake my head.

She continues pulling out Aiden's stars, all of them in order from the last one he wrote on his birthday a few months before he was diagnosed with cancer, down to the ones he wrote when he was a child.

"What's this?" Cameron suddenly asks, pulling a folded-up square of paper out of the bottom of the box after she gets through all of the stars, which are now littered over the wooden floor around us.

Taking the paper out of her hand, I unfold it and see it's a letter that Aiden wrote to both of us. Squeezing in next to her on the beanbag chair, I hold the letter in my hand and wrap my arm around Cameron's shoulders, pulling her against my side.

She rests her head on my shoulder as I read his words out loud.

Dear Cameron and Everett:

I can't believe you read my wishes, you assholes!

Just kidding. I'm probably dead by now, so I guess I can forgive you. I'm sure you're wondering when I wrote this and stuck it in the bottom of my box. I'm currently in bed, looking over at Cameron asleep on a chair in the corner of my room. I had Seth go get my box from the treehouse this morning so I could stick this note at the bottom of it, and I'm gonna have him go put it back the next time he stops by to look at me with pity and tries to come up with something nice to say instead of "Sorry you're dying, man."

I know I don't have much time left, and it fucking sucks. Everything hurts, and as much as I hate saying this, I know it's time for me to go soon. I already wrote a letter to Everett and sent it to him the other day, so he's gonna know I read his box of wishes a few weeks ago when I was having a rare good day and had enough energy to get my sorry ass up to the treehouse.

What I didn't tell him in his letter is that I read your wishes, too, Cameron. Jesus, you're both a bunch of idiots. I hope if you're reading this, that you pulled your heads out of your asses and admitted how you felt about each other. If not, I'm going to come down from heaven where I'm probably soaking in a Jacuzzi with the skanks who have gone before me, and beat both your asses. And you know how much it will piss me off to leave a Jacuzzi filled with skanks, so don't make me come down there.

Since my impending death has suddenly made me come clean about all my wrongdoings, I might as well also admit that I only asked Cameron out to piss you off, Everett. Sorry, kid, but I never really wanted to date you. You're like a sister to me and that's gross. I honestly thought it would make Everett wake the fuck up and do something about his feelings for you. And really, Cameron? You actually accepted? What the hell is wrong with you? You should have smacked me across the face and told me to go to hell. And yeah, I know I asked you out a few more times after that disastrous first date, *but it was hilarious watching you all uncomfortable and wanting to be anywhere but on a date with me. I should be offended by that. I'm hot. Well, I used to be hot. Whatever.*

Anyway, what I'm trying to say is, I love you both. I want you two to be happy. Maybe I went about it the wrong way, but I did what I thought was right at the time. I never expected it would push Everett away and make him stay away for so long, and I'm sorry for that.

I'm also sorry that I wouldn't let Cameron tell you I was sick, man. I realize now that you're going to be pissed and probably feel guilty when you find out, and I never wanted that. I just didn't want you to see me like this. It's bad enough I need help taking a piss and can't even stay awake for more than a few minutes at a time, and I don't want you remembering me like this. I want you to remember me as the guy who was always better looking than you, and better with the ladies than you.

And it's not like I'm exactly thrilled that you have to see me like this, Cameron. That you have to watch me fade away and sit here day after day, waiting for me to die. I'd try to kick you out of this room, but you're a stubborn ass and it would just be a waste of the few breaths I have left. Which is the main reason why you're the only one I want here with me at the end. You're the strongest person I know, kid. You're braver than anyone I've ever met, even if you don't feel like it right now. You're gonna to be okay, Cam. Because Everett is going to come home and finally stop being a fucking idiot and tell you he's been in love with you all his life. And you're going to stop being a fucking idiot and tell him the same thing. You two are going to be happy together, take care of each other, and do all of the living that I won't get to do.

I know I always used to complain about our stupid wish tradition, and all of the wishes you read in my box were superficial and dumb. But the first wish I ever made when I was ten years old was the best and most important one, and I'm attaching it to the bottom of this letter. I'm sorry I won't be here to see you two together, Everett, but the image of Cameron hopefully showing you how good her right hook has gotten before she forgives you for being a stupid shit will make whatever time I have left on this earth worth it.

Don't ever stop wishing on stars.

My wish came true, and so will yours.

Aiden

1,843 days. That's how long I survived in that hellhole. They tried to break me, but I resisted. And I owe it all to the memory of warm summer nights, the scent of peaches, and the one woman who loved me more than I ever deserved to be loved. Now, I'll do anything to get back to Shelby...

Turn the page for an excerpt of
THE STORY OF US.

And find out more about
THE STORY OF US here at...

tarasivec.com/book/the-story-of-us/

Prologue

How much can a man take before he breaks? Is it measured by how many minutes, hours, days, or years he lives in hell? Is it one too many punches, kicks, or broken bones because he refuses to give in?

I wish I knew. As my head whips to the side when a pair of knuckles slam into my cheek again, I wish I knew the exact moment all of this will finally come to an end so I can count down the seconds and know exactly how much longer I need to hang on. Five years, two weeks, four days, and nine hours of the same thing, day after day, and I'm ready for it to be over. But I won't give in. I won't give them what they want even as the punches turn into kicks and the kicks turn into puddles of blood soaking into the dirt floor around me. Marines never give up.

Ooh Rah!

They scream at me in a rapid-fire foreign language. I've learned just enough in my years here to understand how much they still hate me, my country, and my refusal to give them what they ask for. Just like I've done for 1,843 days, I close my eyes and pretend like I'm not getting the shit kicked out of me. I think of her smile, her laugh, the smell of her skin, and her gentle touch. The punches and the kicks morph into soft hands sliding over my chest and warm palms pressed against either side of my face. The metallic scent of my own blood dripping down my face turns into the sweet, crisp smell of fresh peaches and my mouth waters, wishing I could taste her skin one last time.

I wonder if she'd touch me with the same boldness now that scars disfigure my skin. I wonder if she'd love me the same way when she saw how twisted and confused my mind has become just so I can make it through another day.

I wonder if she still thinks of me as much as I do her.

I wonder if she knows she's the only reason I'm still breathing, still fighting, and still holding on.

Blood pools in my mouth and I spit it into the dirt, wishing the dry, packed earth would swallow me up just like it does with the bodily fluids that drip down off my skin.

"Give us names and this will stop. You will live like king and not like dog."

My torturer speaks in broken English, giving his battered fists a break and squatting down to stick his face close to mine. For five years, they've been under the impression I'm some high-ranking military official and can give them the names of top brass with checkered pasts they can extort for their own agenda in this war. I gave up trying to make them understand after the first year. They'll never understand and they'll never care. At this point, it's just a game to them anyway. They don't care about the names; they just care about having another American under their thumb to torture for sport.

"How about we kill your friend instead? Will that make you talk?"

My eyes flicker to the man shackled to the wall a few feet away from me, and the sorry state of his appearance makes me sick to my stomach. He's my brother. My best friend. Everything dead inside me roars to life and my nostrils flare with pent-up rage. I want to make these people pay for what they've done to him. Since we haven't seen a mirror in over five years, I'm guessing he probably feels the same way when he looks at me. Once, the two strongest Marines in our unit, now just shadows of the men we used to be. Bones and ribs sticking out where well-defined muscles used to be, tattered and dirty rags covering our bodies instead of crisp and clean camo pants and T-shirts, long mangy hair and beards that haven't seen a bar of soap or water in years replacing our close-cropped military haircuts and clean-shaven faces.

Through the mop of dirty hair that hangs down over his face, I see him narrow one blue eye at me in warning, the second one swollen shut from yesterday's beating.

Rylan Edwards. My best friend since high school.

We grew up together, joined the Marines together, and went off to fight a war together. It seems only fitting that we'll die together. God only knows what happened to the other men in our unit that were captured along with us. Rylan and I have heard their screams over the years, listened to their shouts of pain, just like I'm sure they've listened to ours. We haven't heard them in a while, which is almost worse. It could mean they're no longer with us, fighting to stay alive. The quietness just gives you too much time to think about the fact that soon we'll be silenced as well.

"Don't do it, man. Don't you fucking do it," he mumbles

angrily around a split lip, the movement of his mouth reopening the scab and letting a trail of blood drip down into his beard. "I can take whatever these fuckers dish out."

I want to tell him to shut the hell up. His words are only going to piss these assholes off, but a part of me wants to tell him to keep going. Don't fucking give up on me and don't let them win. I can't do this alone. I can't survive this alone. If Rylan is still fighting for our freedom, there's no way in hell I'm going to let go and give up.

The piece of scum squatting next to me nods his head in Rylan's direction, the guard standing closest to him slamming his fist into Rylan's cheek, whipping his head back against the wall.

Rylan laughs, like the smart-ass that he is. He laughs loudly from deep in his gut after each punch the little shit levels him with.

"Is that all you got, asshole?" he laughs again, shooting me another look of warning, letting me know he's fine.

He can handle it. He's not giving in. He's not giving up.

How much can a man take before he breaks? When do the dreams stop giving him comfort and he has to accept that he'll never see her again, touch her again or hear her say "I love you" again?

With my knees curled up to my chest and my arms wrapped around my waist to protect my broken ribs from any more abuse, I look into our captor's dark eyes and nod when a particularly nasty punch across the room sends one of Rylan's teeth sailing through the air to land in the dirt right by my face. I've watched them beat the shit out of my best friend for years, and eventually the relentless fists to his face and boots to his stomach turned me numb. But something about this moment shakes me to the core. The determination on Rylan's face, and the pride I feel for him that he refuses to give in, wakes me the fuck up, and one way or another, it ends now.

The monster smiles at me for the first time in five years. I return his smile with my cracked and bloody lips, knowing it's the first *and* last time.

I feel Rylan's eyes on me. I feel his anger and his disappointment from across the room and ignore his shouts to me in between the *thwacks* of a fist connecting with his face.

Pulling my head back from the close proximity of the animal in front of me, I quickly jerk it forward and spit a mouthful of bloody saliva into his face, wanting to throw my hands up and cheer, feeling victorious that I finally found my balls and remembered how to use them.

I picture her smile and I imagine her laugh as he yanks a dirty rag from his pocket and wipes the blood and spit from his face. I hear the soft cadence of her voice, promising to love me forever when he shouts furiously in his own language. I feel her arms wrapped around my waist when, seconds later, two of his men race into the small room, grab me under my arms, and drag me across the dirt floor.

Shouting, the pounding of footsteps and gunfire sound from outside the room, and I wonder just how many people they need to bring in here to kill two weak men who can barely move.

My hands are quickly shackled to a wall above my head right next to Rylan, my broken body groaning in protest. No matter what happens next, I will not give in. I was born a Marine and I will die a Marine.

"Ooh Rah," we both whisper to each other, not breaking eye contact as a loud explosion shakes the walls, rattles our chests, and rains dirt and rocks down on us from the ceiling.

How much can a man take before he breaks?

How much can a man handle before he forgets all the good things and only has regrets filling his head?

I never should have left you. I'll never stop loving you, even if you hate me for walking away.

Closing my eyes to the chaos around us and waiting for them to finally end this once and for all, I let my mind take me away to warm summer nights, the smell of peaches and a woman who loved me more than I ever deserved. I remember how it felt to be loved, wholly and truly loved. I fill my head with thoughts of her, wanting to die with a smile on my face instead of shame in my heart. My cracked and bloody lips tip up at the corners and I hold on tightly to all the good things, refusing to give them up, and refusing to let them go.

Chapter 1

SHELBY

I sigh in frustration when the tiny clasp to the strand of pearls slips from my clumsy fingers yet again. I've been trying unsuccessfully to slip this necklace on for the last five minutes, and my arms are beginning to feel like deadweights. But when another set of fingers entwines with mine at the base of my neck, my breath catches in surprise. I drop my arms and fold my hands together in my lap as he quickly hooks the two ends of the necklace together before resting his hands on top of my shoulders. His palms are smooth and warm against my skin. His touch is gentle and kind, just like the man he is. It soothes me and erases all my irritation, as it always does.

"The pearls look beautiful on you. I was afraid you didn't like them."

I force a smile onto my face as our eyes meet in the mirror, wishing his compliment made me feel happy and beautiful instead of sad and disgusted with the person I've become.

The pearls around my neck feel like a noose, choking the life out of me, and I want nothing more than to rip them off and laugh like a madwoman as the beads scatter across the floor. Instead, I squeeze my hands together as hard as I can until the feeling passes.

"I love the necklace, Landry, it's beautiful," I lie, my eyes flashing to the jewelry box that sits on top of the vanity in front of me before moving back to his face. He smiles confidently, naturally assuming I'm thinking about the countless other necklaces, bracelets, and earrings he's given me recently, neatly resting on the red velvet that lines the inside of the box. He's oblivious to the secret compartment under one of the drawers and that's exactly how I want to keep it.

"Your mother is supposed to be the star of the party tonight, but I have a feeling you're going to give her a run for her money," Landry laughs as I stand up from the chair at my dressing table and turn around to face him.

My stomach churns when he whistles admiringly at the black strapless floor-length dress my mother's stylist picked out for me to wear tonight. Landry McAllister is a handsome man and he loves me. I wish that were enough. I wish I could forget about the life I used to dream of and the plans I used to make. I wish I could stop thinking about those broken dreams, accept my fate and just be happy. All of this wishing and regretting has killed something inside me that I'll never be able to bring back to life. I'll never be able to give Landry what he needs, no matter how hard I try, and I feel a physical ache in my chest, knowing he deserves more.

My hand unconsciously presses against my left thigh when a dull pain throbs through the muscle as I stand. Glancing out the window beyond Landry's shoulder, I see a flash of lightning and the beginnings of a storm send raindrops splattering against the glass. The pain in my leg is never gone, always hovering under the skin, around the muscle and in my bones, making its presence known and reminding me I once had dreams. Dreams that went beyond the walls of this prison I've been exiled to.

Aside from the constant pain, the storm is another reminder of everything I've lost. Everything that was taken from me in the blink of an eye, six years ago, on another rainy night when I lost control. Of my life, my dreams, and my car on that wet and winding road.

Now, I have nothing but memories and regrets. Day after day filled with fake smiles, feigned happiness and pretending like I never hoped for bigger and better things. Twenty-eight years old and every decision about my life is made *for* me, without consideration for what I want, what I need or what matters to *me*.

I wonder if Landry knows how much I want to scream every time he looks at me like I'm the most beautiful woman in the world. I wonder if he notices the guilt clouding my face when he touches me and it never sets my body on fire. I know it would break him if he found out that the only reason I'm with him now is because I have to protect the only person I ever truly loved, and I hate myself for doing that to Landry. I always thought my feelings for him would change and grow. I assumed the love he gave to me would be enough to fix my broken heart and make me whole again, but it's done the opposite. I've become this numb shell of a woman I don't even recognize anymore for a man who probably only used me, but I don't know how to stop. He left this town without saying good-bye and then he left this earth without giving me closure. He left me to pick up the pieces and protect his family and his name and I hate him for that. I've allowed someone else to make all my decisions, rule my life and crush my dreams because I don't know how to stop loving him more than I hate him.

Shouting voices and the pounding of footsteps in the hallway outside my room distract us. Landry walks quickly to the doorway, stopping one of my mother's household staff as she rushes past. With his back turned and his attention focused away from me, I slowly and quietly slide open the bottom drawer of my jewelry box and lift the lid of the hidden compartment. I run my fingertips over the dog tags and wish I could forget how the cold metal used to feel warm against my skin from the heat of his body. How they would dangle down between us, grazing against the skin of my chest when he moved above me. I know I should have gotten rid of them a long time ago, but they're a constant reminder that everything I do is for him, even if what we had was all a lie.

The quiet conversation in my doorway penetrates my thoughts when I hear the staff member tell Landry there's some sort of emergency and it's all over the news.

"Your mother is in a panic and needs all hands on deck."

I close the drawer to the jewelry box right before Landry looks over his shoulder at me. Putting on a smile, I wave my hand at him.

"It's fine, go see what's happening and I'll meet you downstairs," I tell him.

He tells the woman to let my mother know he'll be there in a few minutes, walking back across the room to me when she scurries away. I keep the smile on my face when he grabs one of my hands and brings it up to his mouth, kissing the top quickly and then sighing as he lowers our joined hands.

"I won't be long, I'm sure it's nothing. Your mother panics over everything," he laughs softly.

Landry has been in love with me since I was a teenager

and he worked as an aide for my father, the senator of South Carolina. Ten years my senior, Landry came from a family as wealthy and affluent as my own and my parents never shied away from trying to push the two of us together once I turned eighteen. I wanted to hate him simply because my parents approved of him and because of the pathetic way he followed my father around like a puppy. I spent all four years of high school faking politeness when he'd try to talk to me and every year after that turning down his requests for a date. I'd like to say I did it for the sole purpose of pissing my mother off after my father died and she became obsessed with pushing the two of us together, but I'd be lying. While Landry spent our high school and college years chasing after *me*, I spent those years chasing after someone else. Someone who gave me butterflies each time I saw him, someone whose life was different from mine in every way and someone who took my heart with him when he left, making it impossible for me to ever give it to another.

"And as her financial advisor and the man she's backing to become our new state senator, you're required to panic whenever she does," I remind Landry. "Although considering you have your own things to worry about with your upcoming election, she shouldn't lean on you so much."

Landry chuckles, giving our joined hands a squeeze. "Your mother let me stick around after your father died and helped me make all of the contacts I needed to make a bid for the senate. If I win this thing, it will be because of her. Whatever Georgia wants, Georgia gets."

I paste a smile on my face at his words instead of rolling my eyes sarcastically. Landry kisses my cheek and I watch him leave the room, wishing I had something left to give him. Wishing I wasn't a liar and a fraud. Wishing I could magically glue the broken pieces of my heart back together and give them to him, because I know he would cherish it. He's a good man, even if he *is* one of the sheep in my mother's flock and I was coerced into dating him.

Sitting down on the edge of my bed, I grab the remote from my nightstand and power on the television hanging on the wall across from me, using my free hand to rub the pain from my aching leg. I know I'll be briefed immediately on whatever major crisis my mother is having a conniption over so I won't say the wrong thing if I'm questioned by reporters at her charity event this evening, but since I have nothing else to do while I wait, I might as well get the scoop ahead of time.

When I get to CNN, the reporter's voice fills my quiet room. I'm barely paying attention to what she's saying, busy smoothing down the front of my dress and checking for stray pieces of lint. Every word she speaks runs together in a blur of background noise, until she says a name I recognize. A name I haven't heard or spoken in years, but couldn't stop thinking about every second of every day. A name that makes my heart beat faster and my hands start to shake. My head whips up to stare at the television with wide, unbelieving eyes, and my heart drops into my stomach. They flash a picture of him on the screen from Marine Corps graduation day, but the sight of him in his dress blues isn't what makes my world tilt on its axis. It's the sound of his name coming from a stranger's lips in the quiet room that steals the breath from my lungs, making it impossible to do anything but stare at the television as my hand flies up to cover my mouth and hold back the sobs.

"In a top secret mission yesterday evening, a team of Navy SEALs were sent into the small Afghanistan village of Sangin to rescue Commander Stephen Whitfeld, who was taken hostage earlier this month. We have just been informed that during this rescue mission, several United States Marines who were presumed dead have been found alive. Five years ago, only days away from the end of his year-long deployment, Lieutenant Elijah James was involved in an IED explosion that killed several members of his team and only left behind the men's dog tags as identification. There were rumors that a traitor existed on the team who was working with the Afghan army. But those rumors were quickly put to rest just days after the explosion. Now that Lieutenant James has been found alive, we can only hope no truth will come from those rumors."

The rapid thump of my heart sounds like a drum in my ears, making it impossible for me to hear anything else the reporter says. A wave of nausea rushes through me and I press a shaking hand to my stomach as I stand on unsteady legs while a memory from so many years ago rushes through my mind. Even though I want nothing more than to forget about that moment and the day I signed my fate, I'm unable to stop my eyes from closing as I relive it.

"It's a lie. He would never betray his country. You have to fix this, please!" I begged my mother as I stood in her office with my broken heart clutched tightly in my hands.

She scoffed at me. She didn't care about my pain, the tears streaming down my cheeks, or my conviction that he would never do something like that.

"You don't know anything about him. He used you and then threw you away like a piece of trash," she replied as she stuck the knife deeper into my chest.

I didn't need to be reminded of what he'd done. It had been slowly chipping away my confidence and pieces of my heart every day since he'd left, but unlike my mother, I could separate the man who broke me from the man who fought for his country. The soldier I knew would never do something this appalling.

"He's not a traitor. He doesn't deserve this and neither does his family. Please, Mother, I'm begging you."

She stared at me for a few quiet moments, studying me as I angrily swiped the tears from my cheeks and lifted my chin in the air to show her I wasn't backing down. I would do whatever it took to clear his name.

"I could call in a few favors, but it's going to cost you. Nothing in this life is free, Shelby."

Her words sent a chill down my spine, wondering just how much she would demand as payment, but knowing I would agree to anything in that moment.

"I don't care what it costs. I don't care about anything but making sure he's remembered as a hero. I'll do anything if you just make this go away. Please, I'll do whatever you ask."

The conversation I had with my mother five years ago plays on a loop until I can't stop the voices in my head and I have to grab and tug at fistfuls of hair just to stop myself from screaming.

He's alive.

I promised to do whatever she asked when I feared he'd be remembered as a traitor instead of a hero, and she took everything I had to give as payment. Once she had me under her thumb, it quickly became a slippery slope filled with reminders and threats to keep me in line until I'd fallen so far down the rabbit hole I didn't know how to find my way out.

He's alive.

I can't stop the tears from falling. I can't force back the sobs of relief that something like this is actually happening. How many people lose someone they love, knowing they'll never see them again, never touch them again, never hear their voice again, only to find out it was all a mistake? How many people wish they could turn back the clock for just one more moment, just a few seconds in time so they could look into their loved one's eyes, run their hands down the side of their loved one's face, and hear them speak? It's a dream that everyone who's lost someone has. A dream that slowly turns into a nightmare you feel like you'll never wake up from. Something you know is impossible, but you can't stop obsessing about. I've prayed and I've screamed and I've cried, wanting the impossible, and now, I have it.

He's alive.

I gave up everything to protect him and to save his sister from a controversy that would ruin her in this town. They'd already suffered enough after their parents died—the rumors, the whispers, the finger-pointing and judgment following them everywhere they went…they didn't need anything else marring their fragile reputation. Especially something so completely absurd as Eli being a traitor to his country.

Every dream I let slip through my fingers, every decision I handed over for someone else to make for me, and every piece of myself I've lost in the last five years was for *him*. No matter how badly he shattered my heart, nothing could erase the good memories he left behind. I've wished on over a thousand stars for over a thousand days for closure and to finally have an answer *why*. My heart never healed and I could never let go because I just wanted to know *why*.

Why he lied.

Why he used me.

Why he left the way he did.

The hardest thing I've ever done was get out of bed the morning after news hit that he was gone and live through the pain of knowing he'd never smile again, never laugh again, never speak again, never *exist* again. It was the hardest thing until now.

He's alive.

I could try and pretend this news will finally set me free, but that would just be a waste of time. I know my mother will find a way to make sure I don't stray from the path she's forced me to take.

The hardest thing I'll have to do is face him again and let him see what I've become, knowing I'll never be able to tell him the truth without repercussions. I'll finally get the closure I need, but I know it will cost me. Nothing in this life is free.

"Oh, good, you turned on the news. Can you believe this?"

Landry rushes toward me and takes the remote from my hand, changing the channel to another news outlet. His preoccupation gives me time to push back my feelings, take control of my mind and my heart, wipe the tears from my cheeks, and remove all traces of the hope and fear and desperation that I know are written all over my face. I stare at Landry's profile and watch a muscle tick in his jaw as he listens to the news. A jaw I've run my fingers over and kissed. My eyes move down to his hand clutching tightly to the remote as he switches back and forth between channels. A hand that I've held tightly in my own and felt roaming all over my body. Seeing him standing here next to me is like a bucket of cold water dumped over my head, bringing me back to reality, reminding me of the promises I made and what my life is now.

He's alive.

"Your mother is losing her mind because a reporter did some digging and called her with this crazy story that you had an affair with that Elijah guy they found and they want her to make a statement," Landry says with a laugh. "Didn't he used to work here on the plantation as a stable boy? Shelby Eubanks, the heiress of the Eubanks empire and daughter of the Queen of Charleston, dating a stable boy! The things these people will come up with to make headlines..."

His voice sounds far away and echoes in my ear like he's speaking inside a tunnel instead of right in front of me, pointing the remote at the television and flipping from one channel to the next, while he drones on and on about the impossibility that I would ever lower myself to have an affair with the hired help.

"Lieutenant Elijah James has been found alive..."
"Presumed dead, Lieutenant Elijah James..."
"Elijah James..."
"Elijah James..."
"Elijah James..."

The name I never thought I'd hear again feels like the stab of a knife into my chest each time another newsperson utters it until my vision starts to blur and my shaking legs finally give out. My body crumbles and I stare up at Landry as he drops the remote and quickly turns when he hears me hit the floor. He looks like he's standing in front of a strobe light, his worried face vanishing and then quickly reappearing as my eyes blink rapidly.

I've spent the last five years compartmentalizing things into *before* and *after*. There's a secret place in my head where I've hidden all of my memories of *before* Eli died. I keep those memories buried and refuse to think about them.

I refuse to remember that time in my life when I was young and stupid and so foolishly in love and full of dreams. When my leg wasn't made up of shattered bones with pins holding them together. When dancing, and the love I had for a man who was so different from me, were going to be my ticket away from this town and out of this life.

After Eli died, *after* my dreams died…that's who I am now. Moving through life like a robot and locking the door to *before* is the only way I know how to keep moving, keep breathing, and keep waking up each morning.

I never thought *before* and *after* would collide. I never thought I'd have to unlock that door and be forced to brace myself for the explosion of memories, covering my head and shielding my heart from the pain I know it will bring.

I hear Landry shout for help from far away and I close my eyes, letting the darkness take me away from the name that continues to whisper through my ears.

Elijah James.

He's alive.

And it will cost me.

About the Author

Tara Sivec is a *USA Today* best-selling author, wife, mother, chauffeur, maid, short-order cook, baby-sitter, and sarcasm expert. She lives in Ohio with her husband and two children and looks forward to the day when all three of them become adults and move out.

After working in the brokerage business for fourteen years, Tara decided to pick up a pen and write instead of shoving it in her eye out of boredom. Her novel *Seduction and Snacks* won first place in the Indie Romance Convention Reader's Choice Awards 2013 for Best Indie First Book and she was voted as Best Author in the Indie Romance Convention Reader's Choice Awards for 2014.

In her spare time, Tara loves to dream about all of the baking she'll do and naps she'll take when she ever gets spare time.

You can learn more at:

http://tarasivec.com/

Twitter at @TaraSivec

Facebook at http://facebook.com/TaraSivec.authorpage

Sign up for Tara's newsletter to get more information on new releases and insider information!

http://tarasivec.com/

Fall in love with these charming small-town romances!

BAREFOOT BEACH
By Debbie Mason

Theia Lawson and Marco DiRossi are determined to beat the match-makers of Harmony Harbor at their own game. Both lone wolves, the two conspire to pretend that they've already fallen in love. But just when they want to make their relationship real, a secret is revealed that puts everything Marco and Theia have fought for in jeopardy.

Discover exclusive content and more on
read-forever.com.

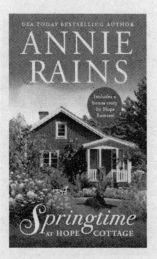

SPRINGTIME AT HOPE COTTAGE
By Annie Rains

In Sweetwater Springs, love has a way of mending even the most damaged heart. When Josie Kellum is sidelined in a small town, she focuses on her rehab to get back to the big city ASAP. But that becomes awfully difficult when she falls for her hunky physical therapist. Includes a bonus story by Hope Ramsay!

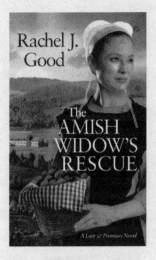

THE AMISH WIDOW'S RESCUE
By Rachel J. Good

Pregnant and recently widowed, Grace Fisher is determined to provide for her family on her own. Elijah Beiler has always admired his neighbor Grace, so standing by while she struggles to support her family isn't an option. Determined to help, Elijah finds it difficult to remain detached. Can he overcome past hurts and open his heart to this ready-made family?

WELCOME TO LAST CHANCE (REISSUE)
By Hope Ramsay

When Wanda Jane Coblentz arrives in Last Chance with five dollars in her pocket, all she wants is a hot meal and a fresh start. But when she falls for sexy musician Clay Rhodes, she never expects a bad boy like Clay to rescue a damsel in distress. Thank goodness Jane plans on rescuing herself. Includes a bonus story!

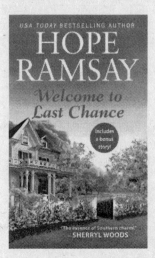

5654

Follow @ReadForeverPub on Twitter and join the conversation using #ReadForever.

THE WAY YOU LOVE ME
By Miranda Liasson

Gabby Langdon secretly dreams of being a writer, so for once she does something for herself—she signs up for a writing class taught by bestselling novelist Caden Marshall. There's only one problem: Her brooding, sexy professor is a distraction she can't afford if she's finally going to get the life she truly wants. Includes a bonus story by Alison Bliss!

THREE LITTLE WORDS
By Jenny Holiday

Stranded in New York with her best friend's wedding dress, Gia Gallo has six days to make it to Florida in time for the ceremony. And oh-so-charming best man Bennett Buchanan has taken the last available rental car. Looks like she's in for one long road trip with the sexiest— and most irritating—Southern gentleman she's ever met.

Connect with us at Facebook.com/ReadForeverPub.

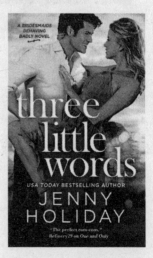